ACCLAIM FOR AWARD WINNING AUTHOR BARRY FINLAY

KILIMANJARO AND BEYOND: A LIFE *JOURNEY*

"If you're the kind of person who c͵   ͺк yourself
out of a great idea this book is tl   ͺc out of your
comfort zone and make things ha҇.   ͺ, Author, *Cameras of
Kilimanjaro*, Australia

"…at once so inspirational and courageous, so human and humane, and so
deeply personal that the reader feels they are climbing right along with this
small and highly determined group." - Reverend Dr. Linda De Coff, Author,
Bridge of the Gods

"*Kilimanjaro and Beyond* is a beautifully written tale about a spiritual journey, a
physical embarking, and so much more." - GoodbooksToday.com

I GUESS WE MISSED THE BOAT: A TRAVEL MEMOIR

"Hilarious at times - a recommended read for those wanting a good laugh." -
Jan Heart

"I Guess We Missed The Boat is a fresh, ironic and jovial travel adventure
novel in which each traveler can recognize himself or herself. It is a travel
book that is amusing and practical at the same time." - Reader Views

"I really enjoyed this book! I think this is a great read. It definitely lightened
my day…" - Shirley Priscilla Johnson

THE VANISHING WIFE

Barry Finlay

The Vanishing Wife

Barry Finlay

Published by Keep On Climbing Publishing

Copyright © Barry Finlay 2014

Cover by ShokVox Productions

This book is dedicated to my family who provide inspiration and support.

ACKNOWLEDGMENTS

The Vanishing Wife is my first foray into someone else's mind and soul, and I must say it has been interesting. Many of the good characters in the book are a conglomeration of wonderful people I have met. It is a challenge (and a bit eye-opening) to place someone else in a dangerous situation that is unfamiliar to them and to try to anticipate how they would react. In case anyone is wondering, the bad characters are a figment of my imagination.

As books always do, this one came together with the help of a number of early readers and people who gave me technical advice. Len Westwood, Claudine Gueh Yanting and Brian Skinner read an early version, offering suggestions on the story line that definitely helped fill in some gaps. A big thank you goes out to them for having the patience to plow through an unedited, incomplete manuscript and offering great advice.

Thank you also to Brian Skinner, who is a retired Superintendent of the Detective Division, Ottawa Police Service, and to Superintendents Daniel Delaney and Uday Jaswal and Staff Sergeant David Zackrias of the Ottawa Police Service for providing technical expertise. Each graciously found time in their busy schedules and patiently answered my questions. I thoroughly enjoyed every meeting and came home knowing that we are fortunate to be in such caring, knowledgeable and extremely competent hands in our great city. After each meeting, I was excited and eager to use the new information in the book. My apologies if I somehow misinterpreted what I heard or used a little literary license in the advancement of the story. Without these individuals and their contributions, the story would not have been complete.

Tom Nickerson, ShokVox Productions, is responsible for the wonderful cover artwork. It is such a pleasure to work with someone who grasps a vision as readily as Tom does. I have often turned to Tom for graphical designs, and the end result is always stunning and representative of my thoughts. Thank you, Tom.

Thank you to Ron Melanson for the profile picture. Ron is a perfectionist at everything he does, and his photography work is no different.

This is the second time working with Editor Extraordinaire Kip Kirby, who once again challenged me and dragged, encouraged and cajoled every last word out of me. Thank you to Kip for the effort she puts into her work. It is always an enjoyable exercise and in my mind, the end result is a better book.

R.C. Butler at Bulldog Press did the layout of the interior and the work to convert to ebook format, and I'm grateful for the effort. It's not an easy task, and it was handled quickly and efficiently.

A big thank you to the people who take the time to read what I have written. Your feedback is precious to me and makes me a better writer.

Finally, thank you to my family who offer moral support and encouragement for my writing and other later-in-life pursuits. My wife Evelyn reads the manuscript almost as many times as I do. Her patience and support are invaluable.

DAY 1

Chapter 1

Mason Seaforth was waiting.

It was 6 o'clock in the morning, and the darkness in the suburbs had begun to ease. The sun would soon make its appearance for another day, causing the shadows to beat a hasty retreat. Mason was now restlessly sitting on the couch in the sunroom that belonged to him and his wife Samantha, or Sami as she was known to her friends. He was staring at the walls and thinking that if he smoked, now would be a good time to light one up.

He hated waiting. Mason was a very punctual man and had always had the attitude that everyone's time is precious. He never wanted to give the impression that his time was more valuable than anyone else's. His wife was no different. She had always had the same attitude as he did, and together they'd earned the reputation of being the "Early Seaforths." That's what made this so unusual and frightening at the same time.

Mason was waiting for Sami.

It had started out to be an amazing 24 hours. They had spent the day relaxing, exploring the area around St. Petersburg, Florida and enjoying each other's company. It was that delightfully peaceful time of year on the beach between the departure of the snowbirds back to the north and the invasion of the tourists from Europe. They had wandered around John's Pass at Madeira Beach, leisurely strolling in and out of the various shops lining the walkways. They had held hands as they walked along the beach, feeling the sun drenching their skin. As they did so, the wind rustled through the palm fronds, sending shivers through the tall grass that separates the beach from the traffic noise on the street. They'd looked into each other's eyes as they enjoyed crab-stuffed mushrooms washed down with Coronas at Sculley's, their favorite hangout.

It was their 20th wedding anniversary and Mason had never been happier. At 48, he was in the prime of his life. He was a mild-mannered accountant who had worked his way into the position of owning his own firm. He worked hard at his one-person operation, but that suited him just fine as it gave him the flexibility to come and go as he pleased. Since meeting Sami 22 years ago, she had become his entire world. She worked as a financial advisor in the bank where Mason kept his investments, but it wasn't until Mason decided he needed additional advice on his current fixed-interest rate instruments that their paths actually crossed. The attraction was instant and intense. As he walked through the door of her office, he couldn't help but notice how attractive Sami was. And when she spoke, Mason's heart skipped a beat. Her dark auburn hair was drawn back off her face, emphasizing her beautiful features. Her green eyes were large and seemed to draw him in as he advanced towards the chair. Her lips were full, a feature he had always found attractive. When she stood to greet him, he noticed her business attire of a pale yellow blouse and dark skirt on her shapely 5'5" frame. Business attire to anyone else, but to Mason it was beyond sexy.

Sami's confidence and professionalism, along with her beauty, won him over in a way no other woman ever had, and after making up excuses to go back and see her a few more times for financial advice, he worked up enough courage to invite her out. After a short courtship, they were married, and life for Mason had been wonderful with every passing year. At 46, Sami was two years younger than her husband, and still very attractive. Mason was only too aware of the admiring glances that inevitably came her way as they walked down the street. But he felt confident that she was more attracted to him than she could ever be to anyone else. Their anniversary had been perfect. They had agreed to celebrate the entire day together, and the hours had flown by as they drank too much wine and ate too much steak and lobster over a candlelight dinner at home. They'd laughed as they donned bibs and sprayed juice from the cooked lobster everywhere while cracking the hard shells. Reminiscences came easily, and they shared memories that would only be funny to them. As she loved to do, Sami teased Mason about how he'd run into the wall in the dark in their hotel room while they were on their honeymoon. She unsuccessfully tried to stifle the wine-soaked gales of laughter as she recalled the black eye that Mason sported for the rest of the trip.

When dinner was finished and the last of the wine consumed, they brought their anniversary to a close by heading into the bedroom early and making love passionately. As Mason reflected on that part of the evening, he recalled that their clothes had come off urgently on the way to the bed with an intensity that was unusual even for them. He also recalled that Sami seemed even more passionate than usual. When they were finished, she had tears in her eyes and her voice quavered slightly when she told him she loved him. But she'd assured him it was only because her feelings were so strong and she was only thinking about how happy she was.

Afterwards, they had both fallen into the deep sleep that only lovemaking brings. Around 4 a.m., Mason had awoken. He felt that something had awakened him. He felt confused and groggy, but he forced himself out of bed and staggered to the bathroom. He was sure his stupor was not only from sleep but strongly enhanced by the effects of the large quantities of wine they had consumed just hours earlier. He could still smell the lingering scent of Sami's perfume. As he stood naked in front of the mirror washing his hands, he smiled at the thought of the last 24 hours, and his tired reflection smiled back. Mason shut off the bathroom light before opening the door so as not to awaken the slumbering Sami. As he felt his way around the bottom of the bed in the blackness, he thought that she must be curled up on the far side because he only felt empty space where her feet should have been. As he climbed into bed, he suddenly sensed an eerie emptiness in the room that shouldn't have been. He reached across the bed to fold Sami into his arms. She wasn't there.

With a jolt, Mason got up again, battling the stupor that he was still feeling, and threw on the blue robe Sami had given him last Christmas. He unplugged his cell phone from the charger in the bedroom and glanced at it as he always did when he first got up. There had been no calls. He went downstairs to the living room. No Sami. Their daughter Jennifer had left for college earlier in the year, and they both missed her dearly so he went back upstairs to check her room. Maybe Sami was missing Jennifer a little more because of their anniversary and had decided to spend the last part of the night in Jennifer's bed. But she wasn't there, either. Mason padded down the hall to the room they had converted to an office, but again there was no sign of Sami. He called out nervously into the silence. "Sami? Sweetheart, where are you?" There was no response.

He decided to check their favorite room, a combination sunroom/entertainment area. They often spent their mornings there sipping coffee, or evenings together with Sami curled up beside him on the couch to watch something that they mutually agreed upon after much playful negotiation. They had splurged a while ago on a 60-inch TV and determined that the sunroom would be the place for it. Now, Mason wondered if maybe Sami couldn't sleep after all the wine and was watching TV quietly with the headphones on. He made his way into the room to check, hoping against hope to find her there. His heart sank when there was no glimpse of Sami.

A creeping uneasiness began mounting against Mason's will. He went to the back door, turned on the outside light, and stared out into the darkness of the back yard through the window. His hand shook slightly as he unlocked the door, hesitated, then called out for Sami into the night. There was no answer. Mason went back inside and opened the door leading from the front hall to the garage to see if she might have gone there for some reason. He switched on the light as his bare feet felt the coldness of the two steps to the grey concrete floor of the garage. He walked around his Audi, checking inside the vehicle as he went. There was barely room to walk between the tools hanging on the wall and the sides of his car, but he squeezed by to open the garage door to the driveway to ensure that her Miata sports car was still there. It stared back, mocking him.

After closing the garage door again, Mason returned back inside. He stood frozen, uncertain and increasingly tense. What was going on? Where was Sami? Where was his wife? Mason couldn't think. He still felt strange and detached, almost as if he was in a dangerous dream that wasn't real. Why couldn't he wake up?

And now it was 6 a.m. The sun would be coming up momentarily. There was no Sami and no question of going back to bed, so Mason finally went to the sunroom couch where he sat despondently, waiting and flipping distractedly through magazines. But he couldn't focus on the words in front of his eyes. The anniversary clock they had been given by his parents sat on the mantle ticking loudly, interrupting the silence that permeated the room. Each tick was a reminder that his wife was gone and he was alone. Then a moment of hope sprang forward: what if Sami hadn't been able to get back to sleep and had decided to go for a walk in their quiet residential neighborhood? It was, after all, a very safe community. She was in all likelihood just out for some fresh air to clear her head, especially if she'd felt as groggy as he did.

Sami never went anywhere without her cell phone, and if she had gone out for a walk, she would certainly have taken the phone with her. He reached for his own phone and dialed Sami's number. The number rang. And rang, and rang again. Mason held his breath. "Please, Sami, please, pick up," he whispered. On the sixth ring, he heard Sami's confident voice message. "You have reached Samantha Seaforth. Please leave a message, and I will call you back."

In a shaking voice, Mason heard himself doing as she asked. "Sweetie, it's Mason, I'm leaving a message. Where are you? Please call me back right away."

It had been two hours since he first noticed Sami was gone.

Chapter 2

Mason had grown up in Valdosta, Georgia while Sami was an import to the south from Minneapolis. Mason loved his home state and its neighbor where he now lived, and his parents were close enough so they could visit periodically. Sami had told Mason when they met that her father had lost his life in a tragic car accident. Her mother had remarried, but then suddenly died from unknown causes just two years later. Sami often intimated that her mother must have died from a broken heart brought about by the loss of her first husband.

Mason knew Sami had not liked her stepfather and had not spoken to him since her mother's death. She had no siblings, and she always said that her school days were not the best years of her life. As a result, they had never gone back to visit her home town, even though he had suggested it on a few occasions. Sami had given Mason the basics, but he had never pressed her on the details, thinking that the thought of her mother's death was just too much for her to discuss. She knew that if she wanted to talk about it someday, he would be there to listen. Mostly, Mason was thrilled that this wonderful woman had moved to Florida, and that providence had brought them together.

The Seaforth home rested on a quiet residential street in the sleepy community of Gulfport. With a population of about 12,000, there wasn't a lot of excitement, although Mason and Sami loved the pretty community with its beautiful views and the local artists who take full advantage of them. It wasn't a hub of activity and tourism such as nearby St. Petersburg, Clearwater, and of course, Tampa. The biggest thing to happen in Gulfport lately was the election of a new mayor, and that didn't exactly generate a lot of enthusiasm among the locals. Gulfport was mostly a retirement community but it was a great place to have your own small business, and there were a variety of leisure things to do. The crime rate was appreciably low. In the previous year, there had been no homicides, and only 28 stolen cars and 23 aggravated assaults. Mason and Sami originally fell in love with Gulfport when they vacationed there the first time, and their love for the community only grew the longer they stayed.

The fabric of the area that they now called home was partly made up of a bar called O'Maddy's by the pier, artisan shops, restaurants, a public library and dolphins in the Boca Ciega Bay. There were festivals throughout the year, which they always enjoyed. They enjoyed watching the sun setting over the emerald water as the waves rolled gently in and out on a never-ending journey back and forth from horizon to beach. The Seaforths laughed at the antics of the awkward pelicans that stopped flying in mid-air so they could plunge beak first into the sea from a few feet of elevation to capture an unsuspecting fish. It was in direct contrast to the dainty shorebirds sneaking along, carefully plucking bugs from the reeds.

They had even enjoyed battening down the hatches when tropical storms pummeled the coast. While they could do without the storms, there was something exciting about hunkering down in bed as the winds howled outside and the lightning eerily lit up the room through the drawn shades. In fact, they both suspected that Jennifer was conceived during a particularly electrifying tropical storm.

Their custom built two-story house was a three-bedroom structure that sat on a street lined with palm trees, and with its beautifully manicured back yard, it was the envy of visitors. They could sit and enjoy their back yard from their sunroom/entertainment room where Mason had thought Sami might be and where he now sat. A look through one of the many windows presented a view of a Chinese fringe bush with its pink flowers and pale yellow gardenias, both of which were in full bloom. On their first visit to the home that would eventually become theirs, the small meandering waterfall with colorful water lilies seemingly sprouting from the wet rocks, babbled away to them as they admired the view and broke down any remaining resistance to buying the place.

Their daughter Jennifer came along 18 years ago, and she was the daughter that everyone could hope for. She had sailed through school, loving every minute of it and accumulating scores of friends along the way. In high school, she'd dated a few guys, but didn't really seem to be serious about any of them. Jennifer was athletic and moved with the grace of a model when she walked. Mason joked with Sami that their daughter had her looks and his athleticism. It may have been partly true, but Sami was no slouch in the athletics department, either.

Jennifer had chosen to go to the University of Miami in Coral Gables. With her excellent academic record and extracurricular activities, she had had her choice of universities, but her parents were relieved when she had chosen one that was relatively close. Jennifer's dream since she was about 12 was to become a doctor, and she knew this school would give her the necessary grounding in all the required subjects to allow her to move to the main medical campus in Miami later on.

Life in Gulfport was everything Sami and Mason had hoped for, but now for Mason, everything was changing. A missing wife wasn't part of the bargain. Mason examined in his mind what might have transpired. He tried to ignore the nervousness that was seeping in. Even though his mind had still not cleared from the previous night's events, he realized he was on the verge of becoming frantic, and that wouldn't help the situation. He reviewed the possibilities. There were plenty of places to walk in Gulfport, but why would Sami do that without leaving a note? And why would she go out in the dark in the middle of the night? Mason decided that no matter how relieved he would be to see Sami walk in the door, she would be getting an earful when she arrived. Because he had to face the truth: he was beginning to get really scared.

Now as the sun's rays had awakened the vegetation in the yard and the shadows had rapidly retreated at the onslaught, Mason put down the magazine that he hadn't been reading anyway and sat staring at the walls. His hands were shaking. A glance at the clock on the digital box connected to the television told him it was now 8 a.m. Four painfully slow hours had gone by while he checked and rechecked the house and yard. With a sudden start, he realized that he hadn't thought of looking for Sami's purse. They mutually respected each other's privacy, and it wouldn't be something he would normally think to do. But this was different and Mason quickly scanned the room. Her purse wasn't visible. A quick check of the kitchen and living room revealed nothing. He thought of the bedroom. While Mason never really kept tabs on where Sami tended to keep her purse, he thought that the bedroom was a logical place, especially given last night's activities. After climbing the stairs once again, he clicked on the light but a quick look around the bedroom left him feeling helpless. No purse, only a quickly escalating sense of dread that something was terribly wrong and he didn't know how to fix it.

At the same time, Mason realized he was still feeling strangely sluggish and slightly queasy. He had shared too much wine with Sami in the past and never felt this bad. Surely it was from the tension of the situation, he decided – what else could it be? As Mason went around to Sami's side of the bed, he thought he could see a red strap peeking out from under the clothes that had been haphazardly strewn across the floor during the previous night's lovemaking. He shuffled the clothes with his foot and uncovered her purse. He didn't know if he was relieved or more worried. He knew that Sami wouldn't go far without her purse, which made Mason think she would walk in the door any minute. Yet why on earth would his wife go *anywhere* in the middle of the night, without him, without her car, without her purse and without leaving a note?

Mason and Sami trusted each other implicitly. They wouldn't check each other's emails, and while they would occasionally poke fun at each other for their respective friends on Facebook, they would never bother to look into it closely because of the mutual trust they shared. But Mason reached down and picked up Sami's purse. Inside was the usual paraphernalia that he would have expected. Makeup, lip gloss, a small brush, the Miata's car keys, Kleenex, a wallet with a few dollars in cash, sunglasses and her credit cards.

There were also a few business cards from her clients at the bank, but that was it. Mason hesitated and then put the purse back down. Was something missing? He knew her house keys were on a separate ring, and they were definitely not there, which would explain why the doors were locked. But was he thinking as clearly as he should be? Or were the thoughts flooding into his head along with the grogginess he was feeling starting to affect his judgment?

He thought for a minute. Wait! Sami's cell phone! He'd often seen her reaching into her purse to pull out her phone. He had called it and it had gone to voice mail, but did Sami even have it? It was an iPhone and Sami's pride and joy. Her life was in that phone and it never left her side, so she had probably taken it with her. He hadn't noticed the phone anywhere during his search of the house, but that wasn't really that unusual. He was looking for his wife, not her phone. He often misplaced his own phone and always tracked it down by calling his own number and wandering around the house waiting for it to ring.

With his cell phone in his hand, Mason dialed her number again, walking slowly through the house, listening for its ring. After six rings, he heard Sami's voice message. Could the phone have become lodged between cushions on the couch or under the bed covers or in the bathroom? The thought gave Mason much-needed hope. He dialed and redialed as he continued his search of the house. Increasingly desperate for any connection to his absent wife, Mason let it go to voice mail over and over just for the reassurance of hearing his wife's familiar voice. Then, without warning, Mason's blood ran cold as he was chilled by a new message on the phone. *"The voice mail box for this user is full."*

Chapter 3

Mason had to think. There were so many competing thoughts running through his head. Where was Sami? Why was her voice mail box full now when it hadn't been just a little while ago? What was going on? It could have been anybody leaving messages to fill up the mailbox, but *this* early in the morning? He wished he could access it. What should his next move be? Should he call the police? Mason had heard that reporting a missing person less than 24 hours after last seeing them would get you nowhere. He decided he needed to clear his head so he could think more clearly. His hands quivered as he filled the coffee pot. He could never remember the number of scoops of coffee that were required, and his foggy brain just told him to throw in a lot – the stronger the better this morning.

He had to get dressed. He went upstairs, threw off his robe and headed in the direction of the bathroom but on the way, he couldn't resist opening Sami's dresser drawers to look for – what? He didn't even know. He moved a few things in her cosmetics drawer and rifled through her underwear drawer. He looked in her closet, moving some of her many dresses aside. His quick search revealed nothing unusual. Another look through the pile of clothes on the floor and through the pockets of the designer denim jeans she had been wearing didn't turn up anything, either.

Mason splashed cold water on his face with his trembling hands. His eyes were bloodshot, and his heart was thrumming like a caged animal trying to secure its release. His accountant mind told him he had to relax and try to sift through the logical next steps. But that was easier said than done. He tried to remind himself that logical steps wouldn't be necessary because Sami would probably be home at any minute. As he towel dried his face, he thought of their daughter Jennifer. He told himself that he should call her soon, but then decided it would be best to wait a little longer. He was trying to convince himself that this was just some bizarre occurrence with an explanation that would be apparent at any minute, but he also knew he was stalling so he could plan what to say to Jennifer. He didn't want to alarm her unnecessarily.

Both parents were proud of Jennifer for remembering important dates like birthdays and anniversaries, and unabashedly letting everyone else know about them. Slowly it dawned on Mason that they hadn't heard from Jennifer last night to congratulate them on their 20th anniversary. Still, she'd sent a large bouquet of flowers, and Mason had noticed a tribute to the two of them on Facebook yesterday morning, courtesy of Jennifer. Maybe that was the new normal, Mason thought. Maybe a public tribute on Facebook had replaced a personal phone call to express congratulations. Mason had to admit it was kind of amazing to see the many congratulatory comments from Jennifer's friends, most of who wouldn't have even known about their anniversary, let alone acknowledged it, if she hadn't taken the time to post the news.

Mason dressed without thinking. His mind was racing in other directions, and it was purely by instinct that he chose the casual business attire that he normally wore to work: tan slacks, a blue shirt and loafers. These were often his chosen outfit, but today, Mason knew he wouldn't be going to the office until he heard from Sami. Out of habit, he checked the mirror on his way past. At slightly over six feet tall with blonde hair that was starting to show signs of grey at the temples, he prided himself on his appearance, an appearance that he maintained by visiting the gym three times a week. He intended to fight off the ageing process as long as possible; and the only testament to the fact he was closing in on 50 were the glasses with stylish designer frames he sported as the result of his astigmatism discovered 30 years previously. But right now, the glasses were hiding dark circles under his red eyes, a glaring testament to the fear that was fighting its way through the fog he was feeling.

Mason poured a cup of the strong brew he had concocted minutes earlier into the large mug that had become his favorite, partly because it had been given to him by Jennifer but also because it was adorned with the phrase, "SUCCESS IS THE BEST REVENGE." He loved the saying and hoped to put it into practice for the rest of his life in accordance with his own broad definition of success. The cold water he'd splashed on his face minutes ago had helped to clear his head somewhat, but he still felt disoriented. Grabbing the cordless phone on the way, he headed back out to the sunroom where he and Sami had spent so many hours reading in the comfortable silence of each other's company. He felt bewildered, unsure and totally at a loss about what to do next.

Without warning, his cell phone trilled. It was Jennifer's personal ringtone, the one he'd assigned to her calls so he would always pick up. Even though he knew by the ring who was calling, he checked the display to confirm it, sighed and answered. There was no time to think about what he was going to say to her, so he decided to play it low key for now. "Hi sweetie, how's it going?" Mason fought to conceal the nervousness he was feeling.

"It's going great, Dad! I have to run to class in a few minutes, but how was your anniversary celebration? How's Mom? Are you two playing hooky today?" He could almost see her smile as she teased him over the phone.

This was just a hint of Jennifer's ability to ask questions. Mason had often suggested she should be thinking about a law degree.

"We had a great time." Mason briefly recounted their day, hoping Jennifer didn't pick up on the muted tension in his voice. But Jennifer was her usual bubbly self, interjecting periodically to ask questions and to tease Mason about being married for *20 years!* The implication was that the two of them were probably married at a time when their vows might have been inscribed on stone tablets.

"I saw your tribute on Facebook, and we received the flowers, Jenn. That was really nice."

"Well, seriously I'm very proud of you two. Most of my friends have divorced parents, so I feel fortunate to have been born into this family. Where's Mom – has she left for work?"

Mason knew he would feel guilty about what he was about to say, but he just needed more time. He tried hard to keep his tone casual. "She had some errands to run. She said she wasn't that busy at work, so she was going to take her time getting there."

"Okay. She just seemed to be a little sad when I talked to her last night, so I just wanted to check in and make sure everything was fine."

Mason's heart hiccupped in his chest. "You talked to her *last night*?"

"Of course, Dad. You know I wouldn't miss calling on your anniversary. Didn't she tell you? She said you didn't have any wine and that you'd gone to the store to get some." Jennifer giggled. "Or maybe you just forgot that Mom told you I called, after all that wine you guys were drinking! I don't want to hear what you did after the wine was finished. Probably went right to sleep at your age." She giggled again at her little joke.

Mason hesitated to probe, but he couldn't stop himself from asking Jennifer, "So what did you two talk about?"

"Not much, but she just seemed kind of sad. I just thought that with the *big* anniversary milestone and me going away to university, she was having some kind of crisis. She kept telling me over and over how much she loved me. It was nice to hear but just a little over the top, you know?"

Mason was silent.

"Well, Dad, I have a class at 10. TTYL, okay? Love you!"

Mason recognized the popular texting vernacular used by his daughter. "Yes, I will *talk to you later* too, sweetie. Take care. Love you too!"

And with that, Jennifer was gone.

Leaving Mason even more perplexed.

Chapter 4

S ince he had awakened before dawn that morning to an empty bed, it felt to Mason like he had done nothing but check the time repeatedly. He couldn't help thinking that any minute, Sami would suddenly come strolling through the front door and the whole nightmare would turn out to have a logical explanation. Another glance at his watch showed time was passing, but not quickly. The phone call with Jennifer had been unsettling, to say the least. If their daughter had picked up on her mother's mood, then it must have been more obvious than he realized. Yet Sami must have done a good job of hiding her mood as they spent their anniversary day together.

Mason set down the cell phone, staring at it as if it contained a clue to his wife's whereabouts. With his shoulders slumped, he walked back into the living room and looked around. He knew he was wandering aimlessly, accomplishing nothing, but he didn't know what else to do. He went back upstairs to the bedroom and scanned the room. His glance landed on the pile of Sami's clothes lying beside the bed. They were an unusual sight in their usually tidy room. Mason knew that if Sami had awakened normally this morning, the clothes would have been folded and put away before breakfast.

The last thing Mason remembered from last night's activities was looking at her through eyes that were half closed and on the verge of shutting completely as sleep settled on him like a fog rolling in from the sea. He remembered Sami putting her white panties and a t-shirt back on and climbing back into bed. As he turned on the lamp on the bedside table, he confirmed that the rest of her clothes were still lying where they had been tossed when they'd first fallen into each other's arms on the bed. *What is she wearing now,* wondered Mason. Had she actually put her clothes back on again while he slept and before she disappeared? Usually the slightest noise would awaken him, but apparently a lot had gone on last night while he slept, and that in itself was strange. Is Sami running around nearly naked now in some kind of medical amnesia episode? The thought comforted him a little, as he realized if that were the case, someone in their quiet neighborhood would soon spot her and call the police, who would bring her home. Then maybe something would begin to make sense.

As Mason descended the stairs once more to go back to the sunroom, he thought again of calling the police and filing a missing persons report on Sami. It seemed like a good idea at this point, yet he hesitated. He still held out hope that there was a logical explanation somehow and that she would appear at any moment. He felt certain the police would ask him what he had done to look for his wife, so he wanted to cover at least some of the bases. He decided to call Sami's co-workers at the bank where she worked. He exhaled slowly as he dialed the number and listened to the phone being picked up at the other end of the line. It was Sarah, Sami's young assistant.

Mason asked if she had heard from Sami.

"No, I haven't, Mr. Seaforth, but Mrs. Seaforth has a 9:30 appointment this morning. Do you think she'll be here soon?"

"Uh," said Mason, holding his breath momentarily, "I didn't want to bother you if she had already called, but I'm afraid you should go ahead and cancel the appointment, Sarah. We're having a bit of a family crisis, so I'm not sure when she might be back to work. Hopefully it won't be long. In the meantime, could you please transfer me to her manager?" Once again, he cringed slightly at the little white lie.

"Sure thing, Mr. Seaforth. I hope Mrs, Seaforth is feeling better soon."

Michael Bublé's voice emanated from the phone as Mason waited to be connected to Willard Smith, Sami's longtime supervisor. Willard was a large, affable, balding man whose front paunch successfully hid his belt. He always had a smile and demonstrated great respect for Sami. Mason had always had a sneaking suspicion that just maybe Willard harbored a tiny crush on her. After a few dinner dates with Willard and his wife, Althea, it became obvious to Mason and Sami that those two just barely tolerated each other. Sami joked with Mason about "sexy" Willard on many occasions over the dinner table.

"Hey Mason, how're you doing? Where's that lovely wife of yours?" His voice was loud but jovial as he answered Mason's call.

"I'm good, thanks, Willard. Listen, I hope you won't mind my calling, but I've noticed that Sami hasn't been herself lately, and I'm a little concerned. She's sleeping right now. Have you noticed anything at work that might have upset her?"

"Not really, although I noticed the day before yesterday that she was not her usual upbeat self. We'd chatted about a client first thing in the morning, and she talked about how much she was looking forward to your anniversary celebration. But then later in the day, I noticed her attitude change completely. She seemed to be sad and angry at the same time. I asked her if she was all right, and she told me in no uncertain terms to leave her alone, that she just needed time to think. Then she closed her office door, and I saw her make a couple of phone calls. I was concerned because of the tone she used with me and she didn't come out of her office until much later. It was strange behavior for Sami, but I expected she would come in today after spending her day off with you and be back to normal. She is okay, isn't she Mason?"

Only silence greeted the question. "Mason, are you still there?"

"Yes, Willard, I'm still here. Look, I'll be in touch, okay? I have to go now."

At the mention of Sami's sadness, heat had spread rapidly across Mason's face and encircled the hairs that were standing at attention on his neck. As he hung up the phone, he thought about the recurring theme that was making him so uneasy. He had noticed Sami's sadness last night after they made love. Jennifer had commented on her mom's demeanour during their phone call. Now her employer had raised the issue again. An awful thought flashed through Mason's mind. Lately the news had been full of stories about cases of undiagnosed mental illness and the ability of sufferers to hide their problems from their loved ones until it was too late. Surely if Sami were suffering some kind of depression, there would have been a sign from a woman he thought he knew so well and whose disposition was always sunny. He decided to push this new thought to the corner to sit with the impending call to the police until he tried the remaining few avenues left to consider.

He tried dialing Sami's cell phone again. Hoping against hope, he held the phone close, listening for her voice, but all he got was the frustrating *"This mailbox is full"* message. His next call was to Sami's best friend, Marcie Kane. The women had met at the gym ten years earlier and had been close ever since. It was as if Marcie and Sami shared a brain. Sami didn't have a lot of close friends since she and Mason spent as much time together as they could. But Marcie would be considered the closest by far. She was a gorgeous African American woman with short cropped black hair, flashing dark eyes, and a figure that she maintained through a regimen of diet and exercise. She was taller than Sami, and was almost always dressed in a striking outfit on the cutting edge of fashion. She could be sweet and then turn around to deliver a cutting remark or a sarcastic, playful comment at just the right time. Sami adored and understood her.

The most outstanding feature about Marcie was her directness. Her politically correct filter was usually stuck in the "off" position. Statements made by Marcie would often be followed by whispers of, "Oh, that's just Marcie being Marcie." Most people accepted her for that quality, except those who didn't quite measure up to her standards. Her ex-husband fell into this latter category, and Marcie was quick to say now that he probably didn't measure up to anyone's standards.

Mason did most of the time, although he had occasionally been chastised by Marcie for the late hours he was forced to put in during the months leading up to April 15 when his clients' taxes had to be filed. So pressing was this deadline that Sami and Mason had carefully scheduled their wedding in mid June for that very reason. Mason knew he would have some downtime to spend with his wife following the tax season. In spite of Marcie getting on his case at the same time every year, Mason knew she had her friend's best interests at heart.

Mason could picture his wife's friend, even this early in the morning with hair done and makeup on, trying to decide what to do with the rest of her day. She would probably be heading off to the gym, as she did most mornings. After announcing it was him and without waiting for a response at the other end, Mason said, "Marcie, can I ask you something? I'm a little concerned about Sami. She hasn't been herself lately, and I'm wondering if there's anything you're aware of that could be bothering her?"

Over the phone, he could hear her derisive snort. "No greeting or anything, Mason? You know, you could learn how to use the phone a little more politely!" Marcie stopped for a second, and then continued more calmly. "Actually I was going to call Sami at work today. The last time I talked to her was two days ago, before your anniversary. She did seem worried about something. I hope you treated Sami well on her anniversary, and maybe bought her something nice? You know, in the manner in which the girl should be treated on her special day?"

Mason ignored the barb about his telephone manners and the fact that their anniversary was *their* special day, something Marcie seemed to have completely forgotten. Mason had often thought that even though Marcie was his wife's best friend, had he been married to the woman, he probably would have left long before her ex-husband had. Anyway, that thought was for another time, and there was that familiar theme again. "What do you mean, she was worried?"

"I don't know," Marcie answered, slowly for her. "She mentioned that there was something bothering her. When I pressed her on it, she said she couldn't talk about it just then. She said we would discuss it later. Why, what's happened? Is Sami all right?"

Mason paused briefly and then decided that he should drop the charade, since the clock was ticking and Sami still had not shown up. With her cocky but upbeat attitude and her total affection for Sami, Mason thought his wife's best friend could be a staunch ally, someone he could confide in. And since Marcie had successfully fleeced her ex, a wealthy professional basketball player, for everything he was worth, she was left in the enviable position of a person with too much time on her hands and more than enough wealth to support her extravagant lifestyle. In short, Marcie was bored. And Mason needed someone he could talk to.

"Marcie, I'm not being totally honest," said Mason, sucking in his breath. "I don't know how else to say this: Sami somehow left during the night and she hasn't returned."

"WHAT?" yelled Marcie. "Your wife left you on her anniversary? What on earth did you do to her, Mason? If you caused Sami to leave, you will have to deal with me!"

"Marcie, please," said Mason, wishing she would calm down. "We had a great day. We celebrated our anniversary the whole day and into the evening. I thought everything was fine, but looking back, she did seem to be a little sad last night, and Jennifer noticed the same thing when she called her. Today I called her boss, and he said he'd noticed she didn't seem like her usual cheerful self. I swear there was nothing wrong between Sami and me. I'm really upset, Marcie, this whole thing is a total mystery to me. I keep waiting for her to walk through the door, but I haven't seen her since last night. I woke up this morning, and she was gone. I've called her cell phone, but her voicemail is full for some reason, and I don't see why it would ever be full. She doesn't get many personal calls other than from you. I guess my next step is to check her computer, if I can access her email. If she doesn't show up by noon, I'll have to call the police."

From the new tone in Marcie's voice, Mason knew he had struck a nerve. "Well, then stop wasting time talking to me. Get on it, man! Go and find the girl. You had better keep me posted."

The phone line went dead, but Mason felt relieved for telling Marcie the truth. There was no doubt in his mind that Marcie was just as concerned as he was.

Chapter 5

Mason wandered into the kitchen, his shoulders rounded from the invisible weight resting on them. He wanted desperately to hear from his wife, to know that despite all appearances, she was all right. The kitchen wasn't that messy to his eyes, but then he remembered that last night Sami had led the way into the bedroom without cleaning the kitchen first. He had been happily surprised when it had happened.

The leftover lobster shells were strewn about, and a few dishes and some cutlery were waiting to be put in the dishwasher. The two wine bottles sitting on the table were only remnants of their former selves, as the liquid they contained at the beginning of the evening had been completely consumed. One had held a Sauvignon Blanc and the other a Cabernet Sauvignon. About the only thing Mason and Sami didn't agree on was wine. She liked hers white and he preferred red. He set the bottles aside on the countertop for recycling later. He felt like he was going through the motions on autopilot. *This is unbelievable*, his mind told him. *Where is my wife?*

He picked up the phone to call the police, but once again, he hesitated. There were other avenues he thought he should pursue first. It was around 10 a.m. now. Sami had been gone for six hours, maybe even longer, but Mason thought it was probably still too early for the police to take action. He knew his secretary of 10 years would be planning his day and wondering where he was, so he had better call her. Myra was in her mid-50s and efficient beyond belief. He had interviewed countless people for the job. Many of the applicants who'd walked through the door were young with an attitude that they were entitled to the job and everything else that life could give them.

Most were more concerned about benefits than they were about the work they would be doing. Some weren't even overly concerned with the way they were dressed. The collection of tattoos, piercings, exposed navels and ripped jeans adorning the over-confident young people who traipsed in and out of his office when he was doing the interviews shocked him. When the slightly greying woman in a professional-looking dress walked through the door to his office, he could tell from her bearing that she meant business. Myra was older, more experienced, and more importantly, she displayed conscientiousness in her answers to Mason's interview questions. There was never a question that she wouldn't get the job, and Mason patted himself on the back every day for making the right hiring decision.

But now, waiting for her to pick up the phone, Mason could feel his pulse become more rapid. This wasn't just a call to tell her he was running a little behind schedule. When Myra picked up the phone on the second ring with her usual efficient tone, Mason told her that he wasn't feeling well and asked her to cancel his appointments for the day. He felt slightly guilty about not telling Myra the whole story. He felt like he was perpetrating a subterfuge on his mother, but he knew he wasn't ready yet to bring anyone other than Marcie in on Sami's disappearance. On the other end of the phone, Myra merely said that she would handle things in his absence and hoped he felt better soon. There was no doubt at all that she would handle things competently in his absence.

Next, Mason thought about Sami's computer. As an accountant, he was skillful with a spreadsheet and relatively proficient on a computer, although he liked to draw on Sami's expertise when he needed some real computer advice. Sami was the computer whiz in the family, and always had been. It was Sami who had shown Jennifer how to navigate around the internet with confidence and how to make the power of the computer work for her when it came to school work. It was Sami, not Mason, who always ensured they had the latest gadgets that technology had to offer.

Although both had their own offices where they went each day of the work week, they had also set up individual workstations in their small home office, which was in an unused third bedroom upstairs. Mason preferred a desktop, Sami loved her laptop. The room had been converted to a cheerful office where they each had a desk. There was enough space that they could avoid tripping over each other. They had two modular desks, and each had cabinets for their work. They'd decided if they were going to spend time in an office at home, the room should be attractive and still functional, so the walls were adorned with a white board and cork board, along with their framed degrees and career certificates to remind them occasionally of how they got to where they were.

While Mason's computer provided basic functionality, Sami used her free time on her computer to build massive civilizations and protect her computer-generated heroes and heroines from plague, pestilence and wars. He could hear the deep rumble coming from the office occasionally as she vaporized computer-game bad guys into dust when he was downstairs watching the baseball game on his own electronic guilty pleasure. He always smiled to himself as the fierce Sami who was boldly protecting her loyal following was a far cry from the gentle Sami who would be joining him in bed after she was sure her adherents would be safe for the night.

Mason pressed the power button on her laptop, and it whirred into action. He marveled at how quickly it started, compared to his desktop computer which Sami teasingly referred to as "something from the Dark Ages." Maybe she was right.

The first screen he came across indicated that it had been locked by the user. That was odd, since they shared everything. He still wasn't thinking all that clearly, but he remembered talking with her about passwords just recently, and they had decided that something easy to remember would be best for them. He would have to think about this later. For now, he was just having too much difficulty keeping his thoughts traveling in a straight line.

He couldn't sit still. Nervous tension was making him unusually jittery as if he'd had far too much caffeine. His thoughts felt fragmented and he couldn't concentrate. It just seemed if something didn't come easily to him, he had to move onto something else. Normally he was a very patient man even under stress, but today was a completely different story. Since Sami's password didn't come to him immediately, Mason decided to go outside and take another look around now that it was full daylight. It was a beautiful morning in their quiet residential neighborhood. He left the computer on, walked out the front door and stood on the step. He wasn't sure what he was looking for, as his eyes scanned the street in both directions. He felt dazed. His heart was racing, and his hands still shook

The sun was shining through the trees, casting shadows on their manicured front lawn, and the breeze was fending off the heat. Mason glanced to one side of his yard. Mrs. Cassidy, their neighbor to the left, was busily watering her grass. Widowed last year after 53 years of marriage, she was a delightful white-haired little lady who always had time for Sami and Mason. In spite of her relatively recent loss and the arthritis that was claiming her mobility, she was always cheerful. This morning, she was hunched over her flower bed in a print dress, looking every bit the lovable matronly neighbor they had come to know and care about since they moved in.

Mason pushed himself off the step in her direction and tried to put on a brave face. He spoke loudly so she would hear him. Raising his voice seemed like such work given the way he was feeling, but he made the effort. "Good morning, Mrs. Cassidy. How are you this morning?"

Deborah Cassidy shut off the water hose and straightened up with a grimace. It was obvious that bending over the flower bed was going to create aches and difficulties for her later when she was done, but she soldiered on. "I'm fine, Mason. How are you and that lovely wife of yours?"

"We're both good, thanks. Listen, Mrs. Cassidy, you didn't happen to see or hear any strange activity outside last night, did you? A car going by or doors slamming or anything like that? I thought I might have heard something, but I could have been dreaming."

She thought for a moment before saying, "No, I didn't hear anything. I have to take pills sometimes to control this damn arthritis, and last night was one of those nights. Besides that, you know I don't hear too well. I slept like a baby."

"Sure, well, thanks. I think I probably just had a bad dream. Anyway, I do need to go, Mrs. Cassidy. Sorry to interrupt your garden work. Take care of yourself, okay?"

As Mrs. Cassidy acknowledged his abrupt conversation with a frown, Mason walked back to his own property. He sensed that he was looking for something - anything - that might offer him a nugget of information. He glanced at Sami's car and thought about the keys in her purse. He went back in the house to retrieve the keys and returning to the Miata, he unlocked the car door. Being a two-seater, there was really nowhere to search. He sat in the driver's seat and reached over to look in the glove compartment. He saw nothing except the Owner's Manual and some peppermints. The car, like the house, was spotless. He opened the trunk, and it too was free of clutter. He shook his head slightly at his tireless wife who was able to maintain the house *and* her car in such condition. As he closed the trunk lid and walked around the passenger side of the vehicle, he glanced once more at the interior of the car. There, lodged under the left front corner of the passenger seat, was a white piece of paper.

Mason opened the door to retrieve the paper. It was a cash register receipt that had apparently dropped out of a shopping bag. He picked up the bill and saw that it was from the Beall's Outlet store in nearby St. Petersburg. He squinted to read it more clearly. It was for the purchase of a complete outfit – slacks, blouse, socks, underwear, watch, handbag – and a hat. A hat? In 20 years of marriage, he had never seen his wife wear a hat. She despised them. This added yet another unexplained dimension. Could the woman he loved so deeply and with whom he felt so comfortable have been preparing to run away? Could she have run off the night of their anniversary? Mason shoved the idea aside. The thought was ridiculous – not even worth contemplating. Had he found the bill any other day, he wouldn't have given it a second thought, but crazy thoughts were taking turns jumping into his head like demented pole vaulters. Why had Sami bought all this clothing? On their anniversary yesterday, Sami had dressed casually and those clothes were now on the floor. The signs were too obvious to ignore: Mason realized that whatever items she had bought were still in the house -- or she was wearing them when she left.

He took the bill with him into the back yard and sat on the chair of their patio set. He gazed at the door leading from their sunroom into the back yard. He thought about the purchase, as the sound of a distant motor boat on the water registered in his subconscious. His eyes moved towards the huge gardenias in full bloom, and he inhaled the sweet scent that wafted on the breeze through the yard. He stared at some bees that were busily flitting from one flower to the next, pollinating each one so they would continue to thrive. He thought that this whole thing with his wife couldn't possibly be happening. Everything else was as it should be. The flowers, the bees, the weather, Mrs. Cassidy... It must be a very bad joke or a dream or something. Sami should be in the bathroom preparing for work or happily making coffee in the kitchen or sitting here beside him listening to the birds in the trees and enjoying the fragrance of the flowers.

But she wasn't.

He looked at the bill again to make sure his eyes weren't deceiving him. The bill stared back, assuring him nothing had changed. He tried to read the date on the receipt. No two cash register receipts were ever alike, and the date was always positioned in a way that made it hard to read. It was one of his personal pet peeves that dates on store receipts were never in the same format. He knew accountants were often accused of being anal, but this one little thing drove most of them to distraction since the date was crucial to applying appropriate month and year-end allocations. However, this one he could interpret easily enough. Sami's purchase was made the day before yesterday - the day before their anniversary.

Mason looked at his watch for the umpteenth time. It was 11 o'clock in the morning.

He had to face it - it was time to call the police.

Chapter 6

Greg Johnson stood towering over the man who lay crumpled in the dirt bleeding and swollen from a number of wounds. Johnson's marching orders had simply been that the guy owed Johnson's boss a lot of money and should pay dearly for it. Johnson never asked questions, only did what he was told -- and did it mercilessly well. As he administered another kick to the inert body, Johnson's mind wandered to a job he had done a month earlier. It was in Tampa, Florida, and he'd been in a condo where he didn't belong, doing what he did best. The condo belonged to James and Joan Briscoe. The Briscoes lived a very affluent life. Their 37th floor condo had a massive window overlooking the water. They could see the boats drifting in and out of the marina, and they could see their own cabin cruiser tied up to its moorings. They could watch people streaming along the pier, stopping at the souvenir shops or buying a snack at one of the little sidewalk cafes. They were close to the bars and restaurants that made up the fabric of the city, and during any of the wide-ranging activities that take place in downtown Tampa, they had a spectacular view of the event without having to leave the comfort of their home.

But during the time Johnson visited them, the Briscoes, who were both in their 50s, were not enjoying their view at all. They were each bound tightly in chairs with their mouths gagged. Joan Briscoe's head hung limply forward on her chest with blood running down her white blouse from a deep gash across her throat. The swelling on her face told the story of a horrific beating inflicted upon her before she died. James Briscoe was conscious enough to know that his beloved wife was dead and that he was going to be next. His eyes were nearly swollen shut and his head throbbed from the force of the blows he had absorbed. Some of his ribs were shattered and so was his life, knowing that if he did miraculously survive this nightmare, he would go forward without Joan. He refused to turn his head to look at his wife, because he couldn't bear to see what this murderer had done to her. It had been bad enough listening to her trying to draw her last breath through her devastated throat. All James Briscoe could think was that this man was an animal.

There was nothing unique about James Briscoe. He had a successful one-man law practice not far from his condo, and he charged his clients exorbitant amounts of money to fight with the Internal Revenue Service on their behalf. James Briscoe was very good at his job, and his acquittal rate was impressive. He knew U.S. tax law better than most senior Internal Revenue Service agents and he made a lot of money, thanks to the power of Congress to impose taxes at will on anybody who had the slightest hint of income. The only people he routinely pissed off were the IRS' own attorneys whom he consistently beat in court. Oh, and his client, the man who had ordered the murders.

The success at defending his clients against the IRS, which was simply trying to claim tax money that was most likely rightfully theirs, bought Briscoe and his wife this beautiful condo, stunning furnishings, a huge boat, and other real estate holdings. But the one thing it couldn't buy them was the opportunity to die a natural death. The one thing that really set James Briscoe and his wife apart from most people was the beating they took in their condo that day.

Greg Johnson, the man administering the beating was known by a nickname among his acquaintances, especially his infantry buddies. They called him "The Force." He was a huge man, and he had always used his size to his advantage, strong-arming people pretty much any way he wanted throughout his life. He took great pride in the work he carried out for his boss. The Briscoes' demise was just another paid job as part of his regular employment. For the most part, Johnson remained emotionless and uninvolved when carrying out his duties, rarely feeling any remorse for ending the lives of people he never knew.

In the military, Johnson learned respect for his seniors. He had done tours in Afghanistan and Iraq, and killed his first man in 2003. It was a lucky shot, and the fact the guy was dead meant nothing to him. He had hoped at the time that there would be more opportunities. He was trained to kill a man in more ways than an average person would imagine possible. His favorite weapon was a folding knife with a serrated edge. He had a variety of military and tactical weapons, but he liked this one for its ease of concealment. He was equally adept with a gun, a rope, his hands or his feet. It didn't really matter to him what he used; but the job sometimes dictated the choice.

For The Force, killing became a little more meaningful in November 2004 when he and his infantry buddies fought their way through downtown Fallujah during Operation Phantom Fury. They had to dodge sniper fire and work their way around improvised explosive devices planted in the ground. He had seen some of his buddies blown up, and that infuriated him. He couldn't wait to get his hands on one of those insurgents and rip him apart.

And it came to that. He turned a corner during an incursion into the depths of Fallujah and was face to face with a young Iraqi fighter equally dedicated to killing him. They had fought brutally for 10 minutes, each gaining ground in turn until the other took over. They were bloodied from punches that connected, and bruised from landing on the concrete that held up the roof of the remnants of the building they were fighting in. They swore and grunted and groaned as they fought for their lives in the dirt. With the last bit of strength he could muster, Johnson struggled backwards as if he was about to collapse and give in. His opponent charged towards Johnson with a piece of concrete raised above his head and a triumphant smirk on his bloodied face, prepared to cave in the head of his adversary. Johnson reached for the knife that had fallen in the melee, raised it and held fast as the hard charging insurgent dove unknowingly into it. He could feel the blade enter all the way to the hilt, and he heard the horrific shriek from his enemy as his life drained away.

Johnson watched him die without expression. It wasn't as impersonal as shooting someone from 50 yards away, but he was doing what he had been told to do. He watched the man's eyes as they dimmed, impressed by his enemy's determination. As a soldier, Johnson had been provided with intensified training to handle these situations. But this guy had put up a fight, probably without the same expert training. It was undoubtedly the sheer desire to stay alive that had kept the insurgent going for so long against impossible odds.

Johnson's reward from the Marines for following orders and killing as many of the enemy as he could during the time he served was a medal and a promotion. And it set his future career. He became a hired gun, a contract killer who carried out orders efficiently and without leaving a trace to implicate him or whoever was paying him. Once he was discharged from the military, The Force continued living up to the nickname he'd been given, killing and maiming people for pay just as he would have for any other job. He didn't really respect his boss, the man he worked for who ordered the work to be done, but he did respect positions of authority. And he liked the paychecks. Killing was what he knew how to do and no one could argue with how effective he was at doing it.

At 47 years old, his face had seen more than its share of abuse. His nose lay flat against his face from an encounter with a baseball bat in a bar fight a few years ago. His hair was long and dark and flowed over his broad shoulders. Besides spending his money on women, he loved to collect art. But for Greg Johnson, "collecting art" only meant body art: the serpent winding its way around his massive left arm or the flag on his right bicep that seemed to wave in the wind as his muscle flexed and relaxed.

Johnson was especially proud of his flag tattoo. It represented his years of service to his country. He was also proud of his skill at not making a mess when he carried out an assignment. But in the apartment of James Briscoe and his wife, he suddenly realized that he had some blood embedded in the bottom treads of his newly-acquired running shoe. It took an unusual amount of effort later to remove it. He had used cold water first with minimal results, but then he found he needed to add peroxide and let it fizz for a few minutes. He should have been more careful.

Johnson had turned to survey the crime scene one last time before he left. Nothing was out of the ordinary, except the two mutilated bodies now drenched in their own blood. He wanted to be certain there were no clues, no fingerprints, nothing that could lead anyone to him. He knew his boss would be waiting to hear that he had administered "proper force" to the Briscoes and made sure their final moments on this earth were not pleasant ones. Although he didn't know exactly what James Briscoe had done to his boss, he had spared no effort at ending two lives in a way that could send a message to anyone else who might need to see just how bad making a mistake with his boss could be.

Johnson's thoughts came back to the present from that time in the Briscoes' condo a month earlier. He administered one last kick to the head of his latest victim, who was unconscious and requiring a number of stitches and casts that would remind him to be a little more forthcoming with his loan repayment next time. As he did so, Johnson knew he would never want to be on the wrong side of the man he worked for. No, that wasn't a good place to be for sure.

Chapter 7

Albert Baker and Tom Finch worked in Patrol District 3, which is an area covering downtown Tampa, East Tampa, the Latin Quarter known as Ybor City and the Port of Tampa. They were an odd couple. Baker was the older of the two with 22 years on the force. He wore suits until they were no longer wearable. He was slightly overweight (a condition he referred to as husky), and his square jaw made him look like the grizzled detective that he was. Baker had the quintessential look that TV detectives are modeled after. But he was hard as nails. Years of running into guys who were some of Tampa's worst had hardened him. Many had run afoul of Albert Baker, and all ended up wishing they hadn't. His years of dedicated service and dealing with the scum of humanity had taken its toll on Baker's stomach, and these days, he kept a bottle of antacid tablets always nearby.

Tom Finch, on the other hand, was a relative newcomer who had gained some respect from his colleagues after taking a bullet in the shoulder in a shootout with a ring of drug dealers in Ybor City. He had long hair usually worn in a pony tail, and his preferred clothing choice was an open-necked sports shirt with casual pants. Finch always looked like he was more likely to pull golf clubs out of the closet and head out for a quick round, while Baker gave the impression of a fighter more likely to take someone into the ring for a quick round. They were indeed a curious paring, but they got along well in their working relationship, and they nearly always accomplished what they set out to do.

They were well aware that their two last names made them sound like a law firm. But what amused their colleagues most and made them the butt of too many jokes was the resemblance of their collective names to former Australian professional golfer, Ian Baker-Finch. Baker-Finch won a British Open but he also completely lost his confidence and shot a 92 at the same tournament a few years later. It was this total collapse under pressure that the colleagues of Albert Baker and Tom Finch liked to tease the two detectives about, even though it had nothing to do with them. As in any police department, anything that provided a source for taunting and chirping was good enough.

Baker and Finch were responsible for investigating homicides in Tampa and its surrounding area. Tampa Bay does not have the worst homicide record in the United States, nor does it have the best. The thing Tampa's mayor was most proud of was what he was careful to describe as "our *declining* homicide rate." An average of 28 murders per year occurs in the city. That's higher than the national average and higher than the state's overall violent crime rate, but it was the declining trend that the city touted. The mayor knew all too well the role crime can play in tourism (and re-election), so he was careful to trot out the more positive aspects of his police department's efforts from time to time.

Yet standing as a giant question mark were Tampa's 24 unsolved murders still remaining on the books, dating back to 1985. Baker and Finch did not want their newest one, sitting fresh on their desks, to become the 25th. The case that the team of Baker and Finch were poring over on this sunny day was that of one James Briscoe and his wife Joan. James was an upscale tax lawyer who lived with his wife in a condo in downtown Tampa, at least until a fateful day about a month ago.

Baker and Finch would be the first to say that solving crimes is not the glamorous job it's cracked up to be on certain television shows. It requires hours of painstaking, mind-numbing research and detection. Things don't conveniently fall into place, but sometimes almost against the odds, there is a break. They had checked and rechecked the crime scene pictures, the information gathered, the post-mortem results, and everything else they could get their hands on related to the case. There was blood splatter everywhere in the condo, indicating that a person or persons, currently unknown, had it in for someone in that particular condominium on that day. Unfortunately, James and Joan were both home and became the unfortunate victims. They were found bound and gagged, sitting in chairs facing a stunning view that neither would ever enjoy again. It was obvious they had suffered significantly before succumbing to the final coup de grâce of having their throats slashed from ear to ear.

There was valet parking and a security guard at the front entrance of the Briscoes' condo building. But the guard said he'd seen nothing unusual that day. He did confirm that a technician had been called to repair the building's security cameras that, unknown to the residents, had not worked for about a month.

The killer (or) killers appeared to have made one potentially-disastrous mistake. There was a a running shoe tread mark left in the blood spatter at the scene, and that was the break they were hoping would give some direction to their investigation.

Baker and Finch had already interviewed everyone who might have had anything to do with the Briscoes, including friends and neighbors. Everyone said they were a perfectly charming couple, and everyone loved them. The two detectives felt that so far they were shooting blanks, as it were, coming up empty with a motive for the murder. They had investigated the couples' finances and tried to identify potential enemies of the pair, but nothing turned up. The only clue they had from the crime scene was the running shoe's tread mark. Running shoe treads can be compared to a car tire that remains relatively constant for an extended period of time of usage. They are known as "pattern evidence," and are unique to specific brands, which makes them a valuable identifier.

Finch submitted the tread characteristics to the searchable databases maintained by the FBI, which simplified the drudgery of identifying the owner considerably. The shoe worn by the presumed killer happened to be made by Brooks from its semi-popular 730 series running shoe. Tread size pinpointed it to be a size 10, a fact confirmed by the manufacturer when Finch placed the call.

It was still painstaking work, but Baker and Finch had a lead, and that's what they lived for as seasoned detectives. With one good lead, they were officially on the killer's or killers' trail. And quite often, it wasn't long before another good lead would show up. They pored over the internet, compiling a list of all the stores in the Tampa Bay area that sold that particular shoe. Since the tread was barely worn, they thought it likely that the shoe had been purchased sometime in the previous few months leading up to the murder. They had to pick a ballpark number, so they chose the previous five months. They took turns calling Tampa area stores to ask for a list of people who had purchased a size 10 Brooks 730 shoe in the five months leading up to the homicide. If the murderer had paid with cash, they were out of luck. There would be no way of knowing, unless a credit card was used or if the stores had asked for an email address so they could send out catalogs.

The stores cooperated, leaving Baker and Finch with a list of 137 customers who met the criteria and whose names they were able to obtain. There was a low chance that their killer's name was on the list, but it was a lead that needed to be followed. If nothing else, they would be able to clear the names of some. Even if a nun with big feet had purchased that particular brand of shoe in the timeframe meeting the criteria, she was going to be questioned just like everyone else on the list.

Baker and Finch decided to tell the people they were calling that they also had a DNA sample from the crime scene. That wasn't a total fabrication. DNA samples had been found at the scene that weren't identifiable; they could have come from friends that had been at the condo at one time or another. The two detectives were also all too keenly aware that DNA samples from a myriad of other crimes were piling up in the overworked, understaffed lab, and that any request to put a rush on a sample would be met with blank stares or worse. Annoying the lab attendants too much could lead to the sample dropping lower on the priority list. The overnight test results that brought perpetrators to a lifetime behind bars were completely foreign to real cops. But at least the samples would give them something to compare to if they needed it. The strategy was to talk to each of the men on the list, verifying their whereabouts at the time of the Briscoes' murder, then run a check on each person's Brooks series 730 shoes if they still owned them, and last but not least, to take a DNA sample from each of them for analysis.

Baker and Finch had now worked their way through 97 names on their list. They had amassed a sizable collection of Brooks 730 shoes, but no one who really stood out as a possible suspect.

Albert Baker reached for his coffee cup. He was about to contact candidate number 98. His name was Mason Seaforth.

Chapter 8

Mason had just come to the decision to call the police and was about to leave the back yard to go inside to make the call when he heard two familiar sounds. The first was the distant sound of his cell phone ringing in the sunroom where he had stupidly left it. He leapt out of his chair in the back yard and tried the door into the sunroom, only to realize that he had relocked it last night after he stuck his head out to call for Sami. Mason thought it might be Sami calling, and he almost lost his footing as he raced around the corner of the house to try to get in the front door to the phone before it stopped ringing.

The second sound that registered in his subconscious as he launched himself out of the chair in the race for the phone was a thumping that practically made the ground tremble. Normally, that sound would elicit grins from Sami and Mason as it moved towards them like the shock of an earthquake with its epicenter just down the street. The same sound would earn a look and a shake of the head from Mrs. Cassidy next door. It announced the arrival of Marcie Kane's car with the stereo in her BMW 128i Cabriolet convertible cranked to thundering levels.

As Mason raced towards the front door, he could only wave at Marcie as the radio clicked off simultaneously with the engine, and she started to emerge from her personal music auditorium. She was driving the metallic blue gift that she had generously given herself as a birthday present. When she brought it over to show the Seaforths on the day of her birthday, she laughingly announced that she wanted to thank her ex, whom she referred to as "He Who Shall Not Be Named," for unknowingly providing her with her brand new set of wheels. The car and Marcie were a perfect match for each other, but Mason had doubts from the first time he saw it that the brilliant German engineers who designed such a beauty considered the load that Marcie would be placing on the speakers. He hoped there would be no collateral damage from flying fragments of the speakers when they exploded under the assault of Marcie's favorites being played at a level loud enough to make the average person's ears bleed.

As he disappeared into the house, Marcie had fully come into view from her car. She was the usual fashionista with her matching red tank top and running shoes separated by black jeggings. She had once spent considerable time educating Mason on the term "jeggings", explaining like an impatient teacher to a student who wasn't picking up the assignment too quickly that jeggings were leggings designed to look like designer jeans.

Mason heard her call shrilly, "Mason, have you heard anything? I want to talk to you." He let the door drift shut as he ran through and raced for his phone. As it closed, he heard Marcie's voice disappearing somewhere in the front yard. The phone stopped ringing when he was about two steps away. When he picked it up, all he could hear was the dial tone. The call display indicated "Private Caller." His spirits lifted as he told himself this could be the call he had been waiting for. At least it could be news. *Any* news at this point would make him grateful.

Marcie burst through the door as he hit *69 on the phone. "Why are you running away like that, Mason? Don't you want to talk to me? Have you heard anything about Sami?"

For the moment, Mason ignored Marcie. As expected but still with much disappointment, he listened as the metallic voice from who knows where on the phone confirmed that the call was from a private number. He looked at Marcie with dismay. He felt the burden of not knowing as he turned to Sami's best friend. "Marcie, I haven't heard anything. It's like she dropped off the face of the earth. I thought maybe this phone call could be her, but it was from a private caller and I got here too late to answer it. It might have been Sami calling from a private number, but there's no message."

"Mason, don't you think Sami would leave a message? If it's a private number, it could just as easily be one of those weirdos telling you that you won a cruise to the Bahamas or your credit rating is in jeopardy or something." Marcie stopped, and when she spoke next, her voice was unusually soft for her. "Mason, look, I just want to say I was a little harsh when I spoke with you earlier. I know this must be awful for you. I'm having a lot of trouble with it, too. It's so unlike Sami to act like this. I'm really worried. Have you called the police yet? What about Jennifer? Have you told her? I want to help in whatever way I can. What do you want me to do?"

Mason took a deep breath. He had the urge to expel some of the frustration and fear he was feeling, and Marcie happened to be in the target area. But he knew that she really was a friend and was nearly as frantic about Sami as he was, so he started to tell her what he had done. He had to think. What *had* he done? It wasn't coming to him quickly, although he knew he had been busy since he'd first wakened to discover his wife missing. Finally Mason took a deep breath and began to recount the story. His memory rebounded from all he'd been through, and he was able to explain patiently that he had already talked to Jennifer and also spoken with Sami's boss. He told Marcie that he had lied to Jennifer, or at least not told her the whole truth, that her mother had been missing since the pre-dawn hours. He told Marcie he had combed the house and yard for any sign of clues, and he had turned on Sami's computer but he failed to figure out her password. He also mentioned the receipt for an outfit of clothing he had found in the car. At the mention of the outfit, Marcie was clearly taken aback.

"Wow," she said with a slight frown," that's strange that she would buy a full outfit before your anniversary and not wear it. But Mason, the really strange thing is the hat. You said the receipt showed a hat? Sami doesn't wear hats. Have you ever seen her wear a hat? That just isn't like her." After a minute, Marcie asked the obvious question: "Where is the outfit? Have you seen it? Her attitude has been just a little off lately. I don't understand any of this!"

Mason said quietly, "They're all good questions, Marcie, and I can't answer any of them. I really wish I could. But I have to ask you a question, which is probably so far-fetched that I have trouble even asking it. But I have to ask because nothing else is making any sense. I have been sitting in the back yard for the last few minutes – just staring and trying to come up with something. I have tossed a lot of things around in my mind and I keep coming back to one question. Do you have any reason to believe that Sami is having an affair?"

Marcie stared back at Mason in a way that only she could do. Since the time he had known her, Mason had observed many people who had the misfortune of saying something that Marcie vehemently disagreed with. He had seen most of those same people wilt under the intensity of the look that Marcie could shoot them when she thought that someone was too stupid to have been given life. "Okay, Mason. I have a question for you that *you* might be able to answer." Marcie's voice rose in pitch from the beginning of the sentence to the end and Mason could sense that he was about to be on the receiving end of one of Marcie's lectures, whether he wanted to be or not. He didn't know whether he was in any condition to tolerate it.

"*Are you completely insane?*" While the pitch was not at full Marcie levels, it was certainly above normal. "That girl may have been smarter to find someone who would wait on her hand and foot and by the way, with her looks, body and personality, I'm sure that there would be any number of guys willing to do that. But for some unfathomable reason, she chose *you* and she loves you more than anything. She would never deliberately do anything to hurt you. So you can forget that thought right now and try to think of something logical that may have happened to her. Don't think I haven't told her that she would be better off with some tall, dark and handsome gazillionaire."

Mason had been listening with his head down for most of Marcie's diatribe, the emotion building inside of him to a point where he was ready to lash out, to strike back. Then he raised his head, only to see a wry smile on her face. He realized Marcie was hurting in her own way, just as he was, and that she was as desperate and distraught as he was, but had to show it her way. He knew that she was trying to lighten the moment. He found a way to smile back as he sensed that there would be no better ally in figuring out this mystery than the tall, strong woman standing in front of him. Then Marcie did something she had never done before. She wrapped her arms around Mason in a hug and with a tremble in her voice she said, "We have to find her, Mason. We have to find what happened to the most important person either one of us has."

Then she held Mason at arm's length and said, "Let's think this through. What should we do next? You give me some guidance, and I will do anything you want me to do to help. Maybe I can be just a little more objective and think a little clearer than you. You seemed to be a little foggy on what you'd accomplished when I asked you earlier. I think maybe you should give the police a call. I know it hasn't been 24 hours yet, but they might have some ideas on what you should do next. And I think you should call Jennifer and be upfront with her. We don't want to alarm her any more than necessary, but she has to know, Mason. In the meantime, I'm going to look for those new clothes that Sami bought. I think I would recognize most of her clothes." Mason was just starting to nod his head, when Marcie took a deep breath, and looked directly at him. "And how would it be if I call all the hospitals to see if she may have been brought in after an accident or something?"

For the first time in what seemed like days but which in actuality was only a few hours, Mason didn't feel so alone. He actually thought they might have the beginnings of a plan. He said, "I think you're right, Marcie. I also think you are a very special friend. Let's get started. Oh, but do you think the hospitals will give you any information if you aren't an immediate family member?"

"Mason, do you think I'm a complete idiot? As of now, I'm officially the black sister from another mother that Sami never had. As far as the hospitals know, I'm the concerned sister she always doted on. Don't worry, leave it to me. There won't be a stone left unturned. After I check Sami's closet, I'll go back into the sunroom and start calling. Good luck with the police."

Mason hugged her again, and they exchanged slight smiles, both knowing that this event had brought them closer through a common cause: the disappearance of someone they both loved dearly. As Marcie headed upstairs to the master bedroom, Mason picked up the phone and listened for the dial tone before suddenly realizing the staccato beep on the other end was indicating an unheard message was waiting for him. Whoever was calling him earlier must have been leaving a message as he was trying to redial their number.

His hands were shaking as he anxiously dialed the number and entered his password to retrieve the message. He hoped beyond hope that the message was from Sami, providing the answers he so desperately needed right now. He called out to Marcie, and she came running downstairs, practically falling on the stairs in her haste and arrived in the room just in time to observe Mason's face turn ashen. He nearly dropped the phone as he slumped into the chair he had been standing beside.

Marcie silently grabbed the phone out of Mason's hand and in one motion hit 1-1 to replay the message. The message that came through the phone line stunned Marcie just as it had Mason. The voice of the caller was serious, and it was clear that it was no joke. His words sent a chill up the length of Marcie's spine. The message said simply: "This message is for Mason Seaforth. My name is Detective Albert Baker from the Tampa Police Department. Please call me back at your earliest convenience." The voice left a phone number, and the message clicked off, leaving Mason and Marcie staring at each other in total silence.

Chapter 9

The shock of what Mason had just heard was like a punch to the solar plexus. Marcie's eyes were enormous and staring at Mason as she hung up the phone. The fact that this detective wanted Mason to call as soon as possible couldn't be good. But Marcie's quick mind switched to a lingering doubt that it was something horrible that had happened to her best friend. If it was terrible news, why wouldn't the police come to the door?

"Mason, snap out of it! You have to call right now."

"Oh my God, Marcie. This has to be bad news."

"Maybe not, Mason. They would come to tell you in person if it was something really bad. Just make the call. I'm here to support you."

Marcie's theory that it might not be bad news cheered Mason a little. There was something to her hypothesis that they would deliver the worst news in person. Still, they must have some news or they wouldn't have called, and he had to find out what it was.

Mason sat in the chair, his knee bouncing up and down as it often did when he was nervous. With sweat beading on his forehead, Mason attempted to dial the number left by Albert Baker. To his frustration, the first attempt was a misdial answered by someone who could barely speak English. Mason felt like throwing the phone across the room, but he tried again. He could feel the dampness in his shirt as he heard his second attempt being picked up at the other end.

"Detective Baker."

It was a full, terrifying sentence in two words. Words pronounced in a fraction of a second that sent more shivers down his spine.

"Detective Baker, it's Mason Seaforth returning your call. Do you have some news about my wife?"

There was a hesitation on the other end of the phone. "Your *wife*, Mr. Seaforth!? That's not what I was calling about. Is there an issue with your wife?"

Mason was taken aback by his question, but he saw no reason to withhold any information from this policeman. "I thought you must be calling with some information about my wife, Sami. I woke up this morning and she wasn't here. I was going to call to report her missing when your phone call came in. I know she's only been gone for a few hours, but this is really unusual for Sami."

He wanted to tell this detective everything, but Albert Baker had his own reason for the phone call. Just as Mason launched into his story, Baker interrupted and said he was sorry but since the Seaforths didn't live in his jurisdiction, it wasn't a case he could help with. He told Mason that there was probably a logical explanation for her disappearance, but he should definitely go in person to his local police station in Gulfport and file a missing persons report on Sami. Baker gave Mason the private number for a Sergeant Juanita Suarez. He debunked the theory that a 24-hour wait is necessary before filing a missing persons report; in fact, he said the faster the police department can start working on a case, the more likely it is that they will be able to solve it. He told Mason to be sure to take a recent photo of Sami with him, to provide a thorough description, and to be sure to obtain a copy of the report.

Mason thanked Baker and started to hang up, forgetting completely that he wasn't the one who had initiated the conversation. He wanted to get off the phone to file a missing person's report as soon as possible. Baker had to remind Mason that he had something to discuss. Mason had trouble digesting that there could be another reason, but he listened as Baker briefly described the murder they were investigating and the running shoe tread mark left at the crime scene. He also asked Mason if he still had the Brooks 730 running shoes. "Yes," said Mason, adding that the only time he wore them was to the gym.

"Do you mind if we take the shoes for a few days so we can do some tests on them?" Baker asked. "Oh, and while we're there, we would also like to take a DNA sample from you if you don't mind."

Mason thought what a strange request it was. A DNA sample? From him? Meanwhile, his wife was still out there missing. But he answered resignedly, "Of course, I'll be happy to give you a DNA sample." He had nothing to hide, and besides, he really wanted to get this phone call over with so that he could turn his attention to the missing person report he needed to file.

"Okay, thanks. My partner and I will be over in about two hours. See you then. Good luck, Mr. Seaforth, I'm sure your wife will turn up at any minute."

Mason hung up and explained everything to Marcie, who had been watching him intently, trying to figure out what was going on. She was incredulous that Mason would receive a phone call about an unrelated crime at the exact same minute he was about to report his wife's disappearance.

The words spilled out as if released by a tap that had been rusted shut for years. "I know it's bizarre, but I can't explain it, Marcie! I just know that I need to go to the Gulfport Police Department right now to make this report. Detective Baker said I shouldn't waste any time. Do you want to come? I'm supposed to bring a recent picture of Sami with me. Maybe I ought to call the Gulfport Police Department just to make sure that this Sergeant Suarez is there – or someone else I can talk to."

Mason took a deep breath as Marcie stared at him, and then dialed the police station. Once again the phone at the other end was answered in that perfunctory, unsettling tone reserved for figures in authority. And again he heard words that he never expected to be hearing today.

"Sergeant Suarez."

Mason introduced himself and almost in a daze, explained the situation. Marcie watched him nod a few times as he listened intently, and she noticed him blanch a little at something that was being said on the other end of the line. After a few minutes, Mason hung up.

"She confirmed that I have to go file the report in person, Marcie. Sergeant Suarez was adamant that I should come over there right away. You're welcome to come if you want."

Marcie considered his request, then shook her head. "I think I would be better off staying here and calling the hospitals," she said. "I'm also trying to think of other things we should do. You go ahead and file your report."

Mason checked his wallet to make sure he still had the photo of a smiling Sami taken at an outing only a few weeks before. It was taken on Mason's phone, of course, but he was so pleased with the result that he had printed out a wallet-size version to carry with him. As he walked toward the door, Marcie asked if there was anything else Suarez had mentioned that could prove useful.

Without looking up, Mason said quietly, "Yes, there was one other place she thought we should check. She said when someone goes missing, no matter how unpleasant, one of the first things people should do is check with the morgue."

Chapter 10

Mason backed his white 2013 Audi A4 out of the garage. He had always admired the Audi brand, and he'd finally allowed himself to splurge a few months previously. He loved that vehicle. But right now that's all it was. Its only purpose at this moment was to get him from point A to point B as quickly as possible; and in this case, point B was the police station. He quickly shut off the radio so that he could think on the short 15-minute drive. As he passed the various stores and restaurants that had become so familiar to him and Sami, he thought to himself that he just couldn't understand any of this. Sami wouldn't just walk away into thin air. He knew her better than anyone, and this was so uncharacteristic that it was beyond belief. They always knew where each other was. They left notes for each other. If one of them was going to be unusually late, they would call. And that was what unnerved him the most: *why wasn't Sami calling him?* What the hell was going on?

The mention of the morgue completely unsettled him. He tried to push the thought out of his mind as he made his way along brick-paved 53rd Street South towards the police station. The bricks on the street had settled in some places more than others, causing Mason's car to roll from side to side slightly as he drew closer. No one in Gulfport complained about the rough streets, as it was one of the features that made the old city unique.

The street was shaded by mature oak and palm trees that offered privacy to the small Cape Cod-style cottages dominating the community. Mason had been to the one-story building that housed the police station a few times as City Hall also occupied the space. He had visited the building to pay parking tickets, and at one time to complain unsuccessfully about his property taxes.

The fire department occupied one end of the building that had been completely refurbished in 1972. As he entered the building, he inquired at the front desk and was directed by an attractive young dark-skinned woman to a door on the left. Another receptionist, who could have been the first woman's sister, greeted him from behind a glass enclosure and redirected him to a phone from which he was able to contact Detective Juanita Suarez.

He took a seat and after a few minutes, a woman in a standard police uniform greeted him. Although she would likely be considered stocky by North American standards, Mason thought she probably didn't have much fat on her frame and that she would easily be able to take down any criminal of any size with the same efficiency as her male colleagues. She was about 5 feet 5 inches tall with reddish tanned skin and long dark hair tied back in a pony tail. Her blue eyes popped against her dark skin. As she approached, Mason noticed the sidearm hanging off her hip on her massive belt, along with all the other weaponry needed to subdue. He recalled reading somewhere that a police officer like Juanita Suarez would probably be carrying stuff like two extra magazines for the gun, a baton, pepper spray, taser, handcuffs, radio and a pouch with gloves and medical supplies. Once again, Mason felt that emptiness in the pit of his stomach and the feeling that this world he had somehow been drawn into this morning belonged to others.

As Sergeant Suarez greeted him, she took him into an austere interview room with only a table and two chairs and wasted little time in handing Mason a Missing Persons form to fill out. She explained that they would be as thorough as possible in trying to find Sami and quoted some positive statistics on the likelihood that Sami would just show up, given the results of other missing persons cases she had been involved in. She told him that the information would be filed in the computer data base to which all law enforcement agencies had access. Mason started to complete the form. It required him to provide Sami's age, weight and height. There was a section on recent contacts in which Mason described her position at the bank and a list of her friends. He wrote down her habits, how cheerful she was, but also the observation that she had appeared to be not quite herself in recent days. He described her level of fitness and that she loved jogging and went to the gym regularly. He noted the fact that she did not take any kind of medication, nor had she ever taken any drugs. Over the years, they had often commented on having attended concerts that might have invited at least a toke on someone's passed-around joint, but neither one of them had ever indulged. They had proudly reminded Jennifer of that fact on more than one occasion.

Finally, after he thought he had been as complete as possible, he sought out the Sergeant. The chair creaked as Suarez sat down and she went over the form with Mason, noting comments where she thought it necessary. The chair swiveled as she turned slowly from side to side, posing additional questions. She asked Mason if Sami had any enemies that he could comment on. He said he wasn't aware of any, and that he just couldn't believe someone like his wife could ever have cultivated some. She asked Mason to elaborate on her friends and work colleagues, which he did. She also zeroed in on Marcie's recent attitude. Mason provided as much detail as he could.

Sergeant Suarez then asked him what he had done so far to try to find her. Mason thought back, and just as he had with Marcie, he realized he was having difficulty remembering what he had accomplished. He attributed that to shock and Suarez nodded slightly, although he noticed her head cock a little and an eyebrow raise as he divulged the information about how odd he had felt when he woke up, almost as if in a fogged-up stupor. She handed him a "Missing Adult Checklist" and went through each item with him. As they went through the checklist, Mason ticked off the relevant items. When they were done, it seemed like so little. He talked of Sami's missing cell phone and the fact that its mailbox was suddenly and mysteriously full of unheard messages. He told her that he had gone through Sami's clothes and purse looking for anything that might help. He mentioned trying to get into his wife's computer but giving up after a few minutes when he realized he didn't actually know Sami's password. He reiterated how he hadn't been able to concentrate on anything. He discussed sitting in the back yard in the early morning light trying to imagine what could have happened, but that his mind just couldn't seem to react with its usual quickness. He mentioned enlisting

Marcie's help and described the friendship that she and Sami had. Last, Mason talked about calling Sami's manager at work, talking to their daughter Jennifer, and the receipt he'd found in Marcie's car. He pulled the receipt out of his pocket and showed it to the police officer.

But the thing that seemed to capture Juanita Suarez's attention more than anything was when Mason mentioned he was a very light sleeper yet he had not heard Sami get up, get dressed or leave the house in the middle of the night. He started to brush this off, recounting the amount of wine they had had for their anniversary, but Sergeant Suarez didn't smile. Instead she asked if he always felt that groggy after drinking similar amounts of wine in the past. She also observed that it really didn't seem like they had had *that* much to drink, considering the time it took to consume it. Mason thought for a few seconds before replying. "Now that you mention it," he said, "I don't think I've ever felt quite that sluggish before, even when we've gone through a couple of bottles of wine on special occasions."

Suarez looked at him with a measured expression. Then she coupled a statement with a question so shocking that it caused Mason to sit back in his seat and gasp. The statement was delivered by the hardened police veteran without much empathy for the state of mind of the concerned husband. The question was delivered by the same person in the tone of an empathetic investigator whose job it was to get to the root of the issue.

First, the statement: "You have to prepare yourself for something, Mr. Seaforth. You mentioned that she was despondent. In cases like this, we have to consider suicide. We have to remain positive and check out all options, but you have to keep suicide as an option in the back of your mind. You have to ask yourself if there is somewhere she would have gone because she was despondent and having a difficult time dealing with life. People sometimes end their life at a favorite spot. Think about any special places your wife liked to go, Mr. Seaforth, and let me know if you come up with a location you would like us to check out. I know this is not easy, and you might think this is an impossible request to consider, but I have seen too many people in your situation where unfortunately things ended badly, and you have to think seriously about the last few days and your wife's unusual demeanor."

Mason looked vacantly at the officer sitting on the opposite side of the table.

Then the question: "Mr. Seaforth, is it possible you were drugged?"

Mason was still contemplating the statement he had just heard when this new question jolted him back to the present. Drugged? This officer actually thought he'd had *drugs* in his system?

He could feel a hotness spreading in his cheeks as his anger grew. Had this woman not understood? His voice rose in an irrational attempt to vent at someone who was trying to help him. "Why would I be drugged? I told you that neither one of us had ever taken anything but prescription medication."

"I'm not talking about knowingly taking recreational drugs, Mr. Seaforth. But doesn't it seem strange to you that your wife was able to get up, presumably get dressed and leave the house without you hearing anything, especially since you claim to be a light sleeper? Add that to the fact you have been less than alert since you woke up. I have dealt with numerous cases of date rape, and the victim has described symptoms almost identical to yours, although if the date rape drug Rohypnol had been used, you wouldn't remember anything that happened last night. And besides that, Rohypnol is not easy to get in the U.S. anymore. However, you could have been given some sleeping pills that contain a substance called BZO and this might well have put you out for a few hours."

To Mason, the roller coaster of the last few hours was not any closer to arriving at its destination. It was just picking up more speed and he felt like it was careening out of control. He was aghast at the thought that his wife could have deliberately knocked him out so that she could sneak out of the house. His head was spinning at the notion that Suarez was planting in his head. But he had to know more.

He shook his head and said softly, "What is BZO?"

"Oh, sorry. BZO stands for Benzodiazepine, and it's found in many over-the-counter sleeping aids. If taken in massive quantities with alcohol, it can be lethal, but with a little extra dosage, it can render you pretty useless for awhile - after you wake up, of course."

Mason shuddered at the thought as the conversation seemed to be getting away from him completely. He tried to bring some common sense into their discussion. "But when we finished the wine, we didn't go to sleep for about an hour. Wouldn't that inhibit any effects of the sleeping pill?"

"Mr. Seaforth, if all she was trying to do was get away without you knowing, the pills would still have the strength to knock you out long enough for her to do that, even if you didn't try to sleep right away. It's possible to fight the effects off until you are ready to sleep. Look, this is all speculation, but I am very suspicious of the way you felt this morning. It's not unusual that fear will cause the mind to fire quicker than usual, resulting in some less than cohesive thinking. Maybe it was just the shock that made you groggy, but if you'll sign a consent form, I'd like to get a lab technician up here to take some samples for toxicology tests. It would be good if you can do it now. They will take a sample of your hair, ask you to pee in a bottle, and draw some blood. We should have the results back in 24 hours. BZO would remain in your urine for about three days, in your blood for anywhere from six hours to two days, and in your hair for 90 days. Believe me, if there is anything, we will find it, Mr. Seaforth. By the way, do you still have the wine bottles?"

"Yes, I think they're still on the counter at the house," Mason said meekly. "But how would she know about the drug and how much to administer? It's crazy."

The sergeant sat back in her chair, shrugged her large shoulders and said dispassionately, "The internet, Mr. Seaforth. You can find anything you want on the internet. It's helped us a lot in finding the bad guys, but the bad news is, it also helps them. Everything is available if you ask Google the right questions."

Mason sighed, signed the form, took his copy, thanked Juanita Suarez and waited for the technician to arrive. Before leaving the room, Suarez told him that she would be over to pick up the bottles later in the day. She also asked if it would be all right if she picked up Sami's hair brush so they could take her DNA for possible forensic analysis later. He agreed and before he knew it, he was back out into the Florida sunshine, thinking that things were truly becoming worse as each minute passed by.

As Mason made his way home, Suarez was returning to her office when she ran into the Operations Commander. He asked how it had gone with the new missing person case. Suarez told him what had transpired and then said, "Lieutenant, I feel so sorry for these people when I have to bring up the possibility of suicide – especially when they are already shattered because a loved one has disappeared into thin air. The husband's pretty devastated but based on what he told me, I think he might have been drugged before she left. I ordered some toxicology tests, and he seemed okay with that. If she did drug him, she had some reason. Why not just leave on her way to work? Why at night? Why not drive away? There are some things that just don't make sense on the surface."

"Well, that's why you make the big bucks, Suarez," the Lieutenant said with a grin. "Good luck sorting this one out. If you need to talk, let me know. You handled everything by the book, so go and figure out what happened to this woman. And let's pray we don't find her in the woods somewhere with the rest of a bottle of sleeping pills beside her."

As he drove through the streets of Gulfport, Mason tried to reject the suicide theory. He knew his wife, and even though she may have been a little sad from an unknown cause, he was sure she would be strong enough to deal with anything. They had a great relationship. Surely she would talk to him about any problems, wouldn't she? There *had* to be another answer to this. Mason reluctantly pondered the possibility that Sami had drugged him to get away. He couldn't believe that she would do it, but even if she had, he knew his wife and he was positive there was an explanation. He couldn't allow himself to think anything else because it just wasn't plausible.

As he pulled into the driveway, he realized he couldn't really remember the drive home. It was like he was on autopilot as his mind swirled with everything that had transpired in the last few hours. Everything -- and nothing. What he really wanted was to be greeted at the door by his wife's smiling face. He was sure that if she was home, she would be heading through the door with open arms to greet him, but it took him no time to realize that wasn't going to happen. Nothing had changed since he left. There was still no Sami anywhere to be seen. Mason took a small measure of relief that Marcie's car was still parked on the street in front of his house. Somehow he couldn't imagine the thought of walking into the house if it were empty. At this moment, that total silence would be just too much to bear.

Chapter 11

Mason unlocked the door and walked in, only to hear Marcie rummaging around upstairs. He dropped his keys on the table by the door and trudged up the stairs with the weight of the day's activities weighing heavily on him. As he went into the bedroom, he called Marcie's name so as not to startle her.

She was in Sami's walk-in closet. She poked her head out when she heard Mason's voice, letting him know that she was looking at Sami's clothes to see if there was anything with a price tag or even some new clothes that she did not recognize. She told Mason that there was nothing there to indicate a recent purchase -- and there was definitely no hat. She also told him that she had called neighboring hospitals and the morgue, and turned up nothing. Mason was somewhat relieved by the news, but in the back of his mind, he was kind of hoping that there would have been news that she was resting in a hospital after a minor accident.

They returned downstairs and sat on the sofa in the sunroom as Mason explained his visit to the police station. Marcie looked stunned at the mention of suicide but like Mason, she quickly rejected the thought. She blew air through her lips as she briefly considered the possibility and discarded it. She made a comment about Sami being the strongest person she knew and asked what else the detective and Mason had talked about.

However, she was stunned again as she heard about the toxicology tests. She started to laugh that nervous giggle that arises somewhere between fear and incredulity when people become aware of something they don't want to believe and for which they don't really want to know the answer. When he got to the part where the detective suggested Sami had possibly drugged Mason to precipitate her leaving, Marcie looked sideways at Mason. "You *are* kidding, right?" Mason shrugged and said in a low, hoarse voice that it *would* explain a few things. Like why he was so groggy when he awoke up and why he hadn't heard Sami leaving during the night.

They continued to discuss Mason's visit to the station and the possibilities surrounding Sami's disappearance. Marcie went to the counter in the kitchen and sniffed the wine bottles, but couldn't detect anything unusual. They were debating what to do next when there was a firm rap on the door. They both jumped at the sound. "What now?" Mason said, completely forgetting about the conversation earlier with Detective Baker before his trip to the police station.

As he opened the door, heat poured into the room. The sunshine was brightly winning the day. He shaded his eyes at the sun glinting off Sami's car behind the outlines of two rather large men standing on the doorstep, and he could see the door of the house and his own image reflected in their sunglasses. The older of the two had obviously done the knocking, as he stood at the forefront with sweat glistening off his brow from the rising humidity. It flashed through Mason's mind that he hadn't even noticed the heat and humidity when he was outside only a few minutes before.

Baker and Finch removed their sunglasses and introduced themselves as they stepped into the house. As they did so, they offered Mason their business cards identifying them as homicide detectives. "Has your wife returned, Mr. Seaforth?" This was from Baker who appeared to be the higher-ranking of the two. "No," answered Mason dejectedly, adding that he had filed a Missing Person report as the detective had suggested. Baker offered his sincere best wishes and reiterated that he thought she would show up soon. Finch added that it must be tough to go through what Mason was going through right now. Mason nodded slightly, thinking to himself that they had no idea what he was feeling. How could they? But he kept it to himself.

Baker and Finch told Mason that he was one of a certain number of people whose running shoes had been identified as having a tread similar to the one found at the crime scene. They mentioned that if a nun with oversize feet happened to own a pair of these same shoes, they would have no choice but to investigate her as well. They chuckled to each other, no doubt conjuring up in their minds a picture of a petite nun in full religious garb with size 10 running shoes sticking out beneath her habit. Mason wasn't in the mood. They asked if they could sit down and go over some necessary details with Mason.

Mason introduced them to Marcie, who stood nearby listening to the conversation. Baker started by asking if Mason had heard of a man named James Briscoe. Mason said yes, that he had read the name in the newspaper but he had also heard of him previously through some of the prominent tax evasion cases Briscoe had handled. Mason pointed out that it was difficult not to have heard of James Briscoe if you were involved in accounting and taxes in the area.

The detectives asked Mason if they could see his running shoes. He got the Brooks out of the closet and brought them downstairs, but before he could say anything, they took the shoes and dropped them in a bag, sealed it and put an identifying sticker on it.

"I've only worn the shoes to my gym when I exercise," Mason said, trying not to be defensive as Baker made notes. Then they started talking about the DNA test they were about to do.

Outwardly, Mason listened politely, but inside, he was becoming increasingly nervous that it was taking up valuable time when he needed to be pursuing other avenues to find Sami. When he indicated this to the detectives, they again offered their sympathy and told Mason it wouldn't take long. Baker was pulling some papers from his briefcase, and Finch brought a small kit from his satchel. Baker told Mason that he would be asking some questions but before he did, Mason snapped a bit impulsively, "You have my running shoes, Detective Baker. Can't you just take the DNA sample from them?"

"Mr. Seaforth, we have to cover every possibility," replied Baker calmly. "There have been cases lately that were lost at trial because the investigators weren't thorough enough in gathering evidence. And there have been other cases where no one would have ever suspected the defendant because of the person's status in society. Did you hear about that Colonel in the Canadian Armed Forces that was convicted of murder, sexual assault and breaking and entering? Williams, I think his name was? He commanded an entire military base in Canada, so he'd be the last person anyone would realistically expect to commit murder. But, he did commit murder, Mr. Seaforth. And that's why we have to be extra careful. In direct answer to your question, how do we know your cat didn't lick your running shoes all over, or your wife hasn't handled them? This would effectively negate any previous DNA that might be on them."

This conversation wasn't helping Mason's blood pressure, especially with the mention of his wife. "Well, do you really think I would willingly give you my running shoes or take a DNA test if I was your guy? Wouldn't I have destroyed the shoes? Isn't this a complete waste of your time *and* mine? What if I don't agree to give you my DNA?"

The response was a patient one. "It's more a matter of eliminating suspects, Mr. Seaforth. You'll get your running shoes back, and assuming you're innocent, your DNA will be destroyed. All we're doing right now is covering all our bases. Let me tell you something else about DNA. We had a case where we knew the individual was guilty of raping and murdering a little girl, but we simply didn't have enough evidence. So we watched his house until one day he moved out. As soon as he left, we went into the house, and we could hear water running in the bathroom. It turned out to be the toilet, which he had flushed before he left. He had dropped a cigarette butt in the toilet, and it was going around and around in the water because the toilet hadn't flushed properly. We took the butt to the lab, got the guy's DNA off it, and convicted the creep.

"This is just to say that DNA is a very powerful weapon for us to use. If you give it to us voluntarily, there will be no problem. If you don't and we have probable cause, we can follow you and pick up your cigarette butts, Coke cans or anything else that you may have touched and dropped. And again, to directly answer your question, if you don't give it to us voluntarily, your name moves further up the list of possible suspects."

Throughout this explanation, Baker had remained calm and gentlemanly, but Mason realized that he meant business. And while the whole explanation might have been interesting if Sami had been sitting beside him listening, the fact was that he considered this to be an infringement on his valuable time, and he just wanted to get it over with.

"Okay, let's do the DNA test. I don't mean to be disrespectful, Detective Baker, but I really feel I need to be focusing on my wife's disappearance right now."

Finch took a stick that looked like a long Q-tip out of the kit. "This is not like CSI, Mr. Seaforth," Finch said. "You've probably seen them take one swab from each side and they're done. What I'm going to do is swab each side of the inside of your mouth 10 times. Can you please open your mouth wide for me?"

When the swabbing was done, Finch said he just had a couple of questions. He started reading from the paper in front of him. The first part was a statement confirming that the DNA would be destroyed if Mason was found to be unconnected to the case. The second part contained questions.

Do you have any knowledge of James or Joan Briscoe?

Have you ever been in their apartment?

Did you come into contact with Mr. Briscoe as part of your job?

Do you have any friends who might have mentioned Mr. Briscoe?

Do you know where you were on the night in question?

At the last question, Mason looked back at Marcie who had been sitting quietly, listening intently. It was a long shot, but he thought maybe Marcie had joined Sami and him for dinner that night or something. She silently shook her head no. Both detectives noted the look between Mason and Marcie and recorded her negative nod in their notepads.

They finally wrapped up their questioning and put everything away. They told Mason it would be as long as three weeks before they would be able to get back to him and return his running shoes. They also admitted it would probably take even longer to process the DNA test because of budget cuts in the lab. Mason was happy to see them go. After they left, he and Marcie exchanged glances. Mason said with some relief, "At least they're gone, and we can get back to the task at hand."

Quietly, they talked about their next steps. For Mason, it meant contacting Jennifer to let her know her mom was missing. Marcie said she knew something about computers, and volunteered to take a look at Sami's to see if there was anything that seemed unusual. Mason also remembered that Sergeant Suarez had said she would be coming by soon to pick up the wine bottles. As Mason took his phone from his pocket, an unexpected ring startled him, and he fumbled to answer it as quickly as possible. Marcie had done a U-turn from the direction of the stairs towards Sami's computer and was hot on his heels.

As he said hello, all he could hear was an unsettling quiet on the line, but he could sense that someone was there. He urgently motioned for Marcie to come over, and they put their heads together with the phone between them. He said slowly but with his voice rising, "Sami, is that you?" There was still nothing. He said, "Sami, if that's you, say something please, sweetie. Are you hurt?"

They could hear breathing on the line and after a few seconds, a rough male voice said, "Where is she?"

"Who IS this?" said Mason, his voice rising. "Who's calling?"

The disembodied voice said abruptly, "It doesn't matter who's calling, Seaforth. Where is your wife? I want to talk to her *now*." The "now" was pronounced as an authoritative command. Mason glanced from the corner of his eye at Marcie, and they both shuddered.

But the caller's demand affected Mason in a different way. He could feel an anger rising in him that he hadn't felt in a long, long time. It boiled from deep inside him and was about to erupt. The day's activities had taken their toll, and he was not about to allow some insolent asshole to make demands on him about speaking to his wife! He didn't expect it, and he certainly didn't appreciate it. At the same time, if this caller had something to do with Sami's disappearance, he definitely didn't want to scare the guy off.

Mason stared at his phone and then said in a barely controlled voice, "Look, I don't know who you are, and I don't appreciate you demanding to speak to my wife. If you would like to change your tone and leave me your name and phone number, maybe I'll have her call you back when she returns." There was an icy pause at the other end of the line, and then the voice spoke again, sending a feeling of sheer panic deep through the bodies of both listeners.

"Listen up, Seaforth, and you'd better listen good. I need to speak to your wife. Got that? You tell her to call me as soon as she gets in. Let her know it's a matter of life and death. In fact, why don't you tell her if I don't hear from her soon, the death will be *hers* when I find her. Have I made myself clear?"

Mason stared at the floor in shocked silence, his blood racing.

"Good. I take it from your silence you understand the seriousness of this situation, Seaforth. So go find your wife and tell her to call me. She'll know who's calling. And one more thing: we didn't have this conversation. Don't tell anyone about it, especially the police. If you say a word to anyone, you can add your death to your wife's."

The phone went dead, leaving the sound of Mason's and Marcie's breathing the only noise breaking the silence of the house. Finally, Mason put the phone down, but before doing so, he checked for a phone number. Once again, it was "private number."

There were so many questions hanging between them. Finally Marcie found her voice and pierced the air with one plaintive question, "Mason, what are we going to do?"

Chapter 12

Mason restored himself from the chill that had descended on the room like a shroud by drawing in long, deep breaths. He and Marcie sat stunned on the couch in the living room. Both were lost deep in thought, but Marcie looked at Mason and wondered if his thoughts were anywhere near as jumbled as hers. She decided to just let him be for the moment. She waited patiently for him to say something. For his part, Mason was thinking about the matter-of-fact question Marcie had just asked. *What am I going to do?* He thought about other problems he'd had, none of which now measured up to this one, and he thought that his best solution was to work through them, taking one step at a time.

Something had happened during that phone call. In an instant, Mason's mind had become crystal clear. The cobwebs that had been created by whatever means were disappearing, and his mind was becoming sharper, more focused. He wasn't going to let whatever was going on with Sami defeat him or his family. More than ever, he was determined to get to the bottom of this mystery.

Finally, he looked at Marcie and said in a clear, calm voice, "I want you to try something, Marcie. You have to look at Sami's computer and see if you can access it. Her system is password-protected, but try to get into it. Sami and I talked about passwords a couple of times, and she always said that simpler was better – that it should be something that you could easily remember but that no one else would think of. Well, you know how she likes to study wine. We talked about some of her favorite labels, and she said a wine name would make a perfect password. She talked about one particular bottle of expensive wine that she really wanted us to try, so maybe she went with that for her password. I remember she always liked to change her passwords at least once a month. Let me think. It was Chateau something ..." Mason thought for a minute. "I know what it was. The wine she was talking about was Chateau Margaux with an x. She said you can buy a bottle for $1,100 and that someday she was going to own one. She always said if she wrote something down once, she would remember it forever." Mason paused. "I suggest you try any combination of the two words with no space, and maybe add the number 1100. She might have added a symbol, like an exclamation mark or asterisk or something. It will be a guessing game -- but if anyone can do it, I'm confident you can, Marcie." He wrote down the name and handed it to Marcie.

She was a bit shocked at Mason's sudden turnaround. Just a few minutes earlier, he was hesitant and unsure and unable to make level-headed decisions. Maybe he *had* been drugged and it was wearing off. Either way, there seemed to be no doubt that Mason Seaforth was back on track.

Marcie started to stand up and head to Sami's computer. She stopped and nodded when he went on to tell her that he was ready to let Jennifer know that her mother was missing. Then he added, "If things go on for much longer, I guess I'll have to tell my parents, too." He knew it would be too much for his aging parents if he just picked up the phone and gave them the news. He couldn't just call them and drop a bombshell like this. They loved Sami like a daughter, so he really would need to drive up to see them in person. It was only about a four-hour drive, easily done if and when the time came. For now, Mason wanted to wait. The more hours that passed made it less likely that Sami would just suddenly come strolling through the door from a pre-dawn shopping trip or something, but he knew he was still clinging to a shred of hope.

Marcie looked at him. "So are you going to tell any of your new detective friends on the police force about the phone call you just got?"

Mason didn't answer for a moment. When he did, all he said was, "No, I don't think so. Not right now, anyway. The man who called was very specific about not telling anyone what he said. I have no idea what he was talking about, but I want to try and get more information before I say anything. I mean, what if the guy finds out that I did tell Suarez or Baker?"

Marcie frowned. "Are you sure that's the right thing to do, Mason? That guy threatened you. He said he would kill Sami and you, too, if she doesn't call him back. "

"I know, but think about it, Marcie. It appears I may have been drugged by my wife. The police found a tread from a running shoe similar to mine in James Briscoe's condominium after he and his wife were murdered. Sami has disappeared. Now this guy calls, threatens my wife and tells *me* not to go to the police. The only good news so far is that apparently he doesn't know where she is any more than we do, which means he hasn't done any harm to her yet. It's all adding up to something. I have no clue what that is yet, I just think it's all connected somehow. I can't help but believe that Sami is safe somewhere, and when we get to the bottom of this, we will get her back. For now, we need to do all *we* can first, before we tell anyone anything."

"Okay, I see your point, Mason. I'll get to work on the computer. Good luck with your daughter. Treat her with kid gloves. She's going to freak!"

"Yes, I know, but she's the one person who does need to know. Don't worry, I won't tell her everything."

Marcie was sitting on the opposite side of the couch from her purse, so she asked Mason if he would mind handing it over. He stared at it, noticing for the first time that it was an unusual shade of orchid with a signature Coach brand label. Sami had told him that some of these designer label bags cost more than a man's suit, and even as much as some people's cars. He had assumed Sami was only joking, but in an attempt to lighten the mood a little, he couldn't help but comment on its weight.

"What have you got in here? Your laptop?"

"Well, Mr. Smarty-Pants, it *does* have a pocket for my iPad, but I think what you're so rudely commenting on is my gun."

Mason gasped. "Your *WHAT*?" His eyes opened wide and his eyebrows arched in disbelief at Marcie's comment. He searched her face for some indication that she was pulling his leg. There was none.

Marcie said calmly, "You heard me. It's my gun." She reached into her purse and pulled out a small gun in a leather holster. "It's a Smith & Wesson 442 Airweight, and by the way, it's not that heavy at all. It only weighs 15 ounces. It only has a two-inch barrel. It kicks a bit when I pull the trigger, but you have to sacrifice something for size. Its accuracy is questionable sometimes because of how small it is, but I've learned pretty well how to control it." Mason saw a sly smile spread across Marcie's face as she regarded her gun with something closely akin to affection as she continued. "Turns out there were two things 'He Who Shall Not Be Named' was good for. The first was the large sum of money he left me so generously in our divorce settlement. The second was that he encouraged me to get a gun and took me to a shooting range to learn how to use it. Oh yeah, he wasn't bad in bed, either. Guess that makes it *three* things he was good for."

Mason remembered that Sami had accompanied Marcie a few months ago to a local shooting range and had even taken a shooting lesson herself that day just to see what it was like. But when she got home, Sami had been very clear that shooting a weapon wasn't for her. She had laughingly said she was going to stick to blowing up bad guys in her various computer games instead. But in answer to Mason's question about how well Marcie had liked it, Sami had turned serious for a moment, saying that from what she could tell, Marcie was a natural, hitting her targets with ease. Sami had said with a smile that maybe Marcie even liked it a little too much.

Mason shook his head slowly, hearing Sami's words replaying in his head, and just watched Marcie as she proudly fondled her handgun and explained its virtues. He couldn't believe the miniature size of the gun. It wasn't much thicker than an overstuffed wallet, and on second glance, it really didn't seem that heavy. Even with its small proportions, though, it was black and ominously deadly.

Apparently misreading Mason's silence as disapproval, Marcie added somewhat defensively, "You may not agree, but if you find out that Sami's been harmed by someone, wouldn't you want to take some action? You can bet I would – and I will, too. If someone has harmed our girl, they will be introduced firsthand to the business end of my little friend here that you've just met. When that happens, take it to the bank that the results won't be pretty."

As Mason went off to call his daughter, he thought to himself what a difference 24 hours had made. At this time yesterday, a conversation about Smith & Wessons and shooting ranges and death threats would have been nothing short of surreal. Mason sat down and readied himself for the call ahead. And as he did so, he knew with a sinking feeling in his heart that no matter how much Marcie tended to exaggerate, right now he believed every word of what she was saying. He had no doubt that Marcie would step up to defend her best friend Sami with whatever means necessary. He just hoped against hope that it wouldn't come to that.

Chapter 13

Mason sat with the phone in his hand for a few minutes, thinking about what he should say to Jennifer. He checked his watch again. It was close to 5:30 in the afternoon. It seemed like about three weeks now since he first realized Sami was missing. He had been so busy, but he also thought that if this went on much longer, there would soon be days when there would be nothing to do. He quickly tried to dispel those thoughts. He missed Sami unbearably. He always talked to her about everything, but she wasn't here now to talk about this.

Just as he was about to dial, the doorbell rang. With the phone still in his hand, Mason walked towards the door. He could see the outline of a police car at the curb through the curtains in the front window. He noticed the sunshine that had been blazing earlier was now replaced by a few raindrops that glistened off the hood of the car. The sky was growing darker, signaling an impending storm. How appropriate, he thought, given his darkening mood. He opened the door to see Sergeant Suarez standing on the doorstep.

"Hello, Mr. Seaforth. Have you heard anything?"

Mason flashed back to the menacing phone call he'd received, the one where a man he didn't know had threatened his entire family and specifically mentioned Sami by name. He hesitated almost imperceptibly, then took a deep breath and did exactly as he had told Marcie he would. For the time being, he thought, I'll say nothing.

"Absolutely nothing, I'm afraid," Mason replied levelly, looking Detective Suarez in the eyes. "We called the hospitals and the morgue. We're trying to access my wife's computer now. It's password protected but we're trying to get into it. I was about to call my daughter and let her know what's happened. I wish there was something more I could do."

The detective stared at him. "Who's 'we,' Mr. Seaforth? Is there someone helping you right now? Maybe you could introduce me." It was a command more than a question.

Mason reminded Suarez about Marcie and called her to the front door for a quick introduction. When she arrived, Marcie suddenly noticed the raindrops on the police car and brushed by Suarez so she could put the top up on her Cabriolet. In her hurry to catch Mason while he was running around the corner of the house earlier, she had forgotten to raise the top. As she came back inside after putting the top back up, she mumbled an apology to Suarez and offered her hand in a conciliatory gesture. Suarez said it was "quite all right" and asked Marcie about her connection to Sami and the last time she had seen her. While Suarez was polite to Marcie, Mason could tell that she was on full alert for anything that might provide a clue. Mason doubted that Marcie would be able to provide anything that he hadn't already mentioned, but understood that the detective had to consider everything.

Finally, Suarez set about collecting the wine bottles and hair brush. She took a pair of thin rubber gloves out of the small medical kit she carried and put them on as she walked into the kitchen. As she picked up the wine bottles, she put them straight into an evidence bag. Then Mason pointed her in the direction of the bathroom upstairs where Sami kept her hair brush. He felt a momentary pang as he saw the detective drop Sami's brush into the evidence bag along with the bottles, and he felt that there was probably nothing she didn't observe as she made her way through the house.

When she got to the front door, Suarez asked him again to call the station if anything at all came up. Mason felt his guard go up as she emphasized the need to tell her *anything* that might have any bearing on the case, no matter how innocuous. It made him uncomfortable, knowing he had already fabricated a few untruths today, something he was unaccustomed to doing, and for all he knew, it showed on his face. But it had become a race with the mysterious caller to find Sami, and if the caller found her first, Mason really believed she could be in grave danger if the police were involved. Besides, Mason really needed to understand what Sami was involved in. He just sensed that right now, it was crucial he keep the threatening phone call to himself.

After Suarez drove away, Marcie went back to the computer and Mason checked the time again, noting that only 20 minutes had passed since he had checked it last. He mentally examined what he knew about Jennifer's schedule and thought that her classes should be over by now. He knew it was past time to share his disturbing news with his daughter, so he called her phone. When she didn't answer after several rings, he left a message asking her to call him back when she had a minute. He wondered if she'd been delayed after a class. Maybe she had stopped to speak with one of her professors or a fellow student. One thing he did know: Jennifer and her phone were not easily parted. In fact, when she was home, he had to remind her to get her nose away from her smart phone for a few minutes so that they could have a conversation. Once he had asked her if she had recently been given access to the command codes for the country's nuclear arsenal because anyone other than the person with his finger on the button should be able to wait for a text reply. His comment was met with a laugh and an "Oh Dad," as she carried on with her texting. It was just one more sign to Mason that technology and social media were racing politeness and the English language out the door.

Sami had joined the texting revolution before he gave in and started doing it himself, mainly because he realized that if he was going to communicate with his daughter as frequently as he hoped, texting and messaging were the most likely ways to do it. Following up his voice message, Mason sent Jennifer a text asking her to give him a call when she was free. He started to add "LOL" for "lots of love," but then remembered somewhere along the way, "LOL" had become "laugh out loud," so he deleted it. He still had some work to do on this texting thing.

Meanwhile, his mind replayed the menacing phone call he had received. Despite the urgency of the threats, he felt he had no choice but to wait. Maybe he should have opened up and shared with Detective Suarez, but he wanted more time to think. He had to know *how* and *why* his wife was involved. Could she have become involved in something illegal? That seemed almost ludicrous, yet nothing at this point was making any sense. He noticed he was feeling hungry and realized that neither Marcie nor he had eaten anything all day. Marcie must be starving. He went back upstairs to the office to see if she had made any progress. He could tell by Marcie's muttering that she hadn't. She had a notepad beside her, and she was busily entering combinations, crossing each one off the list when it was rejected by the computer. "Are you hungry, Marcie? I'm going to order us something from the pizza place down the street. They deliver, and we really should eat to keep our energy level up."

"Sure. Go ahead and order. I just have to figure this thing out. Oh, by the way, did you talk to Jenn?"

"No, she wasn't there. I should hear from her soon. She never strays far from her phone."

As he went downstairs to call for the pizza, he could hear the wind blowing the rain against the windows. It was considerably darker in the room now. He snapped on the lamp by the couch and flipped a switch for the overhead light. He looked outside forlornly and prayed that Sami was someplace safe and dry. It was not a good night to be caught outside.

When the pizza arrived about half an hour later, he gave the soaked delivery man a generous tip for delivering food in such weather. Mason convinced Marcie to take a break and join him downstairs in the kitchen, though neither one felt that hungry. They sat and ate in silence, each lost in thought. Mason was wondering why Jennifer hadn't called, and Marcie was thinking about password combinations that she hadn't tried.

When she returned to the station, Sergeant Suarez dropped off the wine bottles at the lab and went to the locker room to change out of her uniform and into her street clothes. She wore a comfortable shirt that hung loosely over her jeans, along with a pair of sandals. As she was leaving the station, she ran into the Operations Commander again who quizzed her on the Seaforth missing person case. Suarez explained about the possibly-tainted wine bottles and reaffirmed her suspicion that Mason Seaforth had been drugged. She also mentioned that she was starting to wonder if his wife could have left for a love interest. "I just don't think Mr. Seaforth was telling me everything," she told the Commander, choosing her words carefully. He simply nodded and Suarez turned and headed for the door.

Later that night with tremendous effort, Mason dragged his exhausted body upstairs to find Marcie slumped over the keyboard. The combinations on the notepad had grown exponentially but apparently, she'd still had no luck unlocking Sami's mysterious password and had finally fallen asleep from the mental strain of the day. Mason gently shook Marcie's shoulder to wake her and convinced her to go home and sleep. Marcie agreed reluctantly, but insisted that she would be back first thing in the morning to start again.

After seeing her to the door, Mason returned upstairs to the bedroom he shared with Sami. He fell onto the bed, fully dressed on top of the covers. An eerie silence filled the house the way it does when no one is there. Mason had come home before Sami many times, and he always knew as soon as he walked in the house that she wasn't there. This was one of those times. The only sounds he heard were the wind howling outside and his own breathing, which was made more ragged by the anxiety he felt. As a restless sleep finally overtook him, Mason had one thought on his mind that stood out among all the rest: he still hadn't heard a word from Jennifer.

DAY 2

Chapter 14

Mason always kept a pen and notepad by his bedside. He often woke up in the middle of the night, having come up with some solution or another to a problem that had been bothering him when he fell asleep. This night was no different. Around 1 a.m., he awoke with a start and sat up in bed. It took him a minute to surface through layers of restless sleep and to fully understand what had awakened him. *What was Sami doing for money?* He was convinced she was alive, so she must have money to be able to fulfill her purpose. He leaned over in bed and jotted down his question, so that he could forget about it and go back to sleep.

Then the next disturbing thought. *Had Jennifer called yet?* Mason got up to go to the bathroom and checked his phone on the way, sure that any call from her would have instantly awakened him. Still no message. In spite of the hour, Mason called again, but it went directly to voice mail. He forced himself not to think about it. Jennifer was an adult now with a new life of her own. He was sure she would call him as soon as she saw his messages. His thoughts returned to Sami, and wearily, he made the decision that it was time to start letting everyone know that Sami was gone. Maybe collectively, they would come up with something he hadn't thought of himself, something that would bring Sami back home.

Mason's exhaustion was overwhelming, as much emotional as physical. That brought up the question again. Could the wine he'd drunk with Sami on their anniversary night really have been spiked? Did she do it deliberately so he wouldn't know when she got up to leave? The questions confused him once again, and he slid back under the covers, trying to shut his mind off for a few more hours of fitful sleep. Several times he woke up with a heavy feeling, as his mind grappled with the horror of what was happening. No word from his wife and now no word from his daughter. The two most important people in his life were missing and unavailable. He clung to the belief that they were safe, but the silence that hung in the air was sinister and unforgiving.

At 5 a.m., Mason woke again with a shudder of sadness. The empty feeling in the house, interrupted by the odd creak and groan that houses tend to emit from time to time, only intensified the nausea in the pit of his stomach. He glanced over at his notepad and saw the note he had made during the night. *What was Sami using for money?* – He needed to find out if there were any withdrawals from their joint bank account. That would be easy to do online when he got to his computer.

He called the police station to inquire if there was any word about his wife, even though he knew they would call if anything developed. The duty officer answering the phone said that he had heard nothing new. Mason padded down the hall and went into their office, turned on his computer and waited for it to boot up. It was older and slower than Sami's, so it took a little longer for the familiar collection of desktop icons to appear on the screen. Once it was up and running, it took no time for him to access their account balances online and see that nothing looked out of place. He decided to go through each account just in case he spotted something that might help. Each was labeled with a nickname that helped them identify what the account was for. Mason carefully checked the itemized transactions in each account, then he clicked on the one that they had set aside for trips they might want to take. It was called "Vacations," and the minute Mason saw the transactions, a sinking feeling fell over him.

Aside from the regular monthly deposits they both made toward a long-awaited cruise they hoped to take on the Mediterranean, there was a deposit of $10,000. Following immediately was a withdrawal of an equal amount. Both $10,000 transactions had been made just three days before Sami's disappearance.

Mason sat frozen in disbelief. Ten THOUSAND dollars?!!! The unexpectedness of his discovery and the magnitude of the deposit and withdrawal figure sent his body into a state of shock. He leaned in closer to the computer as if it would help him figure it out. Where would his wife come up with $10,000? Why was it deposited first, only to be withdrawn again almost immediately? What had happened to the money? Was this what Sami was using to live on wherever she was now? Mason's mind couldn't begin to grasp this reality. He checked the accounts again even more carefully to see if he could trace a source of the money. The entry in their vacation account was simply titled "Internet Transfer," with a transaction number. He looked for one large amount or a series of smaller amounts in every account they had. Sami hadn't mentioned any financial windfalls, bonuses or large amounts of income that could help explain where $10,000 had come from. Mason thought he had a good handle on their bank accounts and the disposable income they had available.

It required another phone call to Willard at the bank to see what he could tell him about the $10,000 deposit and withdrawal. Yet while Mason knew the money had a definite bearing in what was going on, it also served to reinforce his belief that Sami was alive and needed the money for a specific purpose. If she had taken out $10,000, and the evidence was irrefutable that she had, there had to be a reason. Was she fleeing the country? Was she flying to meet a lover he'd never known about? Evidence might point that way – and probably the police would agree that this was Sami's motive – but Mason refused to believe it. Marcie had flat-out shoved the idea aside, and Mason felt sure that if Sami were having an affair, somehow her perceptive best friend would have extracted the information from her.

It was too early to call Willard at the bank yet, and besides, he wanted to clear his head before doing anything. He asked himself what Sami would do to help her think, if the situation were reversed. The immediate response was that she would go jogging, and Mason thought of her favorite route through Clam Bayou Nature Preserve, not far from where they lived. At that moment, he remembered the conversation that he'd had with Sergeant Suarez the day before. She had told him to think of Sami's favorite places, because people sometimes want that to be the last thing they see. No, it couldn't be. The thought returned again and again. It didn't make any sense with the new information about the money transfer, but he had to see for himself and a run would get him away from the silence of the house for a few minutes.

Mason changed into his jogging shorts and made sure his cell phone was in his pocket. Now was not the time to be missing any calls, especially when Jennifer might call at any minute. He threw on a t-shirt and reached for his Brooks running shoes before remembering that they had been confiscated as evidence the day before by Officers Baker and Finch. It took him a few minutes to find another pair, but he searched them out in the closet, put them on and headed out the door. The sun had poked its head out again after last night's rain, and the lawns were fresh and lush. The smell of wet grass hung in the air.

To save time, he drove down Miriam Street, alongside the path that Sami would take when jogging, past the various yachts that bobbed gently in the water. The expensive boats were in direct contrast to those that were likely mortgaged to the hilt by less well heeled enthusiasts. The yachts were tied off about four feet from the much smaller fishing vessels, protected only by rubber bumpers from slamming into each other when wakes from passing boats or high winds brought them dangerously close together. On the other side of the street was the entrance to Clam Bayou Nature Preserve. Sami loved jogging this route because it offered a little elevation from the flat streets of Gulfport. Mason followed the preserve's paths, which were lined with crushed seashells that provided a softer surface to run on than the brick streets or concrete sidewalks. It was a short but beautiful jog with its mangrove trees, peaceful boardwalks jutting into the inlets and nesting ospreys occupying the highest perches. Joggers would often stop to admire the natural beauty, or smile at the dolphins or manatee that frequently made their way into the coves. But aside from startling two snow-white egrets that ran from his path and squawked their dry croaking sound at his intrusion, Mason saw nothing unusual. He was back in his car and driving home in a matter of minutes. The jog had probably been a total waste of time, and he wasn't a runner in the first place. Yet on some level, he felt better and more closely connected to his wife.

As he drove, Mason pondered the latest discovery about the $10,000 cash withdrawal. What should he do with the information? If he told Suarez about it, she would most likely come to the conclusion that Sami had run off with someone and reduce the attention she was paying to the investigation. If he told Baker and Finch about it, they might jump to a different conclusion and decide that there was a link between Sami's withdrawal and the coincidence that Mason's running shoe was the same size as one found at a crime scene. This could lead them to look more closely at Mason in their Briscoe murder investigation. And what about the threatening phone call? The man on the other end had made it clear that there would be dangerous consequences if Mason talked to anyone.

As he pulled up in front of his house and parked the car, Mason concluded that he would let things progress the way they were for now. He would start alerting friends and co-workers that Sami had disappeared, and he would tell Jennifer.

When Mason entered the house, he felt relieved that he had come to a decision. It helped him feel that he had another game plan and could continue being proactive. He made some coffee and decided to have a quick shower to help him regain a sense of normalcy. After his shower, he toweled off and was just about to put his clothes on when he could hear a rustling at the door like someone was having difficulty fitting the key into the lock. A hopeful rush went through him as he threw on his robe and headed toward the stairs. *Sami!* Bounding down the stairs and trying to tie his bath robe at the same time, he reached the door and flung it open. There, standing on the doorstep with a key in her hand suspended in mid-air, was Marcie. Mason had forgotten that Sami had given Marcie a spare key to look after the house when they were away.

In spite of the early hour and the ordeal they were going through, Marcie looked her usual energetic self. She was dressed in a blue, open-necked shirt and black shorts with high-heeled sandals. "Marcie, you're up early!"

"I know," she said, pushing past him and on into the house. "I've been thinking about possible password combinations for Sami's computer ever since I woke up at half past stupid o'clock. I have a whole list that I've been compiling since I woke up. I'm going to unlock that computer today if it kills me! Oh, and aren't you just the damn exhibitionist with only your robe on. Put on some clothes before I'm forced to wash my eyes!"

Marcie saw that Mason didn't laugh or even smile. Quickly she put a re-assuring hand on his shoulder and said, "Hey, don't worry. We'll get to the bottom of this, Mason. We'll get our Sami back."

"I know we will, Marcie. I appreciate your humor and everything you're doing. It was so difficult waking up to the empty house this morning, and I have a lot on my mind. I was just getting dressed when I heard you at the door. Go pour yourself some coffee while I get changed. I've found something that's pretty significant. I'll tell you after I've changed, and we can figure out what to do next."

A few minutes later, Mason found Marcie huddled over Sami's computer. Her cup of coffee was sitting dangerously close to the keyboard, but Marcie didn't seem to be the least bit concerned that it could present impending disaster. He leaned over to see what she was doing, and at the same time, gently nudged the cup farther away from the keyboard. "Marcie, listen to this," he said, and she turned around to look at him. He told her about the $10,000 transaction in the bank account and how he couldn't find any explanation for its appearance – or its disappearance. He also mentioned that he still hadn't heard back from Jennifer. Marcie's face registered the same shock when she heard about the $10,000, though she didn't seem concerned about Jennifer not calling. "She's in college now. Maybe she's in bed with some football player." Mason tried to ignore that image and carried on. He explained that he thought it best if they just kept the information about the withdrawal to themselves for the time being and got no argument from Marcie.

He left her to continue with the password search and went to call Jennifer for the third time. The phone rang twice before he heard his daughter pick up. "Hello?" she said sleepily.

"Jenn, where have you been? I've been trying to call you."

"Oh, Dad, hi. I'm sorry. I had to study last night and my battery died, so I shut my phone off and plugged it into the charger. I'm still in bed, but I just turned it back on a few minutes ago. Hey, why are you calling so early? Is something wrong? I would have called you as soon as I got up. What's up?"

Mason could picture his techie daughter rolling over and turning on her phone as soon as she woke up. At least she didn't mention rolling over to greet the football player that Marcie had implanted in his brain. He chose his words carefully.

"Honey, I just wanted you to know that your mother had some things come up, so she's gone out of town for a few days. She didn't tell me where she was going. I know it's private and I respect that. I know I'll hear from her soon."

There was a silence on the other end of the phone. "What? She left without telling you where she was going? That doesn't sound like Mom. What's going on? Have you tried calling her since she left?"

Mason knew he wouldn't be able to put much over on his astute daughter, so he elaborated a bit more.

"Sweetie, honestly, I'm not sure. I woke up the morning after our anniversary, and your mother was gone. She must have left sometime during the night, and I can't imagine why. It makes no sense. We had had a beautiful day together, and a lovely evening having dinner and drinking wine. I've already called the police and filed a missing person report. Jenn, I wish I understood what's happening. I'm not sure, but it looks like she may have withdrawn money from our bank account, too. I haven't heard a word from her since she left." Mason hesitated, but then held true to his game plan and omitted any word of the threatening phone call or the fact that his running shoes were being held as evidence in a murder investigation. There was no need to share that with Jennifer.

There was a sharp intake of breath, followed by more silence at the end of the line. Then finally, "This is awful, Dad. I'm scared for Mom. I'm coming home to be with you. Unless you two are having trouble and just haven't told me yet, I think something has happened to her. She would never just leave in the middle of the night."

"No," Mason replied quickly, trying to be reassuring. "Jenn, I want you to stay there for now. You need to study, and it's a four-hour drive from Miami back here. There's nothing you can do here, anyway; not right now. The $10,000 transfer is a good indication that nothing has happened to her. She's just sorting something out. I'm doing everything I can. We'll stay in touch. You can text or call me any time you want, and I'll keep you posted when we find out more. Please do this for me, Jenn. It's how you can be the most help right now. And besides, I have Marcie here to help out."

"Oh God, Dad! *Marcie!?* Isn't she the one who said Mom would be better off with someone other than you?"

"Yes, but she was just kidding, honey. That's how Marcie is. She's being very supportive and a huge help right now. I know this is hard, but just try to stay calm and keep studying. Your mom and I are both very proud of you and want you to be the best that you can be. I promise I will get to the bottom of this and keep you informed. I know it's easy to say, but please try not to worry."

Mason could sense that his daughter was trying to digest everything he had just told her. He waited patiently for her to respond and when she did, he could tell that she was close to tears. She told him in a trembling voice that she knew her mom wouldn't just run away without a good reason. She rationalized that her mom would be back soon and that everything would be clear. That was exactly the response that Mason was hoping for from their pragmatic daughter.

They chatted for a few more minutes, but Mason could not offer anything else. He could only provide vague responses to Jennifer's questions and promise that he would keep his daughter posted.

As he hung up the phone, Mason felt emotionally drained. He was relieved to have told Jennifer, but feeling guilty for not telling her the whole truth. He was heartbroken that he had to give their daughter such terrible news. He felt that he had done a reasonable job of staying stoic and keeping fear out of his voice while they talked. In truth, he was scared to death; but letting his daughter know that would not have helped. He needed to present an air of calm reassurance, and he had done just that. But now, sitting there staring at the cell phone in his hand, Mason realized not much of the burden had been lifted from his shoulders. With his discovery of the suspicious $10,000 deposit and withdrawal from their vacation bank account, Mason thought the heat might have just been turned up even higher.

Chapter 15

Janet Winters had grown up with Samantha Roberts, or Sami as she was known to her schoolmates, in a suburb of Minneapolis. They had been good friends all through school, competing on the same athletic teams and enjoying each other's company. Their lives were relatively normal, except each had had crosses to bear.

Since they had the same body shape and size, they had exchanged clothes for fun on occasion, but Janet hadn't been blessed with Samantha's good looks; she was less vibrant and definitely not as popular. Because of her Plain Jane appearance, she had been overlooked and sometimes even mocked at school. Her hair was as straight as if it had been ironed each morning, and she had eyebrows that lightly met in the middle. She wasn't ugly; there was just nothing distinguishing about her. Janet was simply plain. On more than one occasion, Samantha had actually intervened when classmates mercilessly made fun of Janet's plainness. Sami was happy to set Janet's tormentors straight in no uncertain terms, and had even resorted to using her fists to extract her friend from some particularly difficult taunting. In return, Janet had supported Samantha through parental problems at home.

Janet was sad to see her friend leave for Florida after their graduation. She had organized a farewell party for Sami and made sure that she got a proper send-off. As school chums often do, they had stayed in touch for a while after Sami's departure. But their lives had taken very different paths. Janet heard that Sami had obtained a degree at a university in Florida, landed a good job and married someone nice. Janet's path was different. Despite Sami's best efforts, the tormentors at school over the years had reduced

Janet's self-esteem to a point where it hit rock bottom. She had found some solace in drugs and alcohol. She had found love from men who were only willing to stick around until they grew tired of her. In the end, they always moved on, leaving Janet ashamed and feeling even lower than before, if such a thing were possible.

Janet had gone through a few jobs as a retail clerk, but her late nights of drinking and clubbing would eventually catch up with her. Too many days of showing up late or being less than motivated on the job would always get her fired. That would start another cycle of destructive behavior: going to bars, meeting the wrong kind of men, spending whatever money she had, giving them every part of herself that she could until they left, then finding another job, drinking and smoking the profits, knowing she needed to break these patterns but never quite managing to pull it off, and the cycle would keep repeating.

Her life had chugged along like that for years. She was ashamed of herself, and once in a while she would remember a time when she was happy. In spite of the torment she suffered during her school years, she had enjoyed Sami's friendship so much, and it was definitely the best time of her life. Which is why she was feeling particularly optimistic the last few days. Two things had recently occurred, things that she never dreamed would ever happen in a million years and that buoyed her spirits. She wondered if her life, at long last, was about to change for the better.

The first good thing to happen was that out of the blue, Samantha Seaforth had called her about two weeks ago. It was a completely unexpected call, but Janet was thrilled to hear Sami's voice again. The first thought that crossed Janet's mind was how pleased she was that she had never gotten around to making her number private. She had often thought about it but, like a lot of other things, it just never happened. Sami said she had tracked Janet down through a quick search on the internet. They had exchanged pleasantries and reminisced about some of the happier memories they'd shared. Janet couldn't believe her good fortune that someone as successful as Sami still remembered her and had taken the time to call after so many years.

During the conversation, Janet was surprised that Sami remembered so much about her, including that she had always kept a detailed diary about things that happened in her life. As they reminisced, Sami took the opportunity to ask, "Do you still keep those diaries, Janet?" With a good-natured laugh, Sami had added, "I don't think I've ever known anyone who documented events in their life like you do." Janet replied that as a matter of fact, she did still try to jot down notes, especially when something good happened.

The conversation moved on, but it was somewhat stilted, the result of so much time apart. And then things took a different turn. Sami had asked specifically about one of Janet's many relationships, a guy she remembered Janet dating for a period of time. She said she had seen a name similar to his not long ago in a newspaper article, and she wondered what ever happened to him, and also the man he worked for. Sami had sounded more than a little curious to know if Janet still heard from him and whether she knew where he was these days. Janet didn't know why Sami was asking these questions be-cause the guy had broken off their relationship in typical fashion a long time ago, but she desperately wanted to keep her former best friend on the phone as long as she could, so she was willing to talk about anything. She was tempted to ask why Sami was inquiring about him, but she didn't want to do anything that might abruptly end this conversation with her old friend. And anyway, Janet wasn't able to answer many of the questions about her former lover, because she just didn't know much. When they were together, he had never talked about his work, or his boss, or what he did for a living. Their relationship had been built - as so many of Janet's were - more on physical couplings than on deep conversations. He had called himself "The Force."

Janet believed she had been madly in love with the guy, yet deep down she had a strong sense that he had a dark side. When he was out of town, she often wrote in her journal, noting the dates he was gone and how much she was looking forward to his return. With Sami's curiosity evident on the other end of the phone, Janet graciously offered to copy the information and send it to Sami, although she warned her that some of it was silly and that she probably sounded like a lovesick teenager at times in its pages.

Sami thanked her, and then she brought up something else that had been pushed to the back burner in the ensuing years.

During their school years together, it was Sami who'd stood up for Janet against the school's bullies, but it was Janet who comforted Sami about her abusive home life. Sami was deathly afraid of her stepfather. His behavior often caused them to say that he must have mental issues because no one who was sane would act the way he did. After Sami's biological father was killed in the car accident, Sami's mother had remarried a man by the name of Aaron Marshall. Janet's boyfriend at the time was Greg Johnson, aka "The Force." He had dropped out of school to work for Aaron Marshall before joining the Marines. Sami confided in Janet about some of the horrible things her stepfather had done to her and her mother; and after Sami's mother died, she had told Janet a wild tale of overhearing a conversation that had taken place at Sami's house one night between The Force and Aaron Marshall, her stepfather.

Sami wasn't completely certain exactly what she'd heard, but as she did with everything else, she had confided the details to Janet at the time. Sami had been in the kitchen preparing something to eat while her stepfather and Greg Johnson were having a discussion in the living room. A door separated the two rooms, and Sami decided to check on them to see if they wanted anything. It was one of the duties that her stepfather insisted upon since the death of her mother. The two men were seated in chairs side by side with their backs towards the door, and as she pushed through into the living room, she'd overheard the mention of her mother's name. A tremor had passed through her. Quietly Sami had closed the door again, but she left it open slightly so she could still listen to the conversation. Johnson had laughingly told Marshall that *something* had worked well on the latter's "old lady." It was a word that sounded like "millennium" but it had started with an "s" and she couldn't quite make it out. Johnson had said, "Yeah, I'll keep it in mind just in case I have to use it again sometime. It's hard to detect, unless they do a thorough autopsy and know what they're looking for."

When Sami had heard the word "autopsy," she withdrew back into the kitchen and ran quickly into the bathroom to think. She was shaken by that word, because she knew very well what it meant. She resolved to do some research to try to figure out what the word starting with "s" could have been and what it meant. In the meantime, she acted like nothing had happened. Sami had researched the word days later and told Janet she thought she knew what they were talking about. The information had caused a series of emotions to rain down on Sami, ranging from sadness, to fear, to deep-rooted anger. The word she thought they had used was "selenium." She read that it's an essential trace element that's highly toxic if taken in large doses – *toxic enough to kill a human being.*

At the time, Sami and Janet had debated about what to do with the information, but Sami was afraid of The Force and Marshall, and she wasn't entirely sure of what she had heard. And even if she did hear correctly, with Marshall's power and influence, she was afraid no one would believe her over her stepfather, anyway. Janet had swayed her from going to the police, partly because Sami wasn't completely sure of what she'd really heard, but also because Janet was afraid that Greg Johnson might blame her when he found out, and it would ruin their relationship. So Sami agreed to let it go. Soon after, Sami had moved to Florida and started her new life. That was the last of it – until this phone call.

After Sami left, Janet had also kept it a secret. She didn't even dare write it in her journal. She wanted Greg Johnson to be the one for her, and the last thing she wanted to do was antagonize him in any way. But just as Janet's other boyfriends had done, Johnson left her eventually. After returning from his tour of duty with the Marines, he had come to her one day without any warning and announced he was moving out of town. In fact, he said, he was moving out of the country. He told Janet that the man he worked for had to get away, and Johnson was going with him. It was as simple and as devastating as that. In the ensuing years Janet had thought from time to time of the happy occasions she remembered with Sami and Johnson. And now, for no apparent reason, Sami had called and brought everything up again.

Discussing her old boyfriend with her old best friend had opened the floodgate of memories, and Janet decided to look through her journal notes about her boyfriend, type out everything else she could think of, of and send it all to Sami. Maybe she wouldn't hear from her again, but this gesture on her part would show Sami how much she still valued their friendship. Anyway, she hadn't heard from Greg Johnson since he left so she sure didn't owe him anything. And realistically, she didn't expect she ever would hear from him again. So Janet had mailed the package to Sami, feeling good about her decision.

And that's when the second event took place that defied all odds and had given her reason to think that maybe her life was actually taking a turn for the better. In another completely unexpected turn of events, Janet had received a second out of-the-blue phone call reconnecting her to her past. Now, several nights later, as Janet lay on the bed recovering from an exhaustive session of lovemaking, she reflected upon the man beside her who had just given her another mind-blowing orgasm. It felt so good being back in his arms again.

The guy was big and had tattoos on his arms. He liked to joke about the flag waving on his arm as he showed off his well-toned muscles. His conversational capacity usually revolved around sports, especially mixed martial arts, and his latest escapades at the gym. He was arrogant and often insensitive, but when he went away, he always came back with some trinket for her. She thought her feelings for him were the closest thing to love she had ever experienced. Perhaps his most annoying trait was that he loved to refer to himself as "The Force," even though his real name was Greg Johnson. But she forgave even that so that she could return his love and affection.

When he had moved away, even though she never heard from him, Janet never forgot him. She had continued to look for someone like him, but unsuccessfully. No one had measured up. And then, suddenly, without any warning or reason that she could think of, his phone call came. He had apparently rolled into town from wherever it was he was living and called her. Janet had nearly dropped the phone.

Now, as she reflected happily on all that had happened with a smile on her lips, Greg Johnson rolled over toward her and draped his arm over her. They were lying in Janet's sagging bed. She was unhappy that she had to show Greg that she was still in the same apartment in the same part of town. It was not an area that people would frequent unless they had to, but the rent was reasonable and all that Janet could afford. The building was relatively clean, although it was often visited by police for one reason or another.

Janet lay on the bed with her hair splayed across the pillow. Greg brushed his lips across her ear as he rolled her nipple back and forth between his thumb and index finger. He could feel her nipple hardening to his touch. She looked at him happily and smiled. She sighed and whispered, "You're insatiable – I love it." She traced the outline of his pectoral muscles with her left hand as her right drifted down to that area she loved to touch. She could feel him getting hard against her hand. He took her nipple in his mouth and worked it with his lips and tongue. She could feel herself becoming aroused, even though they had been doing this all night. Then he released her nipple from his mouth, and his hand slowly moved up to her neck. He placed gentle kisses on her as he moved his head up so that his lips were once again at ear level.

"Janet, you used to be really good friends with someone named Samantha Seaforth, if I remember. Have you heard from her lately?"

Janet was in a vague stupor, enjoying every second of his physical attention. She wasn't sure she had heard his question correctly.

She murmured, "What do you mean? Who's Samantha Seaforth?"

"You were friends growing up. I think she was like your best friend maybe."

Janet stiffened slightly as she realized that he was referring to her old friend Samantha Roberts, and she was taken aback that the subject would come up, especially when Sami had just called a few days earlier. It had been years since she had heard from either of them, and now both call, one right after the other. This was too much of a coincidence. Warily, she leaned up on her elbows and stared at Johnson.

"Why do you want to know?"

Johnson didn't reply.

Janet hesitated. She had an uncomfortable feeling in the pit of her stomach. These coincidences were beginning to seem very bizarre. But then the thought occurred to her that maybe, just maybe, Greg Johnson was thinking about getting back together with her, and he was simply making idle conversation. Maybe if she told him something, it would remind him of all the good times they'd shared in the past. After all, Janet hadn't had many positive opportunities in her life and this might be her chance. Maybe at last she was heading toward a future with someone who really seemed to care about her or he wouldn't have come back after so long apart. Attempting to divert the subject, Janet said, "Do we have to talk about this now? I'm just enjoying being with you." A strange look came over Johnson's face, as he continued to look at her, and the silence felt slightly ominous. When Johnson said nothing, Janet made the decision to plunge ahead. What could it hurt?

"Well, it's really weird that you should ask about her," said Janet, trying to act natural. "Sami called the other day. I hadn't heard from her in ages, but it was really great hearing her voice. We talked a lot about stuff we did in school together. She even asked about you. She asked a couple of questions about you and the man you work for. I have no idea why she would ask. You and I never talked much about your business, so of course I couldn't tell her much. I just told her that I remember you were often away for periods of time. She asked if I knew exactly when you were away, and I told her that I had always kept track in my journal of when I could expect you back. I was always so excited and looked forward to you coming home, so I kept track and made notes so that I would be ready for you. Remember how I always greeted you in different ways and different outfits when you returned, just to keep things interesting?"

Johnson was playing his hand over Janet's naked belly as she spoke. "That's interesting," he said in a level voice. "Do you still have those journals?"

"Uh, yes," she admitted somewhat sheepishly. "They're in my closet somewhere. They're not really important, just more stuff that girls write about the guys they date and things that happen to them in life." She stopped, wanting to change the subject. "Mmmmm, that feels good. Why do you care where my journal is? Do you just want to see what I wrote about you?" Janet rolled over and smiled teasingly at Greg Johnson. "You *do* know a diary is personal, right? So stop asking questions and kiss me."

Janet lay back down on the pillow, sighing with pleasure and quite willing to let the conversation slip away. It was hard concentrating with him continuing to arouse her with his well-placed attention to her sensitive areas. He kissed her neck again, on the spot where his thumb had been only a second before. He didn't answer her question, but rather replied with one of his own. "Is there anything else you talked about?" he asked in an even, controlled voice.

"No, not really, that's all that we talked about," Janet said, too casually. The Force didn't react to Janet's revelation other than nodding as he continued to caress her neck, and he punctuated each nod with a light kiss to her lips. His hand moved up her belly and across her breasts. He briefly took his hand away to grab the bed cover, which he brought up so that it rested under his hand and on her throat.

She moaned lightly with each touch, with every caress – until slowly and methodically, he applied increasing pressure. He began to squeeze her throat until she started gasping for air, a look of abject terror rearranging her features. She managed to propel enough air through her stressed vocal chords to utter, "Stop…you're…hurting…me!" as her eyes widened and she struggled against him. Her efforts to dislodge his large body and steel grip were fruitless. Finally, he eased his grip to allow her to catch her breath. She lay gasping beside him.

The Force said again in a quiet, determined voice, "I will ask you again, is there anything else you talked about with your old friend Sami?"

Janet shrank away from the man she had just moments ago thought she loved, the man who had just tried to choke her. In her panic, she sought to escape his grip, but he held on harder and she realized she couldn't move. In a frantic effort to save herself, Janet made a decision that was far worse than any of the bad ones she had made in her life previously. She decided to confess everything.

In a voice weakened by the assault on her neck, she choked out the words. "Sami told me some crazy story that a long time ago, she thought she overheard you and her stepfather talking about poisoning her mother. It didn't make any sense to either one of us, and I didn't bother to tell you because I knew it wasn't true. You would never do anything like that, right? You wouldn't poison someone. I told her she must have misunderstood."

Johnson said nothing, but watched her intently, his face just inches from hers as he pinned her down on the bed. "Sami and I had talked before about what she thought she heard that night, but we decided not to do anything since she wasn't sure she had heard correctly. And then she left town and I didn't hear from her any more. I thought it was strange that she raised it again when she called. It must have been bothering her all these years, because she brought it up again."

Janet hesitated. Was he listening? Did he understand that she knew he couldn't have done anything as awful as poisoning someone? Still hoarse from the choking, she then mumbled, "I sent her copies of my diary."

Janet watched the muscles in Johnson's face tighten and his eyes narrowed as he looked down at her impassively. A shiver of fear stabbed through her. The Force took a deep breath and said with only a touch of sadness, "Thank you for telling me this, Janet, but now I'm afraid you know too much. The poisoning, the dates in your journal, the things you wrote about my trips out of town, well, I'm afraid they could all lead to certain things I've been asked to do by my boss that I would prefer people not know about." He sighed. "I'm really sorry, Janet. You're a nice girl, but it's not going to help you now."

Calmly and quietly, The Force laid his hand on Janet's neck, his grip even more vise-like than before. Janet Winters thrashed helplessly on the bed, but it wasn't in the throes of passion this time. Her thrashing was desperation and fear of imminent death. Greg Johnson added his other hand to the first so that he could apply more pressure. He really wanted to end this as quickly as possible. He ensured that his bare hand never touched her throat, so there would be no DNA to gather from that area. Her hand shot up to grasp his as his grip grew tighter. She kicked and jerked and pulled, but she couldn't loosen the grip of the man who called himself The Force. Her eyes had flown open in shock to see the grim face of the lover who was doing this to her, and they started to bulge as she fought and clawed for breath. Her back arched once, twice and then fell back as darkness enveloped her. Janet Winters took her last breath. At last, she would be at peace.

Chapter 16

The Force looked down at his former lover with some regret. He knew that ending her life to prevent her talking was something he had to do, but though it was necessary, he felt a slight sense of remorse for having done it. Janet was not as attractive as some of the other girls he had been with, yet as his eyes traced the body he would never enjoy again, he knew that in many ways, she had been a good match for him. There was more to an individual than good looks alone. He really had wanted to please Janet during their time together, and when he left Minneapolis so abruptly to go with his boss, he had actually hoped that she would find a better life without him. From what she told him between sessions during the night, such had not been the case.

The Force doubted that he'd really ever loved anyone. He had *liked* people, maybe even cared about a few, but if his boss told him to dispatch them, in any fashion, he would do it. He had grown up with a strong work ethic. When he was a kid, his paper route was handled quickly and efficiently, and he had been promoted to a position of supervising other kids and their routes. He might not have been the sharpest knife in the drawer or even the brightest player on the football team, but he was named defensive captain because he worked harder and longer than anyone else. He learned that rewards came to those who worked hard and well, and so he did his job for his boss as well as or better than anyone could, even when it meant acting coldly and without emotion.

He occasionally felt a brief pang of remorse for ending someone's life, and it was certainly the case this time, just as it was when he finished off that couple in St. Petersburg, but he had no choice. It was just a job, it was something he was told to do, and so he did it. He was a loyal soldier, so to speak.

His eyes took in the inert form of Janet Winters from head to toe and back again. He bent down and kissed her lips one last time and got off the bed. He covered her naked body with a blanket so she wouldn't be on full display when the cops arrived. He didn't want them to have the opportunity to make obscene comments the minute they walked in the door.

Still naked, The Force padded around the apartment doing his clean-up, slowly wiping the things he might have touched and making sure there were no telltale signs of anything that could point to his even being there at all. He had been careful when he strangled Janet to make sure he didn't leave residue on Janet's skin. He had flushed the condoms. She didn't seem to have any close friends, so by the time anyone discovered her, it was unlikely that any of his DNA would be found on her. He had been extra careful when he came in, since he had been fairly certain how it was going to end. It had been his choice to give her a little pleasure before he killed her, though truthfully, he knew it had been a selfish decision that benefited him more than her. But he was quite sure by her passion and vocal utterances that he had at least made her last hours on earth pleasurable. He knew *he* had enjoyed it.

Johnson walked over to Janet's bedroom closet. She had mentioned keeping her various journals there; he just needed to find the one that went back to the time when they were dating and she was still close with her friend Samantha. The closet was small, and it took no time to find what he was looking for. The journals were stacked one upon the other, each annotated with a couple of years on the cover. He noticed that they were in neatly-arranged chronological order, except for one labeled with the years that he and Janet had dated. That diary was conveniently lying on the top of the pile. He surmised that she had pulled it out to photocopy the relevant material to send to Sami.

The idea flashed through his mind that Janet's diaries might make for some interesting reading some day, but clearly not right now. Not when he was standing just a few feet away from the dead body of the woman who'd written them and whose life he had so recently snuffed out with hardly a second thought. The Force leafed quickly through the journal with the corresponding dates, and sure enough, there were they were: incriminating references to his goings and comings with precise dates. These dates were likely to match up too closely with assignments he had been on and murders he had done. He wondered if Janet had actually given Sami any specific dates and sections of the diary, or just a general overview. It didn't matter: either way, it wasn't good. Greg Johnson dumped all the diaries into a briefcase that he had brought with him and set it down on a stand beside the door so that he could retrieve it on the way out.

The new revelation about the overheard conversation from years ago was even more troubling. He wondered who else knew about it. Sami had probably shared the information with her husband, and maybe others as well. The Force was going to have to deal with both those outstanding issues and soon.

As he dressed, he contemplated the next three things he had to do. They all involved phone calls. Two would be from his cell phone; and the third would come from Janet's phone. He returned to the living room and sat down on an old sofa that had seen years beyond its useful life. It wasn't very comfortable, but it was all Janet could afford, he supposed. He rested his large feet on the ancient coffee table that looked like it was made of scraps from old crates. It bore scratches, most likely from other feet that had slid across it as their owners tried to make themselves comfortable on the dilapidated sofa. Greg felt a twinge of jealousy as he thought of the others who might have darkened Janet's front hall and bedroom doorways.

As he made his phone calls, he looked around the room at everything that represented Janet's life. There wasn't much. The remaining sparse furniture was in the same or worse shape as the couch. There were a couple of cheap pictures on the wall, and the flowers he had brought her hours earlier still sat in a plain glass vase on the worn table. Not much for a lifetime.

Both of the first two calls were to former buddies; guys who had the same proclivities for violence honed by tours of duty. Now they did freelance jobs to pay for their gym memberships, because that was pretty much their lives. He had exchanged phone numbers with them after their first tour of duty. After all, they shared something in common: combat. He dialed the first number and waited for the person on the other end in Miami to pick up. He explained what he needed done and the person acknowledged without as much as a question. The response was simply a grunt to indicate that the message was understood and an acknowledgement that he would have the task done in the next half hour. The second call was answered by an equally gruff male voice. Greg never minded reassigning jobs that had to be done to his victims, as it made him feel important. What did they call it? "Sub" something? Oh yes, subcontracting. That's what he was doing. He was subcontracting jobs.

He explained to the individual on the phone that he wanted someone watched. He wanted the person being watched to be presented with a "gift," so that he would be fully aware someone was watching him. And, if necessary, the person being watched just might have to be physically reminded to do as he was told. But the last part was not to be put into action until The Force called again. For now, it was simply to be a display of power to emphasize what they were capable of doing.

The gruff male voice said he understood and hung up. His name was Jason Sage, and he was an old buddy from the marines. The Force had used him for various jobs on previous occasions. He was ruthless and uncompassionate, and just like Johnson, he would do exactly as he was ordered without blinking an eye. He was a loyal soldier.

Johnson paused and looked around the room. How many days and nights had he spent in this place a few years ago? It was too bad that Janet hadn't known to keep her mouth shut when Sami called. She might still be alive if she had. Johnson was in no hurry to leave, as his flight home wasn't for another two hours. He finally got up off the sofa, polished the table where his feet had been and went back into the bedroom to look one last time at Janet, surprising himself just a little with his feeling of remorse. He looked at his watch and realized with a start that time had slipped by. He had one more thing to do before he could leave the apartment and walk a few blocks to a nearby hotel to catch a taxi to the airport.

Greg Johnson went into the kitchen where several dishes were lying in the sink. He picked up a dish cloth, wrapped it around his hand and picked up Janet's phone that was hanging on the wall. He wanted a record of this call, so that the police would eventually stumble over it and become suspicious.

Mason Seaforth answered on the second ring.

With no lead in, Greg demanded coldly, "Put Sami on."

There was a hesitation at the other end of the line until Mason said, "I can't. She's still not here."

"Where is she?"

"I don't know. I'm not sure where she is. Who are you?"

"Have you talked to the police?"

"I told them before you called the first time that my wife is missing. I haven't told them anything since. What do you want?"

"Sami knows who I am, and that's all that really matters. Here's what you need to know right now: you better find your wife, Seaforth, and you better not involve any cops in this. Do you understand?"

"Yes, I understand but why are you so interested in my wife? Who are you, anyway? What do you want? Is it money? I might be able to scrape some together as soon as Sami comes back. But you have to tell me what is going on."

In a controlled and icy manner, Johnson replied, "I don't *have* to do anything, and I'm the one giving the orders here. Got that? What you need to do is listen and stop asking questions or things will start getting worse. And you'd better not go to the police. In case you think I'm kidding here, in a few minutes, there will be a car on the street outside your house. In that car will be a very large, very unpleasant guy who will not blink an eye when it comes to hurting you. He will make sure that you don't wander off on your own and talk to the police. He has done some serious damage to a lot of people like you who didn't take me seriously, and he truly enjoys his job. If I were you, I would pay attention to where that car is at all times and pray that the driver's door doesn't open. If the door does open, it means you have not listened very well. Am I clear?"

"Yes, you are," Mason said, as he heard his voice break slightly over the phone.

"Good. Now I want you to find some notes that your wife has written about her past. It could be a journal or a diary, or maybe some personal notes in a box or even emails or files on her computer. Just confirm what it is. Oh, and Seaforth? You don't want to know what's in those notes, trust me. When you find them, and I am quite confident you will, give them to the guy parked in the car close to your house. He'll know what to do.

"And just a reminder, we have a very long reach. You can expect the man we just talked about to come to your door soon to show you something. What you see should confirm for you how long our reach is."

The statement petrified Mason.

The Force continued, "I want the notes and I want to talk to your wife, Seaforth, and it had better be soon. Find her and have her call me. She knows my number. If you're lucky and do as I tell you, maybe this will all go away."

With that, The Force slammed the phone back into its wall cradle. Mason was left staring at his cell phone. As if things weren't bad enough, there was now this barely-veiled threat about finding notes from Sami's past and men who were going to be watching his house from now on. Mason didn't know what it meant, but it seemed to make things much, much worse.

As he walked the few short blocks to find a taxi, Greg Johnson tossed the dish cloth into a garbage can and wondered to himself again just how much Sami Seaforth knew. Whatever it was, Greg knew it was too much. Samantha Seaforth had to die.

Chapter 17

As Jennifer Seaforth left the dormitory on her way to class at her campus in Coral Gables, she noticed a large disheveled man leaning against a tree about 30 yards from the path where she was walking. Jennifer was always aware of her surroundings, and this individual looked completely out of place among reasonably well dressed, or at least clean, classmates. He wasn't moving, and he seemed to be watching her. Now alert as she walked, Jennifer picked up her pace and headed toward the school building in front of her. As she did so, she sensed the man abandon his spot against the tree and start following along on the path a few paces behind her. Jennifer quickened her pace even more, and it was immediately matched by the stranger behind. She looked around for campus security, but there were none present that she could see. Just as she was about to stop and confront the man, she heard him call out her name. As she turned to look directly at him, the man raised a dark object in his hand.

Jennifer tensed and prepared herself for some kind of attack. Through university-sponsored classes, she had learned how to fight back against a physical attack. Without thinking, she adjusted her stance so she could kick him in the crotch or gouge his eyes or stomp on his instep, all things she'd been taught to use if necessary. She couldn't imagine this stranger would attack her in broad daylight with students passing around them. But he had called her name, so it was obviously personal. She braced herself. But there was no attack forthcoming.

The dark object in his hand wasn't a weapon, it was a phone, and in his other hand he held up a newspaper. Before she could respond or even yell, the man leered at her and snapped her picture with his phone. What a sick bastard, Jennifer thought in disgust. Was he one of those guys that got his kicks from taking pictures of unsuspecting women? She tried to memorize his facial features and his clothes as best she could, so she could alert campus security the first opportunity she got, but right now, she had a class she was about to be late for. And she had her missing mother to worry about. "Pervert!" she yelled, and started after him as he took off in a dead run. It was disturbing that he'd known her name, but she guessed he could look it up in the campus directory or something. She'd been told there are all kinds of freaks in the world who would come to a college campus to try and get their kicks, and obviously this creep didn't belong there. He certainly wasn't a student. Jennifer decided to let her dad know the next time they talked, and worry about it later.

Mason sat alone in the room and once again, the temperature in the closed space seemed to plummet. The guy had mentioned that they had a "long reach." What was that supposed to mean? Who was he? Mason got up and looked out the window, but there was no sign of the car the caller had told him to expect. He called up to Marcie and asked her to join him in the living room. Marcie started talking as she descended the stairs, asking questions in a staccato fashion as only Marcie could.

"Did you talk to Jennifer? What did she say? I heard the phone ring a few minutes ago. Who was that? Is there any news?"

Mason waited until Marcie turned the corner into the living room and sat down facing him. He explained that he had spoken to Jennifer and that she seemed satisfied for now that things were under control, though she was obviously very worried. He knew something had to be done quickly or she would make good on her promise to come home – probably on the weekend, which was only a few days away. He also knew it would be very hard for Jennifer to concentrate at college, not knowing in real time what was happening at home.

Marcie looked at Mason in her perceptive way and said, "Okay, so what was the other phone call?"

With a deep sigh, he brought her up to speed on his second call from the anonymous man, emphasizing the caller's assertion that it would be a grave mistake to involve the police if he ever hoped to see his wife again. "It's confusing," said Mason, frowning slightly. "He's threatening us, yet he doesn't seem to know where Sami is, either."

"I don't understand this at all, Mason," Marcie said, shaking her head and frowning, too. "Why does this guy want to talk to Sami so badly? What could she have gotten herself into? Do you think she has some kind of gambling debt or something? Could it be something from her past that she never shared with you, and now it's come back to haunt her? And where would she get $10,000?"

Mason thought for a minute. "I guess the truth is, Sami was never very forthcoming about her past. I knew about her mother's death, of course, and I know she never liked her stepfather at all. But that was a long time ago. Maybe I should have pressed the issue." They talked for a while, trying to figure out what Sami might have been involved with that would cause her to know this rough-sounding man who was now trying to find her, but came up with nothing. Marcie told Mason that his Chateau Margaux theory about Sami's password had not resulted in any progress, so they agreed that maybe she hadn't had time to change it. They also agreed that getting into Sami's computer was even more important now. Mason reminded Marcie about Sami's theory that something easy to remember was better when it came to passwords. As Marcie went upstairs to work on the computer once more, she glanced out the window to see if any strange cars were parked on the street. She didn't see any, but she did notice Sami's Miata sitting there, and that gave her another idea.

She'd only been gone about 15 minutes when Mason heard a shriek from the office upstairs. Mason's first thought was for Marcie's safety, and he charged up the stairs and rounded the corner into the office, only to find Marcie leaning back in the chair beaming from ear to ear in front of Sami's computer screen as if she had found the Holy Grail. "I got it, Mason! I found Sami's password! It's the name and year of her car – Miata2011! She loves that car, so it makes perfect sense! We should have thought of it sooner."

Mason looked on in surprise, and then realized how obvious it was, right there in front of them all the time. "Marcie, you're a genius," he said, as he gave her a quick hug, and then leaned over her shoulder to look at the screen. He didn't see anything unusual on her desktop, but he knew it would take time to go through her various folders and files. Whatever was on her computer – if in fact, anything *was* on her computer – wasn't going to be sitting out in plain view.

He pulled up another chair as Marcie slid over sideways, and settled in to begin his search. But just as he picked up the mouse, the downstairs doorbell rang, followed by three rapid heavy-handed thumps on the front door that shook it on its hinges. Mason and Marcie both jumped, and then exchanged tense glances. He told her to stay out of sight upstairs, but close enough so she could hear whatever happened. He knew she still had the handgun in her purse.

Mason went downstairs, his heart beating fast, and opened the door, not knowing what to expect. Standing in front on him on the porch, far too close for comfort, was a very large man who appeared to be in his late 30s wearing a windbreaker and jeans. He wore wraparound sunglasses on a nose that was slightly askew on his face. A scar ran down his cheek. He held a cell phone in his hand, and as he held it up, Mason noticed some of his fingers were bent and crooked, as if they may have been broken at some time in the past. When he opened his mouth to speak, the gruff words that came out were barely above a whisper.

"Mason Seaforth? I have something to show you."

He shoved the phone at Mason. As he looked at the screen, Mason felt a sharp pain in his chest and a wave of nausea filled him. He grabbed the frame of the door to steady himself, as his knees began to buckle. On the screen of the phone was a picture of his daughter, obviously taken at the university on her way to a class, judging from the campus buildings in the background. Mason cried out and tried to snatch the phone out of the man's hand, but his attempt was quickly blocked. "Don't touch this phone. Just take a good look." Mason couldn't help but notice that his daughter appeared startled in the photo as if someone had called to her and taken her picture when she turned around.

The man laughed, turned the phone screen back towards himself, and with two fingers, he expanded the image. Without a word, he showed the screen again to Mason. This time, Mason saw something more on the enlarged version. Whoever was taking the picture was holding a copy of the Miami Herald beside Jennifer's face so that the date was visible. Mason peered more closely, and then reeled as he realized the date he was looking at was today's. This picture had been taken today! Had this man just been with his daughter in Miami? Mason struggled to take all of this in and comprehend what was going on as he stared at the photo. It was clear by the newspaper that his daughter's photo had been taken today. But how? Then Mason realized how easy it would be for someone in Miami to take this photo and email it to someone else on the other side of Florida. He felt physically ill.

The burly man put the phone back in his pocket and turned to walk away. Then he stopped, turned around to look at Mason, and in that same gravelly voice barely above a whisper, he said, "The car you see there on the street is mine. I will be here watching you. You can count on it. And if you do something stupid other than what you are told, I will be back to pay you a much different kind of visit. The next time you see me, I won't be on your front porch, I'll be inside your house, and you will be very, very sorry, trust me." He paused, then added, "If that happens, your daughter just might get a visit too."

The man started toward the car that Mason now noticed parked a couple of doors down the street. Drained and stunned, Mason closed the door, and slumped against it weakly. Marcie quickly descended the stairs. He noticed she had her gun in her hand down by her side. "Oh my God. Mason, what did he say? I couldn't hear everything, but it didn't sound good at all." Mason shakily walked to the couch to sit down and told her to put the gun away. He took deep breaths and tried to settle his nerves. Finally, he started to speak in a slow, uneven voice. He told Marcie what the stranger had said and about the photo that he had seen with today's date revealed in the hand of whoever took the picture. Things were escalating, and he felt like he was drowning. The little bit of progress Marcie had made by getting Sami's password was far outweighed by the ominous dangers of the threats he was getting. Would these people, whoever they were, harm his daughter? If they found Sami before he did, would they kill her? Why was he being watched -- was he in real danger? They had indicated as long as he didn't talk to the police again, he would be all right, at least for the time being. What should he do? Should he ignore their threats and call the police anyway? Mason felt so helpless. His family's life was at stake. He sat, lost in thought, wrestling with the dilemma and weighing the consequences, until finally he came to his decision. Right or wrong, he was not going to involve the authorities any more until he had more information. This was his family. If going to the police meant endangering his family, then he would continue going down the path he was on until he was convinced to do otherwise.

Then it occurred to him that the University of Miami had its own police department. That was one of the reasons he and Sami had approved of Jennifer's decision to go there. He would contact them without involving Suarez, Finch and Baker. Somehow he didn't think the campus police were on the same level as the police he had been warned not to talk to. He could tell them that some nutjob had followed his daughter this morning on the campus and taken her picture without permission. He would ask them to talk to Jennifer and keep an eye on her without being obvious, and to watch in case other students were also being followed by the man.

His decision made, he looked at Marcie who had been sitting quietly waiting for him to come to a decision and tell her what their next move would be. Making direct eye contact with her, Mason said, "Marcie, there's one thing I would like you to do for me."

"You should know by now I would do anything for you, Mason. Well, maybe not *anything,* but you know what I mean." She was trying her best to be a steadying influence for him.

Mason took a deep breath, and Marcie knew that whatever was coming was something important. She steeled herself, wondering what it was going to be.

"Marcie, I want you to show me how to use that gun of yours. I have to be ready for anything. I can't believe how much our lives have changed in a few short hours, and I honestly have no idea what's coming next. Can you show me the basics? The guy parked out front is watching me, but he doesn't know you're here. Maybe you can sneak out the back and buy a gun for me."

Marcie had thought she was ready for anything, but she saw that she was wrong. She hadn't been prepared for Mason Seaforth to ask her to show him how to shoot a gun. She knew he must be feeling extremely desperate to make this request. "It's not that simple, Mason," she replied. "First of all, I can't 'sneak out the back,' because I obviously need my car, which is parked out front. Secondly, there is something that 'He Who Shall Not Be Named' taught me about guns, and that is that you have to have respect for them. You can't just pick up a gun and expect to know how to use it. If you point a gun and shoot it at someone, you have to be prepared beforehand. You have to know how to pull the trigger, how much pressure to apply, and you have to be accurate. If you don't know what you're doing, you're just as likely to shoot yourself as your intended target!" Marcie couldn't help but laugh. "When I first tried it, I couldn't hit the side of a shed. It's dangerous if you don't know how to use a gun properly. You can't hesitate, 'cause you may not get a second chance. If you just wound the attacker, it could make them more determined to kill you than they already were. You have to be prepared to kill if you're going to have a gun." Marcie stopped and took a deep breath. "I will do one better than show you about my gun. I will get someone who really knows what they're doing to show you."

"How do we do that? I'm getting desperate, Marcie. My daughter is in danger. My wife is missing. Where can I get this training? How long will it take?" Clearly Mason was feeling slightly frantic and cornered.

"The place I want to take you to is just outside of St. Petersburg. It be-longs to the man who trained me. We need to spend some time there, but we can do it all in a few hours. It will take the guy a few minutes to show you what to do, but you will have to fire off a few rounds to get the feel for the gun." Marcie stood up and pulled the curtain back a little to peek outside. She couldn't miss the navy blue sedan sitting at the curb a couple of doors down the block. "Yep, there he is," she said with a touch of scorn. "Apparently he isn't going anywhere."

Mason thought for a minute. He wanted desperately to get onto Sami's computer and start going through her files, but he also felt vulnerable. He knew now for sure that whoever was calling them was not bluffing. The car outside and the picture of Jennifer proved it. His decision was made. The computer would have to wait. He was even more resolved to learn how to shoot, but he was sure he would be followed if he left the house. That was the last thing he wanted to happen. "Well, he just arrived here, and maybe he doesn't know the neighborhood. Let's move before he gets settled in. You go out the front and get in your car. I'll slip out the back door on foot and meet you at the Super Gas station two blocks over. Do you know it?"

"Sure, I get my gas there all the time."

"I'll watch when you leave. If that jerk approaches you or you feel like you're in any danger, come back in the house right away. Understand?"

"You got it," said Marcie with a small determined smile, and she headed out the door. As Mason watched from the shadows behind the curtain, his eyes widened at the scene on the driveway. He saw Marcie walking stiffly towards her car. Her head was up, and she was standing tall. This was always her way of dealing with things – with bravado. She appeared to be staring at the driver in the vehicle on the street as she walked to her car and opened the door. Then with a flippant wave of her hand and an airy smile, she acknowledged the driver of the parked car with a one-finger salute. Mason stared in disbelief. He heard the sound of her car door slamming, the engine starting and then the front of Marcie's car thumped on the uneven pavement between the surface of his driveway and the street as she backed out at breakneck speed. Once out of reverse, she shifted into drive, and took off down the street, tires squealing in protest. Mason sensed he had just witnessed a display of bravery meant to mask the real fear Marcie was feeling. On the other hand, he thought to himself, she *does* carry a gun.

Mason made a show of opening the drapes and standing in full view as he looked out the window. He wanted to make sure the driver saw him. He could see the driver's head turn towards the house, and he could feel the eyes upon him. He knew he had been seen, and that was enough. Now it was time to put the rest of the plan into action. Mason closed the drapes again, picked up his car keys and phone, threw them in his pocket, and headed for the back door of his house.

The Force felt his phone vibrating in his pocket and picked it up. He listened closely to the voice on the other end recap the details about his visit a half hour ago at the Seaforth house, just before he set up watch from his navy sedan a couple of doors down the street. "I showed him the picture like you said and told him I would be watching his every move. He nearly passed out. I almost laughed. I thought he was by himself, but then I'm sitting in the car watching the house, and out comes this sexy black chick a few minutes later. I'm like, 'What the hell?' Looked like she might've been there all night. The guy's probably getting a little extra while the old lady's away. I know I would with that. She had these cute black shorts on and she was hot, man! I thought the car in the driveway was his, but apparently, she drives this nice BMW convertible, and she took off like there was a gator on her tail. I'm thinkin' maybe they got word his wife's coming home, so she took off like a shot."

The Force thought that maybe this guy shouldn't think. "Okay, listen. Is Seaforth still there? Is there any way he could have gone with her?"

"No, no way. He's there, man. I just saw him through the window. Do you want me to work him over a little? Aside from my little front-door visit to him, he's probably feeling pretty good after screwing the black chick all night. I could fix that."

"No, leave things alone. I told you I'll let you know if you need to do anything other than watch the house and report back to me. Let's let things simmer for now. Just keep watching the house. Make sure you're noticed. Be obvious, and let's hope the neighbors don't start wondering why you're parked there. If he leaves, follow him! We'll scare the hell out of him for now, but nothing else. I'll tell you if you need to go and talk to him again. For now, stay put."

"OK, man! It's your nickel."

As he clicked off the call, The Force sighed with the weight of having to deal with idiot sub-contractors. Sometimes he wished he could be in three places at once. Then he'd know the job got done correctly, the way it should be. Maybe, he thought, supervision isn't all it's cracked up to be, after all.

Mason headed for the back door and slipped out into the yard as quickly as he could, locking the door behind him. He stepped on some day lilies while climbing up on the decorative water feature, which was in the back left hand corner of their yard. The additional height gave him the boost he needed to climb over the fence and into his neighbor's yard behind the wooden privacy fence that separated their adjoining properties. He irrationally hoped that Sami would forgive him for squashing the lilies. He also hoped that the neighbor whose yard he was now trespassing on didn't see him climbing the fence and crossing his yard to get to the street in front of his house. It would raise too many questions.

Mason ran to the Super Gas station, but when he pulled up out of breath near one of the pumps, there was no sign of Marcie's BMW. He waited with a pounding heart in the shadows of the station as cars pulled in and out. After what seemed like an eternity but was really only about 10 minutes, Marcie pulled in and Mason was relieved not to hear the familiar bass-heavy thump of Marcie's stereo that always accompanied her wherever she drove. As he climbed in, she told him that she'd wanted to make sure she wasn't being followed, so she had circled a few blocks before arriving at the station.

Mason nodded and simply said, "Good thinking, Marcie. We need to take every precaution possible."

Chapter 18

Detective Albert Baker was going through his emails. He had worked out a routine for himself so that he didn't check each one as they came in. With the flood of emails that poured across his desk each day, it was simply too distracting to stop what he was doing every time a new one came in. He had even turned off the notification tone because it annoyed him to hear a succession of emails setting off a series of beeps. So his management decision dictated that he would check them every hour or maybe even every two hours when there was something else requiring his attention. He reflected briefly on how times had changed. For law enforcement officers now, their patrol vehicle was their office. Everything they needed was right there in their cars. They could spend the day in their vehicle and be as plugged in as any office worker. But this afternoon, Baker was sitting in his office at the station discussing the Briscoe murder with his colleague, Tom Finch. They'd decided to take a break, so he was checking his messages.

Baker had his email set up in preview mode so he could read the first two lines of each one. That way he could pick and choose to read the ones that would require his immediate attention, and set others aside to file for reading later – or could maybe be dealt with by the weight of one finger on the delete button. They were the ones he enjoyed the most. He got some measure of satisfaction by eliminating emails so they would no longer be there weighing on him as he went about his daily routine. But he loved his job and did it to the best of his ability, so if something caught his attention or intrigued him, he would read that email and respond. Maybe he was a bit old school -- well, okay, probably a *lot* old school -- but he always thought a question deserved a response. If he could not respond right away in detail, he still tried to let the person know he would get back to them when he could. Baker had tried unsuccessfully to instil this same discipline in his colleagues as well. After all, the time they spent complaining about how busy they were could undoubtedly be used more productively by providing courtesy responses to those who were probably equally busy.

So now as he skimmed the preview lines casually and dispatched each response methodically, he wasn't expecting to be stopped dead in his tracks by an email that jumped right out at him and grabbed his full attention. The subject line read, *Query – Mason Seaforth*. Baker immediately clicked on the email and started to read further.

I'm a detective with the 4th precinct in Minneapolis assigned to investigate the murder of one Janet Winters. She was found dead in her apartment yesterday. She had been dead for a while when she was found. We checked the outgoing calls on her phone and noted one to a number of someone living in your area – a man named Mason Seaforth. If you have any information about Mr. Seaforth that you think might help us in our investigation, could you please advise me at your earliest convenience?

Thanks. I look forward to your response.

P.S. I assume the weather is better there than it is here. Lucky bastard!

The signature block at the bottom read David Lawrence, Detective, 4th Precinct, Minneapolis Police Department.

Baker stared at the screen for a moment before he responded, telling Detective Lawrence that Mason Seaforth was a person of interest related to a homicide in Tampa and that his wife had mysteriously disappeared at the same time from Gulfport. He went on to explain the shoe tread that was found at the scene and the details, such as they were, that related to the disappearance. He mentioned that Sergeant Juanita Suarez from the Gulfport Police Department was looking into the disappearance and that he would alert her to the latest information from this new murder. He ended the email by asking how they kept warm in their igloos in Minneapolis.

His partner Tom Finch wandered in just then with a coffee in each hand. They were double-cupped to save his fingers from the heat coming off the steaming liquid. As Finch set one of the coffees down on the desk, Baker showed him the email from Detective Lawrence in Minneapolis. Finch took a minute to read the missive and then read Baker's response.

"Hmmm, this is interesting," Finch commented. "Maybe our accountant friend is not the mild-mannered guy he appears to be."

"I don't know what's going on here, but there seems to be some connection. First the running shoe, then his wife disappears, and now it seems he's connected somehow to a homicide in Minneapolis. Is it possible his wife was running away from domestic violence? If this guy is capable of murder, either directly or by hiring someone to do the dirty work, he could be capable of anything. His wife could be buried in the back yard for all we know. But what's the motive? Right now, we have nothing except a pair of running shoes, a missing wife and a mystery phone call."

Baker picked up the phone and dialed the number for Sergeant Suarez. When she answered, he explained the email he had received. He asked if there had been any progress on the disappearance of Mason Seaforth's wife. As a matter of fact, replied Suarez, there had been one new development.

"I just got the toxicology results from the lab on the two wine bottles they had been drinking from the night she disappeared. They liked different kinds of wine, so they were drinking from different bottles. The lab discovered some BZO in one of the bottles. It will take a little longer to find out exactly what kind of sedative it was, but it appears the little anniversary lady wanted her husband out of the way for awhile, so she apparently managed to get some sedative in the bottle he was drinking from."

"Is there any indication that she might have been trying to kill him?"

"Not really," Suarez replied. "There wasn't nearly enough dosage to do that, but there was clearly enough to make him less functional long enough for her to disappear. So either she didn't know what she was doing and didn't add enough to put him into dreamland permanently, or she did know what she was doing and gave him enough to put him out of commission so she could pull off the great escape. I suppose there's the remote possibility that someone else doped the wine bottle so they could grab her when he was sleeping, but that's really a long shot. The logistics make it nearly impossible, but I wouldn't rule it out altogether."

"What's your next move, Sergeant?"

"I'm convinced there's enough indication of something unusual here that we should notify the local media that she has disappeared. I think we should raise the public profile to shake the bushes a bit. I will be paying Mr. Seaforth another visit to discuss the disappearance further with him. I want to watch his face for telltale signs. Given that we have two suspicious murders and the same guy's name keeps turning up, and coincidentally his wife goes missing at the exact same time, I'm starting to wonder if he might even have given himself the sedative. Or they might have faked it between the two of them as part of some bigger scheme. I'm not ruling anything out." Suarez then added, "I'm going to get him to sign a consent form, so I can bring his wife's computer back to the lab. Maybe we can find something there and if he doesn't want to sign the form, the suspicion will become even deeper."

The conversation didn't do anything to solve any of the mystery, but it did get the three cops – Baker, Finch and Suarez -- thinking in a number of different directions. Suarez was now contemplating the murders in two different U.S. cities, murders that oddly enough, seemed to be somehow connected with the missing woman's husband. Baker and Finch were still digesting the news that Seaforth had been drugged, or at least wanted everyone to think he had been.

Before leaving to talk to Mason Seaforth, Suarez put Sami's photo and relevant information on the police department database and on their Facebook page. She also typed up a press release that would be splashed all over the news tonight. Anyone who wasn't aware she was missing would know by the end of the evening, and the usual flood of responses would come to her desk like a giant landslide. She could immediately discard most of them, but there might be the odd one that would be of interest. Many cases had been solved by someone coming forward as the result of seeing a picture on the news, so it was certainly worth wading through the nuisance sightings if one that meant something actually surfaced.

Once that was done, Suarez drove to the Seaforth house. As she pulled up to the curb in front of the house, a blue sedan was just pulling away behind her. She went to the door and rang the doorbell. There was no answer. She tried it again. There was still no answer. She went back to her car and pulled out her phone and called Mason Seaforth's number. When she heard his voice mail answer, all she could do was leave a message.

The driver of the blue sedan was also on the phone, calling The Force to report the latest development. After circling the block, he expected the police officer to have gone inside the house, but he was surprised to see her walking back to her car. He relayed the information to his boss that Seaforth must have had a short conversation with the police officer. The Force was seething inside, but it was a good sign that the conversation between the police woman and Seaforth was short. He told the driver to be vigilant. It may be time sooner rather than later to reinforce to Seaforth that he wasn't supposed to talk to the police at all.

All the phones were hung up without anyone having any satisfaction.

Chapter 19

Marcie drove north on 53rd Street S. and across the Sunshine Skyway Bridge that would take them to an area just south of Brandon, Florida. As she drove, Mason sent a text to Jennifer asking her if she was all right. Almost immediately he got a response saying that she was fine, but some creepy guy had tailed her on campus that morning and taken her picture while she was on her way to class. Mason's heart sank. He knew exactly what she was talking about, but he didn't let on. He told her to be vigilant and said he would contact the university police on her behalf. But what he didn't mention was that he had already seen the picture, already called the police, or that there was a connection to her mother's disappearance.

Next he placed a call to Willard, Sami's manager at the bank, to ask about the amount of money that Sami had transferred and then withdrawn. Willard checked Sami's term deposits and verified that an amount of $10,000 in Sami's name had indeed been redeemed, transferred to an account labeled "Vacation" and then withdrawn almost immediately. He lowered his voice and advised Mason that he really shouldn't be telling him since the term deposits were Sami's personal financial activity, but he was doing it as a favor to Mason. As soon as he mentioned the term deposits, Mason recalled Sami telling him about a little money she had received from insurance when her Mom died. They had discussed it briefly and Mason told her to put it away for a rainy day. He had forgotten completely about it. He smiled grimly to himself as he thought that this must be the rainy day they had talked about.

Willard asked about Sami as Mason had anticipated, and this time, Mason told him the truth: that Sami had disappeared the night of their anniversary, and he had not been able to find her yet. Willard listened intently without saying a word. "Please go ahead and let people know," Mason told him. "Maybe there's someone she talked to about her plans while she was at work. Maybe they'll remember something." He left Willard in shocked silence as he hung up the phone.

Mason and Marcie were each lost in their own thoughts as they continued the drive. Mason wondered if he should have stayed at the house and continued searching Sami's computer instead of trying to learn how to shoot a gun. He shook his head imperceptibly as he thought about driving somewhere to learn how to shoot, born out of the innate necessity to protect his family. It made him think about society and where it was going. The drive reminded him of the road to Valdosta, Georgia where his parents lived. He and Sami had often pointed out to each other the incongruity of the road signs along the way. They were gigantic, in your face and obviously, available to anyone who wanted to pay. Every few miles there would be one shouting, "Advertise Here." They were interspersed with signs that carried local messages. One had apparently been rented by Jesus as He announced, "Let Go, I Will Catch You." The next trumpeted a relaxing time at an Adult Super Store and Spa and another bragged about the availability of "1000's of Guns." Juxtaposed in the middle of it all was a sign advertising an annual Daylily Festival. He and Sami had often said that there is a market for anything in America, and the billboards backed that up. Now he was about to join the hundreds of thousands of people who felt the necessity of owning a weapon.

He asked Marcie, "So why do you carry that gun around? Is it even legal?"

"Mason, don't be such a wimp! You must be an accountant! All you need is the green eyeshade and the arm bands to complete your supreme wimpiness. Of course it's legal. Where have you been? Thanks to the good old Second Amendment to the Constitution, Uncle Sam gave me and all the other cute chicks like me who might need a little protection once in awhile the right to bear arms. And since he gave me that right, I'm going to use it just in case somebody wants to get up in my face. And as of 2005, Florida is a "stand-your-ground" state, remember? That means that if someone breaks into my house, I can legally presume he is going to do me harm and shoot him in the face. I would be immune from any kind of prosecution unless there is probable cause that what I did was unlawful."

Mason could see her eyes were actually sparkling as she talked about her gun. "I don't even know what language you're speaking right now, Marcie," he sighed. Mason thought with a shudder that anyone who knew Marcie would be a complete idiot to try to break into her house. If they knew she had a baseball bat beside her bed, it would be scary enough. But if anyone with bad intentions knew Marcie and that she stashed a gun in her nightstand, it should be enough encouragement to try robbing someone in a very different part of the country.

Mason absorbed what he had just heard. He couldn't help but wonder what had become of society when someone could be so proud of an object that could end another person's life. The right to bear arms was entrenched in the Constitution at a time when it was a necessity. Surely, that was a different time and man had advanced a little since then. But he also knew that the argument about guns would rage on between the believers and non-believers, no matter how many mass murders there were in his beloved country. Now was not the time to be arguing with Marcie about the validity of hers or anyone else's rights.

They drove through Brandon, and along a country road until Marcie spotted a clearing just to their right. There was no indication that there was anything worthwhile at the end of the tight, rutted road she chose to follow. Mason could hear grass scraping on the bottom of the car as they bounced down the path. Finally, they came upon an old farmhouse. In the distance, Mason could see figures in camouflage outfits running around and crouching low as if in some kind of military exercise.

Someone exited the house and walked towards the car. Mason briefly thought of the characters he had seen on the popular TV show, *Duck Dynasty*. This guy was overweight and also wearing camouflage. He wore a beard that was first noticeable for its length, as it hung down to his waist. It had been black at one time, but now the dark color was highlighted by streaks of grey and it was bushy in a manner that reminded Mason of some of the scrub in the ditches he had seen on the way over here. In fact, Mason thought, there could be any number of creatures living in the beard, and it's doubtful that anyone, including its owner, would know. The big guy's lips were barely noticeable as they were framed by hair, but as he approached the car, they were exposed by a broad grin.

Marcie got out of the car and gave him a big hug. She motioned for Mason to come around to her side of the car to meet the big gentleman who was simply introduced as Leroy. Leroy's beard was only surpassed by his outgoing personality and thunderous voice as he vigorously shook Mason's hand and slapped him on the back, causing Mason to take a step forward. Marcie told Leroy that Mason was there for some gun training.

"How long have you got?"

"About all I can spare is two hours. "We have to get back. There's a lot going on right now. I need to know the basics so I can protect my family if the need arises."

Leroy responded with a hearty laugh. "Marcie, did you explain to your friend here about guns? You know better than that. You must have learned something from Germ…"

"Don't even mention that name in front of me, Leroy. He's now known as 'He Who Shall Not Be Named,' and that's the only name he needs. As for learning anything, don't worry, I explained to Mason that shooting is not as simple as he might think. But he's right; we do need to get back this afternoon, and my friend here definitely needs to know how to shoot a gun. Do as much as you can as a favor to me, okay? We'll have to make do with that."

Marcie gave Leroy some cash, and they headed out to the area where they had seen the figures running around as they were driving in. As they got closer, Mason instantly recognized two players from the Miami Heat basketball team. He realized they must be friends of Marcie's ex-husband, as they all greeted her on the way by. She whispered to Mason, "Don't tell anyone you saw these guys here. This is something they do for recreation and for protection, too."

When they were standing in front of a row of targets, Leroy took a weapon out of the holster that he had on his side. "This is a Glock 17. It's one of the finest weapons around and a lot of law enforcement agencies use these. It's lightweight and easy to handle. One thing to keep in mind, though, is that this gun has what's called a safe action lock system. What this means is that there is no external safety on the gun. There's no switch that turns it on and off. There is no hammer to pull back like you see in the movies. When you pull the trigger, Mr. Seaforth, this gun fires. Got that?"

"Yes, but then why do they call it a lock system?"

"Because there's a lock on the trigger that releases automatically when you pull the trigger. It's there so nothing can accidentally jar the trigger and fire it. But the responsibility is still on the person shooting this gun not to do anything stupid. The guys that invented this model of the Glock were geniuses, really. You know what else is great about this gun?"

Mason thought he would probably fall into the "do something stupid" category as a shooter, and he certainly couldn't really see anything great about any gun, but he waited because he knew he was going to find out whether he wanted to or not.

"The previous version used to kick the empty shells back in your face. This one ejects them to the side so they won't hit you. It's an awesome design! But here's a tip. If you do get hit by an empty shell casing, it burns like hell. I suggest you do up the top button on your shirt so you don't get an empty shell casing down there." Leroy laughed, but Mason could tell he was serious.

Mason could also see the same fire in Leroy's eyes that he saw in Marcie's when she was talking about her gun. He knew he wouldn't be here if it wasn't for Sami's disappearance and the chain of events since. It was surreal and totally out of character for him, but he knew it was something he had to do.

Leroy handed Mason the gun, and he was surprised at the lightness of it, given its size "It's plastic!" Mason exclaimed in surprise. "Are you sure this thing will stay in one piece and not melt when it's fired?"

"Ah hell, they've dropped one out of a helicopter to test it, and it fired just fine afterwards. Believe me, it'll fire. Now, I want you to hold the gun up and aim it at that target. You're good for up to about 20 yards with this little honey." The target was about 10 yards away. Mason buttoned his shirt collar and held the gun up with one hand and aimed it. His hand was visibly shaking.

"Does that feel comfortable?"

"No, it's not that heavy, but when I hold it like this, there's a strain on my arm."

"Exactly! That's why you never hold it with one hand like that. Extend both hands with your thumbs down the left side of the gun. Relax when you hold it. Interlock your fingers. Aim at the target, calm yourself, hold your breath and squeeze the trigger. Don't pull, squeeze it. Give it a try."

Mason squeezed the trigger, and immediately he could feel the gun recoil in his grip – as it pushed itself up about three inches. He could hear his shot echo across the landscape – without leaving a mark in the target sitting there untouched.

Leroy grinned. "Okay, you missed the target completely, but actually did well for your first time. Try a few more practice rounds, and then I'm going to put you in a crisis situation to see how you react. The reason the gun recoiled is because you weren't holding it properly. It's all in the grip. Hold it tighter and it won't jump on you. Try it again. Don't worry about the number of bullets. This baby holds 17 shots."

Mason continued firing and wondered if this was some sort of illegal paramilitary group that Marcie had brought him to. He was sure Leroy had had a few tours of duty in his lifetime and had probably been through some unimaginable situations. The more he focused on the target, the tenser he became, but eventually, he started to hit it. It wasn't pretty, but he thought he was making some headway. Marcie, who was firing beside him at her own target with her small gun, was having a great deal more success and way too much fun.

Mason felt that he was starting to get a comfort level with the gun when Leroy came back. He handed him a different Glock 17 and explained that this one had soft bullets with paint in them. He gave Mason a large paint-splattered shirt, a holster and a helmet and told him to strap on the gun and put on the headgear and head down the path into the woods. He also gave Marcie an old shirt and helmet and told them that it was Mason's job to protect her as they made their way through the trees.

Just as they turned to leave, Leroy said, "I have one more piece of advice before you go out there. Police officers everywhere are trained to fire a controlled pair of shots when they make the decision to shoot. The reason is that your second shot will usually be more accurate than your first because your gun won't be fully extended with your first shot. So squeeze the trigger twice when you decide to shoot. It's called the "double tap.""

As soon as they stepped onto the path, the trees enveloped them, creating a canopy overhead so the light was completely obscured. There was rustling in the woods to their left, but Mason thought it might be a small animal. The deeper into the woods they went, the darker it became. It was downright spooky, and Mason was tense because he sensed something was about to happen. They had only gone about a hundred yards when a gunman leaped out onto the path in front of them. He was yelling incoherently that he was there to shoot the bitch. He raised his gun to shoot, and Mason reacted. He reached for his own gun, but as he was fumbling to get it out of the holster, he felt a splatter on the old shirt and another on his helmet as the paint-filled bullets hit him. He was effectively dead, and so was Marcie.

When they went back to meet Leroy, Mason was met with a look of some amusement. "So what happened out there?"

Mason replied with embarrassment that he and Marcie were both dead.

"Yes, but you don't need to be embarrassed. Police officers are constantly training to shoot. It's a perishable skill that disappears in a few weeks if you don't practice. Your heart rate speeds up when you are in a crisis situation. That takes blood flow away from your hands, so your dexterity is reduced. Your extremities become numb. You get so excited you can't even do the simplest things when you are placed in a life or death situation. It's not like you see on TV. It takes months of shooting range practice for it to become a matter of automatic correct reactions. Understand?"

Mason was wondering if this was such a good idea after all. Leroy set him up in a few more crisis scenarios, and each time he came back with more paint on the shirt and helmet and each time he was dead and Marcie had been summarily executed. Each time he had taken a second or two too long to reach for his own gun. He wasn't able to reflexively reach for it and prepare to shoot. He had gotten the gun out of the holster, but once it got stuck in his shirt. He had frozen on one occasion when he was completely startled by the attacker approaching from behind. He had panicked when two attackers came at him, and he had shot wildly on another occasion when the attacker was in the shadows and coming at them from farther away. The one thing he did right was fire twice in rapid succession as he was instructed by Leroy, but both shots went wild. Unfortunately, when he did get close, Mason noticed that this time his "attacker" was wearing a state trooper uniform and had come to protect him. Had Mason's aim been straighter, he would have "killed" the imaginary law enforcement officer. This last scenario had pretty much frazzled his last nerve.

After they had been there for about two hours, Leroy said to Mason that he had done everything he could do in a short period of time. He imparted some final words of wisdom. "In a crisis situation, your eyes are focused on the source of the danger. You won't see peripherally as well. You can just as easily shoot someone dear to you by accident. A gun also makes you more susceptible to getting shot. The attacker could take your gun and use it on you, or he might have more training than you and shoot you first."

"If you're in a situation where you are chasing or being chased, you have God-given senses that will help you. And it isn't only your sense of sight. It's not your eyes that are likely to save you. If they do, well, good, but it's the other senses I'm talking about. The first is your ears. Listen for the slightest sound that might give away the location of the bad guy. Twigs snapping, footfalls, heavy breathing, the safety being released on a gun or a bullet being jacked into the chamber... These are all things to listen for. And remember; if the guy you are chasing is any good, he will be listening for exactly the same things, so be aware of the noises *you're* making as well.

"Another sense you can use is the sense of smell. I don't care who the person is, in a life and death situation everyone is nervous and sweating, so there is likely to be body odor. Try to be downwind from the guy. He might also be wearing cologne. The smell won't tell you where he is, but it will give you an idea when he is close.

"When it comes time to shoot, do it slowly and with accuracy. When you aim a gun, you have to be prepared to take another person's life. You can't think about their family, or that your actions will be creating misery for some people for the rest of their lives. You have to know in your heart that it's either him or you and think of nothing else. Make sure it's fatal when you shoot. *Shoot to kill.*"

Leroy paused and took a deep breath. "I've saved my best advice for the last. In a crisis situation, there are three things you can do that might save your life." Mason listened intently as Leroy outlined what he considered to be last-ditch, life-saving gambits, and did his best to burn them into his memory. Somehow, he had a feeling, if things went the way they had been, he was going to need them sooner rather than later.

Leroy wished them luck and shook Mason's hand. As they drove back towards Gulfport, Mason and Marcie were quiet. Mason had just been through a sobering and humbling experience, but rather than giving him a sense of confidence, it had almost done the opposite. Now he was wondering if he could deal with things at all.

Most of all, the three actions that Leroy had imparted that might save his life were still echoing in his head.

Hide.

Run.

And if you are wounded,

Play dead.

Chapter 20

"So, Mason, do you still want to buy a gun?"

They had been driving back to Gulfport in thoughtful silence for quite a few miles now. Marcie's words were not spoken with any sarcasm. It was just a question. She had been equally rattled by Mason's experience with the crisis scenarios. Her training had always been simply to shoot at targets, and she had never done this kind of "crisis training." She made a mental note to ask for the additional training at her next opportunity. She knew that with the proper instruction, Mason could handle a gun. But he hadn't had enough instruction. She also realized that in a crisis situation, things would happen fast and he might not react the way he would need to with such a short amount of training. It would be better to be properly prepared if they had time, but time was a luxury they didn't have.

In spite of everything, though, Marcie still subscribed to the theory that having a gun was preferable to not having one, and she would be keeping hers. She smiled to herself. Maybe if she aimed for the bad guy's nether regions, she could hit him in the chest. She could make do with the limited training she had been given, but she worried about Mason. Meanwhile, the time was racing by, and still no word from Sami.

"I really don't know, Marcie. That little exercise scared the hell out of me. I think we should give it some time to let things play out a bit more before I get all crazy and think about buying a gun."

"Okay, I get that, Mason. But what about Jenn? Do you think she's safe?"

"The campus police will make sure she's safe. I've been thinking about that. The guy who keeps calling doesn't seem to know where Sami is, but he desperately wants to talk to her. He wants her to call him. He wants *me* to find Sami, so this makes me think we're safe for the time being. He knows that if Jennifer hears from her mom, she'll let me know. So aside from Sami, I'm their prime concern until Sami shows up. I think the best thing for Jenn to do right now is to stay where she is."

"That makes sense. What are we going to do now?"

"Well, I think we should go back to the house the same way we left. Let me off at the gas station, and drive back to your house. If you want, you can come over later or call me. Whatever works best for you, Marcie, I really appreciate everything you're doing. Unlocking Sami's computer was brilliant. Now I need to get into the computer and see if I can find out anything useful."

"Are you kidding? I'm in this until we get Sami back and life gets back to normal. Just give me a call when you get in the house. Let me know if our watcher is still there and whether I should come over right away."

As he sat watching from the blue sedan, Jason Sage thought about what The Force had said. He had heard him say that he should follow Mason everywhere he went, and he had also heard the questions about whether or not Mason could have been in Marcie's car. He had seen Mason at the window and hadn't seen him leave the house, but it made him wonder. It had been a few hours since the black chick had left, and the house had been awfully quiet. There were no signs of activity. He had watched the windows closely for any more sign of movement. He hadn't seen any.

He didn't want to mess up this gig. He thought he could get more work from The Force or people like him through referrals if he did well on this job, so he took it upon himself to go to the front door. If nothing else, he could rattle this Seaforth character a little more to keep him in line. In the long run, he thought, it could make his job much easier. With a little encouragement and additional pressure, Seaforth would be scared out of his mind and wouldn't dare to try to leave or talk to the police. He got out of his car and started walking towards Mason's door.

Marcie dropped Mason off at the gas station, and he quickly retraced his steps back into his yard. So far, no neighbors had seen him, and no dogs were barking. That was a relief. He put his key in the lock in the back door just as he heard pounding on the front door. Mason silently unlocked the back door, entered his house, and raced to the side of the front window so he could see out to the street. Sure enough, he could see the blue sedan was sitting there as if it had never moved. But the driver's seat was empty. Mason wondered if the guy was going to sit there for 24 hours a day without a break. He went to the front door and slowly opened it, unsure of what was coming next.

The driver of the blue sedan paused in mid-knock. "So you are here, Seaforth. I wondered if you had fallen asleep or something. I know *I* sure would after doing that black chick. It seemed awfully quiet around here. I'm just checking to make sure you haven't done anything stupid."

"I'm following leads to find my wife," Mason retorted, "and you can report that back to your boss. I don't need to be interrupted every few hours or have you checking up on me constantly. My wife has disappeared, and I'm doing my best to find her. You guys are not helping by interrupting my search, which does not include involving the police by the way. If you know where she is, tell me and I will call her. Otherwise, stay out of my way!"

"Okay, just remember you're my new best friend. You and I are inseparable. If the police come to the door again, I'm going to be watching very closely. If need be, I will stay in the house here with you and the black chick. Maybe we can share her while we're all waiting. You would share, wouldn't you, Seaforth? She looks like she could handle both of us. Pretty sweet."

Mason felt nothing but revulsion as he slammed the door in the thug's face. He was disgusted that people like him actually existed. He didn't want to show this guy any weakness. However, he also thought that convincing this idiot that he was weak might work to his advantage later. Mason called Marcie and told her what had just happened. "Come over whenever you're ready," he said, "but when you get here, just ignore the guy in the car. I don't think he'll bother you."

Marcie had turned on the CD player and cranked up the volume as soon as she'd dropped Mason off at the gas station. For her own peace of mind, she'd driven around a few blocks, but hadn't made it back to her house yet, so the minute she got Mason's phone call, she wheeled her car around the corner and back onto Mason's street with the asphalt vibrating beneath its wheels. Kanye was singing something about "Through The Wire" louder than would be humanly possible without amplification. She scraped by the blue sedan with inches to spare and parked in front of Mason's house. When she turned off the ignition, quiet was restored on the street. Before going in the house, she turned around, flipped her middle finger at the watcher, and snarled. She too wanted him to know that they weren't afraid of him, even though truthfully, that was not the case.

It was empowering to know she could act this way right now without any consequences. But it was also an instinctive reaction to the situation they were in. Because this guy was somehow involved in Sami's disappearance, she hated him more than she could ever believe possible. He could even be the guy making the phone calls. She wanted to walk up to him, put her gun against his temple and find out what he knew. She even thought she could probably put a bullet in this man's head without thinking twice for what he and his sleazy companions, whoever they were, were putting Sami and her family through. But she realized that he was probably just hired muscle and most likely didn't know anything. So for now, her middle finger would be her weapon.

She rapped on the door and walked in. Mason was sitting on a chair with his head in his hands. She walked over, put her hand on his shoulder and said, "Mason, we have to be strong. We have to find Sami. Forget about that guy outside. You have to be strong for Jennifer."

"I know I do. I'm just feeling shell-shocked. I just can't believe everything that has happened. It seems like weeks have gone by since Sami left, but it's only been two days. Look at everything that's going on. I should be in the office helping my clients with their accounting issues, not running around trying to learn how to shoot a gun." Mason exhaled and took a deep breath. "Sorry, Marcie. I just needed a few minutes to think about next steps. The local news is coming on soon. There's a good chance they're going to mention Sami. I think I'd better make some phone calls, especially to my parents. I wanted to be there to tell them in person, but I sure don't want them to find out about Sami by watching TV."

"Is there anything I can do? Do you think we should put posters with Sami's picture on local convenience store bulletin boards?"

"I think this is much bigger than posters but I'm willing to try anything. Let's do it. Use my computer, so that I can start going through Sami's later."

Marcie disappeared to work on the posters, and Mason prepared to make his calls. When he picked up the phone, he heard the familiar urgent staccato beep signifying a message. His heart started to race. Sami? He quickly retrieved the message, and listened to Suarez's voice asking him to call her. She added that she wanted Mason to sign a release letting her take Sami's computer. She also said that she was trying to locate Sami's cellular phone by running a trace. Again, she asked that Mason return her call as soon as he could.

Mason looked at the phone. He knew he needed to check Sami's computer before the police did, so he decided to delay returning Suarez's phone call as long as he could. He'd tell her that he had been out talking to the neighbors about Sami's disappearance and that he never did get past the password protection. He placed calls to Sarah at Sami's office and Myra at his office. Unlike Sami's boss Willard, Sarah hadn't noticed a change in Sami's demeanor, but she was relatively new, so that was to be expected. In each case, his news was met with shock and sympathy. Then he called his parents. He wished he could have told them in person, but time was running out and they needed to hear the truth from him. They were peanut farmers near Valdosta, Georgia and had been hard-working people all their lives. Although there was much love in the home and they were good Christian people, they never displayed much emotion, a trait Mason had inherited. He wished sometimes he could display more emotion, but he hadn't thought it was in him to do – at least until now.

When his mom answered, he exchanged quick pleasantries and then said, "Mom, I have something to tell you. Can you put Dad on the extension?" As soon as he had both parents connected, Mason swallowed hard and told them what had happened. He left out any mention of the threats he'd gotten or the man parked outside watching him like a hawk. He also omitted any mention of his experience at the gun range with Leroy. The news he did share about how Sami had mysteriously vanished on the night of their anniversary was already bad enough, and he didn't want them worrying themselves sick. He had a sense that his mother's radar was on full alert and that she suspected there was more he wasn't sharing. He'd always felt that way growing up after a night on the town or when he had done something else that he knew she wouldn't approve of. She always seemed to know, somehow, and this was no different. Nevertheless, she said nothing. He could sense their stoicism over the phone.

His dad asked a few questions, and Mason brought him up to date, warning him that the nightly news broadcasts were probably going to introduce the disappearance of Sami Seaforth from their sleepy little town. His mother assured him that prayer was the most likely thing to bring Sami back. Mason wasn't religious himself and didn't attend church on a regular basis, but he considered himself to be a Christian and spiritual man. His religious leanings were among the undecided. But at this stage, he might be ready to try anything. He decided his best option right now was to end this conversation and get off the phone, so he tried to assure them as best he could and hung up with the promise that he would call them back as soon as he had more news. His mother told him to call whether he had news or not, and with that, he was able to disconnect.

The next call was to Jennifer. She had finished classes for the day, and she was eager to hear any new details, so Mason spent some time talking with her about her mom and speculating about what might have happened. He told her that no one involved in the case had found anything yet, and she asked again about coming back to Gulfport to see him. Glad as would have been to have Jennifer with him, he assured his daughter there really was no reason to skip classes at this time. "Sweetheart, I know this isn't easy for you being so far away, but it would make me feel better if you'd stay put, keep up with your school work, and let me keep updating you. Believe me, if there is anything at all that you need to come home for, I'll let you know." As he hung up and turned toward the stairs to start working on Sami's computer, there was a hesitant knock at the door. Mason knew from the knock that it wasn't their oversized, under-educated watcher this time, so he went to the door and opened it. Standing on the doorstep was the always faithful Myra, with a dish in her hand.

"I thought you wouldn't have time for dinner, Mr. Seaforth, so I brought you something I had in the freezer. It's homemade lasagne. I hope you like it."

The gesture nearly brought a tear to Mason's eye. He realized she must have gone home soon after he talked to her to get the meal. He asked her to come in, but his secretary said she knew he was busy and she just wanted to drop it off. He thanked her profusely and with a promise to help in any way possible, she left.

Mason and Marcie picked at the lasagne and Mason made a mental note to thank Myra from the bottom of his heart for her thoughtfulness. He was sure it was delicious, but his taste buds were not cooperating. There would be a bigger than usual Christmas bonus for Myra. Once they were finished, Marcie went back to working on her posters and Mason sat down in front of Sami's computer.

Now the serious work began. He had to go through all of Sami's emails, folders and files as thoroughly yet quickly as he could before Sergeant Suarez pressed him for the computer. He started with the emails. The first that caught his eye was from a "Joe Cooper." He thought this might be something. It was a normal enough name. When he opened the email, he discovered that Joe Cooper was allegedly a Barrister representing someone named Mr. Jack who had recently passed away. The fortunate recipient of the email would receive Mr. Jack's estate of one million Euros in exchange for an email response with a phone number and address. Sad really. *Delete.*

There were others with subjects like:

Giant Department Store Sale – Everything Must Go! *Delete.*

$89 Hotels! *Delete.*

The Best New Vitamins! *Delete.*

The more he looked at her emails, the more he realized this was going nowhere. He absent-mindedly deleted a few more irrelevant emails that Sami would never miss, and then opened her calendar. When he opened her schedule, there were the usual annotations about dental appointments, dinner engagements that the two of them were expected to attend, and the upcoming artisan walk in the park that they both looked forward to each year.

He needed a break to rest his eyes. He turned around to see that Marcie was surrounded by posters with Sami's face on them. He commented on her progress, and she smiled. He could tell she was exhausted. He suggested she go home and get some sleep, and she said she would after she plastered some of the posters on the local convenience store bulletin boards.

As she left with the posters under her arm, the phone started ringing again. It was a friend of Mason's and Sami's calling to say she had just seen the news. It confirmed what Mason had anticipated: the police had informed the local media about Sami's disappearance. As soon as Mason hung up, the phone rang again. And again. And again. Colleagues, clients, friends – it didn't stop ringing until finally, Mason shut off the phone. There was no doubt the news was out. Maybe this would turn up something of value.

Suddenly, he was overcome with a sense of total exhaustion. He could barely drag himself into the bedroom. As he was drifting off to another troubled sleep, Mason thought about what his mother had suggested. He wondered if a prayer could help. Well, it certainly couldn't hurt. Mason closed his eyes, and in his mind, he said a silent prayer for the safe return of his beloved wife. At this point, it seemed like it would take divine intervention to provide a break in their search.

DAY 3

Chapter 21

The Force was back in his own city, waiting at the airport. He was dressed in casual attire, and he had a sign in his hands bearing the names of two women. He didn't know them yet, but he would know them intimately very soon. He didn't even know what country they were from, and he couldn't care less. He'd been told that they would be from Southeast Asia somewhere, although other women that had been brought in were from Africa and Europe.

The women would have been encouraged to come to the U.S. by his boss's contacts in that area. His boss had many contacts around the world who could find similar women willing to relocate to what they assumed would be a better life anytime he wanted. The women would usually be in their early 20s, although occasionally much, much younger, and they would have been promised a land of opportunity, education and a job as a housekeeper. They would have been given loans to purchase their airline tickets, and their accommodations would be taken care of when they got to their new country.

The Force knew from talking to his boss that the women were always easy to convince. He had come to know the type. They would have many siblings and aging parents, or they were orphans. They might have kids of their own but no husband, and they dreamed of making enough money to support their families. They were willing and extremely vulnerable. With no opportunity for work in their own countries, they were desperate for a way to improve their lot in life. They would have a strong sense of family, and they were always overwhelmed by their good fortune when they were approached on the street with an offer that truly seemed to be like winning the lottery.

They saw it as their golden opportunity, and it didn't matter that they'd never met the stranger who made the offer. But as with many things in life, if it seemed too good to be true, there was a very good chance it was. When these young, innocent, hopeful women arrived in their new country, they would find that the promised jobs had suddenly evaporated.

Picking up these women at the airport was one of the regular duties on The Force's job description, along with straightening out people who made the mistake of owing his boss money, and permanently dispatching other people as he had done in Florida and Minneapolis. There had been many previous trips to the airport like this one. It was The Force's job to make the new arrivals realize very quickly that they were going to have to pay back the money they had been loaned and they had better think of a way of doing it pretty quickly. Interest rates would be astronomical, so it was obviously in their best interests to do something lucrative. They would be in shock and have no clue what they could do to get out of this mess. Once the women realized just how much trouble they were in, The Force would offer a simple solution. He would propose the idea of selling their bodies as an easy way to make money. He would tell them that he would introduce them to the things that Western men liked in bed, and he would practice with them a few times to make sure they got it. It was one of the perks of his job – and probably his favorite. When the women were ready, they would be presented to his boss to enjoy until they were farmed out to their more permanent line of work.

There were a variety of tactics The Force used to keep them in line. He might introduce them to drugs to ensure their dependence on him. They would learn that he was their friend, their savior; the only person they knew in their new country that would help them. At times, he might have to rely on some strong-arming to bring them in line, but then he would pretend to soften so they continued to believe that he was on their side. They would be threatened with far worse if they tried to deviate from what they were told. He made sure that they heard the rumors of other girls in their situation who had "mysteriously disappeared," and this scared them more than anything. Some of the rumors were even true.

After choosing new and exotic names for them, Johnson would then place them out on the streets or with an escort service run by his boss, or perhaps in an illicit massage parlor. He would determine throughout the initiation process where they would be best suited.

It didn't take long for the girls to realize that the land of milk and honey was really a nightmare, although some would think it wasn't all that much worse than the situation they had left behind. But they also realized soon enough when they were paid only a fraction of the money they made, that their usefulness in their new profession would run out long before their loans were paid off.

While The Force was waiting for the flight to arrive, he took a phone call from Jason Sage, who gave him a report on the Seaforth house. He was surprised to hear that Sami hadn't shown up yet. He thought she would be back by now. What was going on down there, anyway? Where had she gone? He also realized that he would have to find someone else to relieve the watcher occasionally. No one could watch a house 24 hours a day without a break. Just as he hung up, he saw two nervous young Asian women heading his way, full of excitement to be on this new adventure and giggling at the sight of their names on the sign. These two were exceptionally attractive. He was going to enjoy introducing them to their *real* new job.

Mason got up early, keenly aware this was the third morning he had awakened with no Sami beside him. He went downstairs, brewed more coffee and choked down a couple of pieces of toast with peanut butter. Food was taking a back seat to everything else during this time of crisis, and he realized he was barely hungry. He silently thanked Myra again for her thoughtful contribution of homemade lasagne the night before. There were leftovers, which he was sure would disappear later in the day. He looked outside to see the car and watcher parked down the street on the curb.

He had touched base with Jennifer to let her know that there had been no developments. They had chatted for a few minutes, just reassuring each other that everything would be all right. Then Mason had gone over to Sami's computer where he now sat, trying to figure out what he should do first. He didn't know what he might be looking for, and he hadn't a clue where to start. No inspirations had come to him during the night for his bedside notepad, and he wasn't sure whether that was good or bad.

He was pretty sure there was nothing in Sami's emails or calendar, so the next step would be her files. Sami always took copious notes, so he wasn't surprised to see files with labels like "Recipes," "Exercise," "Life Events" and "Instructions." The latter folder included instructions for lighting the barbecue and the fireplace, among other things. The "Recipes" folder was full of various subfolders named for ethnic recipes and exotic cuisines from around the world. The folder marked "Exercise" contained physical, nutritional and lifestyle tips, along with specific conditioning exercises for flexibility and muscle strength. Mason swiftly swept through other folders in her Word files and came up with nothing unusual.

And then he opened her "Life Events" folder.

As with her other files, Sami had divided her information into a series of subfolders. There were folders for her school years, her move to Florida, her career path, her friends, and many more that summarized the life of Sami Seaforth. Mason was surprised at the extent of Sami's documentation.

He plunged on. There was one folder that really caught his eye just by its title. It was entitled "Evidence." His nerve endings vibrated, alerting him to the fact that this could be it. Mason felt a chill rolling down his spine as he clicked on the folder to open it. It too contained numerous headings and was written like a journal. He noticed it was comprised of multiple neatly-typed pages sectioned off by various subtitles. Scrolling through, he noticed names that were unfamiliar to him, but one name jumped out at him beyond all the rest: James Briscoe. He realized that he had found what he was looking for and what The Force was after: Sami's notes.

He decided to print off the document and read it in hard copy. Call him old-fashioned, but he felt he absorbed things better with paper in his hands than he could by reading something on the computer. He grabbed each page from the printer as it slowly churned out the document. Once the printing was complete, Mason poured himself another coffee and settled down to read. Just as he did so, he remembered the phone call from Suarez, indicating she wanted to pick up the computer. He had his phone turned off, but he was concerned she might decide to pay him a visit unannounced to get Sami's computer. It probably made sense to make extra copies of the document. Maybe he should give one to Marcie for safe keeping.

Mason plugged a tiny flash drive into the USB port and copied the contents of Sami's "Evidence" folder on it. Then he did it again with another flash drive. He would give one flash drive to Marcie and keep one for himself in a safe place. If Sergeant Suarez showed up, he knew he couldn't withhold the computer. That would just make her suspicious of his motives. He wanted to cooperate with the police so they could help him find his wife; but the thugs had said "no cops." He decided he would delete the information before giving the computer to Suarez. Even though the police could retrieve it, it would buy him more time. Actually, it might not be such a bad idea if Suarez did take the computer. It would also serve to keep it out of the hands of whomever it was that was after Sami.

He started to read again. The first part was familiar to him. Sami was born Samantha Jane Roberts in Minneapolis. Her parents were identified in the document, and she talked of her love for them. It seemed like an idyllic family until it all started to unravel. First came the traffic accident that had torn the family apart. Mason already knew, but the document confirmed that her mother had survived with "serious but non-life threatening injuries." And then without warning, Mason came to a part that was new to him – something his wife had never mentioned and he had never known about. Alarmingly, this section was under the heading "Worst Days of My Life."

Sami's notes documented disturbing things she had overheard or her mother had talked directly to her about. The relationship with her stepfather appeared to have started out well enough, but as time passed, Sami's mother was forced to realize she had married the wrong man. Her mother had confided in Sami, accusing Marshall of extortion, setting up prostitution rings and running drugs. These illegal activities served to make him very, very wealthy with cash which he had no problem squandering at the gaming tables.

There followed a chilling account of long-term physical abuse. The notes outlined how Marshall's losses at the tables would often result in violent outbursts towards Sami's mother. Often another person would be in the house when these outbursts occurred, and he would stand around and do nothing to intervene. Sami identified that person as Greg Johnson. In brackets beside his name, she had typed "The Force."

Mason was feeling physically ill at what he was reading. Waves of nausea poured over him. He had to stop reading before he became totally overwhelmed. He felt anger, disgust, revulsion, fury, but most of all, he felt deep love for his wife. He so desperately wanted to hold her right now. All this evil that she had known growing up, she and her mother, at the hand of a man named Aaron Marshall. And his accomplice, the guy called "The Force." He wondered if Sami had been writing all this while she was supposedly playing games on the computer. But why? Was there a reason after so many years that she would now be documenting all of this? Maybe it was cathartic for her. Or was it something else? Apparently, something had caused Marshall and his henchman to resurface, and now they were threatening Sami with physical harm.

He had the urge to skim the rest of the document first to get a sense of what else was in it quickly and then go back and read every detail, but he prevented himself from doing so. He wanted to absorb every word, to feel what his wife had gone through in her life. He wanted to thoroughly understand every nuance. The sinking feeling in the pit of his stomach told him that there was much, much more to this story, and he had the sense of watching a train wreck, piling up car after car, one on top of the other, as the engine flew off a bend in the tracks. He just couldn't avert his eyes.

As repugnant as it was, he read on. The abuse had gone on for as long as her mother was alive. Her mother had lived longer than Mason had been led to believe. Sami was older than he had realized when her mother died.

There was a scan of the obituary in the document which said the cause of death was natural causes. Sami had highlighted the words. In her notes, Sami pointed the finger directly at her stepfather for having caused her mother's death. Sami wrote in the document that she believed she had overheard Marshall and Johnson discussing killing her mother with selenium, but she had never gone to the authorities because she lived in terror of Marshall. At the time of her mother's death, Sami was in her senior year in high school. Mason could sense relief in Sami's writing, as it was shortly after her mother's death that she was able to use some money from the estate and move to Florida. It seemed that Marshall was happy to be rid of her.

The name of her school was identified, and there was mention of some of her school friends. The only one with a phone number beside it was Janet Winters. Sami and Janet were clearly very close, as Sami described how she would spend long nights talking to her friend about the situation at home. Janet apparently had her own problems at school. She was a victim of bullying, and from what Sami wrote, Mason got the impression that his wife had stood up for Janet against her tormentors on more than a few occasions. Sami and Janet had obviously spent a lot of time together consoling each other. In spite of Sami's protests and advice against it, Janet had had an intimate relationship with Greg Johnson.

The next sections were a series of dates in chronological order, each with a specific act that had occurred on that date, and most of them involved either Aaron Marshall or Greg Johnson. There were dates related to the abuse of Sami and her mother. There were five dates under the heading, "Provided by Janet Winters," with a note indicating that Greg Johnson had been out of town. Sami had also typed a suggestion that the dates Johnson had been out of town could possibly be linked to crimes committed in other cities on those dates.

Mason was fully immersed in what he was reading, trying to reconcile what he had always thought to be true about Sami's background with what he was seeing now, and he barely heard the tap at the front door. Unaware of what had transpired since she had last seen Mason, Marcie breezed in, obviously in high spirits and ready to start working on whatever game plan he might have for her. The situation may have been grim, but Marcie had dressed as if she expected her outfit to keep both their energy levels up. She was wearing a bright multi-colored geometric halter top with matching capris and a pair of flip flops with a similar bright multi-colored strap across her instep. On most women, the outfit would have looked gaudy, but Marcie carried it off with her usual sense of style and attitude. Mason was so involved in the shocking details of Sami's computer folder that he obviously hadn't heard Marcie and her rap group arriving in the car. When she told him that she was late because she'd been delivering more posters to area convenience stores, Mason was shocked to learn that it was already 11 o'clock in the morning.

"What have you been up to, Mason?"

Mason took a deep breath. "This is really hard," he said. "I thought I knew everything about my wife, but it looks like I was wrong." Mason told her about the document he was reading, and immediately Marcie asked to read it. He printed a second copy of all the pages, and handed it to her. She sat down and began to dig in. "Don't skip anything," Mason cautioned her. "It's very disturbing, and I think you're going to be as surprised as I am, unless Sami has already hinted at any of this stuff to you."

Mason watched as Marcie started to read. He wanted to finish reading his own pages, but he also wanted to observe Marcie's reaction. She was only a few pages in when she looked up, her mouth forming an 'O' and her eyes wide and brimming with tears. "I can't believe this is Sami we're reading about. It's horrible to think that she went through all this. And kept it quiet all these years. Why, Mason? Why? How could she hide this from us?"

"I think I might know the answer to that question Marcie, but let's finish reading and then discuss it. It certainly doesn't get any prettier as you read, but let's get the full picture. We will need to read it more than once. You know Sami as well as I do, and you know she wouldn't hide anything from us unless she felt she had no choice. She must have been strongly compelled to cover all this up. I wish she had confided in me, but obviously there was something holding her back other than just bad memories she wanted to put behind her.

We need to find out why, and the answer could very well be here."

Silence descended upon them as they continued reading. It was clear that Greg Johnson, AKA The Force, had worked for Sami's stepfather. It was quite possible that he still was. There were more dates. There was the date that Marshall had moved from Minneapolis with Sami's note that it was "approximate." It appeared that the city was getting too hot for him so he left. But there was no indication where he had gone. Mason paused for a minute, and his unfocused gaze drifted away from the document. The thought occurred to him that Sami had not created this entire document recently. It must be something she had been working on for a long time. He looked back at the "Documents" folder and confirmed the trail of dates when the document had been saved. This was something Sami had been working on for years. And then it hit him: *The last date it had been opened was just before she disappeared.*

He went back again to the document. There was a date about three months ago with the comment, "Met James Briscoe." Mason's blood ran cold. His wife had met with Briscoe, the man whose murder had precipitated Baker and Finch gathering his running shoes. There was a paragraph under this date:

"James Briscoe came into the bank to negotiate a loan on behalf of a client for a large sum of taxes owed on a property in the Tampa Bay area. His client owed $2.5 million to the IRS for back taxes, interest and penalty fees. At first, Mr. Briscoe was reluctant to disclose his client's name. I was shown a file that supported the loan claim, but the name of Briscoe's client had been obscured. The money owing was the result of a high profile tax case which Briscoe (a tax lawyer) lost. It was related to the timing of the sale of the property.

I was only allowed a quick look at the document, but I'm pretty sure Briscoe had accidentally left some documents I shouldn't have seen in the file. It appeared to me from what I saw that the courts had ruled that the date of the sale had been falsified on Briscoe's client's tax return. I knew that not only would this client owe the entire amount of back taxes, penalties and interest, but he would most likely be charged with falsifying IRS documents as well. I recognized the property as being in a commercial mall in a trendy area of Tampa Bay that had been hit by the recession. I advised Briscoe that I could not proceed

*any further without more details on his client. I also told him that I would need to know his
client's current financial situation. Briscoe seemed very nervous, but when he finally agreed
to tell me the name of his client, it turned out that it was Aaron Marshall."*

Although the words didn't convey it, Mason thought his wife must have
been horrified to see her stepfather's name resurface after all these years. He
continued reading, glued to the words on the pages. Sami went on to write
that she asked Briscoe for more information using the need for collateral
from his client as an excuse. Briscoe said that he would put up the collateral
himself on his client's behalf, and that he shouldn't have mentioned his client
at all. Sami wrote that she tried to get more information about the client's
court case, but Briscoe seemed to sense that her questions were about more
than just the loan. She noted that he became red-faced and even more nervous and agitated, and practically ran from the bank.

In her documentation, Sami wrote that this was the first time she had
heard anything about Aaron Marshall in more than 20 years. The section
ended with a notation that she never saw Briscoe again in the bank. Accom-
panying this was a scan of a press clipping detailing the brutal murder of Mr.
and Mrs. James Briscoe by an unknown killer in their Florida condominium.
The report said that the killer was still on the loose and no motive had been
found. Sami had added a note speculating that Briscoe and his wife were
probably killed by either Marshall or Johnson.

Mason stopped a minute to think. Briscoe had apparently lost the case
which resulted in Marshall owing a huge sum of money for unpaid taxes,
which was made worse by the fact they had tried to falsify the records. Mason
speculated that Marshall had become enraged at his lawyer's inability to protect him and ordered a hit on Briscoe. Sami had put two and two together
and realized that her former stepfather was still alive and as evil as ever, and
Mason couldn't help but feel that the wheels of her disappearance had been
put in motion by Briscoe's chance visit to Sami's bank.

Mason continued reading. The next section included more dates under
the heading of "Threats." The dates were since James Briscoe's murder, and
they seemed to be hastily typed. The first referred to threatening calls from

Johnson. The wording beside the date contained a typo, which was highly unusual for Sami, and said, "Johnson calld this morning…demanded to meet." There were many more calls documented, each one a little more threatening than the last and each apparently typed quickly with minimal attempts at grammatical correctness. The final few referred to specific threats to Mason and Jennifer if Sami didn't contact him by the weekend. Mason paused. Those calls would explain why Sami's voice mailbox was full.

As Mason looked at the last section, he saw pictures staring back at him. There was a photo of Aaron Marshall and there were a few of Greg (The Force) Johnson. He stared at the picture of The Force, feeling certain that this was the gravelly voice on the other end of his phone, the voice who had been threatening him if he didn't tell him where Sami was. The picture of Aaron Marshall was grainy and looked like it had been taken years ago, although Mason was unsure if it was just the quality of the scan. There was one typed sheet remaining that Mason had not yet read, and he turned the page so he could see it. It was addressed to him, and it read in bold type:

My dearest Mason, I know you will find this document and read it soon after I leave. Since you have obviously figured out my password now, I hope it helps to explain some things for you. I have to deal with this before our lives can ever be normal. Please DO NOT involve the police or try to intervene. As you may already have figured out, these are very dangerous men, but unless I talk to my stepfather, I am afraid they will never leave us alone. I am hoping this document will help me do that. If I don't do something now, we will always be in fear for our lives. I love you and Jennifer very much. I am so ashamed that I didn't tell you my story. I need time to sort things out. Please don't try to find me. I really need time alone. Please trust me and believe in me. Love, Sami. XXOO

Chapter 22

Mason sat back. Dumbfounded. He thought about what he had just read. He glanced over at Marcie, who was still reading. Her lips were moving slightly, and her eyes widened more and more with each word. Finally, he watched her read the last page, and as she looked up, he could see her eyes were red.

She murmured. "Oh Mason, this is awful. What do you think it all means?"

"I have so many thoughts running through my head right now, Marcie, I honestly don't know. At least we know Sami is out there trying to be a heroine. Let's try to be logical about this. First, Sami mentions that she thought I would be reading this document. So, either she thought I knew the password or assumed that I would figure it out. She probably thought I would enlist your help, so you could help me figure everything out." He said this with a wry chuckle.

"Well, Mason, we know how much she loves that car, so she may have thought we would figure it out. Anyway, we did, and you found the document she intended you to find. It's just all so crazy. Did you know any of this?"

"I knew about the car accident and that her mother had survived. Any time I brought up the subject, though, it seemed like Sami always wanted to talk about something else. I never knew she had been treated the way she was – that there was so much violence and sadness in her past. I did know her mother had remarried, but I never dreamed it was so horrible for her. Sami has always been very loving and I always felt so confident in her love for Jennifer and me. I don't understand why she hid this from us. It feels like a betrayal in some ways. It's like she's been hiding things from me for years. I'm not even sure I know who she is anymore. But I know I need to find her and get to the bottom of this."

"I understand how you feel, Mason, but you can look at it another way. These are very dangerous dudes Sami's talking about. There are references to murder, drugs, young girls, prostitution. My take on it is that she was trying to protect her family the best way she knew how. She loves you two so much that she is willing to do anything to protect you. If she had told you anything, and especially just before she left, you would have wanted to go with her. And if she'd told Jennifer, she would have wanted to get involved.

"Don't you see, Mason? Sami is trying to protect everyone by possibly putting her own life in danger. I think that if these two assholes never resurfaced in her life, this document would never have seen the light of day. But they did resurface because Briscoe happened to walk into *her* bank and shot his mouth off. She decided that she had to do something."

She continued, "But I'm not convinced it's the smoking gun, Mason. There are all kinds of inferences and circumstantial evidence. There are the dates that place the enforcer somewhere away from home which might link him to various crimes. There is the link between Marshall and Briscoe, and Briscoe happened to end up dead. There is the abuse in the early years and the speculation that Sami's mom's death *may* have been arranged by Marshall. But what does any of that prove, Mason?"

Mason sat for a few minutes, just thumbing through the document. Finally, he said quietly, "I'm not sure it actually *proves* anything, Marcie, but it does point fingers enough that the police would have to focus their attention on Marshall, and I'm sure that's not something he would welcome. Sami has done one of two things. Either she has gone into hiding, and that's not like her, or she wants to confront Marshall with the information she has gathered in some misguided attempt to get him to stop threatening us. He *is* her stepfather, so she probably thinks she can reason with him. But I don't know if she understands that she's walking into the lion's den."

As he looked at Marcie and thought about their conversation, he realized that in Sami's mind when she and Mason married, she had started fresh and everything before was history to be forgotten. She had protected herself by writing this document in case her past ever came back. Then she added a computer scan of Janet's handwritten notes to it. She had built a new life that she wanted to preserve. And the way she was going to preserve it was to confront Marshall with the information she had to protect her family. That's what all this is about. He knew that he had to find her, to make sure she was all right, and try to stop her from going to Marshall by herself. Once this was over, they would have a long talk to clear the air, and then he would never let her out of his sight again.

He couldn't just sit and wait anymore. He simply had to find her. He couldn't leave her out there by herself, trying to outsmart these guys. She had said not to involve the police, reiterating what the thugs had said, so it was pretty clear that he shouldn't consider involving them right now – at least directly. He decided he was going to let Sergeant Suarez have the computer, and he knew the police would find what he had found soon enough even if he deleted everything. He picked up the document again and flipped through the pages one more time, but this time with a more specific purpose. He found the phone number for Janet Winters. That was the next step. He would call Janet. He told Marcie what he was about to do, but before doing so, he did a quick search online to determine where the area code was. The search told him it was in Minneapolis. Apparently, Janet Winters had not moved away from the place where she and Sami had grown up.

He dialed the number and as he listened to the phone ringing, his hands were shaking. He watched Marcie flipping through the document again. He was so grateful for her help and support. He didn't know if he would be able to function without her. She had pointed out to him once when she was at their house helping him assemble a barbecue that she was yin and he was yang and that the whole was greater than each individual part. They had both laughed at the conversation and Mason thought it was ridiculous at the time, but he was realizing now that unbeknownst to both of them, what she had said was so true. They were polar opposites, but they were holding each other together at this very difficult time.

Mason didn't want to leave a message, so he was just about to hang up when the phone was picked up at the other end and a gruff male voice said, "Hello."

"May I speak to Janet Winters, please?"

"Who's calling?"

"It's Mason Seaforth. Janet Winters is a friend of my wife's."

"I'm sorry, did you say Seaforth?"

Mason confirmed that he had and was shocked when the person talking on the other end identified himself as a Detective Lawrence with the Minneapolis Police Department.

"Why are you calling, Mr. Seaforth?"

Mason wanted to be careful, so he replied to the question by telling the detective that he could easily call back at a more opportune time. He didn't realize that he was about to be in for yet another shock. The detective responded to his evasiveness by saying, "There is no point in calling back, Mr. Seaforth. Janet Winters is dead."

Mason couldn't believe his ears. He felt he was spiralling into some kind of vortex. Everyone connected in any way to his wife seemed to be dying.

"Are you there, Mr. Seaforth?"

Mason replied in barely audible voice, "Yes, I'm here."

"I strongly suggest you contact Detective Albert Baker in Tampa and tell him everything you know about your wife's connection to Janet Winters. Do you hear what I'm saying, Mr. Seaforth?"

"Yes, yes I will. Thank you very much, Detective."

Mason hung up the phone numbly, and Marcie could tell by Mason's ghostly appearance that once again things had not gone as expected. This was becoming way too commonplace. As he was explaining the brief but shocking conversation, the phone rang again. It was Sergeant Suarez.

"Ah, Mr. Seaforth," Mason heard her say. "I've been trying to reach you, but your phone didn't ring. It just went straight to voice mail. I was just about to come over to your place to see if everything is okay."

"Yes, after the news announcement last night about Sami, my phone didn't stop ringing so I finally turned it off. I just now turned it back on. So I understand you want to pick up Sami's computer." Mason decided to hide the fact they had found relevant information or had even gotten into Sami's computer at all. "I'm not sure how it's going to help you. We haven't been able to figure out the password."

"Yes, I would like to stop by and get the computer," Suarez replied. "Don't worry, we'll get in it." She got straight to the point. "Any idea where your wife might have gone, Mr. Seaforth? Is there any chance she flew somewhere?"

Mason immediately thought of Minneapolis. Then he thought of Sami's now dead friend, and the thought sickened him. "I have no idea, Sergeant. Nor do I have any idea why she would leave town without telling me. It doesn't make any sense."

Suarez decided to be blunt to see if she could get a reaction. "Have you thought about anyone she might have run off with? With the drugs in your wine and the new outfit she apparently bought, it's something that has to be considered, whether you want to think about it or not."

Mason caught his breath. So the drugs had been confirmed. At least his wife would be safe if it were that simple. "No, Sergeant. That is the furthest thing from my mind." Then he thought that a little misdirection couldn't hurt, so he added, "But I would be happy to know if you find something out along those lines."

"Okay, no problem. I'll be over later today for you to sign a release form, and I'll pick up her computer then. Our technicians are well trained to uncover things you might not expect. I'm very sorry, Mr. Seaforth. This must be very difficult for you."

Mason assured her it was and quickly got off the phone. He didn't want to spend any more time talking to the officer than he had to. He sensed that she knew somehow that he was withholding information. But what was that she'd said? About Sami flying somewhere? Something clicked in his brain.

He couldn't quite grasp it. He went back to Sami's computer and opened her email again. He felt there was something there that he'd overlooked the first time. He checked the email file, but nothing jumped out at him. Still, something had definitely clicked when Suarez mentioned flying. What was it? Was it something he had absent-mindedly trashed?

He opened the "Deleted" folder and reviewed the emails he had dumped in it. Wait! There it was -- the one with the Subject line blaring, "$89 Hotels!" This one was from a discount travel site. He remembered when he and Sami had booked a flight to Aruba for a vacation through the same site that that company had followed up with offers of hotels and car rentals at their destination. Mason read through the email carefully, and then he went through it again one more time, even more slowly. It was definitely a follow-up to one that had been sent to Sami previously. But where was that one? He looked in her folder again, but there were no other emails from the same company, so she had probably deleted it. But in her haste to leave, she had forgotten about the traditional follow-up email. The previous one had obviously been an itinerary for a flight because this one was offering great deals on hotels and cars at her destination. *And her destination was clearly visible.* The email listed a variety of hotels and car rental options at various price points starting with the day she disappeared.

Now he knew. He knew where Sami had gone.

On this roller coaster ride of emotions that Mason was riding, he was clearly on the up slope again. He looked at Marcie who was taking notes as she read Sami's document. He got up and wandered around the room. He went downstairs to the kitchen to calm his nerves. On the way, he looked outside to verify that the blue car was still there. Finally, he went back upstairs. Marcie looked up as he entered the office.

"Mason, are you okay?'

"Yes, Marcie, I am. I am *very* okay."

"What does that mean, Mason?"

"Marcie, I know where Sami has gone."

She inhaled sharply. "Well, tell me! Where is she?"

~ 153 ~

His entire body was vibrating from the discovery he had just made. "Sami is in Ottawa, Canada."

Chapter 23

Marcie was the perfect image of the proverbial deer firmly stuck in headlights – staring wide-eyed at Mason while she processed what she had just heard.

"Canada? Why Canada?"

"Well, I'm sure she saw something in Briscoe's folder indicating that's where Marshall is. Now she's gone to confront her stepfather. I think she's trying to protect our family by showing Marshall all the circumstantial evidence she's gathered, and she'll probably threaten to go the police. I think she's got enough there that the police would open an investigation. She's taking an awful risk, though. I guess she thinks her protection is the information she left behind on her computer for either us or the police -- and she is probably counting on Janet to back up her story. She probably doesn't know Janet is dead."

"So what should we do? Just sit here and wait until she comes back? Call the police and tell them everything we have found out?"

"If we notify the police, Marcie, it could endanger Sami. But I'm not going to just sit here and wait either. I can't do that. Sami left a trail for us to read for a reason. She would have destroyed it otherwise. I don't think she intended for me to follow because she was clear about not interfering. But another awful thought just occurred to me. She's probably thinking that even if something happened to her, we would be protected by the information she left behind. She's counting on the police doing something with it. But she underestimated one thing. I'm not going to sit here. I'm going to Canada to help her."

Marcie said, emphatically, "There's one thing wrong with what you just said, Mason. You keep saying 'I.' There are *two* of us in this thing. I'm going with you. I've been with you all the way along, so don't think I'm going to sit here waiting, or else I'm going to have to go back to thinking you're the jerk I first thought you were. I was just starting to like you and think that maybe Sami had made the right decision after all when she married you. Don't do this to me. You're not going to leave me out of this, Mason."

"Okay, let's think about this for a minute. Maybe you should stay here in case Jennifer decides to come home. And now I think Jennifer really should come home, at least for the weekend."

"Why? That doesn't make any sense. With that guy outside, it would make more sense if she went to your parents' place. You don't want her in this house alone being watched by that man. Your parents aren't being watched right now as far as we know, so she would probably be safer there. Besides that, you said your Dad was an Army veteran who fought in Vietnam. Even at his age, I'm sure he could handle anything these guys could throw his way."

Mason realized that Marcie was right and besides, it would be reassuring to have her along. He decided he would call Jennifer and tell her to go to his parents' place. He would let her know that he and Marcie were going away to help her mom. He would tell her to be on her guard – to make sure she wasn't being followed - but not to go into the story in any depth. There was no point in unduly alarming her any more than she already was.

"Okay, Marcie. I agree with you. Now, what do we know about Ottawa or even Canada, for that matter?"

"I know the Raptors play basketball in Toronto, because my ex always talked about what a great time he had when the team was there. I always naively thought 'having a good time' meant that the town had good restaurants – not that he was having a good time with a variety of skanks in his hotel room. Montreal is the other big city I know about, and it's mostly French. I also know that every severe weather pattern that comes into the U.S. seems to come from Canada. I hear CNN talking about 'Alberta clippers' and 'polar vortexes' whenever snow storms come into the northern states. I know it's cold in Canada. The people who don't speak French say 'eh' a lot. The people I've met here from Canada always seem to be really pleasant. Maybe too pleasant. They apologize for everything. Anyway, that's about it. I have no idea where Ottawa is relative to other cities in Canada, nor what's there. It must be a decent size for Marshall to move there, if that's where he moved."

Mason couldn't add much. "I know that Ottawa has a professional hockey team called the Senators. I've seen them play hockey against the Lightning in Tampa, so the city must be big enough to support a professional team. Do some research on the city on the internet while I start looking for flights. I want to leave as soon as we can."

Marcie went straight to Mason's computer to begin researching Canada and Ottawa, while Mason used Sami's computer to look for flights. It didn't take long for Marcie to comment. "It looks like Ottawa has about a million people. It's the nation's capital, so I guess it's a government town like Washington. Why would Marshall go there?" Almost immediately, she answered her own question with, "Ah, it looks like it's between Montreal and Toronto, so maybe that's why. He could hide in Ottawa and run his criminal activities in the larger centers. Maybe that's it! That would make sense. But going to Ottawa is really a long shot, Mason. How are we ever going to find Sami in a city of a million people?"

"We're going to look for Marshall. I think that's what Sami has been doing. If we find him, I don't think Sami will be too far away. Sami said in her document that Marshall liked to gamble. Are there any casinos in Ottawa?"

Marcie's fingers clicked on the keyboard. She found an answer quickly. "It looks like there are two. One is called the OLG Slots at the Rideau Carleton Raceway but it only has slot machines by the looks of it. They have over a thousand slots and some electronic games. They also have horse racing. OLG stands for...let me see, oh yes, Ontario Lottery and Gaming Commission. Not sure what happened to the 'C' for Commission." Now on a roll, Marcie was quiet just long enough to find what she was looking for. "Aha," she exclaimed with a note of victory in her voice. "Apparently there's some controversy brewing that the city is planning to expand there and the owner of the hockey team wants the casino wherever his arena is. Do you think that might be what Marshall is involved with?" She thought for a moment. "Mason, didn't Sami say that James Briscoe was killed over a property deal and some taxes owing. Maybe it had something to do with that."

Without waiting for an answer, Marcie continued reading. "The other casino is called Lac-Leamy in Gatineau, which seems to be very close to Ottawa. It has gaming tables. That would be a better place for a major gambler like Marshall."

Mason absent-mindedly nodded and continued with what he was doing.

"Hello, Earth to Mason. Is anyone out there?"

Mason's response was an unintelligible mumble as he was lost in performing his own search for flights out of Tampa and Orlando.

"And look, it says here the casino is open 24 hours a day, 7 days a week -- and they have poker and other gaming tables. They have some special VIP status for high rollers, too. I'll bet you anything that's where the scumbag hangs out."

She could tell that Mason was involved in what he was doing and only partially paying attention, so she decided to take down the name and address of the casino and discuss it with him on the plane. After making her notes, she continued her research; but now her mind had switched gears to a far more deadly concern. Since they were going to search for Sami who was herself searching for two very dangerous men, Marcie's thought turned to her gun. She had a troubling suspicion in the back of her mind, something she needed to check out. *What were the gun laws up in Canada?*

She knew she would want her own gun with her on this coming trip, but after several well-publicized public killings in the news recently, she had read that every country had a different way of dealing with private gun ownership. She wasn't sure she would be allowed to bring an unloaded weapon in her suitcase through Canadian customs. It sure wouldn't help things if she got hauled away by the Royal Mounties or whoever it was that patrolled the border up North.

Her search brought her to a site belonging to a government organization called the Canada Border Services Agency, or CBSA. They seemed to be the ones who set the rules on such matters. She clicked on a link entitled "Visitors to Canada and Other Temporary Residents." That brought her to a Table of Contents under which she found "Restrictions/Firearms and weapons." She eventually got to a page that referred to restricted weapons, including things like martial arts nunchaku sticks, which was accompanied by a picture of two sticks held together by a chain, as well as wristbands and finger rings with spikes on them. She didn't have time for this. Like every other government document she had attempted to read, it would take hours to find what she was looking for. She decided to Google the question instead: "Who may carry handguns in Canada?" And sure enough, there was the answer, plain and simple: *Either people who require them because of their occupation, or those requiring them for the "protection of life,"* and that category required written authorization. Uh oh! She was not going to be able to get her gun across the border, and neither would Mason if he bought one.

Marcie thought that it would probably be best if she didn't bring this small detail up with Mason. She asked innocently, "Mason, what if we flew into Toronto and drove to Ottawa from there? I don't think it's very far. On the map, it looks like it's about an inch away, so it must be close. We might be able to cover our tracks a lot better so the police can't follow us."

"You read my mind, Marcie." Mason seemed invigorated by all this as if he had found new life. "I found a flight on United Airways leaving for Toronto at 6:45 in the morning. I'm going to make reservations on that one if they have room. I think flying to Toronto would buy us more time. If the police somehow discover our whereabouts, it would throw them off the scent for a while. As much as I would like to, we still can't involve them directly. I like the idea of flying to Toronto first. Let's see how far it is to drive from Toronto to Ottawa."

A quick check on MapQuest revealed that it would take about five hours to travel the route. He realized they would have to get through Customs at the airport in Toronto before they continued on their way. If all went well, they should be in Ottawa soon after lunch, and their search could begin. It was time to get moving. If his hunch was wrong and Sami *wasn't* in Canada, then he would have wasted their time and the price of two plane fares. But somehow he didn't think he was wrong. Mason booked the tickets.

As he waited for the boarding passes to print, he glanced out the window. To his surprise, he saw *two* people in the blue sedan. He turned to Marcie. "Uh oh. We're going to have to travel light, Marcie. That guy in the car is still there, but now it looks like he's got a friend with him. We're going to have to go out the back again and over the fence, so we won't be able to carry much. Depending on how long we stay in Ottawa, we can buy more clothes there. But I came up with an idea while I was booking the flights -- tell me what you think.

"Since there are now two people watching us, most likely it's so they can take turns while one sleeps or eats. The guy I met at the door seems to think you and I are having some fun here while Sami is away, so let's encourage that idea. I'd like you to go home and put on your sexiest outfit. Put some clothes in an overnight bag and make sure they see you when you come back. Meanwhile, I'll arrange for a taxi to pick us up at the gas station. We'll leave the house around midnight to take advantage of the darkness and maybe their sleepiness. If they think we're fooling around together, they'll assume we're in bed and that will explain why they don't see much movement in the house."

Marcie looked over at him and grinned broadly. "Well, well, well, you *have* been thinking, Mason! I like the plan. Nothing like a little deceit to throw them off guard. I know just which outfit to wear. Their dirty little minds will immediately assume we will be shacking up here alone. But won't they think it means you have an idea of when Sami is coming home if we do that? "

"Yes, I guess that's possible. If they come to the door while I'm still here, I'll tell them I heard from her and she was very upset. I can say I don't know for sure when she's coming back, but she told me she needed some time away from me to think about things on her own."

Marcie agreed and left the house to put her part of the plan into motion.

Mason went to the drawer where Sami kept their passports. His was lying there, but as he had halfway expected, hers was gone. To him, it was confirmation that Sami had left the country.

Mason dialed his daughter and was glad that Jennifer answered immediately.

"Hi, Dad, I'm so glad to hear from you! Is there any news?"

"Unfortunately, no, I haven't heard anything from your mom, sweetheart, but we did find out that she may have gone to Canada. It looks like she had some business there that she wanted to handle on her own, but Marcie and I have decided to go help her so she can finish up and come home sooner. Now, Jennifer, there's something I want you to listen to very carefully." Mason went on to explain that the situation was a little more risky than he had originally thought, and that Sami appeared to be dealing with some less-than-honest men, so he wanted her to go to his parents' place for the weekend since he wouldn't be at the house.

"Okay, I can do that, but Dad, the campus police talked to me. They think it was just some creep with no place to go. They said they're going to watch out for him, and I should be fine. Are you sure I really need to go?"

"Yes, it would make me feel better if you would," said Mason, not wanting his daughter to know that the man who shoved the camera in her face was doing so at the request of a very dangerous individual named The Force. "Please do it for me, Jenn. I'll call you when we get there to let you know what's going on, but can you please go to your grandparents' place just for this weekend?" Mason swallowed hard, closed his eyes, and fibbed, "I don't think you're in any danger, but I would rather know that you're safe. Just don't tell anyone where you're going, okay? No one, not even friends of yours on campus."

There wasn't much protest from Jennifer. She was relieved to know where her mom was. She wasn't really surprised that her mom had gone to Canada, as she knew that her business clients could come from anywhere in the world. Her classes ran until late Friday, and she wasn't crazy about driving to her grandparents' house so late at night, but she agreed to go first thing the following morning. She had been rather unnerved since the man had followed her and taken that picture, and she didn't want to have to think and worry all weekend, so it would be nice to have her father's parents to talk to, especially with everything that was going on.

"Okay, Dad. I'll go. Just promise me you'll be careful and text me often."

"I will, Jenn. Thanks. I'll call your grandmother and let her know you're coming."

Mason then turned back to the computer, searching for the folder where he had found Sami's document. He checked all the other folders to make sure there was nothing in them that might confirm where he thought Sami was. Then he plugged each of the flash drives containing all the documents he'd copied into the USB socket on the computer, checking them to be sure everything was there and completely readable. He planned to give one to Marcie and keep one for himself. If things went well in Ottawa, he would find an internet café and attach the contents in an email to Officer Suarez with copies to Detectives Baker and Finch. He brought the document up on the screen one last time and stared at it. He knew if the computer was taken back to the police laboratory, as Suarez said she was going to do, they would be able to recover any deleted material, but he fervently hoped it would take them some time to do that.

At this point, there were just too many people involved at Marshall's end for the police to guarantee his family's safety. Besides Marshall and The Force, there were also now the two bozos in the car outside his house, and the man who had taken Jennifer's picture in Miami. If the police got in-volved, they could all be in jeopardy before Marshall and his friends were ever apprehended.

Mason wasn't sure he was doing the right thing. He had no idea how his presence was going to help his wife in her mission up in Ottawa. But when Mason thought of the alternatives and the trail of evil that Marshall had been part of, he knew in his heart that he had to take action. With the flash drives securely in his pocket, and knowing Sergeant Suarez could arrive at any time, Mason hit the delete button on Sami's computer.

Chapter 24

There was a meeting taking place at the police station in Tampa. In attendance were Juanita Suarez, Albert Baker, Tom Finch and the cop from Minneapolis, David Lawrence, who was sitting in long distance via Skype. The three Florida cops were sitting around a conference table. The table was large enough to accommodate 10 people, but the remaining chairs were empty. The table and chairs had been there since the office was opened many years previously, their replacement derailed by budget cuts. Someone had even taken the time to scratch "DOOLY WAS HERE" onto the surface of the table at one corner during what must have been a particularly boring meeting. The inscription was accompanied by some artwork scratched into the table with a pair of eyes peering over a ledge at whoever happened to be sitting in the chair at that location. Coffee cups littered the end of the table where the meeting attendees were sitting, and Finch was at the front of the room ready to jot down notes on a white board.

While everyone was getting settled for the meeting, Albert Baker zoned out for a minute to reflect on how much life had changed. He wasn't sure he was keeping up. The department had purchased this infrared, interactive, blah, blah, blah whiteboard a few months ago. The user could write on it, and everything written down would be automatically transcribed to a computer. The notes could be attached to an email or printed and distributed within minutes to everyone in attendance – or to anyone else, for that matter. Or whatever was on the computer could be displayed on the white board and the images could be moved around on the board – just like Baker could do on his computer screen. You could even write on the board with your finger or a stylus, or, he thought, you could probably use anything with a point for that matter, and it could be saved on the computer. Albert shook his head and thought he really wasn't keeping up with technology, and that maybe it was time for him to take early retirement and move on to a nice quiet security job.

Detective Lawrence, who was investigating Janet Winters' murder, had called earlier to talk to Baker about Mason's phone call to Winters. As a result, Baker had decided to get everyone's heads together to do some brainstorming and figure out what they collectively knew. Baker was pleased that Lawrence could join them electronically, but he remembered the days when life was simpler; when everyone didn't expect an immediate answer in the space of an instantly-returned email or text message. Sure, the police had some advantages with all this electronic stuff and in many situations, were able to catch criminals sooner. But the bad guys were also moving forward, and crimes were becoming more sophisticated all the time. It was the age-old dichotomy between good and evil that's been prevalent for centuries, each trying to keep one step ahead of the other. One thing was for sure: the police would not be able to keep up if they didn't have the ever-improving technology to do so. Baker knew he was "old school" and his stomach burned with acid reflux every time he thought about it.

He popped an antacid from the package that was never far away and started the meeting by thanking Suarez and Lawrence for joining them. He made a joke about Lawrence appearing a little flat this morning, referring to his two-dimensional appearance on the computer screen. Lawrence fired back that it was because of the cold weather in Minneapolis, and that his features should soon be expanded by the hot air which was about to be pumped his way from Florida. With that out of the way, Baker asked Finch to note on the board the names of the three known victims: James Briscoe, Joan Briscoe and Janet Winters. Then he asked each person in turn to talk about the cases and what they knew so far.

Lawrence started by talking about Janet Winters' neighbor alerting the police to a smell emanating from Winters' apartment, and that a subsequent autopsy had confirmed the cause of death to be strangulation several days earlier. No fingerprints were found, indicating that the crime scene had been wiped clean by someone who knew how to do it. Because of the meticulous way the killer had taken pains to erase any evidence, the murder seemed more premeditated than random. Finch noted under Janet's name "strangulation" and "no prints." It appeared that there had been plenty of sexual activity on the bed, but there was no seminal fluid on the body, indicating that condoms had been used and flushed or removed. Some hair was found on the bed, which was being analyzed. Not unexpectedly, trace evidence of clothing fibers was also found on the carpet, bed and Winters' clothing. The fibers might be a useful link to an assailant's clothing later on. Lawrence noted that the absence of a forced entry and lack of disruption at the crime scene indicated that the victim had, in all likelihood, known her killer, which certainly didn't rule out Mason or even Sami Seaforth completely.

Baker stopped Lawrence there and asked about the process used to gather the trace evidence. He made sure to let the Minneapolis detective know that he wasn't telling Lawrence how to do his job, simply that he and Finch had been involved in a case recently where the evidence hadn't been gathered correctly or retained properly. He knew that there were so many things that could go wrong. A piece of forensic evidence has to be discovered, collected, packaged, labeled, and transported to the police department. It has to be stored until it's ready to go to the lab for testing, after which it has to be removed and transported. At the lab, the evidence gets logged in, stored again and kept from being contaminated by other pieces of evidence. The process is called "continuity of evidence" requiring that at any given moment, someone in authority must know exactly where and under what conditions the evidence is stored, and that no tampering is possible.

In spite of every precaution taken to collect samples in various tubes, vials and sealed baggies, and the fact that the collectors are often in Hazmat suit-like protective clothing to prevent contamination, mistakes can be – and do get -- made. Because of past experience, Baker was more than once bitten and more than twice shy. Lawrence assured him that the police department in Minneapolis was as thorough as any. In spite of Baker's attempt to soften his question by pointing out he had been on the receiving end of poor evidence collection and handling, Lawrence was obviously a little miffed at the implied suggestion that his department might be anything less than professional. "With all due respect, we aren't country bumpkins here in Minneapolis, Detective Baker. We take precautions just like you do. But I hear you. It's always a concern."

Lawrence reined in his anger and went on to say they had checked the phone records and that there had been three calls that appeared to link the Seaforths to Janet. The first had been made from Sami's office at the bank to Janet's phone a couple of weeks earlier. Then there was one from Janet's apartment to the Seaforth residence the day of the murder. And just this morning, there was one from Mason Seaforth's phone line to Janet's cell phone. Finch noted the dates of the calls on the board. Lawrence pointed out that the approximate time of death determined by the autopsy, and the time the second phone call had been made, were similar.

Everyone in the room understood the term "similar." Establishing the time of death could not be done with certainty. If the time the person was alive and the time the person was dead were both known, the time of death could be established with 100% certainty. Any factors other than those two reduced the certainty of the time of death. So it could not be established with certainty how long before her death that Janet made the phone call - or even if she had been the one making the call. For now, the working premise was that Janet had called the Seaforth household shortly before she had been murdered. Still, the fact the phone had been wiped clean could well point to another scenario. Lawrence confirmed that someone had answered the phone at the Seaforth residence, and that the conversation had lasted about two minutes.

Baker asked if Janet lived in a gated community, thinking they might be able to determine the time Janet had returned home. Lawrence told him it was not gated and that Janet lived in a seedier part of town occasionally inhabited by drug users and prostitutes. He noted that her lifestyle could have invited all kinds of problems, and the neighborhood was inhabited by any number of people who would not hesitate to kill someone for a few dollars, but the link to the Seaforths was one that had to be tracked down. Lawrence concluded by saying, "I don't know what the link is between the Seaforths and the Winters woman, but based on the phone calls, there *is* something, and I'm anxious to hear what you folks have. Maybe it will help piece things together."

Finch duly noted everything on the board, and the computer captured everything that was written. Next, Officer Suarez outlined what she knew. She was disappointed that the meeting had come up before she had a chance to collect Samantha Seaforth's computer, but she was glad for the chance to participate in the conversation. She mentioned that one of the wine bottles had contained a substance that could have effectively knocked Mason off kilter for a number of hours. She told the other cops that the DNA results on Sami's hair brush had not come back yet, but they had run her fingerprints taken from the wine bottle through the Integrated Automated Fingerprint Identification System and found the only match were the fingerprints taken when Sami had applied for her job at the bank.

Suarez continued by mentioning that Sami's cell phone had not been found and the locator trace she'd ordered had yielded nothing. She said that Mason Seaforth, her husband, had agreed to sign a consent form allowing her to pick up Sami's computer, which she would be doing on the way home. She concluded her part of the meeting by saying that her gut feeling was that Mr. Seaforth was withholding information. How much she didn't know, but she sensed something wasn't right in his responses. She also speculated whether Sami's disappearance might be related to an affair or a romantic entanglement with someone other than her husband, though she admitted she had nothing to base this on, at least yet.

After Finch had noted Suarez's comments, it was Baker's turn. He spoke about the running shoe tread found at the Briscoe murder site, and how his department was trying to match it to ones purchased within the past year. He explained that one such buyer of that particular model was none other than Mason Seaforth, who had willingly turned over the running shoes to him for sampling. He said that the Briscoes had been murdered in a particularly brutal fashion by a person or persons unknown, leaving a gruesome murder scene, and that his initial impression of Mason Seaforth did not suggest that the man could have personally carried out such a violent crime. He acknowledged that people do crazy things during crimes of passion, and finished by saying, "Of course, the job could have been contracted out."

Everyone was thoughtful for a few minutes as Finch finished writing on the board. Then Baker said, "Well, lady and gentlemen, what do you think we have here?"

Lawrence said, "The Seaforth angle might work for you with the Florida connections, but what about the link to Janet Winters? It may just be a coincidence, true, but I've learned not to put too much stock in that word. All of a sudden the Seaforths, both of whom are possibly linked to the Briscoes, have an interest in Janet Winters who is now also dead. Mrs. Seaforth disappears, maybe to Minneapolis to kill the Winters woman? I just think there are too many connecting pieces for it to be coincidence."

Juanita Suarez agreed with Lawrence. "I want to pick up Sami's computer and see if there is something in there that we can use. It might give us some clues. Mason Seaforth said his wife's computer is password-protected and he didn't know what her password was. It should take our people less than a day to figure it out. Also, if you guys could check the manifests at the airport to see if she headed out of town, it would help me a lot. There's a lot to do and so little staff. You guys know what that's like, right?"

They all nodded in silent agreement, and Baker picked up the conversation. "I tend to agree with both of you. Mason couldn't remember where he was when the Briscoes were killed. We'll press him on that to see if he can come up with something. We're going to continue to run down leads on the Briscoes. We'll follow up with the bank where Sami Seaforth worked to identify if anyone there can help us. I think we need to probe into the Seaforths' backgrounds more closely as well. Oh, and there is one other thing I think we should do, too. We also found some clothing fibers at the Briscoe murder site. I'd like to do a comparison to the fibers found in Minneapolis at Janet

Winters' apartment. It could be a long shot, but let's check it out, anyway, just to be sure."

Baker finished the conversation by thanking everyone for their cooperation, suggesting they all stay in touch and pass along any leads of interest, no matter how casual or seemingly unimportant. When he walked back to his office and checked his computer, there waiting for him were the full written notes from their discussion of just minutes earlier. Baker shook his head and popped another antacid into his mouth.

Chapter 25

There was something Mason needed to do next. It wasn't particularly appealing to him, but frankly, everything he had been forced to do in the last couple of days had been completely distasteful. He knew he would do anything for his family, and this was just one more to add to the list.

He opened the door, walked outside and straight to the car with the two thugs staring at him as he approached. He walked up to the driver's side and motioned for him to roll down the window. Sage stared at him with a look that was somewhere between bemusement and perhaps a little concern. The look he gave him made Mason think that perhaps the driver was concerned he had a gun, so Mason displayed both his hands. He shouted to the driver, "Roll the window down. I want to talk to you."

The window came down just far enough that Mason could see the driver's eyes through the open crack. Mason said, "I just want you guys to know that a police woman is coming over here, and I *didn't* call her. She wants to look at my wife's computer and I can't withhold it. A lot of good it will do her. I can't even access it – can't figure out the password. It will buy me a little time because after she leaves, my friend will be coming back. We plan to stay inside by ourselves and have some fun, if you know what I mean, so I'd appreciate your not coming to the door and bothering us. I would like a little quiet when she's here."

It was like the idiot didn't even hear the first part of Mason's statement. "Want some help? Danny and I could help you out."

Mason managed to control the anger that was seething deep down inside him, but he thought he might have twitched a little at the mention of

Danny's name. He would file that away for later. He knew that these guys were going to pay sooner or later, and he sincerely hoped that if he wasn't the one to do it, he would at least be around when it happened. But he controlled his feelings and simply said with what he hoped would be construed as a dirty chuckle, "I think I've been doing quite well without you until now." Then without thinking, he took what he knew was a risk but it might help with the plan that he and Marcie had worked out.

"I've been married to my wife for a long time, and you know how it goes – sometimes the grass is a lot greener in a different pasture," Mason lied. "I hate to ruin her return, but when she does get back – whenever that is – I'm going to have to tell her the truth: that I've found someone else. So please give me some privacy, and don't be surprised if you don't see any lights in the house for a day or two. I plan to enjoy this time with my friend. And I would also suggest that you guys not be here when the cop arrives. Otherwise, she's going to see you parked here and get curious. I doubt you want that."

The man behind the wheel narrowed his eyes through the partially-lowered window. "So you know where your wife is? I think if you know what's good for you, you'd better tell us. The man I'm working for will be very interested in hearing it. I'm envious of you, man, but that chick you're seeing is starting to piss me off, the way she keeps missing my car by inches and flipping me the finger every time she goes out."

Mason thought to himself how difficult it was for this guy to keep his mind out of his pants. "Look, you seem to be guys who will understand my situation. My wife and I have been having difficulties lately. I think she found out somehow I've been screwing her best friend. She packed her bag and took off. I don't know where. She may have gone out of town to visit friends, for all I know. Or maybe she's holed up in some hotel. She left me a note saying that she would be back in a couple of days and that we'd sort things out then. In the meantime, I'm going to have more fun. And - if she catches me, so what? It's over between us, anyhow. I just want to get away with as little alimony as possible. That's my big goal now."

Through the window, Sage leered at him. "You're quite the guy, Seaforth. I wouldn't have taken you to be such a jerk, but it looks like you are." He looked at his buddy and smirked. "But just remember, we're going to be out here making sure you are what you say you are until your wife shows up."

Mason had to swallow twice to keep his fear from showing. "Yeah, well, I better go. The police woman will be showing up any minute. You guys should make yourselves scarce." As soon as he said the words, Mason realized he had crossed a line. Telling these guys what they should do was clearly a mistake. Sage's manner suddenly became more threatening. "That ain't happening, Seaforth. This is how it's going to work. I'm coming in the house with you, and I'll be just around the corner while you're getting rid of the cop. I'll hear every word you say - and I suggest you don't say much. My buddy will drive the car away for just long enough to get this done. If you say anything contrary to what you just told us, you will regret it. I'm very good at breaking bones. Got it?"

"Yes, I understand."

Trying not to show how rattled he was, Mason turned and walked back to the house. He had difficulty to control the shaking that was overtaking his body, and he wondered if he had gone too far in trying to get these guys on his side. He felt like he needed a shower to wash away the past few minutes.

The two occupants of the blue sedan bemoaned the fact they didn't have their electronic listening equipment with them. It would sure help, but this was only supposed to be an observation job, according to The Force. If they had their equipment, they would be able to monitor Seaforth's conversation with the cop without having to risk going into the house. Second, they could listen in on the passionate evening Seaforth was about to have and enjoy it vicariously, if not as much as he was going to. Third, if they had their electronic listening devices, they'd be able to hear the conversation Seaforth and his wife were going to have when she got home, just for the entertainment value.

In the meantime, it was time for some old-time spying. Jason Sage got out of the car and walked to join Seaforth in the house. The guy on the passenger side of the car slid over to the vacated driver's seat and drove away.

Chapter 26

Mason was still badly shaken when he walked back to the house. The comments about his wife had gone to the very core of his soul. He felt sick to his stomach about the lies he had told and the things he had made up about Sami. He swore to himself again that these two and anyone else involved in this terrible ordeal were going to pay. He was going to protect Sami, even if it cost him his life. His wife and daughter were the most important people on the planet, and he would defend them to his grave, if necessary.

Mason recognized that he was poorly prepared to protect his wife and daughter from homicidal maniacs, but he would have never believed that he'd be put in a position where he would *have* to. Every day they got up in the morning and went about their daily routines. On their free days, their most important decisions were what to eat at meal time, where they'd like to go for an evening together, or whether to buy another plant for the back yard. He could never have dreamed that their safe, secure routine would be interrupted by people intent on killing his wife for reasons he still only barely understood after reading Sami's document on the computer. He felt especially heartsick at the thought that his wife must have known something like this could happen. But that thought was for another time, and he shoved it out of his head for now. His immediate concern was to help Sami out of this mess. There would be time for answers later.

He was upset that his wife had not shared any of her background or the situation she was in with him beforehand. Together they could have found a possible way out. Did she not trust him? But he knew it wasn't that. It had to be that Sami was afraid for him and Jennifer and wanted to spare him what she knew she was going to go through. Now she was gone, he was about to embark on a possibly-futile attempt to find and rescue her – and they were all in danger, maybe even his daughter Jennifer.

Just then he heard an insistent knock on the door. As he opened it, Jason Sage pushed past him and straight into the house. He pulled back his lightweight brown leather jacket as he entered, revealing the handle of a gun sticking out of the waistband of his jeans. "Remember, Seaforth, I'll be listening. And by the way, I noticed how you reacted when Danny's name came up. So for the record, mine's Jason Sage. Since we're going to be in the same house for awhile, we might as well become acquainted, don't you think? But remember, I'm your worst nightmare, just like Jason Voorhees in *Friday the 13th*." Jason's laugh ended in a smoker's choking rasp.

He recovered quickly and added, "Be smart. Seaforth. Don't say something I won't like, or you are going to be walking with a cane for the rest of your life." He walked around quickly and chose a spot in a hall closet where he could hide within earshot of the front door. He took out his gun and waved it menacingly in Mason's direction before pulling the door towards him.

Mason glanced out the window and noticed that the sun was setting on the horizon. A darkening stillness was falling on the neighborhood as the last of the setting sun's rays faded through the thick, overhanging branches of the trees. Mason ran upstairs, taking two steps at a time as adrenaline surged through him. He unplugged Sami's computer from the wall and carried it downstairs so that he could give it to Suarez when she showed up. As Mason returned to the main floor, Sage kept an eye on him through the partially open closet door with an amused look on his face. The bastard was actually enjoying this, Mason thought.

It wasn't long before Sergeant Juanita Suarez pulled up outside the house in her police cruiser. Mason could see her through the living room curtains. He prayed that Marcie wouldn't choose this very moment to arrive in the outfit he had asked her to wear. It would be extremely awkward, to say the least, and Mason was absolutely sure that Suarez would immediately jump to the wrong conclusion. Instead of thinking that Sami had left him to have an affair, Suarez would be likely to think Sami left because her husband was the one having an affair. There were a lot of balls in the air right now. Jason Sage was hiding in the closet, and Marcie could show up any minute in an outfit that would be difficult to explain. Mason wished that this was a nightmare from which he would soon be awakening. That thought quickly evaporated as the Sergeant rapped on the door.

Mason glanced towards the closet where Sage was holed up. He could imagine Sage hiding there, so close to where he would be talking to the police officer. Mason thought he would be standing in the dark holding the gun with both hands just below his chin and pointed towards the ceiling, his right finger through the trigger guard. Mason was concerned that Suarez would sense there was someone else in the house.

Mason nervously opened the door and greeted Suarez. "Hello, Mr. Seaforth," she said as she came into the house. "Have you heard anything at all from your wife?" When he replied that he hadn't, she asked if he thought perhaps she might have left the city or the state and flown somewhere else. "I really don't think so," Mason said. "I can't imagine why she would do that without telling me." Suarez looked at him and said gently, "I'm sorry, Mr. Seaforth, but given how long she's been missing, we have to pursue all the angles. This means we have to explore the possibility that your wife may have run off with someone. I know this isn't easy for you, but we're going to be checking the manifests at the airport to see if she boarded a flight. We need to know if she's left Florida at this point." Mason's heart skipped a beat. If Suarez was about to order checks of the airlines' boarding records, he knew she would easily discover that Sami had gone to Ottawa. He silently thanked God that the detective hadn't put this plan into effect yet or she would already know Sami's real destination, and she would certainly have mentioned Ottawa with Sage listening closely.

"Mr. Seaforth, did you notice your wife exhibiting any unusual behavior before she disappeared? Was she leaving the room to make phone calls, maybe going out on sudden errands at night, staying at work longer? Anything like that? Can you think of any unusual activity on her part that might give us a clue?" Mason decided to play along with this line of questioning, because it would reinforce what he had told Sage earlier out in the car.

"Well, I didn't want to go into this, but yes, unfortunately we have been having some trouble lately. I was hoping we could sort things out over our anniversary dinner, but things didn't go as well as I had hoped. We had a big fight before we went to bed. I guess she couldn't face me in the morning, so she decided to leave and figured giving me the drugs would keep me from waking up in time to stop her."

Mason desperately wanted to flick his eyes to where Sage was standing to alert Suarez but he was afraid Sage would shoot both of them. In spite of the anxiety he was feeling, he had to continue to play along.

Suarez looked at Mason skeptically. "You do realize that we're not a private detective agency, right Mr. Seaforth? We have a lot of work on our plates, and we can't be chasing non-existent problems. I know it isn't 'non-existent' to you and I'm sorry if that *is* what has happened. As long as we don't have any reason to believe otherwise, I'm prepared to wait until I hear from you. However, I've also been talking to Detectives Baker and Finch about the situation involving Mr. and Mrs. Briscoe in Tampa and guess what? Your name came up. Your name also came up in connection with the murder of a Janet Winters in Minneapolis. There are just too many questions here, Mr. Seaforth, for us to drop everything. Now I came to get your wife's computer. We are still going to pursue her as a missing person, despite what you're telling us. Are you still willing to sign the release so that I can take a look at Mrs. Seaforth's computer?"

Mason could feel himself getting more upset by the minute, and he felt the officer's gaze looking right through him. He could sense the presence of Sage in the closet, and he had to get rid of Sergeant Suarez before anything worse happened. "Sure, I have no problem with that," he said. "I want to know where Sami is, and maybe you guys will find something that will tell me where my wife has gone. At least then I could call her." He picked up the paper and without reading it, took out his pen to sign it.

"Please read the document you are about to sign, sir," Suarez told him firmly. "Otherwise, I'll need to read it to you." Then she stopped and looked at him more closely. "Mr. Seaforth, you look a little pale. Why don't we go sit at the kitchen table so you can read this properly before you sign it?" The Sergeant started to move towards the kitchen.

Mason touched the Sergeant's arm as a shock wave coursed through his body. The path to the kitchen passed right by the closet with the door ajar. He said quickly, "Actually, I really don't feel well. Do you mind if we sit on the couch?" He started to move to the couch as quickly as possible without arousing any more suspicion in Suarez.

Suarez turned and followed Mason to the couch. Mason breathed an audible sigh of relief as Suarez said, "I understand that you aren't feeling well. You really do look a little ill. I know this must be an awful strain on you. I can assure you if we find anything on the laptop, I will be back in touch. Either way, we'll get your wife's computer back to you as soon as we've gone through it. In the meantime, if you hear anything, anything at all, please let me know immediately. You should also know that it wouldn't be advisable for you to leave Gulfport right now because I'm pretty sure Detectives Baker and Finch will want to talk to you about the Briscoe killings. In our business, we don't believe in coincidences, Mr. Seaforth. So we have no choice but to follow up on whatever connections you and your wife had with the Briscoes and the Winters woman. By the way, could you tell me why you called Ms. Winters?"

"She's a friend of my wife's from way back. I thought she might have been in touch with Sami. It seemed reasonable."

"Really? Have you or your wife spoken to Ms. Winters in the recent past?" Mason thought quickly. "Sami mentioned her over dinner the night of our anniversary. They used to be best friends at one time, so I took a chance that Janet might know where Sami is. I thought Sami may even have gone to visit her friend, since they were close in school."

"Did you call Janet a few weeks ago?"

"No, I didn't. This was the first time I tried to talk to her. I had no idea that she was dead."

"Okay, well I'm sure the detectives will be in touch. By the way, where's your friend, Marcie?"

"She went home. She's been spending all her time here with me, trying to come up with ideas about where my wife has gone, and she had some things she needed to do."

An uneasy feeling ran through Suarez. She couldn't put her finger on it, but she felt like there was someone very close by watching them. As a trained officer, she had learned to trust her instincts completely, and her instincts right now were on high alert. "Is there anyone else here right now, Mr. Seaforth?" she asked him. Mason felt like he was about to break into a cold sweat. He could picture Jason Sage moving his finger closer to the trigger. "No, there's no one here," he lied, doing his best to keep his voice steady. "As I just told you, Marcie had to leave. There's no one else here."

Suarez didn't say anything else, and Mason went through the motions of reading the release document and signing his name. He just wanted to get rid of Sergeant Suarez before she became any more suspicious. Mason handed Sami's laptop to Suarez, and she tore off a copy of the release form for Mason to keep. "Don't get up, please," she told him as she headed for the door. "You need to get some rest." It took everything he had to stay on the couch and not to usher her out to her squad car. Finally, she was gone.

Sage emerged from the closet and congratulated Mason on his performance. "You did well."

"Yeah, whatever. Look, you need to leave now. My friend will be along any minute. Please leave us alone."

"Okay, I guess you behaved yourself enough for now, Seaforth, but just remember, we will be watching."

Once back in her patrol car, Suarez thought about her encounter with Mason Seaforth. Something definitely felt wrong. His change of tactics, trying to act as if now his marriage was in trouble when he had been so insistent there was nothing at all wrong, his obvious nervousness and sweating, his pale demeanor, her sense that there was someone else in the house – none of this added up to a good situation. The officer searched her patrol car computer and found a number for Marcie Kane. Marcie picked it up on the second ring. "Hello, Ms. Kane, it's Sergeant Juanita Suarez," Suarez said by way of introduction. "I've just left Mason Seaforth's house. He tells me you've been very helpful to him in trying to find his wife." Marcie thanked the officer and said she would do anything to locate her best friend.

Suarez got right to the point, "Are you aware of any marital difficulties the Seaforths may have been having?"

"No, I've seen nothing like that. They seemed to be very happy. I'm Sami's best friend, and I think I would have sensed something."

"Thank you, Ms. Kane. I'll be in touch."

After Sage left, Mason went out to the garage to find some timers that he used every year for their Christmas lights. He had used them since they moved into the house, and every year he left them in a different spot in the garage, all the while resolving to himself that he would eventually put them in the same place two years in a row. After rummaging through a few boxes and drawers, he came up with three. He plugged two of the timers into separate lamps on the main floor and ran upstairs to the bedroom where he plugged the third timer into the bedside light. He set them to go on and off at different times for the next week. He threw a thin towel over the nightshade in the bedroom to provide some ambient lighting that should be barely visible from the street.

As he descended the stairs, he heard a rumble coming from down the street outside and he recognized the classic sounds of Mick Jagger and the Rolling Stones complaining about getting no satisfaction. He thought to himself that Marcie must have finally broadened her musical horizons.

He decided to watch Marcie's entrance from her car, so he edged up to the window behind the curtains. And emerge she did. As if in slow motion, first one long leg appeared from the car, slowly followed by the second. Marcie was in full performance mode. She was wearing a tight blue short-sleeved mini dress cut thigh-high. The hip-hugging material drew attention to her round behind. One side of the dress was off the shoulder and the depth of the blue, which could be compared to the darkening evening sky, accentuated her dark skin to perfection. She wore clear plastic shoes with a six-inch stiletto heel. Mason thought the shoes were stunning, but he desperately hoped she had running shoes in her overnight bag, because she certainly couldn't move fast in what she was wearing. The thought occurred to him that it would be possible to fill the soles with water and put goldfish in each one. Maybe some designer had already thought of that. She was carrying a small white handbag. Then he had another thought. Marcie wouldn't be able to carry her handgun when she donned that outfit, because concealment was impossible. In short, she was absolutely stunning.

Marcie was obviously enjoying her role. As she got out of her car, she made a show of bending over to retrieve an overnight bag from the back seat. Mason was quite sure her mission of attracting the attention of the watchers was successful.

Marcie strutted up the driveway, placing one foot carefully in front of the other, teetering on her six-inch heels, as she made her way up to the house. At the door, she turned, looked directly at the car and flipped them her finger. She had a self-assured smile on her face, but as she turned and entered the house, her resolve quickly disappeared. She slumped with her back against the door, no longer looking like a confident model on the catwalk but more like a beautiful woman who was feeling miserable after a terrible date. Her head thumped back against the door, and her eyes searched the ceiling. After what seemed like a full minute, she let out a breath. "Oh my God, I have never been so self-conscious and scared in my life! Do you think they bought it?"

"You did great, Marcie," said Mason encouragingly. "You look amazing. Believe me, those guys will be envious of what they think I'm going to be doing in here with you. But your overnight bag is really small. Do you have enough clothes for our escape later?"

"Yes, I've got running shoes and some clothes. I packed really light.

Suarez called me and I told her I didn't think there was anything wrong in your marriage. I hope that was all right. Is everything okay with you?"

Mason was a little worried that their stories didn't match, but it was too late for that. There was no reason for Marcie to know if there was a problem with the stories. He didn't tell her about the visit from Sage, but he did let her know about giving the laptop to Suarez.

"Now we have to get on with our plan, Marcie. There are candles in the drawer. Could you please get them out and put them on the dining room table? There are candle holders in the hutch, and I've got a bottle of wine in the fridge. I'm going to order some Greek food from the restaurant down the street. We'll light the candles in a few minutes."

Mason placed the call to the restaurant, and Marcie set the table so that Mason was at the head and she was to his immediate left with her back to the window. Their shadows would be visible through the drapes. They decided to leave the blind up for now. When the meal arrived, Mason paid the delivery man while checking the street to be certain the blue sedan was in place. It was, and even in the dark he could make out the shapes of its occupants staring at the open front door where Mason knew his form was illuminated by the light in the hallway behind him. Once the transaction was complete, he retreated back into the house, closing the door behind him.

Neither Mason nor Marcie was very hungry, but they lit the candles and started eating, and as they did so, Marcie leaned over as if to kiss Mason on the lips. She held her head in front of Mason's and whispered, "We have to make this appear authentic, Mason. I could see your outline against the light from the outside as I came in this evening. Just pretend you're kissing me, and let's make it look real."

Mason almost laughed, thinking that with the situation they were in, this was probably the *least* romantic mood he had ever been in. Nevertheless, he did as she suggested, and they repeated the performance off and on until the meal was finished. They pretended to pour each other generous amounts of wine, they fed each other bites of the Greek food, they threw their heads back in fake laughter at something that one of them had apparently said, and they appeared to cuddle affectionately. They felt like they were giving a very believable performance, one that would convince the two men outside their romance was genuine.

At 10:48, Marcie got up from the table as planned and went upstairs. Lights started to go off as Mason had set them on the timers, and at exactly 10:50, the timer clicked in the bedroom and the lamp came on. At exactly 10:51, Mason stood up from the table, carried their empty dishes out to the kitchen, pulled down the blind and extinguished the candles. The downstairs was now in darkness. By 10:55, Marcie was in the bathroom off the master bedroom changing from her eye-popping blue mini-dress and spike heels into a pair of indigo stretch jeans, slim white t-shirt with a lightweight tweed jacket and a pair of running shoes. While Marcie folded her dress and put it along with the spike heels in the closet, Mason took his turn in the bathroom and changed into blue jeans and a dark grey sweater. He put on a light jacket and a pair of Reeboks. By 11:20, Mason had packed a light carry-on and Marcie had freshened her makeup. At 11:28, they crept silently downstairs and waited at the back door.

At 11:30, the light in the bedroom clicked off, the house was plunged into complete darkness, and Mason and Marcie were out the door and on their way to Canada.

DAY 4

Chapter 27

There were anxious moments as they retraced the path Mason had followed earlier to get to the gas station where he had met Marcie for the gun training. They waited in the shadows at the gas station, expecting to see the blue sedan roar up and the occupants jump out to shatter their plan. But the taxi arrived, and they spent some restless hours trying to get some sleep on a bench in a corner of the Tampa Airport. They lay with their heads on their bags to ensure no one tried to run off with them. Finally, they were able to board at 6:15 a.m., and they were on their way to Toronto. They talked a little on the flight, but for the most part they were absorbed by thoughts of everything that had transpired and what might lie ahead.

When they arrived at Pearson International Airport in Toronto, they each grabbed their carry-on and disembarked quickly. They cleared Customs easily, declaring that the purpose of their travel was pleasure. They were given only two options, and the second choice of "business" didn't seem to fit their purpose any better than the first. Once through Customs, they entered the arrival lounge and Mason noticed Marcie looking around. Just as he spotted the car rental door, she stepped forwarded and greeted a tall man who had apparently been waiting for her. She told Mason she would catch up with him while he went to get their rental car. Mason knew that Marcie had been to Toronto a couple of times with her husband when his team had played the Raptors, so it wasn't unusual that she would know someone there. She had obviously contacted him before they left.

Mason made the arrangements for the rental. He signed for a Toyota Camry from Thrifty and was just finishing the transaction, adding Marcie's name as a secondary driver, when she sidled up to him. She was carrying a box of some heft that the man had obviously given her. "Sorry, that was a friend I met through my ex. I thought it would be a chance to say 'hello.' Mason told her it was no problem and that the clerk just needed her driver's license so they could be on their way. He said, "I made sure we have a GPS to help us navigate."

As they were leaving the car rental counter, Marcie spotted a Tim Hortons. She had read it was one of Canada's largest fast-food chains and a Canadian staple. Knowing they had to eat, she pulled Mason to the small restaurant with tables and chairs set out in front of the counter. Mason ordered a medium coffee with milk, and Marcie ordered a cup of café mocha to drink there and a large coffee with double sugar and double cream to go. "Ah, you mean a double double," said the smiling clerk behind the counter. They each had a steak and cheese Panini. They ordered some of the trademark donuts for the road. As they finished their meal, Marcie mused that it was pretty good. "Maybe now that Burger King has bought Tim Hortons, we will see some of these in Florida."

They continued towards the parking lot where the rental cars were located, checking the license plates as they went. They noticed that the Ontario plate slogan was "Yours to Discover." They both realized that nothing could be truer. But what they really wanted to discover was Sami. They found their car, got in and Mason programmed the GPS to take them to downtown Ottawa. The screen announced that their drive would take four hours and 48 minutes from their current location at Pearson International Airport. They fastened their seat belts as a pleasant female voice on the navigation system told them to turn left.

It was a house that was often admired by those who drove down the trendy street along the historic Rideau Canal in Ottawa. It wouldn't be the first thing you'd notice, as visitors' attention is automatically drawn to the canal and all its delights in summer and winter. But most people driving along the canal would envy anyone fortunate enough to be able to live within eye-sight of the waterway. Originally opened in 1832 to ensure a continuing sup-ply and communication route between Montreal and the British naval base in Kingston in case of invasion, the canal was inscribed as a UNESCO World Heritage Site in 2007, recognizing it as a work of human creative genius.

In summer, tourists and locals alike can be seen cycling or walking along the sidewalk adjacent to the water, lying in the grass soaking up the sun's rays, enjoying a drink on one of the patios overlooking the water, or even pleasure boating on its placid surface. In winter, it changes to a white wonderland as thousands of people skate its five-mile length. During a break, skaters can enjoy a cup of cocoa or a local delicacy of fried dough pastry stretched to resemble the shape of a beaver's tail.

The house overlooking this beautiful space in the nation's capital city was a brownstone featuring a large balcony on each of the two floors. Its most impressive feature on the inside was a dramatically-curved mahogany staircase with a wrought iron railing that led from the main floor to a turret housing a den. There was an enormous blown-glass chandelier hanging from the coffered ceiling 14 feet above the dining room table that could be ad-mired in detail while climbing or descending the staircase. A large floor-to-ceiling stone fireplace dominated the living room. The many windows at the front of the house allowed beautiful vistas of the canal.

Modern conveniences, such as an indoor barbecue in the kitchen, were in stark contrast to the old beauty of this historical building. But there was one other modern convenience that visitors would be surprised to see, if they noticed it at all. Among all this beauty and history was an advanced security system, which protected its owner from any uninvited or unwanted visitors.

None of the beauty within or outside the beautiful house was even a consideration of the occupants on this day. The owner of the property was in full rage. He sat at his desk in his den. The room was adorned with expensive paintings that he loved. He felt that he had earned the right to surround him-self with beauty, and he took pride in the artwork that adorned the walls. The desk was solid hardwood with contrasting maple inserts. Only folded copies of the local newspaper and Toronto's *Globe and Mail* interrupted one corner of its pristine surface. On the other was a replica of the "Bronco Buster" sculpture, the original of which was created by Frederic Remington in 1865. He particularly liked the sculpture because it depicted a strong-willed cowboy in mid combat with an equally strong-willed horse. The ultimate winner was left to the imagination of the observer.

A wall-to-wall bookshelf that matched the desk loomed behind him. A variety of books of different genres crammed its shelves, but if one looked closely enough, there was a common thread among many, with names such as "All or Nothing," "Double Down" and "Secrets of Winning Roulette."

He had earlier poured a glass of The Macallan Sherry Oak Scotch for his guest. The Scotch was 12-years old. He had better Scotch in his collection: his personal favorite was a 33-year old Glendronach that was available only in select stores and carried a hefty price tag of around $350 a bottle. But he saved the good stuff for people who were more refined than the man sitting in front of him. He never quite understood why anyone would ruin the taste of good Scotch with ice, which is exactly what his current visitor did. The owner of the house considered himself a connoisseur, and he felt that adding ice or water dulled the taste. Ice froze the delicate aromas of the whiskey, which could only be considered sacrilege. But it wasn't merely the fact that his guest put ice in his Scotch that caused him to be particularly irate at this moment. He didn't like what he was hearing. Not one bit.

The man was Aaron Marshall, and he was displeased that the where-abouts of his stepdaughter, Samantha Seaforth, were still unknown. Marshall was a tall, stately-looking man. At just over 6'1" and 64 years of age, he carried himself ramrod-straight. His hair had turned solid gray but was full and swept back in a pompadour, much the same style worn by Elvis in the mid–'50s. He had a goatee that matched his hair color and enhanced his handsome, elongated face. He wore a starched white shirt with a pale blue tie. When he was angry, which was often, his face turned an ominous shade of red that was in sharp contrast to his goatee, and his deep voice seemed to drop an octave lower. Rocking back and forth in his executive chair at an ever-increasing speed was another indication that Marshall was reaching fever pitch. His rage was partially directed at the man sitting in front of him, who was sipping his Scotch with ice. That man was Marshall's trusted lieutenant and confidant, Greg Johnson, otherwise known as The Force. But mainly, Marshall's anger was directed at the situation he found them in.

The Force occasionally lived in a spare room in the house, if Marshall felt there was a need for some personal protection, but he was also the owner of a small farm just south of Ottawa. That's where he trained the girls Marshall imported from other countries. Right now he was suffering Marshall's wrath and dreaming about his quiet piece of property and the two Asian girls who were currently locked in the house.

"You better tell me again. This is not making sense to me. What do you mean you don't know where Samantha Seaforth is?"

Johnson told his boss everything he knew, except about the police taking custody of Sami's computer. He wasn't happy when Sage had told him about that. But he reasoned there was really nothing they could have done. And anyway, with Janet Winters dead and once Sami was out of the way, any information they found on the computer would be circumstantial at best.

"We know we're getting closer, but we still don't know where she is yet. Her husband seems to be fooling around with some black chick, and it looks like Sami walked out on him. He seems to think she will be back soon, but he's taking full advantage of her absence. He's shacking up with the chick, while his wife's away – at his own house, no less. My guy in Florida overheard the detective that's working the case – Suarez or something Mexican like that - say that she's suspicious that Sami may have flown off somewhere. It's possible she may have gone to Minneapolis to see Janet. It will be a big surprise to her when she finds out Ms. Winters is no longer with us." The Force chuckled a little in the hopes of defusing the situation.

But Marshall was seething. He leaned forward as he thumped the desk with his palms and yelled, "*Yeah, well, what if she flew here?* I'm glad *you* think it's funny! She just can't leave it alone. Don't you understand that? Maybe we should have let sleeping dogs lie, but when Briscoe mentioned my name to her, everything opened up again. Your damn girlfriend Janet had to keep that diary and send it to her! Johnson, I don't like the way things are moving, and *you* had better *fix* it. I want every copy of Winters' diary destroyed, and I want that Seaforth woman dead." Marshall slowed his words down for emphasis so there was no chance of confusion. "AM. I. MAKING. MYSELF. CLEAR?"

Johnson knew there was no point in debating this further. He nodded that he understood, and decided that he would try a different tack. "I think you're going to enjoy the two new Asian girls. They are cooperating well. They are very willing to do whatever I ask. They're scared to death and will comply easily. I think they will be great in one of your parlors in Montreal. I trust that Alexandra is working out well for you?"

The mention of the parlors in Montreal triggered another round of anger from Marshall, but this time his rage was more controlled - and more dangerous, as The Force well knew from previous episodes. Marshall said through gritted teeth that he had heard from his source in Montreal City Hall that there were as many as 15 applications *a day* for new massage parlors in Montreal. He talked about the fact that there were more than 420 locations in the greater Montreal area offering sexual favors and that didn't bode well for supply and demand economics. "I can't make any money if the field gets too crowded, especially if some of the new places lower their prices to compete. I've also heard the new mayor in Montreal wants to crack down on the number of erotic massage parlors in the city. We can't let him do that."

Marshall glared directly at Johnson. "Listen to me. When this mess is finished with Samantha Seaforth, I want you to pay a visit to some of these upstart establishments and remind them who's in charge. You have my authority to buy them out or *burn them out*. Hire as many men as you need, but I want the supply reduced. Maybe we can take care of the problem before the mayor and his bunch of do-gooders step in. Understand?"

Johnson said he did, and after the two held eye contact for a minute, Marshall started to relax. His chair slowed to normal rocking speed. Johnson drained his glass of Scotch. He knew his boss considered it sacrilege to cut the drink with ice, so he always made a point of tossing the remnants of the ice into his mouth and crunching them loudly with his teeth. He respected his boss and he didn't want to lose his job, but some of his idiosyncrasies were just too much to take sometimes. He didn't really like Scotch, but he drank it to appease his boss. Even with ice, it left an aftertaste that he didn't care for. But he could choke down a glass of the stuff every once in a while if it kept his boss in a better mood. And the small goal of aggravating his boss by loudly chewing the ice was a little piece of satisfaction he savored.

He thought of the other occupant of the house, Alexandra. She was a 17 year-old Romanian beauty who had been brought over recently and subjected to the training of The Force. She would be leaving for Toronto soon where she would be put to work. In the meantime, she was locked in the bedroom. He knew that Marshall would start to feel a little better once he was able to take his frustration out on someone. And he knew his boss would feel even better later when they made their usual trip to the casino.

Jennifer thought long and hard about what her dad had said. The stress of studying for exams, and the fact her mother had gone to Canada for some reason, were taking their toll. She understood why she should go to her grandparents' place. But it was a long drive, and she had to be back for classes on Monday. She was a mature university student now, and she was quite sure she could handle herself. Besides, she really wanted to be home when her parents got there. She wanted to give her mom a big hug before telling her never to disappear like that again. She made the decision. She would leave Saturday morning just as she'd promised her dad, but instead of going to her grandparents' house, she would go to her parents' place in Gulfport. It really shouldn't upset anyone. She would call them all when she got there.

Sergeant Suarez resolved on the way back to her office from the Seaforth residence that she was going to shift this case to the back burner. She had no time to pursue wayward housewives, and the more she thought about it, that's what she thought this case had become. If she followed cases of disappearance for reasons of marital discord, she would be doing it 24-7. There were just too many men and women having affairs on the side out there. Mason was still a person of interest in the murders of the Briscoes and Janet Winters, but that was for Baker and Finch to investigate. She would have the technical people look at the computer, but as far as she was concerned, this was pretty much Baker and Finch's show now.

Baker and Finch were in somewhat of a holding pattern as they waited for the results of the forensic tests. They were gathering data on Mason, Sami and Marcie. So far, all three individuals seemed to be model citizens and unlikely to have committed the crimes. But there were "unlikely" suspects before who had pulled off heinous crimes for a variety of reasons. Perhaps this was one. Baker could recall neighbors of victims saying over and over in television interviews that they just couldn't believe this could happen in their neighborhood. So they had to run down every lead.

David Lawrence was busy in Minneapolis looking into the life of Janet Winters, trying to piece together what he could.

Sami Seaforth was still missing.

Chapter 28

Mason and Marcie spoke very little on the drive through downtown Toronto to the 401 highway headed towards Ottawa. Midway through Toronto, she pointed out the CN Tower looming to the south of their vantage point on the road. Traffic was about the same as it would be at this time of the day driving through Tampa. The flow was obviously aided by the multiple lanes stretched from one side to the other, but there were plenty of cars pouring on and off the main road onto entrance and exit lanes. Drivers had to be vigilant at all times as cars whizzed by on both sides. Based on what Mason could tell, the speed limits were relatively the same as Tampa's, although metric, and just like in Tampa, they were apparently posted for everyone other than those actually driving the cars. The Tower was clearly visible against the blue sky with vast Lake Ontario in the background. Marcie made idle conversation by noting that she had eaten at the revolving restaurant atop the Tower, and she talked about her recent discovery that thrill seekers could walk along the open edge of the 5-foot ledge near the top of the Tower totally hands free, prevented only by a thin safety harness from falling 1,200 feet to a horrible death. Mason ended that conversation with a very unenthusiastic "No, thanks!"

They drove on in silence, only speculating occasionally about what they might find in Ottawa. The conversation was nervous and awkward. Mason kept it quiet, but throughout the drive he questioned himself over and over if he was doing the right thing. He didn't arrive at a definitive answer during the drive, but he was committed to seeing it through.

The GPS turned out to be an excellent estimator, as they arrived in the outskirts of Ottawa almost precisely at the predicted time. They had seen a sign miles earlier indicating that they were entering Ottawa, a city of a million people, yet their drive continued through farmland and open spaces. They saw a herd of deer in one field surrounding newborn fawns that were in need of protection from four-legged predators. Marcie couldn't help saying as they drove through the countryside, spotting only the occasional farm yard or dilapidated barn, "Where is everybody?" They decided any real evidence of habitation had to be off the beaten path, as it certainly wasn't visible from the highway they were traveling on.

As they turned onto Highway 417, which would take them most of the way into the downtown area of Ottawa, the city stretched out before them. Most notable was a series of large Gothic-style buildings in the distance on their left, with a central clock tower dominating the skyline along the Ottawa River. Marcie noted that it must be a beautiful, romantic view at night with the lights illuminating the buildings and reflecting off the river. She also observed that the buildings that were so dominating must belong to the Canadian federal government, as only a government would be located in structures like that. It would turn out to be true, as they would later find out they were looking at the Canadian Parliament Buildings. But their enthusiasm for sightseeing was completely dampened by the reason they were there. They were in Ottawa to find Sami and to somehow deal with her stepfather. Mason had only answered monosyllabically in response to Marcie's questions, but she understood and was empathetic. He had withdrawn into a dark place that she didn't want to invade right now. While she preferred to talk when she was stressed, she recognized Mason's need for quiet and she respected that.

They found a hotel just off the Queensway, which Highway 417 had somehow magically become somewhere after they entered the outskirts of the city. They paid for rooms with their credit cards. Mason knew they were leaving a paper trail for the police, but that wasn't a bad thing. He really thought everything would have been brought to a head by the time the police located it. Mason and Marcie agreed to freshen up and reconvene in an hour.

Marcie tapped on Mason's door at the appointed hour and entered the room after Mason removed the chain from the slot in the secondary door lock. There was nothing special about the room. A king size bed dominated the space with a desk in the far right corner. A leatherette chair rolled on a plastic carpet protector in front of the desk. There was a small table in the far left corner of the room as she entered. Marcie carried the box that she had picked up at the airport. She told Mason that she had something to show him, but she had to explain it to him first. Mason looked disinterested as sat on the rolling desk chair while Marcie sat facing the window on the side of the bed with the box beside her.

She said, "Mason, you were preoccupied when you were searching for flights, but do you remember me saying that Canada has very strict gun laws?"

Mason shook his head, "I don't really recall discussing it in detail, but I remember you said something about Canada's laws being stricter than ours. I think their laws must work, because you don't see the mass murders and multiple shootings in the news, at least as frequently as we have them in America. But why did you ask me that? "

"Well, do you remember that man I met at the airport in Toronto? The tall guy I spoke with while you arranged for the rental car?"

Mason was starting to become a little agitated. "Yes, I remember. Is this 20 questions we are playi…?" His voice trailed off. He had an awful feeling he knew where this was going. "Marcie, you didn't…"

Marcie took the top of the box off with a flourish and inside wrapped in tissue were nestled two guns. They obviously weren't new, but Mason recognized one as being similar, if not identical, to the Smith & Wesson 442 that Marcie carried back home, and the other looked very much like the Glock 17 he had used at the shooting range, although he wouldn't know one gun from another. Mason's eyes nearly popped out of his head. "Marcie, you may know how to use that thing, but I don't! And besides, they *aren't legal here*. What if we get caught with them? You have to get rid of them *right now*."

"Mason," Marcie said, and this time, her voice was very low and serious. "These are very bad dudes we're dealing with, Mason. They won't think twice about killing innocent people. We came up here to find Sami and protect her, but the truth is, we're all in danger: her, you, me. We *need* some protection, Mason. Look, we can leave them in the glove compartment of the rental car. If we get caught, we'll just say we didn't know they were there. They can't be traced. The serial numbers have been filed off. Somebody could have put them there to get rid of them when we left the car unlocked in a parking lot, for all we know. If we handle them carefully, we don't even have to leave fingerprints. I'm telling you, we're keeping the guns. I paid a lot of money for them, and the bad news is, I'm afraid we are going to need them. I hope I'm wrong. I hope we don't need them. I hope we find Sami and she's just up here on a little vacation, and Aaron Marshall and that other guy say, hey, we were only kidding. We didn't mean any harm. But the guns stay, Mason. I'm taking them down to the car with me when I go, but I'm keeping mine in my room at night. You can do what you want, but I don't want to have to save your ass because you aren't within reach of yours."

Mason realized that what Marcie was saying made sense. He wasn't happy about it, but from everything he'd seen already, Marshall and his men were bent on finding and harming Sami. He realized there was no point in arguing. Besides, Marcie had made up her mind, and that was that. He finally agreed.

Marcie brightened after Mason started to settle down, obviously relieved that she had told him. The guns, and how she was going to present them to Mason, had been weighing on her since they left Toronto, so she was glad to get that out of the way. "Well, we're here. What are we going to do first?"

And there it was: the big question. While the guns had been weighing on Marcie's mind, it was the question of what they were going to do next that had been distracting Mason since they had embarked on this crazy plan. If Aaron Marshall was really involved in illegal criminal activity here, he wasn't going to be advertising his address to the world. He had obviously moved to Canada with some legitimate business, but based on his association with Briscoe, it was probably real estate holdings that wouldn't be advertised any-where. Mason thought of checking the local newspapers on the off chance that there might be something that would catch their attention, but he thought it would be a long shot at best. He really thought their best option was to check out the big casino later that night and see what was going on. Maybe they could ask around to see if anyone at the casino knew Marshall. This really was going to be a fishing expedition, and the result could mean they were snagging the deadliest catch, but Mason was sure if they found Marshall, Sami wouldn't be far away. Something told him down in his gut that this was the right thing to do.

He checked his reasoning again. He really thought that Sami was going to confront her stepfather with the information she had and threaten to go to the police with it. Her protection was her notes and documentation that she hoped would precipitate an investigation by the police if anything happened to her. He thought for sure that Sami had not yet found Marshall since The Force was still looking for her. It was the only explanation he could come up with that made any kind of sense. Mason desperately wanted to be on the right track for the sake of his family.

He brought Marcie up to date on the next part of the plan - if you could call it that.

Chapter 29

After they climbed into their rental car, Marcie carefully placed the guns in the glove compartment. She had waited to take them to the car until they both left the room. "You have no idea how uncomfortable this makes me feel," Mason said. "I can't convince myself we should have them. How likely is it that we're going to have to shoot somebody? And for that matter, how likely is it that we actually CAN shoot anybody?"

"Well, I can think of a few people I could shoot right now," Marcie retorted, "and if you don't stop complaining, you're going to be the first!" With that, she took a CD out of her purse and plugged it into the player in the dash. The hip hop sounds of Jay-Z filled the car. Mason glanced at Marcie with something between a smile and a grimace on his face.

"What! This is one of my favorite albums. It's called *The Black Album*, and it's on Rolling Stone magazine's list of the top 500 albums of all time. This is *music*, Mason. Just enjoy it! Now let's go find your wife."

Mason decided that he would have to put up with Marcie's idiosyncrasies for a while longer, so he let it go. He put the car in gear and headed up the ramp into the Ottawa evening. As they drove, he suggested to Marcie that she gather as much about her surroundings as she possibly could as it could come in handy later. He promised that he would do the same. He drove north on Metcalfe Street in the direction of the Parliament Buildings, which were exercising their control of the skyline at the end of the street. Behind the buildings lay the Ottawa River that separated the provinces of Ontario and Quebec. Mason and Marcie both thought to themselves that they would love to come back and visit when they had more time and fewer things on their minds. But neither one expressed the thought out loud. They were there for far more frightening reasons. They didn't see much obvious security in front of the Parliament Buildings, not at least compared to political buildings in the U.S., and they both thought it was amazing how different the two neighboring countries were in many respects. The route took them right on Wellington Street and ultimately across a bridge into the French province of Quebec. The first thing they noticed was that the signs were in French first, with the English lettering much smaller, if it was there at all. It was like being in a different country. "I guess every country has its differences," remarked Marcie. They could see a fountain in the distance that Mason recognized from his research as the water spouting up from Lac de la Carrière. When he saw it, he wondered how it would be pronounced. Marcie's guess was that it would be the same as the pronunciation for "career." The main building that dominated the skyline across the river was the Hilton Lac-Leamy hotel, which Mason assumed could be seen from any direction as it towered above surrounding buildings.

They were able to understand enough from the signs to get them to the casino. There was one that directed them to Boulevard du Casino and their destination was designated number 1 on that street. The building was an inviting white with a circular structure on the top, a rounded glass front and a series of spikes rising from the roof. A series of lights in the shape of fountains guided them down the boulevard in the direction of the casino. They followed the crescent-shaped road in front of the casino which deposited them in the parking lot where there was room for thousands of cars. Mason and Marcie stared at each other as they got out of the car. After three days of searching night and day for Sami, Mason couldn't help but think that the trail had now reached this place where nothing made any sense to them. But he also knew time was running out. The moment had come to get some answers.

Chapter 30

As they approached the door leading into the casino, they noticed a handful of people in identical blue jackets with a gold shoulder stripe milling about out front. Mason noted one had the name "Voiturier" emblazoned across the back of his uniform and assumed that would be the person's surname, but when others turned around, he noticed they all had the same designation. He remembered that they were in predominantly French-speaking Quebec, so he deduced from the uniforms and number of people wearing them that it was "valet parking," and then he realized how much he felt like a fish out of water here. With no English translation, a visitor would have to fend for themselves. But then he realized it would be no different if they were in France. It was just that Canada was so close to home. He stopped to talk to one of the young men who had moved away from the pack that was apparently assigned the job of parking cars for the well-to-do, some of whom probably wouldn't be able to afford the tip when they exited the casino later that night. The valet was a good-looking young man with deep-set brown eyes and an engaging smile that flashed perfect teeth. He would undoubtedly be popular with the ladies.

Mason pulled out the picture of Aaron Marshall that he had printed from Sami's computer files.

"Good evening. I'm wondering if you can help me with a little information."

The young man looked down at the picture and then back up at Mason. "What kind of information are you looking for, sir?"

"I'm in town from Florida," Mason said. "It's the first time I've ever been to Canada, but I understand an old friend of mine lives here and occasionally frequents this casino. I have a business proposition that I would really like to discuss with him." Mason handed the valet the photo along with a folded American $20 bill. He hadn't had the time to exchange the bills for Canadian money. He noted the valet's name tag identified him as Andrew.

"Ah, I see you understand the value of the exchange rate, my friend," the young man said, flashing a big smile as he took the money. "We always appreciate American tips, because the casino always pays out in Canadian dollars." Andrew looked at the photo again. "I'm not totally sure, but this picture looks kind of like a younger version of one of our regular guests. His name is Aaron Marshall. He usually shows up on Friday and Saturday nights. He must do pretty well, because he's a very generous tipper. That's why I know of him." Andrew looked at Mason and smiled. "The only time you want to avoid him is if he has a bad night at the tables. He gets real ugly then. Was he like that when you knew him?"

Mason said nothing, but he felt a shiver run down his spine.

"He usually stays away from poker, except for blackjack. We have a Texas Hold'em room upstairs on the third floor, and my buddies inside tell me he never goes up there. He plays over on the far side of the ground floor where the tables are. Sometimes it's roulette and sometimes blackjack. Every Saturday night around 8 o'clock, he goes upstairs and eats at Le Baccara restaurant with his bodyguard. You can set your watch by him, and probably even your calendar. My girlfriend works in the restaurant, and she tells me the guy goes downstairs to choose his own wine from the 13,000 bottles they've got stored down there. They give the staff a tour once in awhile to remind us how the other half lives. I guess it's supposed to encourage us or something. Anyway, I haven't seen your buddy yet, but it's Friday night. He'll be here."

As Andrew was finishing the last sentence, a yellow Porsche Cayman S drove up with its twin exhausts at full throttle. It stopped in front of Andrew, and the driver's door opened. A set of long legs barely covered by a short white dress emerged, along with their owner who was a stunning blonde. The dress was as low at the top as it was high at the bottom, which earned her admiring glances from the other male valets, who might also have been a little jealous that Andrew was in the right place at the right time. By contrast, a toss of the keys to Andrew accompanied by a seductive smile earned the blonde an eye roll from the lone female in the group.

Andrew tore his attention away from the dress and its occupant, who at that moment was hustling from the car and the cool night air into the casino, and looked back to Mason. "Ah, the lifestyles of the rich and famous," he whispered loudly. "Sorry, I gotta go, man." Andrew waved the $20 bill. "If you want to send any more of these Jacksons my way, I'll see if I can give you something more on your buddy. The guy's obviously loaded. Hit him up for some free drinks." He laughed as he climbed into the Porsche and drove away.

As Andrew roared off to park the car, Mason was more than happy with the information he'd just received. They appeared to be on the right track. Mason and Marcie had been discussing their approach. They knew that the casino would be armed with highly-sophisticated security cameras, so even if they saw Marshall from a distance, they wouldn't be able to create a scene. If it came down to a war of Marshall's words against theirs, as a casino regular he would undoubtedly win. So they decided to keep a low profile and merely observe for tonight. Maybe Marshall might actually lead them to Sami's whereabouts if they just bided their time.

They had already looked at the casino's web page and found that photos and videos were allowed inside as long as they weren't obtrusive to customers. They could also use their cell phones away from the tables, so they decided they would split up and stay in touch by text. As they entered the casino, they were greeted by the unlikely sight of a bamboo forest rising up out from the first floor and onto the second where they now stood. The bamboo shoots reached towards the high ceilings, and Marcie commented that they were probably used as much for sound-deadening purposes as for aesthetics. Mason was surprised she could think of that at a time like this, but what she said made sense.

There were walkways on either side of the forest, and on the left was a long staircase leading to the third floor. Both walkways would take them into the heart of the casino, so they chose the right-hand side and deposited their coats at the coat check. As they entered the main casino, the decibel level picked up appreciably. They were bombarded with the metallic sounds of the brightly-colored slot machines spread out across the floor in all directions, tempting gamblers with the possibility of untold riches. Many of the 1,800 slot machines were in use. People seemed totally oblivious to their surroundings as they stared blankly at the rotating lines of cherries, bars, numbers, and other symbols in the lifeless machines that held their fate.

The people held captive by the spinning rows of symbols knew in a matter of seconds after each spin whether or not their ship had come in or sailed away yet again. When the symbols all matched up in one of the machines, the noise level increased, causing nearby players to plug their tokens into the machines with even more fervor. Yet for all the energy in the casino and the din of the gaming machines, the overall sound was surprisingly muted by the casino's high ceilings, large plants, thick carpeting and other soundproofing devices.

Mason had read once that the machines which paid the best dividends were located in high traffic areas so they would attract more customers. That wasn't really a concern tonight. They weren't there to play the slots – or any other casino games. But Marcie and Mason agreed that they would each find a slot machine somewhere near the tables so they could keep an eye out for any sign of Marshall. They wandered through the casino, getting their bearings.

The gaming tables on the left side of the casino held the attention of a number of well-dressed Asians, but for the most part, attire was very mixed. There was no black dinner suit and waistcoat, buttons on the sleeves and traditional black bow tie. Instead, people at the tables were dressed no differently than those sitting at the slot machines, which meant everything from sweatshirts and blue jeans to sweaters and skirts.

It was now time to split up and begin their detective work. Marcie continued to wander around the casino while Mason went up the long staircase to check out Le Baccara restaurant on the third floor. But instead he found more slot machines, the room for Texas Hold'em that Andrew had been talking about, and a restaurant called Banco Bistro. The halls on the way to the poker room were adorned with soothing murals of cave drawings in earth tones. But no restaurant called Le Baccara. He checked a sign by the elevator which identified everything by floor. Sure enough, there it was: Le Baccara Restaurant, third floor. Mason was baffled, but thought he'd somehow passed it without noticing the entrance. Or maybe Marcie would find the access to it as she walked around downstairs.

Mason glanced at his watch as he descended in the elevator back to the second floor where they had entered the casino. If Andrew's information was accurate, Marshall should be turning up at any minute. He wondered what his reaction would be if he actually saw Marshall and his bodyguard. From what Andrew had said, Mason was pretty confident that the source of the threatening phone calls would be with his boss tonight. His heart was racing as the minutes ticked by.

And then – there he was. Amidst all the hundreds of people walking in and out of the casino and sitting at the machines and tables, Aaron Marshall still stood out on very first glance. He walked ramrod-straight and gave off an aura of self-importance. He was wearing a casual beige jacket with a contrasting brown crew neck sweater, black slacks and expensive loafers. Mason noted that he was one of the better dressed in the building. In perfect lockstep with him to the side was a man that Mason knew from the photo was his bodyguard, Greg Johnson. The Force. Johnson wore a black turtleneck and jeans, and his eyes kept darting from one side of the room to the other, doing his job as the thug that he was. The staff treated them with respect as they made their way to the tables, indicating they'd had previous experience with both Marshall's money and his moods.

Mason felt physically ill at the sight of these two. He felt intense frustration that he couldn't just confront them and get out of them what they knew about his wife. But he was in no position to do that. He had to bide his time.

Marshall's game of choice tonight was roulette. The game Marshall was about to play called for a croupier to spin a wheel one way and a ball the other. The tilted wheel will eventually lose momentum, the ball will fall into one of the colored numbers, and the bettor will either win or lose. Marshall undoubtedly understood gambling and house odds, and he understood money, and knew that every casino is in the business of making lots of it. But he was apparently willing to play, even though there is really no way to win at roulette other than through sheer dumb luck.

Andrew had mentioned that the week before, Aaron Marshall had had a wonderful night of playing blackjack. Staff at the casino also benefited as Marshall doled some of his winnings to the dealer, the drink servers, and of course, to the young man who parked his car.

Tonight Marshall was ready for an evening of fun. He hoped the odds were going to be with him at the table, because the discussion with Johnson was still in the back of his mind. He didn't like the way the search for Sami Seaforth was going, and he certainly didn't like the way his massage parlor profits were shrinking in Montreal with too many new competitors applying for licenses. His session with the mostly cooperative Alexandra had relaxed him somewhat, but tonight he just wanted to enjoy an easy evening at a mindless game to take his mind off everything. The Force was sitting just off to the side, keeping an eye on things.

As he sat there with seven other players at the roulette table, Marshall never realized that there were two other pairs of eyes watching his every move. With Johnson at his side, Marshall felt safe anywhere he went, and the casino was no exception. There was no reason for him to suspect that his moves might be under surveillance by two people he had never met, yet with whom he had a very real connection.

To get a better view, Mason and Marcie had taken up well-placed locations at the banks of slot machines adjacent to the tables. There were gaps between the machines that let them both observe what was going on at the roulette table. Marcie sent a text from her vantage point to Mason. "Did you find the restaurant?" Mason texted back no, it was listed but he couldn't locate it. Marcie's next text was short: "What do we do now?" Mason replied with, "Nothing tonight. Let's follow them when they leave to find out where they go."

Periodically, Mason pressed the button to cause the numbers and sym-

bols to spin on the machine just enough times not to appear obvious. Sometimes he won, but more often he lost. From his location, he was able to
watch Marshall place his bets on the felt table and he could see the croupier
spin the wheel. All the croupiers had some things in common. They all appeared to be pleasant and they all looked very professional, dressed the same
in black shirts and brown patterned vests. To Mason, many of them seemed
to be a little bored, but Marshall appeared to be enjoying himself, which was
all that a casino cared about.

About two hours later, Marshall gave his bucket of tokens to The Force
who was now standing in a line-up in front of the cashier, two people ahead
of Mason. Another gambler walked up behind Mason to cash out, and Marcie
came next. Mason glanced around to confirm Marshall was still there and as
he did so, he noticed that Marcie was holding her bucket with both hands,
obviously supporting some weight. He understood that casinos operate on
the premise that the easier a game is to understand, the lower the chances are
of you winning at it. Yet somehow Marcie had sat there for two solid hours
and come out ahead.

They got their coats and followed a safe distance behind Marshall and
Johnson. He didn't want the parking valet to see them or say anything that
might be overheard by Marshall, so they hurried out facing the other way and
walked quickly to the rental car in the parking lot. It seemed to take forever
for Marshall's car to be brought up from the valet area, and their hearts were
pumping while they sat there with the engine running. Once Johnson put his
foot down on the gas, they pulled out but made sure they stayed far enough
back that they wouldn't be noticed in the rear view mirror. Mason knew The
Force was trained in spotting trouble, so he didn't want to alert him in any
way. At one point, they were separated by a red light, and Mason worried
about what to do if another car turned in front of them and blocked his view
of Marshall's silver Cadillac XTS.

Their route took them across the MacDonald-Cartier Bridge back into
the province of Ontario and past the historic Byward Market, which featured
a colorful conglomeration of retail outlets, dining establishments and side-

walk kiosks. The cars wound their way along the Rideau Canal and eventually to a large two-story brownstone. Mason stayed back far enough so that there was no chance he and Marcie would be noticed.

As The Force drove into the driveway, Mason continued past and circled around the block twice to make sure that this was likely to be the home of Aaron Marshall. The silver Cadillac still sat in the driveway, although both occupants had apparently already gone inside. He and Marcie drove back to the hotel with mixed emotions, and on their way up to their rooms, they stopped at the lobby bar to discuss what to do next. Getting to Aaron Marshall meant getting past Greg Johnson, his bodyguard. It was obviously going to be a challenge, but Mason couldn't think of any other tactic that could work. He wanted to use the same approach that his wife was apparently going to use: to confront Marshall with the information Sami had gathered. If he could do it first, maybe he could save Sami from getting involved. The threat would hopefully be enough to get them to leave his family alone. The smartest and safest idea, Mason decided, was to hold the confrontation at a public place, because to confront him in private with no one around except the ever-present bodyguard, would most likely result in him and Marcie being found at the bottom of the Canal when it was drained in the fall.

After talking it over, they decided that their best option was to attempt to meet Marshall on Saturday night at Le Baccara Restaurant – if they could ever find it.

Baker and Finch were once again brainstorming in the boardroom. Sergeant Juanita Suarez had called Detective Albert Baker and told him she thought that the Seaforths were acting very strangely, that now she had decided they were a pair of philanderers, and that, in her opinion, the only murder about to be committed by them might be of each other. She mentioned Mason Seaforth's suspicions that his wife was having an affair, and added that she wouldn't be surprised if it were Mason himself who was up to no good with his friend, Marcie. She spoke of a rash of robberies that had taken place in her precinct and that her commanding officer was concerned about a gang formation right there in Gulfport, both of which were taking all of her resources.

Baker thanked her for her efforts and said that he and Finch would take over that part of the investigation and get back to her. He thought if Sami really had left town, they should find out where she had gone as soon as possible. He decided that they had enough cause that a judge would sign a court order to let them look into Sami's cell phone records, so he suggested to Finch to get right on it. The more he thought about it, the more he realized that they really didn't know what any of the family had been up to. As Finch was leaving the room, Baker added, "Tom, let's add major credit companies and cell records for the whole family. We never know what might turn up."

DAY 5

Chapter 31

Jennifer was up early Saturday morning, and with little traffic on the road, she made the trip from her dormitory to her parents' home in Gulfport in about four hours. Her route had taken her along the famous Alligator Alley corridor, but the drive was no novelty since she had driven it many times before. At Exit 18, she turned towards 26th Avenue, which would take her into Gulfport. She always felt a sense of warmth coming home. Although she had moved out to go to school, she always felt comforted when she came home. Even though she knew neither of her parents would be there when she arrived, she still felt reassured to be back.

As she drove up to the house, she noticed a blue sedan across the street with two men sitting in the car. They seemed to be looking toward the house. She thought it was probably nothing, but she made a mental note to check later to see if they were still there. She pulled into the driveway beside her mom's Miata, got out of her own car and went to the front door. She put her key in the lock, turned it and opened the door. For just a brief second, she hoped that her mother and father would be there and everything would be as it always was - but when she walked through the door and into the living room, she knew instantly that the house was empty and silent. She heard nothing, no familiar greetings from her parents, no sounds of life or activity anywhere, and she realized that she was completely alone in the house she'd lived in for 18 years.

Jason Sage and his colleague were very surprised to see Jennifer drive up to the house. Sage said, "Huh. Now this is interesting. I think that's the daughter. She's probably not going to like what she sees when she walks in on her father and that black chick going at it hot and heavy." He laughed lasciviously. "Awk-ward!! This is better than watching any soap opera! I'll call the boss and let him know what's going on. Bet he didn't count on this happening ... "

Mason was sitting in the hotel restaurant around noon sipping a coffee and picking at the lunch buffet. His appetite, which had been slowly waning during the past four days, was just about gone altogether. If he couldn't find Sami, he wondered how he would ever eat again. When Marcie sat down, she noticed he looked tired and pale, and his features were drawn. It was clear he had not slept well.

He acknowledged Marcie's "good morning" with a barely perceptible nod. He said quietly, "It was too late when I got in last night to call Jennifer, so I called her this morning instead. I am very upset. She didn't go to her grandparents the way we discussed."

"What do you mean she didn't go? Is she still in Miami?"

"No, she drove up to the house. She said at the last minute, she felt like being at home instead of with her grandparents. I told her to pack her stuff and get out of there immediately."

Marcie exhaled sharply. "Mason, this is awful. She has to get out of there now! Those guys are probably still outside, thinking that you and I are inside together. If Jennifer is there, they're going to expect to see some activity, and they're going to be expecting to see you and me!"

Mason's voice was barely above a whisper. "Jenn said she noticed a blue sedan when she drove up. I told her to just walk out to her car like nothing is wrong and leave. I didn't give her details, I just said she needs to get out of the house and drive straight to her grandparents. Right now, the men will still think you and I are there, so they won't do anything to Jennifer. They can't follow her, because they're under orders to watch us. I told her to call me as soon as she was on the freeway."

Marcie held her breath as she watched Mason distractedly chase some egg around on his plate. "And...?"

Mason looked up and said, "I'm still waiting to hear from her. There's been no call."

Marcie's shoulders sagged. "So what do we do now?"

"I guess we do the only thing we can do. We wait some more."

At that very moment, Greg Johnson was on the phone with Jason Sage, and it was Johnson's turn to express his anger.

"Why didn't you tell me earlier the daughter was there?"

"She just drove up a few minutes ago, man. She hasn't come out."

"Have you seen any sign of life in the house? Are you sure Seaforth and the woman are still in there?"

"We could see through the window they were getting pretty cozy, and we've been sitting here the whole time. Everything's normal at the house. Someone turned the lights on this morning and no one has come or gone other than the daughter. I'm sure they're still there. You know, the neighbors are starting to get nosy. The old guy across the street came over this morning to ask what we were doing. I told him about Seaforth's wife disappearing and that we were undercover cops here watching the place. I told him it's an on-going investigation, and I couldn't say anything more. He seemed to buy it. But if the real cops drive up, we're going to have to split."

Johnson's concern was increasing as he listened to Sage. "Okay, listen, this is going nowhere. I don't know where the woman is and the boss is start-ing to get really antsy. If we don't get a break in this soon, there's no telling what he'll do. If the girl comes out by herself, I want you to grab her. Don't hurt her, but take her somewhere and keep her hidden until you hear from me. Check and make sure Seaforth and the woman are still there - and be sure he sees that you have his daughter. Maybe when we grab the girl, it will encourage them to move a little faster. And if she doesn't come out by herself soon, go and get her. I don't have to tell you this, but make sure no one sees you – maybe show her your gun to keep her from screaming. I'll be busy with the boss for a while, but call me back later when you have the girl. Got that? "

With the affirmative response from the other end of the line, Johnson hung up.

Jennifer was standing alone in the house, staring at her cell phone. She had just hung up from talking to her dad, and she was scared. He sounded very upset that she had gone home instead of to her grandparents, and he had told her under no circumstances to stay there any longer than it took to get her bag and leave. His words had scared the daylights out of her, and now she regretted not doing as he originally suggested. She glanced outside and sure enough, the men in the car were still there, but she averted her gaze quickly and moved toward her car. She didn't want to give them any indication that she had seen them. She didn't see them start to move as she stepped off the doorstep, but she heard the sound of a car door opening and began to move faster. Trying to act as normal as possible, Jennifer got into her car and put the key in the ignition, but it was too late. She sensed, rather than saw, one of the men running toward the driver's side of the car and the other closing in on the passenger side. Their movements were swift, and their techniques echoed their Special Forces training. Both car doors were flung open before she had a chance to hit her automatic lock switch.

As she looked left, she knew someone was getting in on her other side and she flung her right fist out in a futile attempt to stop the intruder. She connected with nothing but air. As the driver's door was opened, she could smell a sweet, pungent odor and felt a wet, cold cloth over her mouth and nose. She resisted the urge to breathe as long as she could, but her assailant was too strong, and she couldn't move the hand that was firmly clamped over her face. She struggled with everything she had, but her arms and legs quickly became weak, then numb and finally completely non-functional. The sound of the birds singing and the wind rustling through the trees faded, and her attempt to look at her assailant through wide, fearful eyes became futile as her vision blurred. Just as he'd been instructed, Jason Sage now had Jennifer Seaforth in his control.

Danny wordlessly exited the car and went to the doorstep of Mason's house to pound on the door. Jason glanced out the car window as he pushed the unconscious Jennifer over to the passenger seat and angled her head up against the seat rest so that it looked like she was sleeping. He fastened the seat belt around the comatose girl and waited for Mason to respond to Danny's repeated knocking. When it became apparent that was not going to happen, Jason could only see Danny's back as the latter fiddled with the lock on the door and let himself in. Danny wasn't gone long and when he re-turned he shrugged to Jason on his way past Jennifer's car and got back in the blue sedan, which he drove away from the curb. Jason started Jennifer's car, backed out of the driveway and fell in behind the blue sedan with Jennifer propped up in the seat beside him.

Only a few minutes had elapsed from the time Jennifer got in her car with the intention of driving to her grandparents to the time Jason drove her away to a completely different destination. Jennifer was unconscious and totally unaware of what was to come.

Mrs. Cassidy, the neighbor next door, quickly closed her drapes, trying to make sense of what she had just seen. She didn't want to be thought of as the nosy neighbor, but what she had seen was extremely disturbing. There had been two men sitting in a car for quite some time, and they appeared to be watching the house where Sami and Mason Seaforth lived. She hadn't seen Mason since he had come over to ask her if she had heard any noise during the night. What was going on next door?

Her arthritis was really acting up today, nearly confining her to her chair, but she really liked the Seaforth family and something seemed very wrong. She and elderly Mr. Davis across the street had been discussing the blue sedan and the two men sitting in it over the phone and wondering if they should notify the police. When Mr. Davis approached them, they told him they were undercover cops, so they had decided it was probably better if they didn't get involved. But after what she had just seen, or at least thought she had seen, she was having second thoughts. It all happened so quickly, and her eyesight wasn't what it used to be. But it sure looked to her as if a young woman – possibly the Seaforths' daughter – had been mugged or grabbed outside their house as she was trying to get into her car. She couldn't be sure what took place in detail, but she had the distinct impression that when the car drove away, one of the two men from the blue car was behind the wheel. Mrs. Cassidy made up her mind. Difficult as it was, she decided to hobble over to the house, knock on the door, and talk to Mason Seaforth himself. And if that didn't work, well, for the first time in her entire life, she was going to dial 911.

Since it was Saturday afternoon, it would take Finch a while to find a judge to sign off on the court order allowing him access to the past phone records, airline boarding manifests and credit card information for the Seaforth family. With the apparent disappearance of Sami Seaforth, and the connections of members of the Seaforth family to the murdered Janet Winters in Minneapolis, as well as to the late James Briscoe in Tampa, there was enough to support getting a court order with no problem. The minute the official document was signed, Finch went into action. He sent a copy of the order to the phone company by email and his questions were answered in a subsequent phone call. He was surprised at the response he got. He contacted the credit card companies in the same way, and the information he received supported what the supervisor at the phone company had told him. A quick check of the airline manifests with the new information re-confirmed his findings.

Finch got up hurriedly from his desk and headed into Baker's office, only to find his colleague on the phone. Baker held up one finger, indicating that Finch should wait until the call was finished. Baker was furiously taking notes as he listened to someone on the other end of the line. A couple of times, Finch saw Baker's eyes widen in surprise, and once he sat upright in his chair and drew his breath in. When Baker hung up, he turned to Finch and said, "That was David Lawrence, that police officer we've been dealing with from Minneapolis. He's been doing some digging of his own, and guess what? It seems that Janet Winters used to go with a guy by the name of Greg Johnson. The guy calls himself "The Force" and while he's never been convicted of anything, he's been suspected of being involved with a bunch of different crimes. He's smooth and he's tough. "

Baker consulted his notes, then looked back at Finch. "Wait, though, it gets better. This Johnson guy works for a guy by the name of Aaron Marshall, who just happens to be *Sami Seaforth's stepfather*. Marshall and Johnson disappeared from the Minneapolis scene shortly after Sami's mother died of mysterious causes. Lawrence told me that Marshall came under a lot of suspicion for having had a hand in her death, but it was never proven and there was no evidence to link him to the death. In fact, there was never enough evidence to even investigate it. Marshall and Johnson dropped out of sight for a while, but apparently they left the country entirely and moved to Canada shortly after Sami's mother's death. Since nothing could be proven, the Minneapolis police force put it in a file and moved on to something else. The police force there lost track of Marshall and Johnson, but now Lawrence is wondering if there might even be some connection between Marshall and Briscoe that would tie everything together. It's a long shot, but he was hoping maybe we could follow that up from our end as well."

Finch nodded. "Well, I just might have even more answers to make this whole thing interesting. What if I told you that when I checked the flight manifests for the day that Sami Seaforth went missing, it turned out that she went straight to the airport and boarded a flight for Ottawa, Canada the day after her anniversary? As if that weren't enough, now her husband and his friend Marcie Kane flew up to Toronto yesterday. So somehow he must have figured this out, though I don't know how. According to the phone records, Mason called his daughter's phone number from Ottawa this morning, so they must have rented a car in Toronto and driven there, but I haven't checked that yet. It will be easy enough to find out. There is nothing in the phone records to indicate any contact between Seaforth and his wife. But why would they both be there and leave the daughter here?"

Baker picked up the phone and dialed Mason's number. He wasn't surprised when there was no answer. He left a short, firm message that Mason should call him back as soon as possible. Then he addressed Finch as if there had been no interruption in the conversation. "That's a good question," Baker said, leaning back in the chair with his hands behind his head. "I think the first thing we should do is talk to the daughter. Maybe she knows what's going on. Then we'll follow up on the rental car agency angle. I wonder if we need to call Canadian Border Services or the Royal Canadian Mounted Police." He really wasn't sure which organization would be in charge. Since it wasn't a case involving immigration at the moment, he suspected that the RCMP would be the first point of contact. All he knew for sure was that things were happening pretty fast, and the last thing they wanted was to find someone else turning up dead.

Finch stood up and prepared to leave Baker's office, but was stopped at the door by an officer assigned to phone answering duties that day. "Sorry to bother you, Detectives," the officer said, "but a call has been transferred to you from Sergeant Suarez in Gulfport. It's an old lady named Mrs. Cassidy and she wants to talk to someone about a possible abduction. She says she's pretty sure she saw two men kidnap a girl who looked a lot like Jennifer Seaforth."

Jennifer could feel a tingling in her leg. As she slowly began to regain her senses, she realized the tingling was being caused by her cell phone vibrating in her pocket where she had left it. She felt nauseous, and she had no idea of where she was, but she could feel the movement of the automobile. *Her* automobile! She could hear voices talking, and finally realized that the driver had the radio turned to an all-news station. Slowly the realization came to her that she had been kidnapped. She didn't move, not wanting her abductor to know she was awake yet. She knew she couldn't answer the phone, but instinctively she covered it with her right hand to silence the noise coming from the vibration.

She could feel the acid from her stomach shoot up into her esophagus. She thought she was going to be sick. Involuntarily, a low moan escaped from her throat as she tried to fight off the effects of the chloroform combined with the movement of the car. She tried to gather her senses enough to look out the window but the moment she did so, she felt the cold, disgusting cloth once again over her nose and mouth. She turned away from the driver who was holding the steering wheel with one hand and the cloth over her face with the other, but she couldn't get far enough away from the offensive fabric to avoid contact. Desperately, she plunged her thumb and forefinger into her jeans pocket to retrieve her phone. Her intent was to press the speed dial number for her dad, but for the second time, she succumbed to the chloroform and everything turned black. As the light faded and her extremities lost their function, the phone slipped out of her fingers and fell down beside the door. As it did so, it slid along on the slippery surface of the floor carpet to a final resting point under the seat.

For the second night in a row, Mason and Marcie arrived at the Casino du Lac-Leamy in Gatineau, Quebec. Mason was now worried sick about his daughter. He had left several messages, but had heard nothing. By now, she should have reached her grandparents, but he didn't want to call them and get them upset. He felt frantic and helpless, and terrified when he thought of the two men sitting outside his house. They would have seen Jennifer. Had they gone to the door to talk to her? Had she tried to leave and they stopped her? *Where was she?* Not knowing anything was the worst, yet there was nothing he could do. If he notified the police at this point, it would tip off Marshall and The Force and whoever else they had working for them. And it could endanger Sami even further, wherever she was.

Mason felt a sense of hopelessness enshroud him. His family – his wife and daughter, the two people he cared most for in the whole world – were now both missing. Instead of getting closer to the truth, he felt he was falling farther behind.

The evening air was cool, mixed with dampness from a steady drizzle that chilled both Florida residents to the bone. Mason and Marcie had spent quite a bit of time during the afternoon discussing how they were going to confront Marshall when the time came, and they had finally decided that the best way would be to do it without Johnson there. Realistically, though, neither one knew how to pull it off. The Force probably never left Marshall's side unless told to, and when he did, someone somewhere usually paid a steep price for his visit. Mason had a copy of Sami's confidential journal documentation describing the conversation she had overheard between Marshall and Johnson after her mother's death, along with the other information. He was carrying the pages in a brown manila envelope tucked away in an executive portfolio.

Mason was glad to see Andrew working valet services again when he drove past the casino entrance. He found a parking spot, and he and Marcie walked slowly towards the building. He had made a reservation for 8:15 at Le Baccara restaurant in order to be there shortly after Marshall and Johnson arrived. They just had to find it. Mason approached Andrew who was chatting casually with one of the other patrons. When he saw Mason, Andrew wandered over.

"How's it going?" Andrew said good-naturedly. "Did you run into Mr. Marshall last night? He must have had a good night. He gave me a really nice tip for parking that big mother of a Cadillac XTS for him. He wasn't in a great mood when he arrived, but he was doing better when he left, that's for sure."

"Well, first things first, Andrew. Where is that restaurant you were telling us that they eat at every Saturday night? I couldn't find it when I walked around on the third floor last night."

Andrew chuckled. "It exists. You just have to go all the way to the back of the casino. There's an elevator. Take that up to the restaurant. You will see signs to point you in the right direction. Or you can take the stairs. It's a bit of a hike, but you'll end up in the same place."

"Sounds like they don't really want people to find it," said Mason with a slightly annoyed tone in his voice. "Well, we'll find it tonight. I made us reservations." Mason took a deep breath and thought, okay, here we go . . . "I was just thinking that it's going to be hard to get Mr. Marshall to look at my proposal with all the casino noise and activity level going on. I wonder if there's a way I could show it to him privately where no one else is around us. His bodyguard is always hanging around, so it's difficult to discuss anything with him in private. It seems like my friend doesn't trust anybody." Mason stopped and Andrew looked at him, waiting to hear what he was going to say. Then came the big question, which Mason tried to deliver almost as an afterthought. "Andrew, do you think it would be possible for you to separate them somehow? Not for long, of course, but it sure would be nice to show Mr. Marshall my proposal without having that bodyguard staring at us."

Andrew shifted uneasily from foot to foot. "Like I said, they have a standing reservation for 8:00 on Saturdays." His eyes darted to the huge illuminated "C" at the beginning of the word "Casino" that spread across the right side of the building, informing anyone who hadn't figured out by now where they were. His eyes drifted back to Mason as he put his hands up in front of himself in a defensive pose. "Boy, I don't know. I've never seen them apart in the whole time I've worked here. And what you're asking is not in my job description, either, sir. I don't want to mess with those two. Rumor around here is that the bodyguard, who calls himself "The Force," by the way, has killed people. In fact, people say the two of them are involved in human trafficking and a bunch of other stuff."

"Well," Mason said as he pulled a $100 American bill out of his pocket. "How would it be if we just tried it the old-fashioned way that you see on TV? What if you were to place a phone call to the reservation desk at the restaurant about 8:25, disguise your voice and tell them to let Mr. Johnson know there's a policeman who would like to see him at the front door. Then hang up. It's as simple as that. He'll never know who called, and you will have $100. "

Andrew was obviously interested in the proposal, or more likely in the money, but he also looked very nervous. Once again, he looked away toward the "Casino" letters as if seeing them for the first time. It was obviously a stall tactic to give him time to think. Finally, the valet turned back to Mason. "All right, since you're waving around a Benjamin now, I'm in. I'll make the phone call, but that's all I'm doing. As soon as I say there is a policeman waiting for him, I'm hanging up like you said. And if anyone overhears me when I pick up the phone, I won't make the call. I'm not going to jeopardize my job for this, no matter how much money you're offering. Whatever happens after that is not my responsibility. I'm done. I'll deny ever having this conversation with you. Mr. Marshall is one of the best tippers of anyone who comes here, but he also has a mean temper and I don't know what would happen if he found out that I'd made the call." As he reached out his hand and took the $100 bill from Mason, Andrew added, "I hope he really likes your proposal, because I've never seen him without his bodyguard, and if anything goes wrong, you could regret separating them."

Mason added a twenty and said, "Andrew, my friend and I don't exist. You and I never had this conversation. No one will ever know. Just be sure to place the call right at 8:25. That's important." Andrew nodded, and turned to go grab a set of car keys for a man exiting the casino. Mason hoped he was not putting this nice young man's life in danger as he and Marcie continued through the doors. But he also thought silently to himself that with any luck, Andrew's volatile tip machine customer was about to get put out of business

permanently by the end of the night. And as far as he was concerned, that would be the best thing that would ever happen at this casino.

Jason Sage drove Jennifer's car into a parking lot behind one of the many closed businesses hit hard by the recession. The faded sign out front identified the building as a discount golf store, but not even the tourists had been able to keep this one open. Grass had started to overtake the parking lot, as the owners had apparently simply walked away without any hope of recovering their investment. For them, it seemed, bankruptcy was their best hope of starting over.

Jason was followed closely by Danny in the blue sedan. Danny pulled up beside Jennifer's car, where they were both out of sight from prying eyes due to a tall, battered fence separating the store from residential houses. Any gaps in the fence had long since been filled in by the overgrowth of vegetation. Jennifer was still passed out from the second application of chloroform. Danny said, "How much did you give her? I thought she would be awake by now."

"I didn't give her much the first time. I'm always worried about this stuff. Too much can kill a person, and I don't think the boss would be happy if all of a sudden, she ended up dead. You and I would be treated to a necktie someday and it wouldn't go well with a suit, if you know what I mean. She started to wake up, so I gave her a little more. She'll be fine, although I'll bet she has a huge headache."

Jason grabbed under her arms and Danny took her feet, and they moved Jennifer to the back seat of the blue sedan. Jason looked in her purse, grunted and then pulled her jean pockets inside out, not being overly careful where he placed his hands. "Huh, I would have thought she'd have a cell phone. She must have left it behind. Oh well, it won't do her much good there. Let's get her to your house and wait for The Force to call."

It was a 10-minute drive to a community of row houses. Making as little noise as possible, the two of them carried the still-unconscious Jennifer into the one owned by Danny and took her upstairs where they laid her down on a bed. Even if the neighbors were watching, it would not be the first time any of them had seen Jason and Danny helping a drunken female into the house.

Mason and Marcie finally found the elevator to Le Baccara at the back of the casino. When they got off the elevator, they were greeted by a narrow hallway leading past a showcase of expensive wines and an impressive display of awards, indicating the restaurant had one of the world's most impressive wine lists. A large leather armchair sat below the awards, and the entrance to the restaurant had a large drapery, preventing those in the hallway waiting to be seated from staring at those who were enjoying their meals. The restaurant had two distinct rooms. Mason had requested and been granted a romantic seat for two by the expansive floor to ceiling windows overlooking the lake. They were seated in the restaurant at precisely 8:15 in the first dining area. Marshall and Johnson must be in the second dining room, which offered more privacy. He looked around and noticed that chefs were preparing the meals in full view of the patrons in the first dining room where they sat.

Mason wanted to relax, but the business at hand had his stomach churning, and he was also worried sick about his daughter. It had been hours since they had talked, and he had warned her to get out of the house as fast as she could. He was beginning to fear that Sage and his accomplice had done something to Jennifer. Mason grabbed his cell phone and dialed Jennifer's number again. He listened to the phone ring and ring, but there was still no answer. Mason left another message in a voice that he knew was shakier than it should be. "Jennifer, please, sweetheart, I'm worried sick about you. Please call me immediately. What's happened? Where are you?" Marcie watched him, but didn't say anything. When the waiter arrived at their table, they each ordered a glass of Merlot.

The restaurant had the dark ambience of a high-end establishment that created a romantic mood for its patrons. That played perfectly in Mason and

Marcie's favor. They stared out at the lake and the lights on the other side. Or so it appeared. The darkness of the room combined with the blackness outside gave them a perfect reflection in the window of what was going on in the inside of the room. And that's what they were focused on. They were waiting for Andrew to do his job and make the phone call.

Marshall and Johnson had arrived at the restaurant at precisely 8 p.m. as predicted by Andrew, and were looking over the menu. The menu had its usual assortment of regular appetizers, entrees, salads and soups, but each night, the chef featured several unique specials du jour, which Marshall always wanted to hear about in detail. Johnson didn't really enjoy eating meals with Marshall, but it was part of his job. He had to admit the food was the best he had ever tasted – and he never had to pay. Marshall ordered the seared beef tenderloin with mushrooms, marbled spinach and potato fried in duck fat. Johnson ordered the duck supreme roasted skin-on with lavender honey glaze. Rather than choose a bottle of wine from the cooler, Marshall chose a glass of Cabernet Sauvignon, while Johnson selected a Pinot Noir.

Just as their wine was being delivered, Johnson's cell played its familiar tune. Marshall allowed Johnson to take phone calls until the meal was served, after which his phone had to be shut off. Johnson quietly berated the caller for interrupting his dinner, but then listened attentively as the person on the other end spoke. Johnson smiled a little at first, but soon a frown came over his face. He became increasingly agitated as the conversation continued, until finally he abruptly disconnected. Marshall stared at him inquisitively, waiting for an explanation. Dreading what he was about to have to tell his boss, Johnson relayed the basics of the call. He explained that he just received confirmation that Jennifer was now drugged and in the hands of Jason and Danny in St. Petersburg. And then, holding his breath, Johnson told Marshall that Seaforth and Marcie were no longer at the house. They, like Sami, had vanished into thin air.

Johnson watched as Marshall's anger manifested itself in the form of the bright crimson color that came over his face. He leaned forward and hissed at Johnson, "Call Seaforth right after dinner and tell him we have his daughter. I'm getting sick of these people. And YOU are failing miserably at your job. You better start to make this right, Greg." He sat back, straightening the lapels on his jacket and trying to compose himself. Then, incredible as it seemed to Johnson, with his lips caught between a smile and a grimace, the man had the audacity to demonstrate that all was well to anyone who might have caught any of the conversation by raising his glass in a toast.

They didn't get a chance to clink glasses as a waitress approached the table. This was an unexpected intrusion and one that Marshall didn't appreciate. First Johnson's phone call and now this! He had made it clear to restaurant management that once he had ordered their wine, they were not to be bothered by the normally discreet staff until the food was delivered. He didn't want anyone overhearing any of his conversations, so he ensured staff was tipped well to stay away and approach only when needed.

She was not a new waitress. Her name was Cheryl, and she knew the rules. She approached timidly and apologised profusely for the interruption. She said, "I'm sorry, I just received a call from the front desk of the casino. They said there is a policeman who urgently wants to see Mr. Johnson downstairs."

Johnson's radar antennae immediately went up, but he said, "I'm going to let him wait. It can't be anything important." Marshall disagreed. "I think you need to find out what this is about. Let's not raise any unnecessary suspicions. I'll tell them to hold our meals until you return."

At 8:27, Johnson emerged from the second dining room. As he walked purposefully into the first dining room, Mason saw him do a sweep of the restaurant with his eyes, but Mason knew that the thug wouldn't expect to see them here, and in the darkness he wasn't too concerned. He and Marcie continued pretending to stare out the window, both turned a little more than

they would normally be, so their faces were somewhat obscured. But they could clearly see the reflection of Johnson striding to the door. To the casual observer, they were lovers enjoying each other's company and intent on drinking in all the sights they could. And if they were recognized, Mason would just have to confront Marshall earlier than expected. He knew they were safe in a crowd.

Mason glanced over at the doorway to the second dining room where he knew Marshall was seated, and he felt tremendous distaste for the men who had put his family in this situation. He couldn't imagine hating anyone more than he hated Aaron Marshall and Greg Johnson right now, and he knew that somehow, some way, this was going to come to a climax tonight. Mason knew this was it. Andrew had done his job, and the wheels were in motion. He reached for the portfolio and took out the manila envelope with all of Sami's documentation. He looked at Marcie and said, "This is it, Marcie. It's time to move. You stay here. If anything goes wrong, get out as quickly as possible. Call the police and explain everything. I don't think you'll need to do that, but just in case."

But just as Mason started to stand up, envelope in hand, he noticed a woman striding through the doorway into the dining room. She wore blue jeans and a tan jacket over a light blue sweater. She had glasses with large frames that gave her a serious, professional look but it was offset by a base-ball hat on top of a mane of blonde hair. In her hand, she carried a brown manila envelope identical to the one that Mason was holding, and she was completely focused on the door leading into the second dining room . . . the intimate, elegant room where Marshall now sat, alone and unaccompanied.

Mason's heart leaped into his throat. He didn't recognize the blonde hair and glasses, and the baseball cap was completely unfamiliar, but the stride, upright posture and full lips were unmistakable. There was no question in Mason's mind.

They had found Sami.

Chapter 32

Mason slumped back in his seat, and almost involuntarily reached out and squeezed Marcie's hand hard. The strength with which he did it startled Marcie, and she looked sharply at him. As she did so, she saw Mason's eyes dart quickly to the right and back to her twice. It was obviously a signal, but it took Marcie a few seconds longer to understand where he wanted her to look and why. As she turned her head, she froze and her mouth dropped open. Without thinking, she rose quickly from her seat, but Mason grabbed her arm and motioned for her to sit down. Without saying a word, he nodded to a point about 15 feet away, and there was Greg Johnson, rapidly closing in on Sami. His strides were twice as long as Sami's, and he caught up with her as she reached the entrance to the second dining area. Mason and Marcie watched as he showed why he'd earned the nickname The Force. He grabbed Sami's arm roughly and spun her around to face him. He pulled her close with a leering expression, almost as if they were lovers in the midst of a nasty spat. Their faces were only inches apart as Johnson leaned into Sami and in almost the same motion, reached down and suddenly seized the manila envelope from out of her hand. It all happened so quickly that nobody else in the room seemed aware of what was happening. They were all eating and chatting with their dinner companions, oblivious to the drama just a few feet away.

Mason and Marcie sat in shock, as if watching a movie with no sound. They could not understand what was being said across the room, but it was obviously not good. From where he was seated, Mason wasn't able to see Sami's face, but he could see The Force's and the man was looking at his wife through narrowed eyes and an expression bordering on repressed rage. Mason could barely breathe. He debated what to do. He had never counted on Sami turning up just as he and Marcie were ready to confront Marshall and Johnson with the evidence. But he realized that Sami's resolve in heading straight for the second dining room indicated that she had been scoping out Marshall's habits just as he and Marcie had. He knew Marcie couldn't see Sami's face, either, but her expression showed that she was ready to stand up and jump in. It was tempting, but as much as he wanted to leap up and confront Johnson, he felt it would be a mistake with possible serious repercussions. What should he do? His mind spun furiously like one of the casino's slot machines. And then, suddenly, without warning, his mind was made up for him. A few seconds after Johnson sharply elbowed Sami forward into the adjacent dining room, Mason felt a vibration from his cell phone. Mason reached down into his pocket, picked up the phone, and looked at the screen. He was horrified to see that it was a number he had seen before, and he instantly knew it was coming from the next room. *Johnson was calling him!*

When he answered, Johnson said, "Hello, Seaforth. Surprise. We've got your wife *and* your daughter now. If you want to see them alive again, I strongly advise you to hand over all of the information Janet Winters sent your wife the last time they spoke. I believe you've already met my colleague in Florida, Jason Sage. You know who I'm talking about – he's been watching your house for the past three days. I'll give you his phone number, so you can make the arrangements. Do it quickly. My boss and I don't have a lot of patience, so get on it. If you go to the authorities, you will regret it in ways you can't even imagine. We will always know where your daughter is and your wife, too. If we decide to let you see them again, just remember we will always be able to get to them if you decide to go to the police. You get the picture. By the way, Seaforth, you are already testing my patience. I know you're not in the house. Where are you?"

Mason swallowed hard. He felt damp and numb. The news that they had his daughter paralyzed him. It was like the floor opened up, and he had plunged through. There was nothing to grab onto. He was stunned into silence, but terrified that at any minute, Johnson or Marshall might decide to walk back into the first dining room. The sight of a man seated with an African American woman and talking surreptitiously on a cell phone while sweating profusely would be more than enough to draw Johnson's attention. Johnson broke in on his thought process, "Seaforth, you're not answering my question."

"I don't know how you got my wife and daughter, but there is no need to hurt them. They haven't done anything to you, and neither have I. I haven't gone to the police. I don't know what kind of information you're talking about. My wife never mentioned anything about any Janet Winters sending her information. I don't think she and Janet were still in touch with each other. But either way, that's no reason to kidnap them."

At the sound of the word "kidnap," there was a muffled sound and Johnson said in a low, threatening voice, "If you know what's good for you and your family, Seaforth, you'll do what I've told you to do. But you'd better not waste any time. My colleague will track you down, so I also suggest you get back to the house." There was a click and then silence. The Force had hung up, leaving Mason ashen and badly shaken.

Marcie had been trying to piece together the conversation. "What did he say?"

His voice barely above a croak and averting his head in case Marshall or Johnson suddenly materialized from the next room, Mason replied, "He said they have Jennifer. They must have grabbed her when I told her to get out of the house. He said the only way I can protect Sami and Jennifer is to give up the information Janet sent Sami. He obviously doesn't know about all the other stuff she has documented. He knows we have left the house, but I hope he still thinks we're in Florida."

Marcie took a deep breath. "Oh my God, Mason, what are we going to do?"

Mason simply stared straight ahead and said nothing. And that's what Marcie saw when she looked into his eyes. Nothing. It was as if the light behind them had been extinguished. The familiar accountant and husband of her best friend had been replaced by this shell of a man she didn't even know. She sat there, waiting and watching helplessly. She felt so sad.

But then there was a transformation before her eyes. Mason's facial muscles tightened. She could almost count every muscle in his thin face as they tightened, forcing his eyebrows together. His lips clasped tight. He was gathering bunches of the tablecloth in each hand. He swung his dead eyes back to Marcie's, and it appeared that in that instant, he stopped breathing. It looked like it took considerable effort as his lips barely parted and he said through gritted teeth, "The time for doing something in public is over. My family and I will never be safe if we don't settle this thing right now. Thank you for bringing the guns. This ends tonight."

Chapter 33

Mason threw some bills on the table to cover their wine and headed for the door of the restaurant. Their startled waitress could only stare as he rose from the table and hurried through the door with Marcie right behind him. They ran for the stairwell, and as they did so, Mason saw a bench around the corner in the hall away from the sightlines of the elevator or the entrance to the restaurant. He sensed that Sami had been sitting there the whole time, that they had been only feet away from each other, neither knowing that the other was there. Or she could have simply been hiding in the stairwell. Either way, they had practically been within touching distance of each other. Maybe, he thought, if I had seen her, everything would be different now. Still, The Force's two henchmen apparently had his daughter in Florida, and that had to be dealt with quickly.

Marcie and Mason raced down the stairs, knowing they had to get out of the casino before Marshall, Johnson and Sami exited the elevator. They walked as fast as they could through the left side of the casino, trying not to draw attention. They grabbed their coats at the checkout and headed straight for the rental car. They were completely oblivious to the weather, but the drizzle had stopped, the sky had cleared and the moon, which was nearly full, was illuminating the night. The clear sky only seemed to enhance the sharp chill in the Canadian air.

Andrew had waved as they went by, but they paid no heed. Mason was unseeing as he plowed ahead with Marcie in tow. As soon as they got in the car, Mason asked Marcie to check the guns and make sure they were ready to be used. He took the Glock out of Marcie's hand and placed it on the seat between him and the center console. Marcie tucked her Smith & Wesson in the waistband at the back of her jeans. Then Mason decided that it was time to let the police in on what he knew. He picked up his cell phone and dialed Albert Baker. Baker picked up on the second ring.

"Mason, for God's sakes, where are you? We've been trying to find you."

"I'm sure you have, Detective. Don't talk, just listen." The words came out in a rush. "I don't have time for the details now, but listen closely. My daughter Jennifer has been kidnapped from our house in Gulfport. The guys that have her are Jason Sage and Danny somebody. I don't know his last name and I don't know where they've taken her, but you have to find her, Detective. They will kill her if you don't. My friend Marcie Kane and I flew to Canada yesterday and drove from Toronto to Ottawa. I had good reason to suspect my wife might be here in Ottawa, and I was right, only she's in terrible danger. Sami is being held here by two guys by the names of Aaron Marshall and Greg Johnson. Johnson calls himself The Force. Marshall is Sami's stepfather, and she thinks he was responsible for her mother's death. I have information that should help put them both away forever. Tell Suarez the password for Sami's computer is Miata2011. Tell her to have her technicians dig out a file I deleted yesterday. It's all there. Marshall and Johnson have threatened to kill Sami, but I know where they are. I'm following them right now. I will call you back when I know where they're going. Baker, you've got to find my daughter or something awful is going to happen to her."

Baker said calmly, "We know a lot about what's going on, Mason. We know that your daughter has been taken, because your neighbor Mrs. Cassidy called the police about two strange men in a blue car. She saw them kidnap your daughter when she was trying to leave your house and we're triangulating your daughter's phone so we can track her. We also know about Marshall and Johnson. We have contacted the Royal Canadian Mounted Police and Border Services there in Canada. Let us take over, Mason. I don't know what you mean by saying you are going after them, but you aren't equipped to deal with those two. We can take this from here. Where are you?"

Just then Mason could see through the clear glass front doors of the casino that Marshall, Johnson and Sami were gathering their coats at the coat check. He yelled into the phone, "I have to go. *Just find my daughter.* Please!!! *Hurry!*"

With that, Mason pressed the button that ended the conversation, and he and Marcie slumped down in the front seat of their rental car to continue their vigil.

Baker slammed the phone down on the desk in frustration. He sat back and sighed. The detective knew they had been doing the best they could do with the little information they had. Their job was to track every lead and often, cases like this ended up being domestic squabbles or marital issues, so naturally at first, the focus was always on the spouse. But now it was obvious that this situation wasn't faked. There really were lives in danger, and questions that hadn't been answered, and now it seemed kidnapping had been added to the list.

Even more, Baker thought, leaning back in his chair, was the state of mind of the man he had just talked to. That was not the mild-mannered Mason Seaforth they thought they were dealing with. The experience he was undergoing obviously had changed him, and things like that get people killed. He hadn't been completely honest with Seaforth. They had already determined Jennifer's cell phone wireless provider. Thankfully, Jennifer had the latest iPhone, which meant that it used at least 12 satellites in low-earth orbit rather than three towers to identify its location. Had the old tower method been used, they could have located her phone, but only to within a few hundred feet, which means a more time-consuming search process. Since Jennifer's phone was still on, signals were constantly being streamed back to the wireless provider who, in turn, was able to pinpoint its precise location to Baker's team.

Baker thought it odd that the phone was still on. He would have expected Jennifer's captors to have confiscated and destroyed it. Or maybe they had just left it somewhere. He would soon know. The location had been determined and the team dispatched to find Jennifer's phone and hopefully, although he would be surprised, the young girl safe and sound along with it.

Just then his phone rang. Baker picked it up and listened. The field officers were on the scene already. They had surrounded the car and moved in with guns drawn. But the car was empty. There was no sign of Jennifer or her captors. Worse still, the phone had been found under the seat. *Just what I was afraid of,* Baker thought. He reached for another antacid.

Mason thought about what Sami must be feeling, but it was too frightening. Instead, he turned to Marcie and said, "Marcie, I want you to get out of the car and go somewhere safe for the time being. There's no reason for you to stay here now." Even in the shadows, he could see by her face that she was taking his statement as he'd expected. She started to interrupt him in protest, but he continued. "Just hear me out. I don't know what's going to happen tonight, but I've got to do everything I can to protect Sami and get her away. I don't want to put you at any more risk than I already have. You're a true friend, and I wouldn't have been able to crack the password without you. Your support and strength have meant the world to me. I'm so glad you thought of the guns. If it weren't for you taking me to Leroy, I wouldn't even know how to carry a gun, let alone fire one. But this situation has gotten too far out of hand. I want you to leave now before it's too late. I wouldn't be able to forgive myself if something happened to you. Please, Marcie, get out of the car *now.*"

Mason was staring at the casino doors as he enunciated the last word. He didn't know if he really wanted to proceed without Marcie. He was trying to remain tough and project a strong, confident image to the woman sitting next to him, although nothing felt farther from the truth. He suspected, frankly, that Marcie was actually more prepared for difficulties than he was because until now, his life had been relatively drama-free. But he couldn't put this lovely woman in danger any more than he wanted Sami and Jennifer to be in danger. He sat waiting for the full brunt of Marcie's Category 5 wrath to descend on him – but it didn't come.

Marcie was amazed at how calm Mason had become. Gone was the trembling she had noticed at the beginning of this ordeal. His hands were still as they rested on the steering wheel, and his leg was not pumping up and down from anxiety. She put her hand on his arm. "Thank you for your concern, Mason. I appreciate it, I really do. I have really come to learn who you are through this, and I know what your family means to you. They mean a lot to me, too. But you might as well save your breath. I'm going to be there when these guys go down. Besides that, I've seen you shoot! Don't think for a minute that I'm not staying."

At that very moment, Mason squinted and his jaw set. Marshall had come out the door of the casino and was talking with Andrew. Mason tensed up. Was there a chance that they might be discussing him? What if Andrew asked whether his old friend had happened to catch up with him while they were in the casino? That would be enough to completely change everything. But everything looked normal, and neither man was looking around. Mason cast a quick glance sideways and smiled slightly. He put his hand on Marcie's and simply said, "Thank you." He knew he stood a better chance with Marcie at his side. And fortunately, as far as he could tell, they still had the crucial element of surprise. Neither Marshall nor The Force seemed to realize that they were being watched – or that they were about to be followed.

Two minutes later, Andrew drove the silver Cadillac up to the front of the casino and Johnson and Sami joined Marshall on the steps. Johnson had his hand firmly on Sami's arm, but from a distance, they appeared to be a normal couple about ready to leave for the night. It was only by looking closely at Sami's face that anyone would be able to tell she was in distress. Marshall uncharacteristically got in the driver's seat, and Johnson shoved Sami into the back seat where he joined her. From his parked location, Mason could see that Andrew displayed no emotion whatsoever, even if he thought something looked a little strange. Andrew had undoubtedly seen many strange, curious or suspect things in his line of work at the casino, but he knew enough to remain discreet. The Cadillac drove off into the night.

Inside the Cadillac Johnson was looking at the information Sami had in the manila envelope. He was unpleasantly surprised at the level of detail and realized that, in the hands of the police, the notes would cast enough suspicion to cause an investigation. Especially troubling was the part describing Sami's speculation about her mother's death and the conversation she thought she'd overheard about possible drugs administered to her mother. As he flipped the pages, he said offhandedly to Sami, "I can't believe you'd think I would fall for that stupid television trick of having someone call me at the casino with an urgent message. As soon as I got that message, I knew something was up. It's always a pleasure dealing with amateurs. It makes life so easy."

Sami was terrified, but she tried not to let on. "I don't know what phone call you're talking about. I didn't tell anyone to make any phone calls. No one even knows I'm here."

From the front seat, Marshall, who had remained quiet until now, said, "Why *are* you here, Samantha? What was so important after all these years that you just couldn't let things go?"

Sami's voice rose, partly out of fear and partly out of anger. "*Because I know what you did to my mother!* I wasn't sure I heard you correctly at the time. I couldn't believe what I was hearing. Then James Briscoe came into my office. I saw your name in a document he had, and then there was a reference to tax fraud. Then all of a sudden he and his wife were murdered. It was too much of a coincidence. Who knows how many other people you've hurt? But I was still going to let it go. Then the threatening phone calls started from Greg. You obviously thought I knew too much. Why couldn't you just leave us alone? I decided a long time ago to document everything, and I added to it when everything resurfaced. That's obviously not the only copy you have there. If you leave my family and me alone, I won't do anything with this. If you don't, I have left word that it is to be released to the authorities. It may have already been given to the police."

Marshall listened and Johnson merely laughed, although he was subconsciously troubled by Sami's claim not to have to have ordered the phone call. He chose to believe she was lying. "Your husband doesn't seem to know about your notes, but he's looking for them and when he finds them, he has been instructed to give them to my colleague in Florida or he and your daughter will die. We have your daughter now too. You will disappear, and so will any threat to us."

Sami's resolve was fading. Now they had Jennifer!? She thought they'd be concerned about what she knew, but her news didn't appear to be having any effect at all. Had she miscalculated? Had she played this all wrong and put her family in even more danger by trying to do everything herself? She was only trying to protect them. She could feel tears welling up in her eyes, but she played another card. She was nearing hysterics, and she was shouting, "There are other people who know about my mother's death. It's just a matter of time. You can't stop all of us."

Johnson laughed even harder. "If you're talking about Janet Winters, you can forget it. Your friend met a most unfortunate and untimely death recently. It was too bad. I liked her, as you probably remember But, you know, loose ends…"

Sami's heart sank in her chest. Her blood ran cold. She laid her head against the car window, shaking and pale. What on earth had she been thinking, coming here by herself without any protection, without a single alternate plan in her pocket? Why did she ever think she could reason with them? She understood now with a sickening reality that she had badly miscalculated. How much better it would have been to confide in Mason about her suspicions so they could go to the police together and let them handle things. If Marshall and Johnson could be linked to the crimes, she and her family would have been free. Maybe somehow her family could have been put in a witness relocation program or something. But now look at the mess she had created. And the thing that hurt the most was not being able to tell Mason and Jennifer how much she loved them.

She felt hot tears come to her eyes as she thought of her sweet Mason and innocent Jennifer and how she had brought them into this, completely unsuspecting. Her vision blurred as the tears streamed down her face. A deepening feeling of dread descended on her like a shroud. She looked out the window in despair. And then, as she ran her hand across her eyes to dry the tears, Sami Seaforth resolved that she was not going down without a fight.

Chapter 34

Mason pulled out of the parking spot after allowing a respectable amount of time to pass. He didn't want to follow too close for fear of Johnson realizing they were there, unlikely as that was. He really needed to maintain the element of surprise. As they drove, he was pretty sure the destination was Marshall's house. The small convoy retraced the route over the bridge separating Ottawa and Gatineau and once again past the Byward Market, along Queen Elizabeth Drive and finally, to Marshall's home.

Mason drove past, only to see the silver Cadillac pulling into a garage. He said to Marcie, "This is it. This is where it all ends. Let's find a parking spot." He could feel tension mixed with anxiety in his stomach as he drove around the block to park. He picked up his gun as they got out of the car. The Glock felt uncomfortable down by his leg. Marcie had her Smith & Wesson in her hand. They rounded the corner and headed for the house. But just as they did, the garage door rose and the Cadillac quickly backed out. Mason stopped Marcie and pushed her down behind the shrubbery decorating the roadside. He hoped they were invisible in the shadows.

Mason could see that The Force was driving, and he appeared to be the only one in the car. Several things occurred to him. The first was that they had already killed Sami, but he quickly shoved the thought out of his head. He didn't think they would do it here at Marshall's house. Marshall was not the one to deal with Sami. That's what he had Greg Johnson for. Mason didn't think they would have time to subdue Sami and lock her up in the short time that had gone by after they got to the house. There left only one conclusion. He felt in his gut that he was right. It was like his wife was telling him how to help save her. But if it turned out he was wrong, it would be the worst mistake he had ever made in his life. He needed to make a decision, and he had to make it now.

As the car shot into reverse, Mason and Marcie were silently crouched by the shrubs. He thought he could hear a muffled thump and what sounded like the distant sound of an anguished female voice. It wasn't coming from the house. It was coming from the back of the car. Or was it his imagination? Was it a sound he wanted to hear to help him know where Sami was? Or was it simply the wind soughing through the trees? More than anything, Mason wanted to believe his wife was trying to let him know where she was, although she couldn't possibly know he was there.

The car continued on its path in reverse, thumping on the uneven pavement where the driveway met the road, stopped, jerked forward and peeled away, leaving a trail of smoke from the tires. Mason quickly got up and said, "We have to go, Marcie."

Marcie obviously hadn't heard the same sounds from the Cadillac as Mason. "Where are we going? It's just Johnson in the car. Sami must be in the house."

"No, I think she's in the car. She's either down on the back seat where we can't see her or she's in the trunk. I think I might have heard her in the trunk, but I can't be sure."

As they ran towards their car, Marcie thought about arguing. Did it really make sense that they wouldn't leave her in the house? She didn't want to second guess Mason because she knew he was going through hell right now, and she also knew it would be even worse for him if he was wrong. So she went along. They reached the car without incident and drove off to continue the chase of the silver Cadillac.

The Cadillac drove along Hunt Club Road before turning south past a large church that loomed up out of the darkness on their immediate right. The significance of the church was lost on Mason as he didn't realize he was saying a silent prayer, or at least hoping that he had made the right decision by following Johnson. He desperately hoped that the sound he had heard was Sami, and that she was all right. He was scared to death that the police in Florida wouldn't find Jennifer in time, but there was nothing he could do about it. He had to rely on Baker and Finch and their team. The weight was almost too much to bear. He felt like pulling over, shutting off the car and giving up but he knew he couldn't. His family was relying on him, and he was going to see this through.

Mason asked Marcie to call Baker and find out what the status was with Jennifer. She was also to tell Baker where Marshall lived. He said to also mention that Marshall was armed and dangerous, and that he most likely had a hostage. Mason was covering all bases in case Sami was still there. He had no clue that the Romanian girl, Alexandra, was being held captive at the house.

Marcie connected with Baker and asked about Jennifer. Baker brought Marcie up to date on most of what he knew so far, which wasn't much more than they already knew. Then Baker asked, "Where are you now?" Marcie glanced at the GPS map on the dashboard and said to Baker, "We're following Marshall's silver Cadillac on Prince of Wales Drive and we just passed some huge church. Greg Johnson is driving the car, and we think he has Sami." Baker once again asked them to stand down and let the police take over, and when she hung up, he was blustering about her and Mason being accessories after the fact and conspiring to hinder an ongoing investigation, among other things. When Mason asked what Baker had said, Marcie told him that they had not yet found Jennifer, but they were pursuing leads. She explained that the lead with Jennifer's phone had evaporated, but Baker had offered reassurances that everything would be all right. When Mason pressed Marcie on what Baker was saying at the end of the conversation, she replied that he had wished them both a "nice evening."

He had no clue where they were going, so Mason attempted to stay far enough back from the Cadillac that Johnson wouldn't notice he was being followed. Fortunately, traffic was light enough that he could keep the car ahead of him in sight, but he knew it also made them more obvious to a man with the trained eyes of Greg Johnson as they had made each turn in lockstep with the Cadillac.

The speed limit past the church and through the community was 50 km an hour. Mason wasn't familiar with the metric system and had no idea how fast 50 km per hour was, but he kept the speedometer at 50, anyway. Johnson seemed to pay no heed to the posted limit, as he blasted through the area. It put a good half a mile between the two cars, but Mason didn't want to be stopped by the police while Johnson pulled away. He thought that if a policeman stopped Johnson, it would probably be the last stop the unsuspecting cop would ever make. For about 15 minutes, Johnson had been driving south, past a mix of million dollar homes on the left and middle class residences on the right that ended abruptly as they suddenly entered a rural area. The disparity in the speeds of the two cars had opened an even greater gap, but Mason thought that was still okay because he could still see the taillights of the Cadillac ahead. It was a costly decision. The Cadillac went over a rise, but when Mason and Marcie reached it, there was no sight of the silver car. It had simply vanished.

"Shit," Mason exclaimed as he thumped the steering wheel in frustration.

They both strained their eyes to try to find the missing car. There were more rises in the road, so Mason sped up to see if the Cadillac had pulled that much further ahead. "He must have pulled off the highway somewhere. I'm going to turn around." He pulled over to the shoulder and did a quick U-turn on the highway. Marcie wasn't even sure he checked the road as a car roared by blowing its horn, but Mason simply straightened the car out and slowly went north again. They realized they had two choices. Side roads went east and west within a few hundred feet of each other. Mason knew that the wrong decision could be critical and cost Sami her life, assuming he had made the right decision in the first place.

He didn't know why but he ignored the first turn to the right and went to the second, which turned left. After a five-minute drive, two farms became visible in the moonlight on either side of the road. Since Johnson's car disappeared so quickly, Mason wondered if he might be at one of these farmyards.

The one on the right had lights blazing in the barn. Too obvious - probably just doing chores, Mason thought, which meant that his target was probably at the one on the left. Mason took a deep breath and once again went with his gut. He felt that he had done more gambling in the last half hour than he had done at the casino, with far higher stakes. He just hoped he was right. He didn't want to consider the consequences if he was wrong.

He drove about a quarter of a mile down the road and pulled onto the shoulder with the car leaning severely sideways towards the ditch on the passenger side. Marcie virtually tumbled out of the car and Mason had to force his door open on the high side, but he thought it would be better if they approached the farmyard on foot. Marcie came up out of the ditch, and Mason told her not to follow too closely. The farmyard they were approaching appeared to be in total darkness, and Marcie stayed a few feet behind Mason.

Mason thought of calling Baker again, but what would he tell him? He had no idea where they were, and he was terrified that every minute they delayed to wait for the police could cost Sami her life. He was certain there was only one reason The Force would have dragged Sami out here alone: to kill her. Mason knew the police would find his rental car parked on the road soon enough. And he had to act.

They couldn't get a clear view of the yard as they came around a clump of high trees that obscured their sightlines. Both held their guns down in front of them. However, once they came out in the clearing they could see an old farm house, an equally-old dilapidated barn, and what appeared to be some kind of very large shed. Mason could barely make out the back end of the Cadillac parked in a space that had obviously been cleared for it between the shed and the clump of trees. A dim light shone from the partially-opened trunk lid of the Cadillac, further convincing Mason that his fear about Johnson's motive for coming out here so late at night were true. Mason motioned for Marcie to stay back by the trees as he crept forward to the front of the shed, relying on the shadows to his advantage. There were two doors: one was a large closed door as tall as it was wide, big enough to allow enormous farm machinery through. The other was a normal door that was slightly ajar on its hinges, which would allow people to enter the shed. Suddenly, without warning, Mason felt the hard, cold end of a gun barrel pressed against the back of his head.

"Ah, you must be Mason Seaforth." The Force said it without any emotion. "I've halfway been expecting you. Drop the gun. Though you're probably just as likely to shoot yourself as me. Have you ever shot a gun before, Seaforth?"

Mason dropped the gun on the ground. He decided to play along. "No, I've never shot a gun before, but I'll do whatever it takes to save my wife. Where is she? Where's Sami? I know she's here."

The Force ignored the questions and turned Mason around to face him. "I'm the one giving the orders here, Seaforth. You aren't nearly as smart as you think you are. When I got that phone call at the casino telling me someone had an urgent message for me, I knew something was wrong. That's an amateur trick. Then when your wife told me she didn't arrange for the message, it confirmed my suspicions that someone else was in play here. It didn't take long to figure out who. See, my buddy Jason in Florida told me you weren't at the house when they grabbed your daughter in the driveway. Two plus two plus two . . . see how this is all playing out, Seaforth?

"Then there were the headlights. I knew a car had been following since I left the house. Maybe even before that, but I couldn't be sure. Obviously, it was you. It was easy to put everything together. After my tours in Afghanistan, you start to learn certain habits of your enemy."

Mason watched him, trying not to show anything on his own face despite his churning emotions. He was also listening closely for any signs or sounds to indicate where Sami might be. So far the only thing he had picked up on was that Johnson had used the pronoun "I" when he talked about leaving the house. Had Mason made a serious mistake? Was Sami really at Marshall's house? He asked one more time, trying very hard to keep his voice steady. "Where is my wife?"

Johnson responded with a question of his own. "Why don't you tell me where that girlfriend of yours is? From what my friends tell me, she's pretty hot. Then maybe we can discuss your wife."

Just then Mason saw a slight movement off to the side. Before he had time to think, there was a sickening crack, and Johnson fell to the ground. Marcie had managed to sneak up behind Johnson and hit him over the head with a piece of wood she had found somewhere. Mason could clearly see the impact mark on the side of Johnson's head. Blood starting to ooze from the cuts, caused by the jagged piece of timber Marcie had wielded. Mason stared at her. "Do you realize he could have pulled the trigger when you hit him? I could be dead right now. I expected you to use that gun that you've wanted so badly to use."

Marcie said, "You could say 'thank you.' Well, the truth is, I started to come over with the intention of shooting him, but in the dark I tripped on some wire that's rolled up back there, and I dropped my gun. I freaked out, but I knew I had to do something fast. So after I lost my gun, I felt around until I found that piece of wood and clobbered him. I was afraid he would hear me, but thank God he didn't. As for you, Mason Seaforth, *you* should be grateful!"

"I am, Marcie. But we have to find Sami. We don't know how long he'll be out cold before he comes to. She's here somewhere." Mason retrieved his gun from where he'd dropped it, and pointed it at the unconscious figure lying in the dirt. *Pull the trigger!* His mind screamed. *Kill him!!* Mason knew he couldn't kill a man in cold blood. He couldn't even pull the trigger and shoot Johnson in the leg. It was just too much for him. He glanced around and saw some twine rolled up near the door. He untangled it and tied it around Johnson's hands and feet as best he could. It was slippery and Mason's knot-tying skills had not been used since he was in Boy Scouts as a teen. It wouldn't hold Johnson for long.

He picked up The Force's gun, turned back to Marcie and said, "Let's find Sami."

By now, Marcie had gone back to her hiding spot and retrieved her gun from near the barbed wire where it had fallen. When she came back, he suggested that she search the shed while he tried the barn and the house. He told her to watch her back in case Johnson came to and got out of the simple restraint. She pushed the door of the shed open that had been slightly ajar and went inside.

Mason ran to the old barn and searched for a light switch. He called out Sami's name as he ran. He had to flip the switch with his wrist as he had weapons in each hand now like a gunslinger from the old west. As he did so, he stopped to listen for any sign of his wife. His calls were met only with the sound of a slight breeze whistling through the holes in the boards covering the sides of the ancient barn. He ran inside and checked each stall that had once been a home for the farm's horses or cattle. But there was nothing to give him any indication that his wife had been there. On the run, he exited the same door through which he had entered. He slowed to glance over at the front of the shed where they had left Johnson but it was too dark, despite the moonlight, to see enough to be sure.

This time, Mason raced to the front of the house and up the stairs to a porch. The screen door protested with a noisy screech, begging for a drink of oil, as he swung it open. He was part of the way through the door when two shots rang out from the direction of the shed. The first was a distinct popping sound followed closely by the sharp retort of a far larger weapon. It suddenly flashed through Mason's mind that he and Marcie really were amateurs. He had The Force's gun, but it dawned on him now that a professional like the man he and Marcie were trying to deal with would have more than one. The Force must have shrugged off Mason's clumsy attempt at tying him up.

Mason ran back towards the shed, knowing with dread that he was making mistakes that could cost him, his family and Marcie dearly. As he ran, he threw the heavy gun that belonged to Johnson as far as he could. He didn't know how to use it, anyway, and he couldn't see himself blazing away with two guns if it came to a shootout. He would do the best he could with the Glock, with which he had some familiarity, however meager.

He sprinted past the old barn and slid to a stop just before he got to the door of the shed. Johnson was no longer lying where they had left him. He peered around the corner into the shed but in the darkness, all he could make out were the outlines of huge farm equipment. Mason couldn't have known that one of the neighbors had asked to store some extra equipment in Johnson's shed, and so Johnson rented out the space. The neighbor's tractor and combine were now parked in the shed until later, giving the property the feel of a real farm.

As Mason stepped inside, warmth hit him indicating that the shed was heated. He could see a light switch, but he realized turning on the light would make him an easy target. He waited a few seconds for his eyes to adjust to the dark, and the large machinery loomed up as it came into focus.

He debated which way to go. On the right was a huge combine used for harvesting crops; and on the left was a tractor. Mason could see that there was some depth to the shed. He also knew that Johnson would know every inch of the shed and that he could be hiding anywhere, such as in the cab of the tractor or the combine.

He thought he heard a soft moaning coming from his right – at the side of the combine. He quietly stepped in that direction and quickly put his head around the corner. He could see a small form crumpled in the dirt, and he knew immediately it was Marcie. He slowly crawled over to Marcie's position with his gun at the ready. He knew very well that he was an easy target, but he had to get to her. She had fallen on her side after being shot. Her gun was still in her outstretched fingers. He was seething with anger, and he felt more than ready now to stand up and pull the trigger if he had to. He should have shot Johnson when he had the chance.

He could see Marcie moving slightly, and she was softly groaning. As he got close, he could see a small dark spot of blood on her white shirt and that a pool of blood had accumulated under her back. Her lips were moving slightly. Mason bent over with his ear close to her lips. Through clenched teeth in a voice that was barely above a whisper, Marcie struggled with her words: "Sami's...here...Mason. Johnson...has her...go... find her." Marcie said something else that Mason couldn't quite make out. He leaned forward, but just then another shot rang out and Marcie's body lurched a little as the bullet tore through soft tissue and muscle. Mason dropped down prone beside Marcie with his right arm draped over her. He knew the shot was intended for him and he had sensed its hot breath microseconds before it slammed into Marcie. Why had The Force missed? It was dark, but he must be used to operating in night time conditions. The only reasonable explanation Mason could think of was that Johnson was dealing with a struggling Sami at the same time as he pulled the trigger.

From his prone position beside Marcie, he hoped beyond hope that she would survive. Mason was in a panic. He could hear Marcie's ragged breathing, and he could feel the arm that he had draped across her body erratically rise and fall as she struggled to breathe. At least she was still alive. But as much as he wanted and needed to stay with Marcie to keep her alive, he had come too far to stop now. Sami's life, Jennifer's life, Marcie's life, even his own life depended on what he did next.

He could see straight ahead without moving and even in the darkness of the shed, he could make out two pairs of legs below the back end of the combine. One pair was thick and obviously masculine and the other thinner and feminine. He prayed it was Sami, but he didn't want to lift his head higher for fear that The Force would detect movement. Tonight he had made some tough decisions. And he had made some mistakes. And now, the time had come for another potentially life-altering choice.

He thought that arrogance probably came naturally to a man like The Force and Mason was counting on the darkness to mislead Johnson into thinking he had hit Mason with the shot. And because of that, Johnson would think that Mason was either dead or incapacitated, so he would deal with Sami first and then come back to make sure the job was finished.

Mason thought back to what Leroy had said only a few short days before in the bush in Florida. It seemed like ages ago since he had had that gun training, but he remembered as if it were yesterday a rule that Leroy had emphasized to him. It stood out because he thought at the time that he would never in a million years be able do it even if he *was* under the threat of death. Rule number 3 was that if you are hit, play dead. Mason wasn't hit, but he was going to play dead. He was going to count on a struggling Sami to make it too difficult for Johnson to drag her over to where he and Marcie were lying to finish them off.

Mason lay on the concrete floor and listened because he remembered that was another of the lessons Leroy had taught him. He waited and listened. He knew his only possibility of success against a man of far superior skills was to wait for the right moment to strike. But he also had to make sure he did so before any harm came to Sami.

The shed walls were made of industrial corrugated steel, which tended to deaden the sound. It was well built so that machinery running on the inside would not deafen the people operating them, nor release a lot of the sound to the outside air. Mason and Marcie were lying about halfway along the floor's length, but from his vantage point, he could hear his wife struggling against The Force. He was sure now it was his wife. He could hear muffled sounds coming from Sami, as if Johnson had a hand across her mouth. Then Mason heard a loud noise followed by a grunt, and the shed became deathly quiet. He knew his worst nightmare was coming true: Johnson had silenced Sami.

The next sound Mason heard was a door opening on squeaking hinges. Of course, Mason thought – there's a back door. But the sound could be a trap. He could no longer see the legs from his position. He saw the moonlight illuminate the end of the shed, as the door had apparently been swung open. It looked like whoever had been there just minutes before was now gone out the open door. The spot was empty. Mason decided he had to move. He slowly got into a crouch and used the shadows of the combine to move towards the door. He could feel the perspiration on his back and trickling down his arms. He was scared to death, but adrenaline pushed him forward as he crept towards the end of the building. As he got to the end of the combine, he peered around and all he could see was the open doorway.

Mason thought of what his adversary might do. He could have moved back into the building. The moonlight shining through the door cast a blue hue where it illuminated the inside of the building, but there were many shadows where one could hide. Mason could see dust particles hanging lazily suspended in the light of the moon as if only half awake after being rudely aroused from a deep slumber by the door being yanked open. Mason peered down at the floor in the moonlight, and he could make out drops on the cement. He couldn't tell how far they went since the angle of the moon sent its rays away from Mason's location, but the drops appeared to have originated where Mason was standing right now. They were probably oil droplets, as an industrial shed like this would be full of them. Even as he thought of it, he could smell the oil and grease that kept the machines well lubricated.

His thoughts flashed back to Marcie's attempt to speak, and suddenly the words he was unable to understand came to him in a flood as clearly as if she had said them to him when they were sitting in the car. He wondered if he had rejected the thought because it just wasn't plausible. But like anything else Marcie was involved with, this was something that Mason should have just accepted as fact. He understood now what Marcie had said with the clarity of a thunderbolt striking him. He became acutely aware of the tiny droplets on the cement. The phrase that became so clear to Mason was, "*I think I hit him.*"

He crept forward on hands and knees, propelling the gun along the concrete floor with one hand while trying to be as quiet as possible. He arrived at the area of the floor that was illuminated by the moonlight where one of the drops was clearly visible. He tried to stay in the shadows just on the edge of the moonbeam, because he realized that to do otherwise would make him easy prey. But he had to know. *Was this Greg Johnson's blood?* He leaned forward and touched one of the droplets. It was fresh, all right. His fingers felt blood's characteristic wet stickiness. He brought it to his lips and tasted it. It was blood. Either Sami or The Force had been hit by Marcie's shot. Mason thought The Force would be using Sami as a shield, so it could have just as easily been his wife that was hit. No matter what, though, he knew he couldn't blame Marcie for taking the shot. She did what she thought was right at the time.

Mason looked around. There were no sounds at all, and he was sure that his prey had somehow made it outside. It was time for another life altering choice: stay or go? Mason knew he really had no choice. Even as the thought was still forming in his mind, he was already up, creeping toward the open door in the moonlight after his wife and her killer.

Chapter 35

Baker and Finch were disappointed that the cell phone hadn't yielded any results. But they knew that in this business, if something didn't pan out (which was often the case), they just went on to plan B. Sometimes they got well down the alphabet before pieces of the puzzle started to click into place. Sometimes, though, the pieces never did click together, and that's when they hated their jobs. If a piece never fell into place, someone usually paid with their life or a loved one's life.

The two detectives knew they were racing against time. They had the full name of one of the suspected kidnappers and a partial on the other. Finch was busy checking with Florida Highway Safety and Motor Vehicles to obtain a picture of Jason Sage, as well as a license number of the car. Their usual source for photos, which was social media, yielded nothing as Sage was apparently one of the few people left in the world who didn't have an account on Facebook, Twitter or LinkedIn, at least under his own name. They wondered if he had an alias or a pseudonym. However, thanks to the efforts of the Seaforths' elderly next-door neighbor Mrs. Cassidy and her friend Mr. Davis across the street, they now had a license plate number for the blue sedan, and an all-points bulletin had been issued. A call to the Department of Motor Vehicles was required to confirm that the license number was valid. But Baker was pretty sure that Mrs. Cassidy's information would be accurate. Older people tried very hard to get things right when dealing with authorities, he'd found.

Baker was all too familiar with the statistics: 90% of abduction cases are resolved within a 24-hour period, and his gut told him that this needed to be one of those or it could have a very bad ending. Things were happening quickly. At least now he knew approximately where Mason and Marcie were. The Royal Canadian Mounted Police had been alerted, who in turn had contacted the Ottawa Police Service. The latter were headed at that very moment to Aaron Marshall's house, and on the lookout for Sami and Mason Seaforth.

Finch rushed into the office, holding photos of Jason Sage and waving his address. It was an apartment in East Central Tampa, an area known to be high-risk. Baker decided to call in the Special Weapons and Tactics team. He knew they were up against highly-trained individuals who would be heavily armed. You didn't go into a situation as volatile as this without your own highly-trained team.

The SWAT team consisted of snipers who worked in pairs, along with a negotiator (since this was a hostage situation), and an entry team who were armed to the teeth with everything from concussion grenades to MP 5/10 submachine guns and Remington 12-gauge shotguns. SWAT-team members were actually part-timers: they all carried regular police shifts as well, but their rapier-sharp skills were kept honed through constant training.

The team rushed to Sage's apartment on the third floor of the apartment building and took up their positions covertly. They had already forced the evacuation of the apartments on either side of Sage's. They could hear a noise on the other side of the door. The snipers were spread out on the rooftops surrounding the apartment building. Two officers stood on either side of the door with guns drawn. A third loudly pounded on the door, announcing their presence and waited for an answer. Nothing but loud barking and low growling, punctuated by scratching at the door. The officer in charge at the door radioed to the squad members outside, asking if they could see any movement in the apartment. The answer came back negative.

Baker, who was standing with Finch off to the side behind two heavily-armed SWAT team members, shook his head in Finch's direction. He had the sickening feeling that this was another dead end, that there was no one inside. After waiting several minutes and trying a few more attempts to raise someone in the apartment, the team hammered the apartment's front door with their battering rams to break in. Flimsier than it looked, the door shattered easily.

The SWAT team crouched and entered with guns ready to unload their deadly cargo at the slightest provocation. The source of the growling, a pit bull, lunged snarling at the first officer through the door, but was swiftly subdued with a muzzle around its snout. A swift pass through every room quickly determined the one-bedroom apartment was empty except for the dog, and the tactical officers reluctantly gave the all-clear. Baker and Finch entered to see a living quarters that was well used – but obviously not recently.

A strong smell permeated the apartment, mostly from a sinkful of dirty dishes that had apparently been sitting there for days. The living area had a couch and a single chair with floral patterns that would have been well placed in the seventies. A couple of cockroaches scurried past the officers and disappeared behind the quarter round moulding at the base of the wall. An old tube television set sat on a stand in one corner with a stack of DVDs piled beside it. One blanket hung haphazardly off the couch with copies of military, ultimate fighter and porn magazines thrown about on the floor beside it. As he came in and shut the door, Detective Baker had observed a wrinkled, tacked-up "No Smoking" sign with the universally-accepted illustration of a cigarette behind a red circle with a line diagonally through it , but judging from the thick stench of smoke still hanging in the air, whoever lived here smoked incessantly. A number of marijuana plants greeted Baker as he stepped out onto the balcony. They were positioned to be slightly below eye level and out of the sightline of curious neighbors, but their leaves were able to take full advantage of eight hours of sun a day. There were enough plants here to keep quite a few people stoned for months.

The bedroom was in even worse condition, with paint peeling off the walls and bed clothes tossed across the room. More CDs and magazines were stacked in the closet. It was not a place Baker could imagine living in for long, and it said volumes about the kind of person Jason Sage was and the lifestyle he lived.

Baker had seen all of this before – on other raids at other times. The forensic investigators could go through all the stuff that made up Sage's home. But Baker had learned from years of experience to ignore the things that people collect that make them like everyone else in their daily lives, and look instead for things that might define them. There were two items in the bedroom that immediately caught Baker's practiced eye amid the squalor. The first was a shadow box neatly hanging on the wall displaying an Afghanistan Campaign Medal. Baker had seen the medal before and knew that it was awarded to any member of the U.S. Services who had served within the borders of Afghanistan for 30 consecutive or 60 non-consecutive days.

By the way it was neatly framed and displayed, it was obvious that Sage was very proud of his service to his country. But it was the second item that really caught Baker's eye. It was a photo in a cheap frame, likely purchased at one of the myriad of dollar stores around town, which showed a group of five soldiers posing for the camera. They were equipped with a variety of weapons, including machine guns, grenade launchers, automatic pistols and knives. They were all grinning from ear to ear and Baker recognized one of the men as the same one on the driver's license belonging to Jason Sage. Baker took the frame off the wall, removed the photo, tossed the frame on the bed and flipped the picture over. Sure enough, there were names scrawled on the back of the photo. Maybe they had caught a break at last; one of the names on the back was the same as the one mentioned by Seaforth - Danny. The last name was Harris.

Baker and Finch left the investigators in charge to search the room as they went to their portable office in the car to find an address for Danny Harris. They told the SWAT team to stand by. They were rewarded for their search with an address that was only a few blocks away. They engaged the siren and with a squeal of tires, they headed off for the location with the black SWAT vehicle following close behind. They turned off the siren when they got within two blocks of the building and pulled up in the parking lot at Danny Harris' address. Not completely to their surprise, a blue sedan sat in full view in the parking lot. Its license plate matched up with the numbers provided by Mrs. Cassidy.

In the building, Jennifer was bound and gagged in an upstairs bedroom of Harris' townhouse. She had awakened earlier and her head was thick with the after-effects of the chloroform she had been given. She had a foul taste in her mouth and she retched, not wanting to vomit with the tape across her mouth for fear of choking to death. She could hear two male voices downstairs but even though the walls of the poorly-constructed building were paper thin, the sound was muffled and she was unable to make out what they were saying. She decided her best option was to remain still to give her head a chance to clear and to fight off the nausea. She glanced around the room to see if there was something sharp that she could use to cut the material binding her hands behind her back, but it was a plastic cable zip tie designed for holding electrical wires together. It was tight, and it had made her hands numb. She worked her fingers to try to regain some circulation, but it hurt, and the struggle seemed futile.

She wondered with mounting dread what was going to happen to her.

The call had come into RCMP Headquarters in Ottawa from a Detective Finch in Florida, and after listening to the conversation, the officer had redirected it to the Ottawa Police Service downtown. They could hear real urgency in the voice of Detective Finch, and the Staff Sergeant in the police station immediate sprang into action.

The phone call set off a chain reaction of events. Police constables raced towards Marshall's house with sirens blaring and roof lights flashing to get around the traffic, but as soon they got closer, they went into stealth mode so as not to aggravate whatever situation they were facing. In the meantime, a Zone Alert was sent out over the Canadian Police Information Center advising all local law enforcement agencies at exactly the same time about the situation. They were also given a license number and advised to watch for a rental car being driven either by a Mason Seaforth (Caucasian, U.S. citizen) or an African-American woman named Marcie Kane.

Officers on patrol that night in Ottawa responded. In addition, each officer at stations around the area would either be wearing their uniform or have it in their locker so they could be available, if necessary. The Staff Sergeant remained at the office supervising the campaign, making sure that hospitals were notified, a K9 unit was available, a plane was on standby so that they could track Marshall if he made a run for it, and an ambulance was waiting in case of casualties. City of Ottawa workers put up barricades to close Queen Elizabeth Drive and taxi companies and the city's bus transit service were alerted of road closures.

And the tactical squad was called out.

The Ottawa Police Service Tactical Unit was originally formed in 1976 in anticipation of the Montreal Olympics but the impetus came earlier because of the 1972 summer Olympics in Munich. With Ottawa's central location between the main venues for the events, the decision was made to establish a highly trained tactical group that would be available to attend to and deal with a situation at a moment's notice.

The group was now comprised of 32 full time members making up four teams. It was one of these teams that headed out to Marshall's house. An outer perimeter had been established around the house and controlled by the Patrol Officers. No member of the public would be allowed beyond this border for as long as it took to flush Marshall out. Everyone outside that ring was known as RTW (Rest of the World). The world inside this large circle now belonged to the Ottawa Police Service.

When the black Chevrolet Suburban SUVs and the truck that could have been mistaken for a hydro repair vehicle, screeched to a stop, the members piled out. A second invisible circle was laid out inside the first, which was controlled by the Tactical Unit. The layout was simplified by the fact that Marshall's house was fronted across the street by the Rideau Canal. Within the secondary circle was the Immediate Action Team who had the green light to go at any sign that Marshall was going to harm himself or anyone else that might be in the house.

If Marshall decided to make a run for it in any direction, the Ottawa

Police Service could call in the Ontario Provincial Police, the RCMP and the Gatineau Police and have 150 heavily armed men available. The Incident Commander was in charge of his triangle, which included himself, a hostage negotiator and the Tactical Sergeant. Everything was in place without Marshall's knowledge that anything was happening outside. Then the negotiations began.

It had been an unbelievable few minutes for Mason Seaforth and Marcie Kane. On a farm in rural Ontario, Canada, Marcie had temporarily disabled a killer with a piece of wood and Mason knew he was close to rescuing Sami. It appeared to Mason that Marcie and The Force had exchanged shots in the darkness of a shed and both had hit their mark, but Marcie lay dying in the dirt while The Force was obviously less wounded and on the run, dragging Sami with him. Now Mason peered out the open door into a meadow of about 100 yards in depth that led to a wooded area. He could see a path through the meadow leading to an opening in the woods. He listened intently as Leroy had told him, but he couldn't hear anything that would indicate someone was walking or running on the path through the woods. The wind was obliterating any noise that would help him.

Mason calculated that there were a number of things lining up that were clearly not in his favor. First, The Force could easily carry an unconscious Sami through the woods on the run because he was in tremendous shape. It seemed that he had been hit by Marcie's bullet, but unless it hit a major organ or something, it wouldn't even be an afterthought for someone like The Force at a time like this. Also, Johnson would know these woods like he would know his own car. He had probably been through them on many occasions. Finally, he would be all too keenly aware that Mason was in pursuit. It would take nothing for The Force to throw Sami down on the ground while he ducked behind a tree, waiting in ambush to pump a few rounds of ammunition into the unsuspecting body of Mason Seaforth. Mason was at the mercy of his enemy. With each step he took along the trail, he could be walking into a killing ground.

It was time for yet another life and death decision. Mason was so clearly out of his depth now that he might as well be standing in the middle of a shooting range in front of a Special Forces team intent on killing him. How had he ever imagined that he could singlehandedly wrest his wife away from experienced, professional murderers? He was so completely out of his element that for a single minute, he found himself considering turning back. Giving up. At best, he might come upon Sami but be ill-equipped to actually get her away from Greg Johnson. At worst, well – he didn't want to think about the other scenario he faced. He thought again how he should be at home working on someone's accounting records, not trying to rescue his wife by chasing a military veteran through the woods in the dark. But there was no turning back now. He had to finish this.

His body hummed with adrenalin as he sprinted as fast as he could in a zig-zag pattern across the meadow in the moonlight, almost waiting for a bullet to cut him down. He wondered as he ran if he would feel anything or if it would just be instant blackness. But nothing came. When he reached the trailhead leading into the trees, he stopped again to listen, but all he could hear was his heart pounding and the blood rushing through his veins. The combination of the run and the anxiety he was facing brought a pain to his chest, and he had to take a few moments bent over to catch his breath. His shirt was wet with perspiration. He wondered if he might be suffering a cardiac arrest, but he put the thought out of his mind.

He peered along the path in the forest, but it was pitch black. Mason hated the dark. He was always bumping into things at home when he got up at night. There was the black eye he acquired in the dark on their honeymoon that amused Sami so much. But as the neurons in his brain fired uncontrollably, he was instantly transported back on the trail where he had been with Marcie only a few days ago when Leroy had been trying to train him. Then his heart grew heavy at the thought of Marcie lying back in the shed, bleeding on the concrete floor, but he pushed the image out of his mind. For everyone's sake, it was critical that he stay focused.

Mason pushed forward into the darkness, using the trees as cover and trying hard not to step on anything that might give away his location. Every few steps, he would stop and listen intently for a twig snapping or a branch rustling in the stillness of the night. But the quiet was only broken by the constant humming of some amorous male crickets trying to attract a partner by rubbing their wings together. Mason sniffed the air in the hopes of catching a whiff of cologne – Sami's or Johnson's. In the end, Mason knew that this time, he would not get a second chance. When it came down to it, he would have to pull the trigger and he would have to hit his target, something he had not yet done successfully, not in training and not when he had The Force lying on the ground back by the shed. Mason worked his way from side to side along the trail, stopping often to listen. He couldn't see more than a few feet in front of him. Branches tore at his jacket and pants and slapped his face as he pushed through the bushes, opening little cuts and scratches that he didn't pay any attention to.

Just as he reached a particularly vulnerable spot in a clearing between the trees, he heard a motor start up and lights simultaneously lit the night just a few hundred yards down the path and off to the side. Mason dove for the underbrush, momentarily stunned by the noise that broke the stillness of the night and the sudden brightness cast by the lights. He was unsure of the exact source, but he knew it was a machine of some kind. He had landed on some thick, spiky brush and he could feel the branches scraping him again as he picked himself up. The engine of the machine was laboring as it strained at whatever it was doing.

Mason's heart raced. It had to be The Force doing something. Mason crept closer so he could look through the trees. He knelt down and pushed branches aside so that the machine was visible. He had seen one like that before when his friend Taylor had had a pool installed next door to him in Gulfport. It could be used for lifting, but right now it was serving another purpose. It was a white tractor-like machine, about the size of an SUV. It ran on tracks and had two hydraulic arms running down each side connected to a wide scoop at the front. Mason remembered the name of the machine was "Bobcat" because he and Taylor had joked about firing the cat up and taking it for a run when it was sitting idle in Taylor's backyard one night during the pool construction.

Mason couldn't see the operator of the machine. All he could see were the lights illuminating the scoop that was digging in the soil at the end of the arm. The operator was digging a crude hole by pushing the dirt forward. When Mason squinted and looked more closely, he saw just off to the side of the hole his beloved wife Sami, crumpled up in a fetal position. It took a few seconds to sink in, but then it struck him like a ton of bricks. *The bastard was digging a shallow grave! He was digging a grave to put Sami's body in!* And if he finished, undoubtedly there would be not one but three graves before he was done: one for Sami, one for Marcie, and a final one for him as well. The Force's intention was clear. The three of them were supposed to die tonight.

Mason tried desperately to see if Sami's inert body showed any signs of life, but she was too far away for him to detect movement. He was frantic. Time was running out. He had to get to her as soon as possible. If she was injured, he had to get her to a hospital. If Johnson had already killed her . . . he would find a way to kill him with his bare hands, otherwise he wouldn't want to live any more. It was time for another decision. Mason raised the gun and calculated the approximate distance from the lights to where The Force would be sitting in the darkened compartment. Damn, he wasn't close enough. The machine was working about 40 yards from Mason, which he recalled was a little out of good range for the Glock. He had to get closer.

He pushed through the trees to his left. He felt the branches grabbing at his legs as if they wanted him to stop this madness. He neared to about 20 yards from the machine, but he was now perpendicular to it. It was darker from this vantage point, but he could still see what was happening. The engine was even louder now as its scoop dug into the earth as deep as it would go and pushed the dirt forward towards the growing pile. The engine barked with every scoop of earth. He could smell the exhaust every time the machine bellowed smoke into the air.

Suddenly the action slowed. It seemed that Johnson was satisfied with the hole he'd dug because he reversed the machine and manoeuvred it so that Sami's inert body was in a line between the machine and the hole. Once again, the hydraulic arms lowered the scoop to ground level and Mason realized what he was about to do. He was going to push Sami into the hole. *If she was alive, he was going to bury her that way!* Mason flashed to what Leroy had told him about holding the gun, and steadily, Mason placed both thumbs down the left hand side of the barrel. If he didn't do it now, he knew he never would. Once again, almost involuntarily, he calculated the distance from lights to target. He sighted down the barrel, interlocked his fingers on the handle, with the exception of his index finger, took a deep breath and held it, barely moving a muscle.

For Mason, all went silent.

And he squeezed the trigger.

Chapter 36

Jason Sage could feel the same nervous energy coursing through his body that he had felt on patrol in Fallujah. He knew something was going to happen, he just didn't know what. He knew someone was going to die tonight, whether it was in Ottawa or here, and he was going to do everything in his power to make sure it wasn't him or his comrade-in-arms, Danny Harris. He had just got off the phone with The Force. Apparently, things were going well in Canada. At the time of his call, Johnson had Sami Seaforth in his trunk and was on his way to get rid of her. But apparently, Sami's husband and his girlfriend had somehow got to Canada, and they were stumbling around trying to play detective. The Force had told Jason that he wasn't sure how much the police knew and to be on guard. There was a remote possibility that the Florida police had been notified and would somehow track down the location where Sage and Harris were keeping the girl.

Sage had smiled at the thought of the police arriving. He and Harris were more than adequately prepared. They had automatic weapons, handguns, and a variety of explosives that they could use to hold off the police should they show up, at least long enough for them to escape. Sage thought they should avoid a shootout with the police, so they were going to clear out. They would both make enough money from this job to move somewhere. Come to think of it, maybe *he* would go to Canada. He kind of liked the idea of four seasons, and he was sure there were places he could hide for the rest of his life in a country that big. Sage told Danny to keep an eye out the windows, and his colleague was busily doing just that, observing the street for any sign of movement.

While Danny acted as lookout, Sage had just one thing to do before they left. His orders were to kill Mason Seaforth's daughter. It was too bad, really. She was really pretty and he knew she was going to college, so she was probably more intelligent than most of the girls he had had the pleasure of meeting. Maybe he would have a little taste before he got rid of her.

While Sage was on the phone, Jennifer had been lying on the dank, carpeted floor in the pitch-black room where her captors had unceremoniously dumped her. She forced herself to sit up, although the movement caused the room to spin and brought another wave of nausea in her stomach. Her shoulders and legs ached from the pain of being bound up for so long and from exertions that had stretched her ligaments in unnatural ways. She scanned the room for something – anything - that she could use to free herself, but there was nothing. As her eyes adjusted to the light, she could see that the room was sparsely decorated with only one double bed in the middle with no covers. There was a cardboard box in the corner sealed with duct tape, and Jennifer thought that it could benefit from the same kind of sharp instrument she needed to free herself.

She managed to roll over onto her knees, and with her athleticism and by leaning against the bed, she was able to clumsily force herself into a standing position. Hoping nobody could hear her, the girl shuffled over to the door and angled her body sideways to the knob so she could reach it. The pain in her shoulders was excruciating as she tried the knob. It was too much to hope that the door would open as it was obviously locked from the outside. There was really no surprise there. Next she shuffled over to the closet, and using the same awkward stance, she pulled open the door. There was nothing in the closet other than a few mismatched hangers on the rod. Her captors didn't spend much time here apparently, and she wondered if there'd been other girls in this room and whether they had been allowed to survive.

Jennifer leaned on the wall, trying to relieve the pain the ties were putting on her wrists and ankles. She glanced toward the window, and then suddenly thought maybe there was a chance she could get it open and jump to the ground. It took forever to work her way over to the window, but finally Jennifer was standing there, peering out beyond the curtains. She could see a street light, but oddly, it didn't look like it was working. As her eyes scanned the street, she realized that none of the street lights were now lit. Was there a power outage in the neighborhood? No sooner had Jennifer formulated the thought than she thought she saw movement out of the corner of one eye. It was just a quick flash, like someone running from one area to another. Then she looked closer as more helmeted dark shapes came into view. She smiled to herself when she realized what was going on. The house was now completely surrounded and at this very moment, she couldn't count the number of weapons trained on the house. The cavalry had arrived!

Just as the words echoed in her brain, she jumped at the sound of a deep male voice barking out loud instructions over a megaphone: "JASON SAGE AND DANNY HARRIS, COME OUT NOW WITH YOUR HANDS UP." She could hear scrambling downstairs and she imagined her captors rushing to the windows to check outside. She wondered if maybe they couldn't see what she was seeing from her vantage point, but a few seconds later the sound of automatic gunfire erupted from the house and one of the shapes on the street slumped to the pavement while the others dove for cover. Horrified, Jennifer moved away from the window for a few seconds but it was like watching a true crime scene on TV, and she couldn't avert her eyes for long. She thought there would be a hail of return gunfire, but there was only silence.

She thought to herself. *"They don't even know I'm in here."* She once again forced herself to her feet and banged her head on the window in the hopes of attracting someone's attention out on the street. But she couldn't see any shapes now. All signs of life had vanished at the first sound of gunfire. She could hear pounding on the stairs and she knew one of her captors was running toward the locked room. Jennifer literally hopped over to a corner of the room, sunk to the floor and slumped down in an effort to make herself as small as possible.

She could hear a key fumbling in the lock and the door swung open, crashing against the wall, leaving a deep indentation where the knob struck it. She immediately recognized the one who had been driving the car when she came to for that brief instant before he put that filthy rag on her face again. She screamed through the duct tape, but the sound was muffled and as she did so, she heard sharp volleys of automatic gunfire downstairs. The man grabbed her right arm and literally dragged her out the door of the bedroom into the hallway. Jennifer struggled as much as she could against him, trying to throw him off balance as he dragged her toward the head of the stairs, but with no use of her hands or feet, she was at his mercy. The man seized her by one arm and dragged her down the stairs like a sack of potatoes with her bound legs thumping on the stairs. Her shoulders screamed as the ligaments were stretched to their limit. At the bottom of the staircase, smoke hung in the air from Danny's weapon. At the same moment, Danny turned back from the window and said to Sage, "I don't see them anymore." There was simply an eerie silence from outside as if the entire SWAT team had somehow vanished.

Sage looked at Harris. They both knew there was no way they were going to get out of this easily. The SWAT team had merely regrouped, and it was only a matter of minutes before they struck again. Mutually without words, the two men decided they would have to use Jennifer as a bargaining chip. They could kill her later, but right now she needed to stay alive. She might be their ticket to freedom as long as she remained their hostage. Sage knew that an assault was imminent. Then, the gates of hell opened up for Jason Sage and Danny Harris.

It started with an explosion at the back of the townhouse, which was quickly followed by a device tossed through the newly-created hole. As it rolled across the floor, the device emitted a thick screening smoke that made it virtually impossible to see anything and made breathing difficult. Simultaneously, the front door burst open with splinters flying in all directions and heavily-armored officers raced in with automatic weapons drawn. The hole in the back wall had initially been a diversion, and as the team came in the front, more swarmed in through the hole in the back and some had mounted ladders and were coming in the windows on either side of the townhouse.

It was a breach of massive proportions and if seen from above, it would have looked like armored beetles streaming through openings in the front, back and two sides of the building. Each tactical officer was dressed in full black combat gear with heavy Kevlar vests and goggles to allow them to see through the thick smoke pouring out from the canister lying on the floor. They were barking instructions at the top of their lungs for Jason and Danny to drop their weapons. For a moment, it seemed that time had stopped. The challenge now hung in the air. Would the two men drop their weapons and surrender, or was an all-out war about to break out? If so, Jennifer knew she was a sitting duck, a target for any stray bullet – or for a shot directly from Sage himself. He was probably under orders to kill her at this point, and she was close enough for him to shoot at point blank range before anyone could stop him. Jennifer sagged against Sage, shaking with fear. Tears filled her eyes, burning from the smoke.

Then as if in slow motion, Sage turned towards the front door, as his arm with the hand holding the gun to Jennifer's head was grabbed from behind and forced away from Jennifer. A second member tackled Sage to the floor, landing on him as he went down and the air expelled from Sage's lungs in a whoosh. A third member simultaneously tackled Jennifer, throwing his body on top of her as a shield and forcing her to the floor.

Danny Harris had his back to the wall, but could dimly make out shapes in front of him through the smoke. At that instant, he was back in Fallujah, and instinct took over. He raised his gun towards the form of an onrushing member of the team and two shots rang out. Two small holes appeared in Harris' shirt and a trickle of blood started to drip from his chest. He pitched forwards in a slow motion fall to the floor, life seeping out of him with every passing second. At the same instant, Jason Sage was surrounded and subdued on the floor with his hands behind his back. His weapon had dropped to the floor where it was swiftly grabbed and removed. The operation was clean, efficient, quick, and most of all, successful.

As members of the team were securing Jason Sage, another grabbed Jennifer and carried her outside, away from the choking smoke inside the house. As they reached the street and fresh air, the street lights magically came back on in response to an unseen signal. A paramedic talked to the officer who was apparently the one Jennifer had seen pitch forward as he appeared only to be winded from the bullet that hit his vest. Baker and Finch rushed over to Jennifer, who had been gently placed on a blanket on the grass and covered for warmth. A knife quickly unbound Jennifer's hands and feet, and someone carefully removed the duct tape across her mouth as medics began to work on her. The warmth from the blankets started to alleviate Jennifer's involuntary shaking. The girl was clearly in shock, but seemed to respond to Detective Baker's calm tone and the medication she was being given. She flexed her shoulders to alleviate some of the pain she was still feeling. A handsome paramedic bathed her eyes to remove the effects of the smoke. She would be whisked away to the hospital to be treated for shock and to ensure there was no other physical damage.

Once the townhouse was swept for explosives, with the exception of some tape around the house designating it as a crime scene and police coming and going for a while, life would go back to normal on the street.

As Baker and Finch drove away, Baker thought to himself, it's times like these that make this job all worthwhile. There would be little in the news about it, of course, because these types of things happened too often. Now he just needed good news from Canada and there would be no need for an antacid tonight.

Chapter 37

When Mason took the shot, he hadn't even thought of the metal bars surrounding the operator that protected him in the event of rollover. And of course, he couldn't see the bars as he pulled the trigger because of the darkness. Mason heard the whine of the bullet as it ricocheted off the metal. But the shot stopped the machine's forward motion, and its driver immediately shut the engine down. The machine's lights probably controlled by a separate switch, stayed on, still highlighting the ominous hole and mound of dirt behind it. Sami's inert form now lay about three feet from the shovel and about five feet from the hole that was intended for her.

Mason realized instantly that his shot had missed its target. Did he have another chance? Hell, yes, he did. Filled with the rage he'd been repressing ever since Sami's disappearance, he aimed again and pulled the trigger over and over, letting out all the emotions that had built up in him over the past few days. Each squeeze of the trigger jarred his entire arm. The gun lifted several inches each time a bullet raced down the barrel. He knew if he were holding the gun properly, there would be little movement, but right now he was just intent on firing. The sound of each shot echoed in the calm night air, one was barely fading when the next one started. Mason rained a hail of gunfire at the machine and prayed that at least one of them would find its mark. If he missed, there would be no second chances, no repeats to get it right, and they would all die at the hands of The Force.

Finally, Mason stopped firing and stayed still to listen. As the echo of the barrage of bullets stopped, he heard nothing other than the ringing in his ears from the sound of the gun. He forced himself to wait, but he was desperate to reach Sami and make sure that she was still breathing. Still he heard nothing. Was the driver (whom he was certain was Greg Johnson) still alive, just waiting for Mason to come forward where he could pick him off with a single shot? Or had Mason accomplished what he'd set out to do? Once again, Mason understood it was decision time for him, this time with the highest stakes yet. He crept out of his hiding place and crawled into a clearing where the moonlight was so bright, it felt like he was in the city. At any moment, he expected to feel the bite of a bullet shredding through his body, and he knew that if this happened, he was sealing the fate of his entire family. They would all die with him.

He quickly closed the distance between his hiding place and the machine, barely breathing through his anxiety, but there was no gunfire. When he arrived at the cab of the Bobcat, he ducked low and grabbed for the door, only to discover to his shock that Johnson wasn't there. In the moonlight, he could see drops of pooled blood on the floor of the tractor. Were they from one of his bullets, or perhaps the result of Marcie's well-aimed shot in the shed? The thought of Marcie still lying there sent a shiver of dread through him, but he was helpless. He had to stay focused on finding Greg Johnson before the man caused any more deaths. Mason moved stealthily around the back of the machine, ready to fire any bullets he had left, but there was no body as he had hoped. Johnson must have jumped off the side of the tractor away from where the shots were coming from and disappeared into the brush.

Mason ran back around to the side of the machine he had been shooting at and to the front where Sami lay. He could see that her hands were tied in front of her, but her feet were free. While keeping his eyes and the gun pointed in the direction of the bush, he knelt down beside her. He eased the tape away from her mouth and bent over her to see if she was breathing. She surprised him when she opened one eye and weakly whispered, "I'm okay. He thinks I'm dead. Watch out. He's nearb..." Sami had no time to finish her sentence before Mason sensed, rather than saw, a figure rushing at him like a locomotive. It was too late. The figure was noticeably limping as he ran, but he hit Mason with the speed of a linebacker, and Mason felt the air rush from his lungs.

Mason's gun went flying as he was hit. Stars were stabbing at his eyes. He lay gasping in the grass as he tried to find some air - any air - to re-inflate his empty lungs. The Force stood up, and roughly hauled him to his feet. Through gritted teeth, he hissed, "Why couldn't you just do what you were told, Seaforth? Why did you have to follow me here? You're an accountant, for God's sake. What did you think you were going to do? Did you really think you were going to be able to beat me – with *my* training? I've killed more trained killers in Afghanistan than you want to know about."

Mason's wind was starting to return. In the moonlight, he could see a dark stain on Johnson's pant leg, indicating his leg was bleeding and his head was still oozing from Marcie's earlier attack. Through gasps, Mason said, "It's something somebody like you will never understand in a million years, Johnson…it's about *family*…you messed with my family. And besides, look at you. Your head is bleeding, and you were shot by a girl who has only shot a gun a few times in her life at a range." He used the term "girl" to emphasize his point, sneering as he said it. Mason drew in another breath and uttered, "How did you manage to let that *happen,* Johnson? Can you answer that?"

Mason could feel Johnson tense in front of him. He knew that the taunt had hit its mark with the former soldier. Mason hoped that by distracting Johnson, it would give Sami a chance to make a run for it. He just hoped she was strong enough, considering Johnson had probably squeezed her carotid arteries to render her unconscious as quickly as he had back at the shed. He also knew his taunting could very well end up being fatal to him.

"Well, you can say goodbye to your family now, Seaforth." Johnson was screaming, "YOU'RE ALL DEAD! You hear me? You two and that black *girl* will be buried here where no one will ever find you, and your daughter will end up in the ocean somewhere. My boys in Florida have probably already taken care of that little problem…although they may have had some fun before they did." With that, Johnson moved his gun to his left hand and used his right to hit Mason in the solar plexus with such force that he doubled over in pain. Whatever air he had accumulated since Johnson had tackled him ebbed out of his body for a second time, and he found himself again on the cold grass, retching with spasms over and over. He didn't want to give Johnson the satisfaction, but he could hear himself moaning. He thought it was all over, that he had failed in his attempt to save his family, but at least he would die knowing that he had tried. He hoped it would end quickly.

Johnson grabbed him again and brought him to his feet. Mason was still gasping to draw a breath. His stomach was in such anguish that he didn't know if he would survive another hit. He was hunched over, holding his middle and leaning against the hands that were holding him up. He could never have thought possible the spasms that he felt when he tried to straighten up. He had never known such pain, but he wanted to stand up against this monster. Johnson hit him again, this time in the side of the head and Mason lost consciousness for a moment or two as he dropped to the ground. His glasses had flown off with the attack. His ears were ringing, but off in the distance, he thought he heard sirens. He needed to prolong this by trying to antagonize the Force. As he regained some form of awareness he mumbled in a voice he hoped was loud enough for his adversary to hear, "You're a coward, Johnson. Pretty tough against defenseless people."

Johnson took out his gun and aimed it at Mason. Johnson said, "I'm sorry I have to do this, Seaforth. I'm just doing my job." Mason knew this was it. His life was over. But Johnson casually tossed the gun aside as he laughed. "You didn't think I'd let you off that easy, did you? Not quite. I changed my mind. It will be easier to bury you in pieces." With that he pulled out his favorite weapon, the knife that he coveted, and tossed it casually from hand to hand. Mason tried to push himself up on his elbows, but it was difficult. Stars were swirling in front of his eyes, and his head felt twice its normal size. Nausea and dizziness made him lie back down with his hand over his face. He was drifting in and out of consciousness, but as Johnson slowly approached him, he thought he could hear a voice in the distance. It sounded like Sami. What was she saying? Had she succumbed and was calling him to join her?

He looked up, his vision blurred by the blow and his missing glasses and could see that Johnson had stopped and was slowly turning around. A shot rang out. But Mason didn't feel anything. Was this what's it like? No sense of feeling, just life oozing out of some little hole in your body? In his dazed condition, Mason remembered that Johnson had a knife, not a gun. At that split second, he looked up just as Johnson pitched straight forward. In the moonlight, Mason could see that much of his forehead was missing. Blood and other matter streamed down his face. Mason managed to roll away from Johnson just before his lifeless body crashed to the ground with a thud.

Mason swung back and sat up with a motion that was too sudden for the treatment he had just received. He could feel his left eye closing shut, his head was swirling and his stomach was still protesting, but even in his hazy condition, he could make out the form of his wife holding the gun Johnson had discarded between her bound hands. She had used the training she received when she had gone with Marcie to the shooting range. Sami dropped the gun and stumbled toward Mason.

Sami knelt down beside Mason, ignoring her own pain, as they simultaneously said, "Are you okay?" Sami leaned over and kissed him, but Mason pushed her aside as he leaned over and vomited, still feeling the effects of the blow to his stomach. Sami was holding his head and shuddering, her body wracked with sobs. Through her tears, she managed to say, "Oh, Mason, this has been a nightmare. It's all my fault. I never meant for things to end up like this. Please forgive me, Mason, I'll explain everything. I'm so, so sorry."

Through the buzzing in his head, Mason could hear the sirens getting louder. His left ear was ringing from the blow Johnson had delivered, and the entire side of his face felt like an over-inflated soccer ball. He didn't even realize yet that his face and arms were covered in welts from the branches he had pushed through. He tried to undo the binding around Sami's wrist, but he was too weak. He put his arms around his wife, and they leaned their heads against each other. With great physical effort, he gasped in a voice barely above a whisper, "We're going to be fine now, sweetheart. Everything will be fine."

In just minutes, they saw flashlights bobbing through the trees heading toward them. Sami called out, "Over here," and the rescue team closed in around them. They were safe. Yet Mason still felt dread. What about Jennifer? What about Marcie? And what about Aaron Marshall, the man who employed The Force? Greg Johnson might be dead, but Aaron Marshall represented a threat possibly even worse. Mason was sure that as long as he and Sami lived, Marshall would never stop trying to hunt them down. This night – and their nightmare -- was far from over.

The policeman who approached them introduced himself, holstered his weapon and untied Sami. He told his men to stand down and advised Sami and Mason that he had orders to place a call to Albert Baker in St. Petersburg as soon as he was in contact with either one of the Seaforths.

Mason sat, drained and exhausted, holding Sami. Both were shaking uncontrollably. He didn't want to tell Sami about Marcie and Jennifer, so he waited with trepidation while the phone call was made. Sami still had tears streaming down her cheeks. The police officer had walked out of earshot as he placed the call, and it looked like he was filling Baker in on what had happened. When he returned, he walked over to Mason and handed him the phone. As he was doing so, he said, "It's on speaker. There's someone who wants to talk to both of you."

Mason and Sami whispered hello simultaneously and on the other end, Jennifer yelped with happiness. Then her emotions poured out and through tears, she started to explain what she had been through. "Oh my God, I was so afraid I would never see either of you again. I was so scared. I was kidnapped by two guys, and then there was a shootout. I don't know if I will ever sleep again. When will I see you guys?"

Mason knew they couldn't possibly explain everything over the phone, so he tried to reassure Jennifer as best he could and ended the conversation by saying they just had to talk to the police and that he and Sami would let her know when they would be on their way home. As he did with Sami, he said, "Everything is going to be fine now." But he knew everything would require family time and healing.

Mason retrieved his glasses, which were badly twisted, and asked the officer about Marcie. Sami looked up in consternation. "Marcie? What's happened to Marcie? She's not up here in Canada with you, is she, Mason?" Mason didn't know what to say. The last thing in the world he wanted to have to tell his wife after all she'd just been through was that her best friend was lying on a shed floor with gunshot wounds. He looked over toward the officer, hoping for an answer, but nothing came. With a heavy heart, Mason put his arm around Sami and prepared to give her the truth.

"Sweetheart, Marcie has been with me every step of the way since you disappeared. She's the one who unlocked your computer, she took me to get shooting lessons, and I could never have done any of this without her help. But Sami, she got hit by one of Greg Johnson's bullets shortly after we followed you up here. I had to leave her to save you. Sweetheart, I don't know how to say this, but Marcie . . . Marcie may . . . she may not have made it, Sami."

DAY 30

Chapter 38

It was an idyllic day as the Florida sun beat down from a perfectly clear blue sky into the backyard in Gulfport. The lilies had survived the trampling they had so unceremoniously received more than a month earlier. They even seemed to be thriving as their yellow flowers blossomed, seemingly happy in the knowledge that they were back together with the occupants of the home. The decorative meandering water feature was babbling away, doing its best to attract the attention it deserved. An Eastern Grey Squirrel raced along the fence, completely oblivious to everything that had transpired recently. Unlike the flowers and the babbling brook that welcomed the couple, it stopped every few feet to scold intruders into the yard to which it had laid claim. Had the couple sitting there peacefully been able to understand squirrel language, they probably would have realized they were receiving a lecture on squatter's rights.

Mason and Sami's lawn chairs were close enough together that they could hold hands. Sami's hair color had returned to normal, and she had abandoned the oversize glasses that she wore at the casino. They had spent every day since that last night with The Force just being together as a family with Jennifer, talking about enjoying each day and each other. Jennifer had taken a short leave of absence from college to be with her parents. There had been so much joyful laughter, and there had been tears as well. Healing was not going to take place overnight. Sami had many issues to deal with. She knew now in her own mind that she was right about what she had heard after her mother died, although it had not been confirmed. She was dealing with post-traumatic nightmares about what she had put her family through, and the fact that she had not been completely honest on the front end with them.

She understood now that not telling the whole truth was the same as lying to those who loved you, even if you believe you're doing the right thing, and she was coming to grips with this through their heart-to-heart conversations.

Mason had had many discussions with Sami in the last few days. Mason just let her talk, and once she started, the floodgates opened. He thought it was therapeutic, and her psychologist affirmed it. She talked of her troubled relationship with her stepfather, not holding anything back. She confirmed that she had learned from the internet how to administer enough drugs to the wine to make Mason woozy without harming him. She apologized over and over. She talked about buying the wardrobe and hiding it in the garage so that she wouldn't awaken him when she dressed before escaping into the night. "I transferred the money from my mother's inheritance and used cash to travel to Canada. The voice mail box on my phone was full because of all the threatening calls I received from The Force. I dropped the phone into a storm drain when I left." Mason asked very few questions, but he did confirm that Johnson started harassing her after Briscoe had told Marshall about the inquisitive lady named Samantha at the bank.

She explained over and over how she had only intended to protect her family. "I really thought I could convince my stepfather to leave us alone with what I knew. I thought I could reason with him. I thought if I threatened to tell the authorities what I knew, he would leave us alone. I was so wrong. But I thought if something happened to me, you would find my notes and go to the police with them. I tried to make my password simple enough that you would figure it out, but difficult enough that it would take you a while to do it because I needed time to do what I had to do. And if you couldn't figure it out, I knew the police would be able to break the password. I was desperate. I hated leaving on the night of our anniversary. I wanted to celebrate with you, but there was so much pressure on me to do something. I could have left sooner to deal with things, but I wanted to be with you on our anniversary. If something happened to me, at least the last good thing that happened to me was our night together."

She couldn't seem to say it enough despite Mason's reassurances. Then there was the trauma of being kidnapped and nearly killed. The night brought cold sweats and bad dreams and nightmares about shooting and killing Johnson. She had flashbacks that were very intense and disturbing. She would need therapy for some time. Mason had his own thoughts to deal with, but he was always by her side and she knew beyond a shadow of a doubt that he would love and support her as long as he lived, in spite of the guilt she felt for her actions.

And then there was Jennifer. Their daughter was dealing with her own issues. The abduction, everything she had gone through with Jason Sage and Danny Harris had left scars on her young psyche, but age was on her side. Youth is more resilient, her therapist told Mason and Sami, and her healing time would be quicker. She had been through a few sessions with Sami's psychologist, but she would soon be going back to resume her studies at the University of Miami.

The one thing they hadn't really talked much about was what the future held. But now they were ready. They'd asked Albert Baker to meet with them to bring them up to date on Marshall and where everything now stood. As they quietly chatted among themselves, they heard Baker whistling as he sauntered down the path towards them. They had told him they would be in the backyard, and they had a chair waiting for him. He greeted them warmly and sat down beside them. After some pleasantries, he said, "Well, are you ready to hear what's happened since we last talked? I know the memories are painful, but I think you're going to be pleased to hear where things stand now." Mason and Sami looked at each other as they squeezed each other's hands, and said they were as ready as they thought they could be.

Baker said, "The standoff with Marshall went on for 18 hours at his house. As with any negotiation like this, the longer it goes, the more likely the chances for success, and that was the case here. Eventually Marshall wore down and he gave himself up." He continued, "A Romanian girl by the name of Alexandra was found in an upstairs bedroom." When asked if Alexandra would testify, Baker said she likely would because of the sexual abuse. He told them about the two Asian girls found locked in a room in The Force's house. Then he said something surprising. "Quite often girls lured to North America don't testify, especially if they are brought over illegally to act as house servants. The job in North America, even though not that good, is still better than what they would go back to so they simply prefer not to testify."

Baker explained, "The documentation you have, Sami, along with your understanding of what you heard will go a long way toward convicting Marshall." He said it was not unusual that they had not found evidence of poisoning before because they would not have been looking for it. Sami didn't ask the question, but she knew they would have looked closer if she had said something at the time.

Baker went on to say that they had found records in Marshall's home related to illegal young European and Asian girls in various venues in Montreal and Toronto and that charges would be filed for luring, sexual touching, living off the avails of prostitution, human trafficking and potentially, for ordering the murder of the Briscoes and others. Then there was the issue of tax evasion that Briscoe had inadvertently brought to Sami's attention. He had no doubt that their case was strong enough to put Marshall away for the rest of his life.

Baker went on to say that there would be negotiations between the Canadians and Americans, since both sides wanted to nail Marshall, but Baker had no doubt that he would never see the light of day, at least as a free man. "Marshall could very well prefer to be tried in Canada, because the jail conditions would be better," he told them, adding "Either way, jail is still jail."

Jason Sage was spilling everything he knew in the hopes of receiving some sort of plea bargain. While he didn't know a lot, the information he did share would certainly contribute to putting Marshall behind bars. Baker had never been so confident about his ability to get a criminal off the streets as he was with this case.

Baker couldn't resist telling the Seaforths that police were trained in matters like these for a good reason, and that they were entirely capable of handling situations professionally. In future, he strongly suggested, they would be wise to trust them to do their jobs and not try to handle things by themselves. Somewhat sheepishly, Mason and Sami nodded their heads, privately praying they would never need that kind of help again.

After he had finished, Detective Baker got up to leave. Before he did so, he reached down to pick up a bag he had dropped by his chair when he arrived. He handed the bag to Mason.

Mason had a puzzled look on his face as he looked at the bag, but when he turned it around, he noticed the word "Evidence" in bold black lettering on the outside. Upon closer examination, he saw lines with handwritten notes for Case Number, Date, Time and Location of Recovery as well as the name of the officer recovering the item. On another line were the names of the victims, James and Joan Briscoe, the type of offense, and the Chain of Custody, indicating the levels of authority that had handled the contents of the bag. Mason's puzzlement turned to a smile as he realized what he was holding. He opened it, and reached inside. As he did so, his hand felt around and he pulled out his pair of Brooks running shoes. Baker smiled and said, "By the way, Mason. You've been cleared in the murders of the Briscoes."

Albert Baker winked at Mason, and the detective got up to leave for the second time. Mason looked at his wife's puzzled expression and said, "I'll explain later." Baker looked back, waved to the two of them, and resumed whistling as he strode away with a very satisfied look on his face.

Mason and Sami continued to sit in the shade watching the sun create rainbows in the water feature, quietly holding hands. Mason's bruises and scratches had healed, but he was still emotionally disturbed by the thought of Marcie's body lying on the cold, concrete floor. He blamed himself for putting her at risk and endangering her life, although he knew she wouldn't have had it any other way. His thought process was interrupted by the hard-driving thump of a car stereo announcing its arrival about a block and a half away. Sami and Mason noticed that Mrs. Cassidy, who had been tending her garden next door, simply shook her head with a little smile on her face and slowly hobbled back into her house. They looked at each other and laughed.

The noise grew louder and louder as the car approached. This time it was Eminem singing from his album, *Recovery*. Finally it reached a crescendo that abruptly stopped as the car was shut off and a door slammed. It took a few minutes for Marcie to come around the corner with a blue sling contrasting with her starched white shirt. Even in dark blue jeans and with the medical device supporting her arm, she looked like she had strutted out of a fashion magazine.

Sami stood up and gave her a hug. "How are you feeling, girlfriend?"

"Better than I was in the hospital in Canada. They treated me really well and the medical treatment was awesome, but after two weeks there, it was just nice to come home, you know? After they dug the two bullets out of my shoulder, I was ready to get out of there. Fortunately, my own doctor told me yesterday there's no permanent nerve damage. I was so worried. But he says I'll be back to normal with time."

"Whatever *your* 'normal' is, Marcie. By the way, I'm not sure why you're driving with one arm. You're a menace to society." This was from Mason.

"I can drive better with one arm than you can with two, Mason Seaforth, and don't you forget it." Mason smiled, got up and gave her a big hug. Marcie returned the hug with all the conviction she could muster with one arm, and they both knew their banter would continue forever.

Marcie sat down and in a quieter voice, she said, "Guys, I think I've decided what I want to do with my life. With your situation, Sami, and those poor girls Marshall and Johnson were working with, I see a real need to help young girls any way I can. I think there are many ways I could get involved. Girls need education to avoid getting into bad situations, others need help getting out of situations like that, and still others would need counseling after they have been through it. I'm going to research the subject. Then I'll take some courses and go from there."

Sami and Mason exchanged glances as they realized that Marcie was serious. Sami said, "Congratulations, Marcie. I think that's awesome."

Mason added, "Yeah, as long as you don't scare the girls half to death."

That comment prompted a kick from Marcie, which Mason deftly avoided since he had been expecting it. He said, "Are you ready to go?"

"Yup, I'm ready."

Sami was a bit startled, "Where are you going?"

Mason looked at her and said cryptically, "Didn't we tell you? We have someone we would like you to meet, Sami, someone to whom we owe a lot. But we have to make a stop first. You're coming with us."

Marcie said, "I'll take my car."

"Uh, no." Mason quickly overruled that thought and went to get the Audi.

After Mason backed the car out of the garage, they all got in with Marcie in the back seat and Sami sitting on the passenger side beside Mason. Mason drove to the nearest liquor store and quickly ran inside. When he came back out, he was carrying a large bag. Sami looked inside and with a startled look, pulled out the biggest bottle of Jack Daniel's Tennessee Honey she had ever seen.

Mason started the car with a little smile on his face. It was time to repay a large debt of gratitude to a man who had instilled enough courage in an accountant to get him through an ordeal that he never could have imagined. The Seaforth family was going to be fine, and now it was time to say a big "thank you" to a large bearded man by the name of Leroy.

Thank you for reading *The Vanishing Wife*. If you liked what you read, please consider taking a moment to leave a review at your favourite online book store.

Photo by Ron Melanson

Barry Finlay

is the award-winning author of the travel adventure, *Kilimanjaro and Beyond –
A Life-Changing Journey* (with his son Chris) and the travel memoir, *I Guess We
Missed The Boat*. Barry was featured in the 2012-13 Authors Show's edition of
"50 Great Writers You Should Be Reading." He is a recipient of the Queen
Elizabeth Diamond Jubilee medal for his fundraising efforts to help kids in
Tanzania, Africa. Barry lives with his wife Evelyn in Ottawa, Canada.

CPSIA information can be obtained at www.ICGtesting.com
Printed in the USA
LVOW07s0030150515

438558LV00003B/391/P

9 780993 891007